THE GLASS DAGGER
The Afterlife Chronicles

Book 1

Written by Stephanie Hudson
Illustrated by Caroline Fairbairn
First Edition

COPYRIGHT

This book is copyright material, therefore its text and images must not be copied, reproduced, transferred, distributed, leased, licensed or publicly performed or used in any way except as specifically permitted in writing by the author and illustrator as allowed under terms and conditions under which it was purchased or as strictly permitted by applicable copyright law. Any unauthorised distribution or use of this text and images may be a direct infringement of the author's and illustrator's rights and those responsible may be liable in law accordingly.

Copyright © 2017 Stephanie Hudson
Copyright © 2017 Caroline Fairbairn
All rights reserved.
ISBN: 9781973152927

This book is a work of fiction. Names, characters, places and incidents are either a product of the author and illustrator's imagination or are used fictitiously. Any resemblance to actual people living or dead, events or locales is entirely coincidental.

Cover and image design by: © Caroline Fairbairn

DEDICATION

This book is dedicated to Amber, Marley, Ava and Jack, who are the shining lights in our creative souls.
This poem is for you.

Dear Love

Putting my world to paper, I see my vision come to life on the pages,
My stamp on the world, I hope will last throughout the ages,
But then as I hold you in my arms, it is a beauty like no other,
Our daughters and sons held in the arms for the first time as mother.

The feeling of fear and emotions of love become a recipe for life,
One you follow and live each day as a mother and a wife.
A heart overflowing with utter joy, love and pride,
With just one look at the beauty you made, all smiles and wide eyed.

Your greatest creation, there for all the world to see,
And as you grow into the lady and gentleman I know you will be,
I thank the faith I held in the choices I made,
And know them to be an everlasting love that will never fade.

Dear Amber, I love your feisty nature and artistic flare,
Your love in all things gothic and Doc Martins we share,
The way you feel about great movies and books that come alive,
And the way you always work your hardest to succeed in life and thrive.

Dear Marley, I love your caring heart and all the things you share,
The way you make me smile as you dance from here to there,
Always on the move but never saying no to a hug from Mum,
Then your dashing through the world again, living life to the beat of your own drum.

Dear Ava, my little bird of joy and energy galore,
You light up a room with your smile as soon as you enter through the door,
You sing, you dance, and laugh a lot whilst stamping your two feet,
And all the while you fill my heart with joy with every beat.

Dear Jack, the second I first saw you, I felt my love reach out and bloom,
From that first little smiles made and steps taken around the room,
The innocence of love and cuddles you gift are quite simply adored,
I wonder what you will be in life and what goals you will work toward.

So, here's to our young inventor and our beautiful artistic girl,
To the song and dance of an Ava bird and a toddler in a whirl.
Here's to the kids of tomorrow and where our legacy really starts,
Here's to our perfect ending and the tomorrow days that fill our hearts.

All our love
Caroline and Stephanie
Aka 'The Mum's'.

About the Author
&
Illustrator

Stephanie Hudson has dreamed of being a writer ever since her obsession with reading books at an early age. What first became a quest to overcome the boundaries set against her in the form of dyslexia has turned into a life's dream. She first started writing in the form of poetry and soon found a taste for horror and romance. The Afterlife saga is a series of eight books that kickstarted the Afterlife world in which the Chronicles is based.

When not writing, Stephanie enjoys chatting with her fans and spending time with her friends. Being with her loving family as much as she can including her wonderful daughter Ava, son Jack and supportive husband and personal muse Blake, who is there for her no matter what.

Caroline Fairbairn has always had a passion for all things creative and has being putting her beautiful stamp on the world since she could hold a pencil. Originally from London she trained as a ceramist but left the pottery world behind for a journey far more rewarding when she decided to create a family. Since then she has turned her artistic hand to many colourful endeavours, some of which include painting Jane Austin book benches, rhino's, life-sized zebras and pigs for charity auctions. She has also illustrated two children's books, 'Marching to a Royal Beat' and 'Noel's Ark' which are both aimed at a younger audience.

When not holding a pencil, brush or manoeuvring giant fiberglass animals into her home, she enjoys spending quality time with her family and friends. She can always rely on the supportive help from her high school sweetheart, husband Jamie who has been there with her from the very beginning.

WARNING!

This book has been written by a UK Author with a mad sense of humour. Which means the following story contains a mixture of Northern English slang, dialect, regional colloquialisms and other quirky spellings that have been intentionally included to make the story and dialogue more realistic for modern day characters.

Thanks for reading x

I
Blind Truth

'Our story begins in the not so distant future, when legends are written in the sands of time, like footsteps left there to follow. When the heroes of this world are children who rise above the strength of men and bend the will of their blind elders. For this story is only the beginning, so before you continue, you must ask yourself...

Are you brave enough to take the first step into a frightening world of the unknown, without ever looking back?

You are? Very well then, let us begin with the start of every great story, with our Hero...'

"Yeah right, what a load of bull!" Theo said slamming the book shut and stuffing it back onto the shelf in the airport gift shop. He was trying to pass time before his long flight but even he wasn't that desperate to wasting precious brain power on what he considered utter nonsense.

"I believe that one is on sale and I hear it has a shocking ending." An old woman said startling him as she nudged his arm. Theo took an automatic step back away from the woman making it obvious he didn't appreciate the contact. He'd never really liked being touched by others ever since he was a child, as there were too many times he had accidently hurt people. It was something he could never fully explain but after years of being blamed for something he couldn't control, well let's just say he'd learned pretty quickly to keep his distance from people.

"Sorry lady but I am not interested in books like that," he told her honestly, even though at one time this would have been a lie. She gave him a toothless grin, causing her sagging cheeks to wrinkle around her eyes. She was dressed a little like an old gypsy woman you would have seen telling people's fortunes and spinning tall tales hunched over a glass ball. Theo wanted to shiver at just the sight of her as old people had always had an effect on him. He didn't know if it was because some of them looked so close to death that he feared his accidental touch might cause more than a trip to the hospital and more like a one-way ticket to a funeral home instead.

"Do you not believe there could be heroes in our world?" she asked still smiling that creepy smile of hers. Theo was taken aback by the question, thinking it odd from someone he didn't know or more importantly, someone who *didn't know him.*

See Theo had a secret and it wasn't only the unexplainable effects his touch could inflict on another but one he felt he had been cursed with. It was something that he wished for ever since he had been a small boy. In fact, it was his first memories when he arrived at the Children's Home in London, when he was just a baby.

Now I know that most people don't remember anything from their first years on this earth and Theo knew this too but that didn't mean that his memories weren't real. For even then he'd dreamed of being a great Hero and saving the world even before he knew what it really meant. He'd seen the world differently from the start and it was only as he got older that he began to realise that others around him couldn't see the things that he did.

He would see the shadows around his crib, moving and playing with him, keeping him entertained when he couldn't sleep. Smiling adoring faces would wink at him from inside the mirror when the room he was in was empty. Whispers from a different but wonderful world that awaited him would echo around the walls like wind blowing through his curtains when his window was shut.

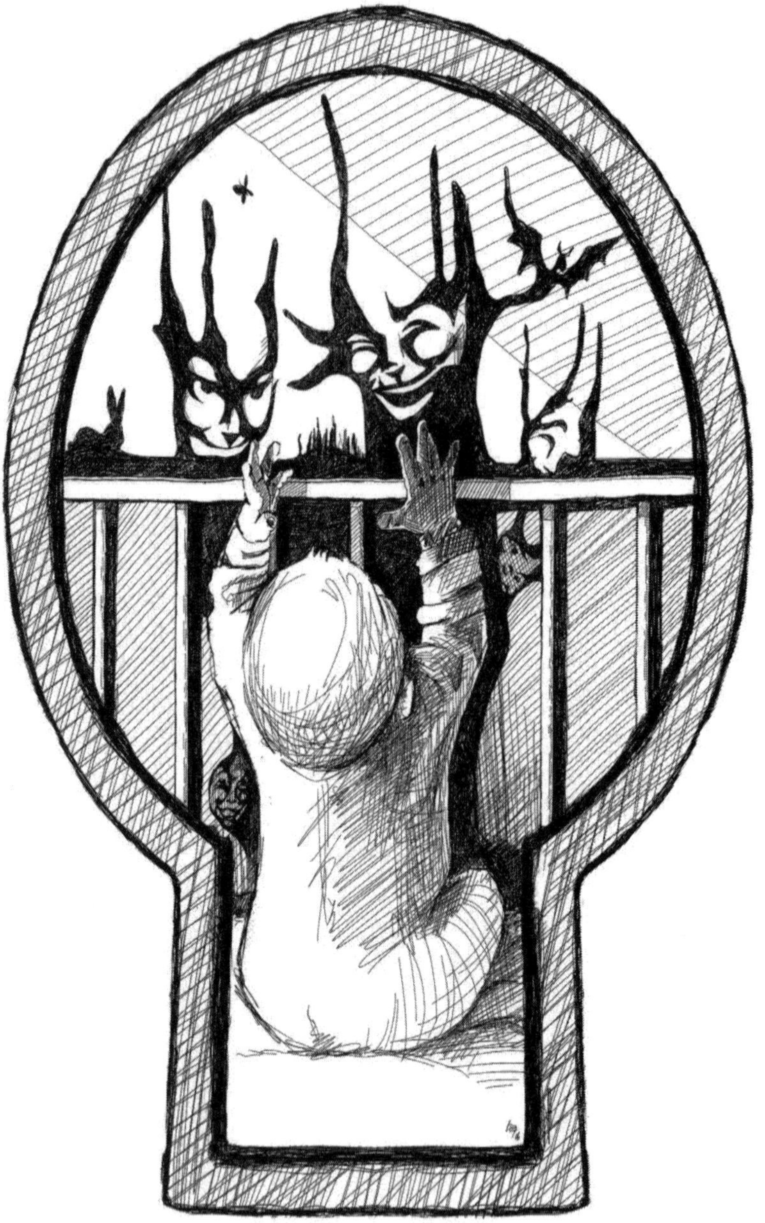

Now these sound like scary things to happen to a child but he was never afraid. In fact, there wasn't anything Theo was afraid of other than the
thought of hurting innocent people. All his life he'd felt as if his brain had been hard wired to protect people. So much so that Theo spent all of his free time growing up reading and researching all about the Heroes of our history. But one day that all changed.

Theo suddenly shook these thoughts from his mind as if seeing his past playing out in the reflection of the shop window and answered the old woman.

"I don't exactly believe in fairy tales." The old woman laughed at Theo's response.

"Now that is a shame..." she said turning away from him and before he could stop himself he asked,

"Why?" The old woman stopped in her tracks just before leaving through the shop's exit and looked over her hunched shoulder at him.

"Because, they believe in you," she whispered cryptically. Theo frowned and shook his head a little trying to make sense of what she meant by that.

"Now listen to old Nesteemia and run along young hero, this is one fight you will not want to miss," she added confusing Theo even more.

"I think you meant to say *flight*," Theo said correcting her but she gave him a cackling chuckle and said,

"Did I now? We shall soon see young Theo...*soon indeed.*" Then the same book that he had been looking at suddenly flew off the shelf and landed at his feet. He looked down at the bent spine showing him the front cover that only held three words…

'THE GLASS DAGGER'

"Wait, how did you know my…name?" His question tailed off when he looked back up and saw that the old woman had disappeared and was nowhere to be seen.

'How did she know?' he asked himself again but his thoughts were abruptly cut off when a woman's voice came over the tannoy informing passengers that this was the last call for his flight. In the end, he didn't have too much time to think about the strange gypsy woman he had encountered as he ended up running to catch his flight, and thankfully *he was a fast runner.*

It was over a ten-hour flight to Portland's International airport in Maine and Theo had little trouble sleeping through most of it. Even if his dreams had been of a creepy gypsy woman who had lured a young blonde girl from her family at a fairground. Theo had jarred awake when he heard a child crying further down the aisle of the plane. It was a scream that had mirrored the young girl's scream in his dream.

He tried to shake away the memory of seeing the gypsy's silver dragon ring turn into something real and sinister when it bit down hard into the innocent girl's hand. She must have been no more than six or seven years old. Theo couldn't help but feel something for her as he usually did whenever he felt an injustice had happened in the world. But no matter how he tried, the uneasy feeling clung to him like oil on his skin as he made his way off the plane and into yet another busy airport.

He didn't know what to expect would happen when he arrived there as vague was the only word that came to mind when he was first told he had to leave the Boy's home in East London, where he grew up. It wasn't easy growing up as an orphan with no idea of where you came from. And it was that age-old story of being left on a doorstep as a baby that wasn't just a cliché in Theo's case, but more a way of life. In fact, he was the only one without any clue as to who he was other than the boy that had been there the longest and had never been adopted for reasons he still to this day didn't know.

Most had, at the very least, some sort of background story to tell and the more stories he heard over the years, the less he started to feel sorry for himself and instead considered himself lucky. He had heard it all in his sixteen years, so much so that he left that place being thankful he wasn't walking away with his own 'woe is me' story following him like a dark shadow.

No, the only story he had to tell now was the next chapter of his life and that was something he had little clue about. He clutched onto the letter he had crumpled in his jacket pocket as if it brought him some comfort. It was the only reason he was here now and even though he had read it what felt like a thousand times, it still held no clues as to why him?

Theo wasn't considered much by his teachers in school or by the other students for that matter. But don't be fooled. This wasn't because he wasn't smart, which he was or because he wasn't athletic, which once again, he was...*extremely*. It was because he hid away any side of him that would draw unwanted attention by his fellow students and even his teachers. So he played himself down in front of everyone.

He became good at being the loner. The living ghost of the school because he chose to be that way. So, if a girl came up to speak to him, he appeared rude and disinterested. If he was picked for a team he would purposely play badly, so he wasn't ever picked again. And he never raised his hand in class, no matter how much he knew his answer was correct. He simply blended into the background knowing it was what was best for everyone because he could never risk himself getting close to someone...*not again.*

He decided the only thing left to do now was to pick up the hand me down suitcase his guardian had fished out of the attic for him and make his way to the arrivals lounge in hopes that someone would be there waiting for him. He couldn't help but wish he had demanded for some more information from his guardian the day he was asked into his office and handed the letter, one he knew would change his life forever. No, instead he simply walked out the door feeling different and gripping onto the letter he held now.

The one addressed to him personally...

AdVitam Academy.

Dear Theo Quinn,

I have the greatest honour and privilege to inform you that you have been selected for a full academic and financial scholarship at the AdVitam Academy for the gifted youths of our time.

If you choose to accept this scholarship you will find your flight details and tickets enclosed within. An Academy delegate will be waiting for you when you land, ready to escort you and your fellow candidates to your new school.

We wish you a safe journey and look forward to welcoming you to your new home.

Yours sincerely.

Dominic Draven,

Headmaster and Scholarship Benefactor.

…And with those few cryptic words, that was it, he was shipped off saying goodbye to all he had ever known with everything he owned fitting into just one bag and shamefully, one with room to spare.

"Great, what now." He muttered to himself looking around not knowing what to expect. He also couldn't help but wonder since receiving that letter, who this Dominic Draven was? He knew he was obviously the Headmaster and one footing the bill in all this, as the letter had stated but the main question was *why?*

Ad Vitam Academy

Dear Theo Quinn

          I have the greatest honour and privilege to inform you that you have been selected for a full academic and financial scholarship at the AdVitam Academy for the gifted youths of our time.

If you choose to accept this scholarship you will find your flight details and tickets enclosed within. An Academy delegate will be waiting for

you when you land, ready to escort you and your fellow candidates to your new school.

We wish you a safe journey and look forward to welcoming you to your new home.

Yours sincerely

Dominic Draven

Headmaster and Scholarship Benefactor.

Or more to the point, why *him* exactly?

"Theo Quinn?" Hearing his name coming from behind him made him stop abruptly so that one of the other passengers bumped into him accidently. Theo sidestepped quickly getting out of the man's way and cringed when he saw the man put a hand to his forehead as if he suddenly felt ill. He watched a few seconds longer just to be sure the small contact didn't have any lasting effects on the man. Theo released a held breath when he saw him meeting up with what must have been his family, knowing that the man had gotten off lightly and must have shaken off the moment of weakness.

"It is Theo…right?" Theo turned his attention back to the short skater girl that had called his name. She definitely wasn't the type of person he had been expecting to see and he had to wonder if the school had sent one of the older students to meet him instead of a teacher like he would have thought.

She looked no older than seventeen, maybe eighteen years old and she wasn't exactly wearing a school uniform. She wore an old band T shirt that had a skeleton demon playing guitar and looked as if it had been bought new back in the eighties. She wore this with combat trousers that had been cut off just below the knee, a studded belt and Doc Martin boots in worn, scratched up cherry red.

"Yeah, I'm Theo," he told her finally looking up at her face. He couldn't help his reaction when he hissed air through his teeth. The girl was obviously blind as most of her eyes were white except for two creepy black dots at the centres. There were also raw scars that looked like burn marks all around her eyes and creeping their way down her cheeks. He couldn't help but wonder, had someone done this to her? Theo started to get angry at just the thought of it.

"Great, well I am Rue, your official Afterlife guide!" she said holding her hand out for him to shake. He was almost glad she couldn't see the confused look on his face as he took her hand, still wondering what she meant by 'Afterlife guide'.

"Are you sure you have the right person?" he said feeling like he had to ask. She laughed taking back her hand and held it to her temple in salute before saying,

"I might be blind but I am a great scout!" Theo didn't know what to say to that and even if he did, he was too busy staring at

the strange tribal eye symbols that had been tattooed on the palms of her hands.

"Now let's get going, the rest of your bunk buddies are already on the bus waiting for us to shake tail," she said, pulling down the large mirrored aviator sunglasses she had perched on top of her head hidden amongst her spiky black hair. Theo ducked under the barrier having no patience to walk all the way around and it was a good job as Rue might have been shorter than him and visually impaired but she could certainly move quickly. He ended up half jogging to keep up.

"So you're our guide to the school?" he asked making sure one last time that she hadn't made a mistake.

"Sure am," she said surprising him at how easily she manoeuvred around the place without even bumping into anyone, she didn't even have a stick or anything.

"But back there you said that you were our official 'Afterlife' guide."

"And?" she said in a tone that suggested she had no clue as to where he was going with this.

"*And...* on the letter it said our new school was called the AdVitam Academy," he informed her hoping now she would understand why he thought she might have the wrong person, although that wouldn't explain how she still knew his name.

"And what do you think AdVitam means exactly?" she asked on a laugh, one that only managed to frustrate Theo as he didn't like being left out of what he considered an important loop, especially when he was smack bang in the middle of that tightening life lasso!

"I don't know, add vitamins to your diet, the school of healthy eating…Hell, you could worship broccoli for all I know! So you tell me, you're supposed to be the guide." Rue laughed at him instead of getting angry at his sarcastic tone, one which Theo was often gifted with.

"Oh Hell might have something to do with it, but trust me when I say, it isn't broccoli we worship," she said winking at him and with her creepy eyes, it went well with her Hellish statement. But Theo shook off the bad vibes he was getting and said,

"Yeah right, now just tell me what it really means."

"AdVitam is Latin," she said grinning and Theo dropped his suitcase to the floor and crossed his arms, forgetting that she couldn't see how unimpressed he looked by her dragging out the answer.

"For?" he prompted rolling his hand around and again ignoring the pair of blind eyes that couldn't see him but not the knowing smile he could see obviously mocking him.

Then she gave him his answer, one he wasn't sure he wanted to hear…

"It's Latin for… the Afterlife."

2
After Death

Theo was left standing there as if a ghost had just walked through him, leaving their mark in the form of little bumps all over his skin. He wasn't quite sure why hearing the name 'Afterlife' had such an effect on him. All he knew was to trust his instincts and right now they were screaming one word...

Run.

Now Theo usually always trusted his instincts and he felt it had got him this far without being damaged along the way. Like the time some school bully and wannabe tough guy thought to challenge him by acting like a coward when sneaking up behind him. Theo had the sudden thought to duck at just the right moment so that the guy's fist slammed straight into Theo's locker instead of the back of his head like the bully had intended.

"Turd sandwich," Theo muttered to himself, thinking back to how he would have loved to have shown that guy a lesson but in the end, he knew the best thing was to just walk away. The one touch rule was what Theo lived by as those few seconds was all it took to really hurt someone.

In truth, the darker side of Theo's personality had mentally visualised the scenario of simply placing a fingertip to the jerk's forehead and watching the effects of what such little effort could do. To stand there and witness as his veins would have bulged, his eyes no doubt growing wide with panic and his skin quickly paling to a sickly shade of grey before he sacked it to the ground into what Theo knew would be a scary state of unconsciousness. He had heard once before the type of nightmares even the briefest of his touch could deliver, once they lost their mind into the oblivion that seemed to feed Theo's world and unknown power. It was why he kept this side of him locked away in the shadows where it belonged, no matter what the bully had intended. The lesson to be learnt wasn't worth the endless madness that would no doubt follow him around for the rest of his life, even if it managed to save a few students from his Butt hole behaviour!

Shaking these memories from his mind he decided for the first time in his life he wasn't going to let instincts rule over this major decision in his life. No, he was going with his heart on this one, as there was something in his heart that said this was the right path to take, almost as if that path was going to lead him…

Home.

"Yo space cadet, you coming or what?!" Rue shouted from inside the automatic doors. He still had no clue how she knew where to look to find him but find him she did. Maybe she had some of her sight? He thought about it but after one more look into those milky depths, he very much doubted it.

Theo didn't answer her but instead just grabbed the handle of his suitcase and when it snapped it looked like he wasn't the only one on the last leg of the journey.

"Great, just great!" he moaned picking it up in his arms and along with it killing all illusions of trying to be cool in front of anyone who might be looking. Well at least Rue couldn't see him struggling in the only awkward way anyone could look when hugging an oversized suitcase to their chest, he thought more with sarcasm than seeing any sight of a silver lining.

Jogging to catch up wasn't as natural looking as he hoped and he was just glad for the moment when he could finally put the stupid thing down. In fact, if it hadn't been soon he would have been tempted to just set fire to the damn thing and put it out of its aging misery. Seriously the thing had half a roll of duct tape just holding it together and the zip looked ready to fling off at any moment and take out an eye!

When he saw the vehicle Rue had stopped next to Theo frowned. Looking up at the black school bus he had slowly walked over to he decided it looked more like something the Adam's Family kids went to school in. He wanted to ask if this was a joke but Rue spoke first.

"Let me guess, a throwback from the sixties?" Rue said nodding to broken suitcase.

"Actually I think it was the first one invented…did they have suitcases when dinosaurs roamed the earth?" Rue laughed at Theo's joke and he liked the sound. He had always had a good sense of humour but rarely was he given the opportunity to show it.

"Hey, you're funny, kid." On hearing this Theo dropped his smile.

"Don't call me kid," he said affronted by the thought. Okay, so Theo knew at aged sixteen he was still technically considered as 'Underage' but that didn't mean he ever felt like it. Quite the opposite in fact, as a lot of the time he looked at most adults as if they were the children. Especially given that most adults he had heard about certainly didn't understand the concept of responsibility that was for sure.

Rue held up her hands as if Theo was waving a gun at her.

"Sorry dude, didn't realise you were older than you look. How old are you anyway?" Theo raised an eyebrow at her and said,

"Sixteen, So I doubt enough years younger than you for you to be calling *me* Kid." he said.

"*I am* older than I look… Now trust me on this," she said and opened up the side panel on the bus before picking up the suitcase one handed without needing to feel around for the pieces of broken handle. Then as if she was some Olympian shot putter she threw the case in making him glad he didn't own any breakables…although he wasn't sure his old 90's Gameboy had survived Rue's mighty swing.

"Jeez, remind me not to hack you off any time soon." Theo commented sarcastically. Rue winked at him and said,

"That's a really good idea there, kiddo," then ruffled his head making him groan out loud, realising he had just set himself up to be called 'Kid' or 'Kiddo' for the rest of eternity when around Rue. Maybe he would have to start wearing aftershave to mask his smell so she wouldn't know when he was in the room. Of course, first he would have to learn how to play guitar and go busking on the streets for money, as like most orphans, he didn't have a penny to his name.

He followed Rue to the bus doors wondering not only why the school bus was black but also why all the windows were blacked out.

"What type of school is this AdVitam anyway?" Theo had to admit the name didn't exactly roll off the tongue, like St Johns did.

"You will soon see, won't you?" she answered pressing the release button at the side making the doors snap open. Theo looked up at the few steps feeling that familiar shiver snake down his spine, which only meant one thing…*run.* But once again, instead of ducking, dodging, running or jumping from the danger he could sense coming, he did the opposite and took his first real step into the unknown.

"There you go," Rue said to herself as if she could sense his hesitation, something that embarrassed him to know. He didn't like people thinking he had a weakness of any sort and for the

most part people would give him a wide berth, being fooled into believing that he had none. After that incident with the bully, he quickly developed a reputation of being a bad ass and in a way, I guess they weren't wrong.

It was a powerful thing for a crowd of students to watch as a young boy was about to get pummelled by a boy twice his size, only to walk away as though it had been nothing to fear. To simply duck his head and without a backward glance, make his way down the hallway without so much as a flinch. Needless to say, his reaction scared the bully into never trying it again and hopefully also never underestimating anyone else smaller than him. But inevitably from then on the rumours spread like a bush fire and ended up alienating Theo even more.

But that was all in the past and now it was time for a new start. He was even starting to let himself believe that this time he might be able to make a friend. Well, that was if he could think of a decent excuse as to why he never touched anyone. Either way, as he mounted those steps, it was enough to allow him to believe that this time it was going to be different...

"Or maybe not," he muttered under his breath as the biggest lad he had ever seen stood up and completely blocked the aisle. Theo's eyes widened as he looked up and up and up until his neck was arched, just to enable him see this guy's shaved head. And as someone who was classed as tall for his age, Theo wasn't used to having to look up to many people, let alone crack the bones in his neck just to see the guy's chin!

"Holy..." Theo was about to swear when the beast spoke, cutting him off.

"Ivan," he said with a heavy accent in a surprisingly gentle voice.

"Uh...Hey..." That was all he knew to say in the presence of meeting a real life giant in the flesh. In fact, he had to bite his tongue from asking the guy if he bench pressed motorbikes in his spare time. He looked like one of those guys you saw off the TV that were competing for World's Strongest Man title.

Ivan was at least six foot six tall with a massive gut that hung over his red and white basketball shorts. His shoulders looked big enough to balance tree trunks either side and his biceps, well they looked strong enough to crush them into splinters. Theo wasn't scared of a fight if it came to it but even he knew just by looking at this guy he would be dead after one punch. In fact, images of this guy actually knocking his head clean from his shoulders would have been animated in a bubble above his head if this were a cartoon.

"I happy meeting you," Ivan said in broken English and before Theo could stop him Ivan outstretched his massive arm and had his hand enclosed in his bear sized paw. Ivan shook Theo's hand, one he held in his vice like grip and Theo looked on in amazement that his touch wasn't having a single effect on him. He couldn't help wondering if it wasn't to do with his colossal size or was he just different like him?

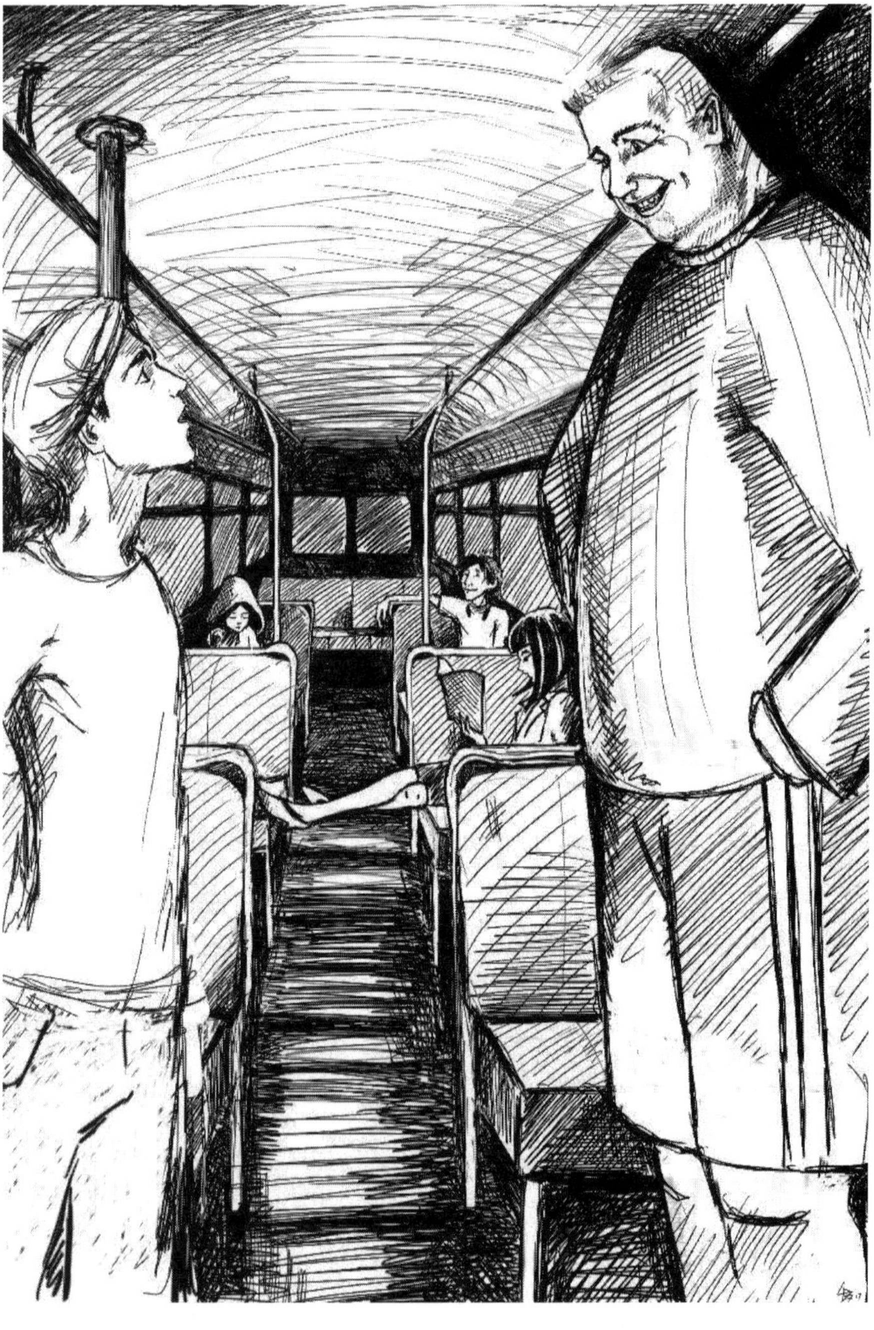

"Cool meeting you too, big guy," he said after Ivan let go of his hand and even though Theo was tough he still had to flex his fingers in and out a few times just to get the feeling back in them. He chose to do this behind his back as he didn't want to upset the guy. Hell, he never wanted to upset this guy…*ever!*

"Imya?" Ivan said and Theo raised his eyebrow in question.

"Sorry?"

"He's asking your name?" A girl's voice came from further back and Theo had to sidestep in front of one of the seats to see past Ivan. There he found an Asian girl with her head in a book and feet on the next seat, not even bothering to look up at him.

"Name's Theo," he said giving his attention back to the giant, who so far was the only person in the world that seemed immune to his touch.

"Very good. I be happy knowing you," Ivan said and patted Theo on the back making him choke on inhaled air from the impact.

"Ah me sorry. Me no, not own me strength," Ivan said getting his words mixed up. Theo tried not to cough again but instead cleared his throat, saying in a croaky voice,

"No worries dude, but you're definitely on my team for sports," Theo said only half joking because he guessed anyone who went up against this guy was going to be on the losing team. It even surprised Theo to think this way, considering Theo never played contact sports for obvious reasons. Was he really expecting things to be that different for him at this new school?

"I yes, basketball I like much…my team," Ivan added punching his chest and looking down at his huge hooded sweater that could have doubled as a blanket for a big bed. Theo smiled up at him and nodded telling him he understood but not really knowing what else to say as he'd never followed basketball before.

"Right, lets crack on should we?" Rue said clapping her hands and Theo looked back at her releasing as she took her seat that she was also the bus driver in this bizarre situation! He watched as she nodded for Ivan to sit, probably realising that Theo couldn't do much with the big guy still stood in his way.

"Ah, me yes sit."

"Magic!" Rue said once a blushing Ivan got the hint and sat down. Then she threw herself into the driver's seat and started the engine. Theo looked at the others he could now see sat on the bus with the same amount of concern as he had letting a blind person drive them anywhere. Theo couldn't help taking a step towards Rue, strangely feeling responsible for this little group and deciding it was his duty to speak the obvious. But before he could Rue held up her hand without looking at him and said,

"Save it and don't sweat it kiddo, I have been driving longer than when you were first giggled at." Theo frowned not really understanding what she meant by that comment but knowing that he didn't like it either way. However, before he had chance to comment, Rue put her hand on the gear stick, putting it into first. One that just so happened to be a chrome skull which had black tears dripping down in what looked like glitter paint.

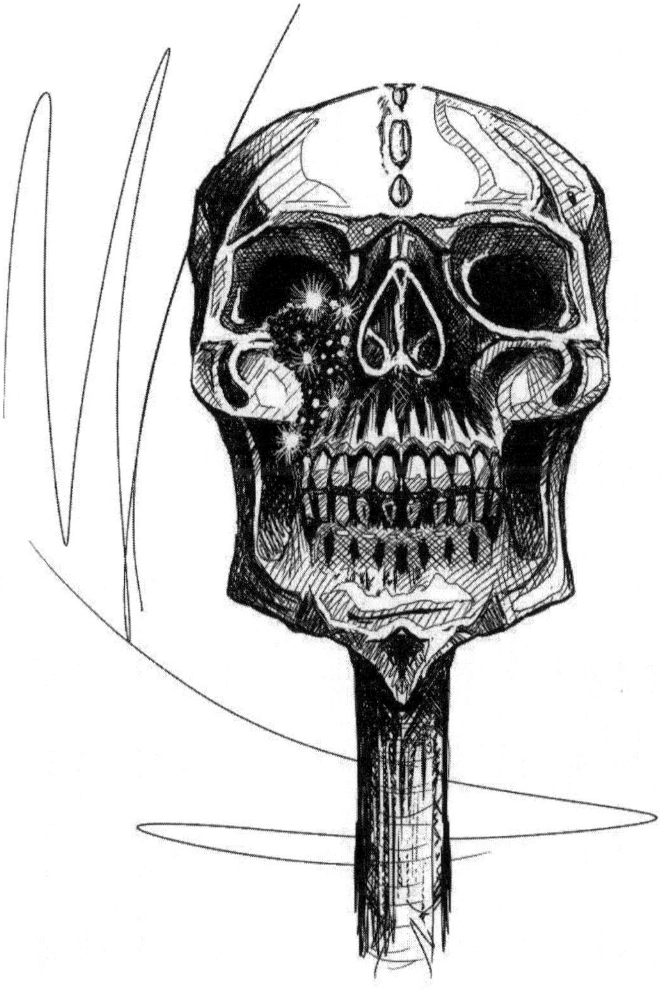

"Sit." Rue warned before pulling away and Theo, feeling as though he had little choice in this strange turn of events, did as he was told. He walked down the centre nodding to Ivan who gave him a beaming smile, one you would have expected to see on a young child just before biting into the biggest piece of cake. Well, he may have been big and intimidating in size but his facial expressions told a very different story.

With his kind soft eyes that lit up and almost disappeared altogether when he smiled thanks to a pair of chubby cheeks, the word used to describe this gentle looking giant would have had to have been *endearing*. Even his double chin and big neck added to the friendly nature he expressed as Theo passed. However, this friendliness didn't last as he approached the next person a few rows down.

"Hey." Theo said to the hooded figure with her head hunched over in a protective manner. He barely got a glimpse of her dark hazel eyes before she looked away quickly, barely giving him a murmur in reply. One look at her and two words crossed his mind… 'Issues and Goth'.

She wore an oversized jacket on top of even more layers hiding herself away from the world. But it was the way she cradled one hand to her chest, hidden inside her jacket as though she didn't want anyone to see her hurting.

Theo had to force himself further along the bus, squashing down the urge to stop and ask her if she was alright. No, he could read the signals easy enough when someone wanted to be left alone but he had to confess that he was surprised to see someone looking so fearful actually on this bus. The other girl on the other hand, now she looked like she belonged alright. Talk about complete opposite to goth girl, this was preppy on a whole other level.

"Theo huh?" she said without moving her feet that were blocking him going any further. It was obvious she had the spoilt teen act down to a fine art and added to the attitude was the look to match. A navy blue blazer of what looked like her previous private school was what she chose to wear. But for some reason the patch that would have been able to confirm his suspicions looked like it had been ripped off, which only managed to make Theo even more curious.

Completing the school girl look was the buttoned cardigan in dark green that matched the colours in her pleated tartan skirt and black knee high socks with platform heeled black school shoes.

Theo would have this girl pegged as the class brain if it hadn't been for the rebellious red streak she had flashing colour amongst her jet black hair and the killer heels she chose to torture herself with. Even the harsh way her hair was cut told him that this girl didn't like to follow the rules and being a team player was the furthest thing from her mind.

Theo didn't know how he knew these things about people but he just did. He didn't believe it was anything corny like having a sixth sense or any rubbish like that. Instead he simply put it down to being perceptive and he always found that a person's appearance could tell you a lot about the personality that went with it.

Like the way she hadn't yet looked up at him but still spoke to him with her eyes glued firmly to her book. This was clearly a statement made to tell him one thing…*I don't care what you think of me.* However, the reality was telling him a very different side to the one she was hoping to portray and that this was more likely an act she put on when she was feeling vulnerable.

Although he knew she would probably swear on her kidneys that this wasn't the truth. And even though Theo wouldn't have blamed her for feeling this way, he knew it was best to just act right along with her. After all, they were all vulnerable right now…especially with a blind girl behind the wheel of the school bus, driving them to God knows where, Theo thought dryly.

"And you are?" Theo asked giving it what he thought was long enough before answering. He used this as a tactic sometimes, fighting attitude with attitude.

"Ena, Ena Douglas," she answered, finally gracing him with a pair of unusual light blue eyes that he hadn't expected to see on an Asian chick. Actually he didn't know what shocked him more, her beautiful eyes or her last name.

"Douglas?" he found himself asking before he could stop himself.

"Yeah, you got a problem with that, English?" she snapped.

"Not really, just didn't expect a Scottish last name for a Chinese chick." Theo answered honestly and not biting to the obvious confrontational tone she was looking for.

"I'm Japanese genius and Douglas is my adopted name if you must know." Theo looked surprised for a moment and couldn't help but glance back towards Ivan and the Goth, wondering if they too were orphans like him?

"Right, so you speak Russian as well as Japanese?" he asked nodding back to Ivan and referring to when she translated for him about Ivan wanting to know his name. But this was one question that she obviously didn't want him to ask and Theo couldn't help but revel a little in the shameful blush that speckled her cheeks with pink at the question.

"Well I…" She was suddenly cut off when Rue pulled the bus forward on a jerk, causing Theo to grab on to one of the headrests to steady himself.

"She's a wildcard that one." A boy's voice said from one of the seats behind Ena and Theo looked up to see another Goth nodding towards the erratic driver. He was the last student on the bus making them a clueless party of five.

Theo decided it was safer siting down so nodded to Ena's outstretched feet and cleared his throat.

"Uh…do you mind?" he said when she obviously didn't get the hint or more like blatantly ignored it. Ena rolled her eyes but at least moved so Theo could pass. He couldn't help but feel as though she was going to make things difficult for not only him but also everyone else on this bus.

"Yo man, it's Theo right?" said the last student, one sat a few rows away from little Miss Japanese Attitude. He stood up and offered Theo his hand, which was something that always made

Theo nervous. He didn't want to be rude and knew sometimes he could get away with the slightest touch, so he took a chance and slapped a hand to his in greeting. It was only when he looked completely unaffected that Theo could sigh his secret relief and say,

"Yeah dude, and you are?" Now that he could see him up close he realised he wasn't a goth like he first thought but more of an Emo. He, like Ena, had jet black hair which was straightened and styled forward in front of his face. On this he wore a grey worn beanie hat that looked like it never left his head. He also wore a 'Fall Out Boy' band t-shirt and a pair of ripped skinny jeans that looked to have paint stains on one side. A junky pair of old charity shop Doc Martins completed the look and these also had splattered paint marks at the toes. Even without the paint on his clothes, it was obvious from the dirty, charcoal dyed fingertips that this guy was an artist.

"I'm Zane Ververs," he said with a slight accent Theo couldn't place.

"Ververs?" Theo asked just because he was curious to know where he was from.

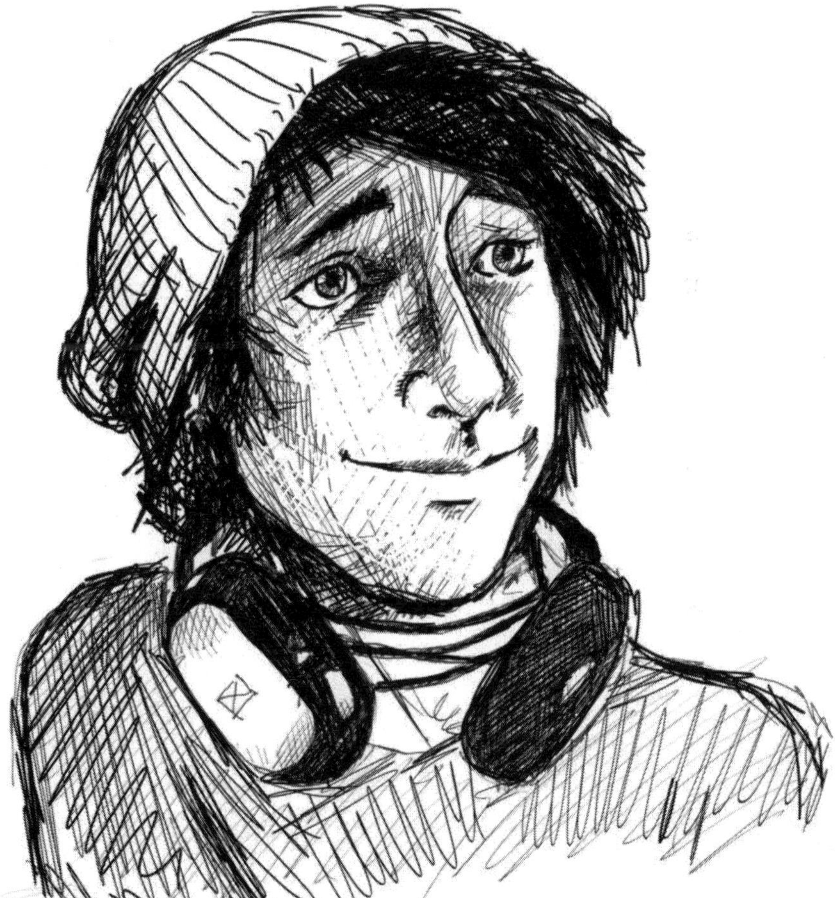

"It's Dutch. I learned English through music," Zane said as he reached into his jeans' pocket to turn off the music he still had blasting from the sticker covered headphones hanging around his neck. Theo decided to take a seat opposite Zane, who also seemed like the most logical choice for conversation.

"That's cool. So you're from the Netherlands?" Theo asked knowing this was the only place he could remember from Geography where they spoke Dutch.

"Yeah and from the sound of your accent, I would guess you're from London?" Theo nodded and for some reason once again put his hand in his pocket to grip tightly onto the letter, as if it brought him comfort knowing it was still there.

"Look man, I have to ask, what do you know about this place we are going to?" Theo asked as if the question had burst from within the same dark place deep within him that he kept locked away. Zane's soulful eyes widened for a second as if he too had been burning to ask someone this very same question. He scooted forward, sliding over to the seat closer to the aisle and leaned forward, causing Theo to do the same.

"Did you get the letter?" Zane asked on a whisper. Theo's hand clenched tighter around the battered piece of paper before forcing himself to relax.

"Yeah, I got the letter but it didn't really tell me sh..." Theo was about to swear when all suddenly Rue slapped on the brakes, launching everyone to brace onto the seats in front of them. The poor goth girl screamed in shock and Theo looked up over the headrest to see Ivan was looking at her with concern.

"Every all things is fine now." Ivan said, once again getting his English mixed up.

"Th...then...who is that?" The girl asked stuttering her words in fear and pointing her shaky finger out to the front of the bus. All eyes followed her direction to find a man stood in the middle of the road, stopping Rue from going any further without knocking him down. Theo was the first one on his feet.

"Oh you have got to be kidding me!" Rue said in clear frustration after holding both her hands out and palms up towards the window. Theo watched as the man in the middle of the road tilted his head to one side as if trying to hear something. Then he slowly moved towards the bus and didn't even flinch when a huge truck went speeding past, beeping his horn as he went.

"What are you...?" Theo asked when Rue pulled the lever that operated the bus doors, causing them to swing open. But his words trailed off as it was too late, she was letting the stranger inside.

Everyone watched in hushed silence as a well-dressed man stepped onto the bus wearing a beige coloured suit. He was unusual looking with steel coloured eyes and a full head of silver hair that didn't look that way due to age. He also had with him an old looking briefcase and Theo, along with everyone else on the bus, couldn't help but wonder what a businessman like him was doing in the middle of the road.

"Really, you're choosing *now* to do this?" Rue said throwing her hands up as though she didn't only know this guy but obviously knew exactly what he was doing there. The business guy gave her a sly and creepy looking smile before reaching into his left pocket and pulling out a small palm sized book. Then he flipped it open and said the words that made the hairs on the back of Theo's neck stand on end.

"But my dear..." he started to say with his smile widening, showing an eerie amount of pointed teeth before he finished his haunting statement...

"You know that Death waits for no man."

3
A Brief case of Death

LAKE HELL~~ION~~
→

Hearing what sounded like a threat, Theo couldn't fight his nature as he stepped out onto the centre aisle to face the man.

"Easy there, Theo." Rue warned as he slowly approached, letting him know there were occasions she knew not to call him Kid. The businessman looked briefly surprised when hearing his name and Theo couldn't help but wonder why.

"So for once the rumours were true?" the man said looking to Rue and she rolled her white blind eyes before answering him without giving the information he had requested.

"They're just kids Carrick, have a heart man."

"Oh I have a heart young one and it beats more than you know, especially for those I am about to take...*now drive.*" The man named Carrick said this in a way Theo could only describe as with a purely evil depth to his voice. In fact, it sounded like something not quite of this world.

"Look Jackass, I don't know who you think you are but you can't just walk on this bus and order her around!" Carrick gave Theo a quizzical stare back for a silent moment and then smiled.

"Remind you of anyone?" Rue said sarcastically as she took her seat and started up the bus once more.

"Your name is Theo?" Carrick asked with an authoritative tone that Theo cared little for.

"Yeah but not that it's any of your business, old man." Theo snapped feeling his temper rising as he walked closer.

"That's where you are mistaken young Theo, it is very much my business." Carrick said smiling and before Theo could respond the way he wanted, the creepy guy held up one hand to stop him and continued with,

"In fact, you shall soon see just how *deep* this business of mine can get."

"That sounds like a threat to me, what do you reckon, big guy?" Theo said as he looked back to Ivan who he could see was also frowning at the man.

"I little believe in violence and like not fear in ladies," Ivan said referring to the scared Goth girl cowering in her seat and forcing him to take a stand against what he too believed in. As he raised up behind Theo, Carrick was obviously surprised by his size as his eyes widened briefly taking in the beast that had Theo's back.

"I think you're out numbered here, dude." Theo looked behind him to see this statement had just come from Zane who also had his back. Theo couldn't help the cocky smirk that emerged when he looked back at Carrick knowing Zane was right, this guy was going to be no match for the three of them, not when they had their own Russian Tank!

"It appears that way doesn't it...?" he said still smiling and Rue interrupted him, growling her warning,

"Carrick, they don't know." But Carrick ignored her caution and instead held up a single pale finger and said,

"Then let's teach them their first lesson shall we... *turn here."* Rue sighed as if it was the very last thing she wanted to do but instead of putting up a fight with the rest of them, she spun the wheel too quickly and nearly caused them to tip over as she turned onto the dirt road. Theo held on like the rest of them and looked out the window just in time to see the old broken sign that said, 'Lake Hellion' only the 'ion' had been crossed through with red paint.

"Now I think it's time to return to our seats, gentlemen," Carrick said and this was when Theo had had enough at practising the art of patience.

"And I think this is your stop!" Theo replied before cutting the distance between them deciding it was about time to take some of the wind from this guy's sails, right along with energy from his body.

"Theo no!" Rue shouted just as Carrick moved both his arms outwards and Theo stopped in his tracks to look behind him just in time to see both Ivan and Zane get thrown sideways back into their seats. Goth girl and Ena screamed in fear at the impossible act they had just witnessed.

"Now *that* is interesting," Carrick said calmly, looking at him with his head tilted in a curious manner and drawing Theo's anger back into focus. It didn't take a smart ass to know that this Carrick was obviously surprised that his powers hadn't worked on Theo and he was questioning what that reason could be.

"No but it's about to." Theo warned knowing what he had to do. And just as he was about to run at the guy to take him down with his touch, Ena screamed his name,

"THEO, LOOK OUT!" But the warning came too late as the last thing he saw before he too was thrown forwards was Rue driving them deliberately into...

'Lake Hell'

Theo must have hit his head as he was briefly knocked out for a minute before he opened his eyes under water. The shock of his new situation made him raise his head quickly and take a deep breath. A brief moment of panic set in from not knowing how long he had been out of it but he quickly gathered from the murmured sound of screaming and gushing water that it hadn't been long. He got up from where he had fallen in between the seats onto the floor and tried to shake the pain from his head enough to focus on what was happening. He pushed the wet hair from his eyes and tried to take in the deadly situation around him.

"WE CAN'T MOVE!" Ena shouted and just as his blurry vision started to finally come into focus he knew what was happening. The lake water was rapidly flooding the bus and quickly looking at the other students, Ena was right, none of them could move...not even Ivan.

"Think Theo, damn it, think!" he said out loud frantically looking around the bus for answers, that was when he heard the chuckle. He growled down at the floor feeling his rage build within him when hearing the sound coming from the man responsible for all this.

"What did you do to them?!" Theo snarled turning his head to the murderer in a cheap suit.

"You really want to help them?"

"Of course I do you freak!" he shouted back angrily.

"Then leave them. Actually, better yet...*sit down and join them.*" Carrick said this last part in some strange sort of demonic purr and Theo had hit his limit.

"Better yet, *I stop you!*" And like before, Theo charged him running through the rising water as though not only his life depended on it but theirs too.

"Let's see if you can run through this, youngling." Carrick said just as he pulled his briefcase around to hold in front of his chest and after he spoke his warning, Theo watched as the ancient looking locks on the case flipped up. Then as though this was all happening in slow motion, he saw the case lid drop and when he was but a hair's breadth away from touching him,

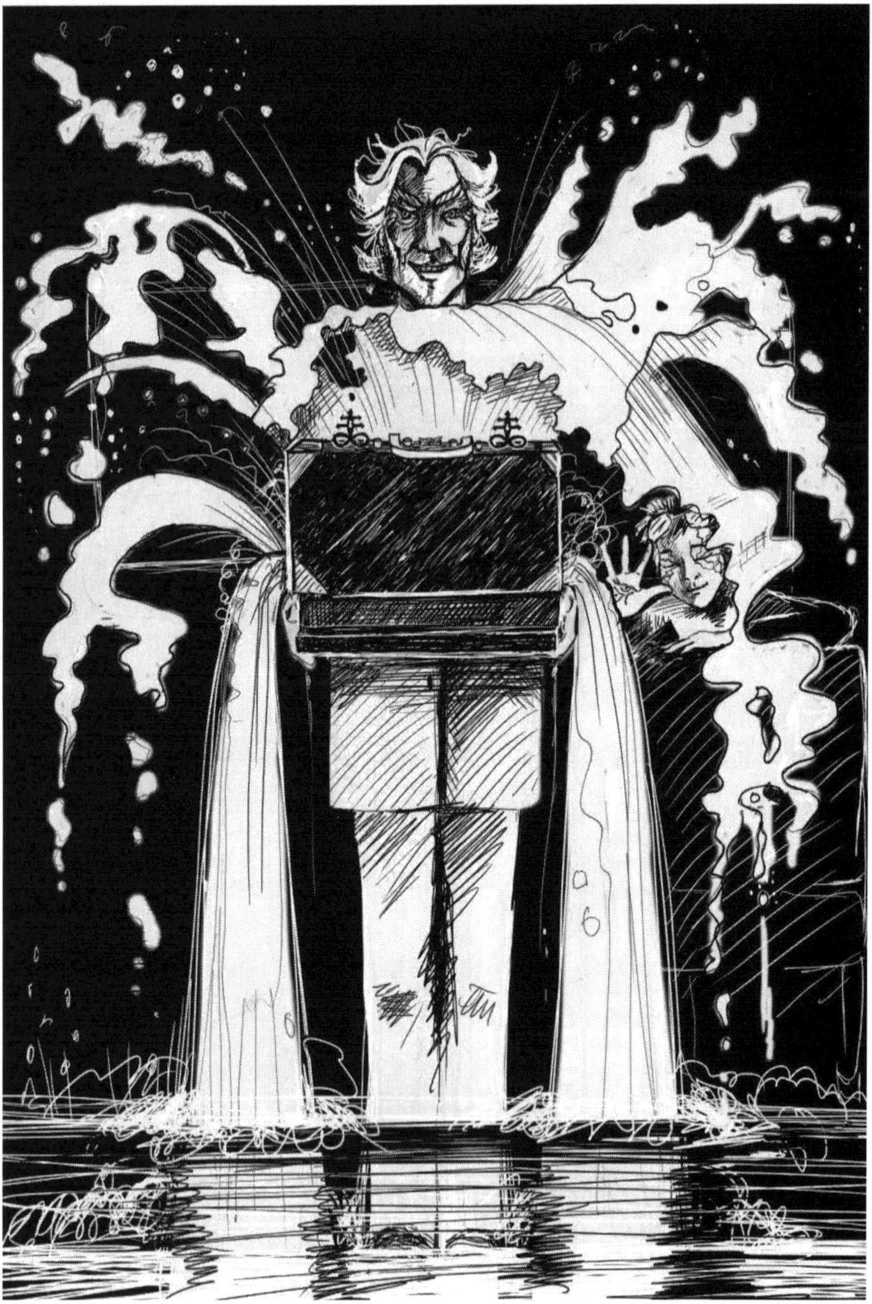

putting an end to all of this, disaster came pouring out of the case.

"NO!" Theo's screams died as he was swept back by the torrent of water that came crashing into him like a battering ram and all from that small black square Carrick held in his hands. Theo couldn't understand any of it and had little time to even try and comprehend how he was doing any of this or most of all why. No instead his mind was consumed with only two needs, *survival and rescue.*

When the chaos the gushing water caused finally calmed enough for Theo to get his bearings he knew that he was, like his new friends, quickly in a world of trouble. The bus was nearly completely filled with water now and he along with the others were barely holding on to what little air they had.

Theo swam to the surface and took a needed breath before ducking back under to try and pull the others from their seats. He first tried the girls but it was no use, they wouldn't budge and it was only when Ena shook her head at him that he gave up. She frantically nodded to the monster that had done this, reminding him that they were still under the guy's spell. Theo knew what he needed to do. Lucky for Theo he was a strong swimmer and could hold his breath longer than most.

So with that in mind, he turned his attention back to the cause and swam back at Carrick, channelling all of his anger into strength. It was obvious that by the time Carrick finally saw him coming, that it was the last thing he had been expecting. The shock on his face was what gave Theo the last push needed to quickly reach him and when he did, he wasn't the only one surprised by what happened.

Theo first reached out and touched the briefcase lid, trying to push it closed. The case not only slammed shut but it sizzled under Theo's hand, creating a wave of tiny white bubbles to rise to the surface. Only when the burning stopped, did Theo remove his hand and the first thing he saw was the scorched mark of his hand print now forever embedded in the thick leather on the case. Carrick screamed under water as he himself had been burnt by Theo's touch and he moved back clutching his briefcase to him in what now looked like fear.

"What are you?" He saw Carrick mouth the question under the water and he was amazed at how this guy was surviving without any air. As for Theo, he was quickly running out of it and when he swam up to the surface, the haunting reality became clear...

He had failed.

Theo only just managed one last gulp of air just as the bus became completely submerged under water, which thankfully managed to give him enough strength to try and kick out the window closest to him. When that failed he looked around for Ivan and this was when he noticed that the others were now free from Carrick's hold. However, from the way they all floated weightlessly in the water, he knew it didn't look good. It was almost as though they were suspended in time as each of their clocks had stopped.

He reached out trying to grab Ivan's hand that was floating closest to him in a last ditch attempt to bring him round. He figured that with their combined strength, they both might be able to break the window.

"You don't give up, do you?" Theo jerked back when he suddenly heard Carrick's voice speaking in his head. He looked around to see Carrick watching him with nothing short of wonder in his expression and strangely enough, a soft kindness in his eyes.

"You want to be a hero?" Carrick asked him, both shocking and scaring him at the same time. Theo didn't want some murdering freak poking around in his head and especially not if these were his last moments on earth. He knew he should have listened to his gut as his heart was nothing but a traitor to him now.

"You can't save them," Carrick warned and Theo shook his head in anger. He couldn't believe that, he just couldn't. He had to try...he had no choice.

"You always have a choice, in this world and the next," Carrick continued to speak to him and no matter how Theo tried to ignore it, he found himself being drawn further and further into his words. No! he couldn't let himself go there! He was stronger than this! So with one last reach, he grabbed onto Ivan's hand and as soon as he made contact, unbelievably the large Russian opened his eyes. It was almost as if his touch had caused an electrical current to repower his body, jarring him back into life.

Theo nodded frantically to the window and began kicking out at it so that Ivan got the hint. The big guy moved back, getting into position and with his first kick, smashed the whole panel out of the frame. Theo knew he couldn't help the others without first getting the desperate air he needed, so shook his head at Ivan, telling him with one look that they couldn't help the others without first helping themselves. He knew they were useless if they were both dead.

The last thing Theo saw before swimming through the gap was Carrick shaking his head as though disappointed it had all happened this way. Theo didn't fully understand the look or where it was coming from but right then, he didn't care.

Ivan followed him as he turned his back to the Monster responsible, as he needed to focus on saving the others. The vast lake water looked dark and gloomy, making it hard to see what was around them but it was clear that sunlight was leading the way to the surface. If anything, it looked almost as if they were reaching up for Heaven.

Almost there, Theo said over and over in his mind knowing they were so close. He looked back at his friend making sure he was still with him and Theo almost smiled as he was so sure that they would make it. But then something started happening and for the second time that day he saw something else he couldn't explain.

"Look out!" Theo mouthed the panicked words of warning, releasing the last of his air to do it but it was too late. Shadowed serpents deep from below them started to rise up like giant water snakes and as Ivan was below Theo, they got a hold of him first. Ivan's eyes widened just as he felt the first tug downwards and

Theo reached down, stretching out his hand for him to grab. Their fingertips barely touched before he could tighten his grip and with one last tug, his new friend was gone.

"NO!" Theo's scream also meant the end for him too if he didn't reach the surface. So, with nothing left for him to do, he looked back up at his only survival and pulled himself up, using his weakened arms to drag his body through the water.

"You might have their spirit boy, but you don't yet have their power, not until you die Theo." He heard Carrick's voice in his head again and just as his hand emerged out of the water first, that's when he felt his own deadly tug from the serpents. He looked down as they entwined themselves first around his legs and then slid through the water up the rest of his body. Once there Theo started to twist himself free but it was no use as they started to squeeze themselves tighter, getting a better grip on him and snarling at him under the water. It was now he noticed that they looked like demonic eels made of black oily ink that had at some point slithered into the lake and had come alive as if for this very purpose.

Theo knew when he had been beaten and it was as if Carrick knew it too.

"That's it, just let it happen." This was said out of comfort and as Theo closed his eyes, he knew it was the last voice on earth he would have wanted to hear this from. But for some unknown reason all

© Caroline Fairbairn

he felt was comfort and it was as though someone was also in the background, telling him to just accept it.

To just let go.

And then it came with Carrick's last words of

"Welcome to your Afterlife..." and with it,

His Death swiftly followed.

4
The Afterlife

Theo inhaled sharply as if taking his first breath all over again and he half expected to feel the burning pain of water flooding his lungs. But that wasn't what happened. He was no longer freezing cold from being plunged into the wintery depths of Hellish Lake and he was no longer feeling the strain on his muscles as he tried to fight for his life.

It was the complete opposite in fact. A warmth like no other enveloped him in a comforting cocoon and surrounded him as though the heat of the sun was giving him strength. He suddenly felt strong in ways he never had before and with this, combined with the peaceful calm of the darkness that surrounded him, he knew then that this was not the end...

It was only the beginning.

So when Theo awoke the last place he expected to find himself was still on the bus travelling down the road as if nothing had happened. Was he dreaming now or had he been dreaming then? He looked down at his clothes expecting to find them all dripping wet but they were bone dry. Then he looked around at the others to see everyone was doing the same as him. Even the bus was just as it had been before crashing into the lake and Theo couldn't help but put his fingers to the glass just to check it was actually still there.

"Okay, so what just happened?" This came from Zane who, unlike him, wasn't questioning the possibility of any of it being a dream. Ena was touching her hair and Ivan had his large sweater pulled out in front of him as he too was checking himself over.

"Cause I don't know about you guys but it kinda felt like I had just died." Zane added as if needing to be sure that everyone else was on the same dark page as he was.

"I don't know man, but I doubt we all dreamt the same thing." Theo said rubbing the back of his neck as if this would help relieve some of the tension.

"This is impossible," Ena muttered to herself but Theo was more concerned with the Goth girl as she was quietly weeping in her seat.

"Hey, are you alright?" Theo leaned over his seat and asked her, remembering himself before he touched her shoulder.

"I...I don't know...I feel...*weird,*" she whispered on a shaky breath.

"Yeah, well she isn't the only one!" Ena said getting that bite of attitude back in her tone.

"Did...did we...really... *drown?*" the Goth girl said, finally turning her head and looking at Theo for the first time. Big brown teary eyes met his and even through the black eye makeup streaming inky tracks down her pale skin, he could see the beauty she tried to hide under her hood.

"What's your name?" Theo asked using a softer tone and purposely reining in his temper to do so.

"Janie," she said rubbing her eyes with one hand and Theo didn't have the heart to tell her she'd just smudged all those black lines sideways, across her cheeks.

"Alright Janie, I'm Theo and that there is Zane, Ena and Ivan." Theo said nodding back to the others and was happy that she received kind looks from them all, especially Ivan who went as far as to give her a wink. Theo ignored her blush and carried on,

"I don't know what happened to us but whatever it is, I can promise you this...you're not alone. We are all in the same boat here."

"But we on bus," Ivan said looking confused and Ena smacked her forehead, muttering,

"Give me strength." Theo shot her a dirty look that told her to have some patience. Janie however giggled which was a much better sound than her fearful crying.

"Boat, bus, whatever. My point is that are we all in agreement that whatever just happened...well, it actually happened to all of us?" Theo asked addressing the whole group.

"Well if you mean some creepo in a bad suit just stepped onto our bus and kicked our asses with some water, a freaky voodoo briefcase and drowned us all, then yeah...I would say it happened!" Ena said sarcastically but at least she was straight to the point.

"What she said," Zane said shaking a thumb her way.

"I no understand," Ivan said shaking his head and having to place his hand on the seat in front as if he would soon pass out from it all.

"No me either, but I know someone who will." Theo said through gritted teeth, getting up and trying to ignore the fact that his legs wobbled, feeling as though his bones had been replaced with rubber bands. He made his way down to Rue who lifted up her hand towards the mirror as if this was how she was seeing who was coming. Hell, but after what felt like had just happened, he wouldn't have been surprised if the blind girl could see with her hands.

"Look Kid, before you give me attitude you have to know that this was not the way it was supposed to go down." Theo frowned and nearly let his mouth drop open in shock. He didn't know what was more surprising, the fact that she hadn't automatically started denying it and passing it off as nothing or the fact that any of it had been real and actually happened!

"You drove us into a damn lake!" he shouted making her wince and bunch her shoulders up, which only highlighted her guilt.

"Well yes, there was that," she said and Theo thought he would actually growl he was getting that mad.

"I think you'd better start explaining things here Rue…don't you?" he said trying not to make it sound like a threat, he really did, but that was going to be a mission for anyone considering he was obviously now talking to someone who had been an accomplice to what should have been his death.

"I wish I could but I can't," she said turning off the main road onto a single lane that was covered either side by thick forest. Theo tried not to wonder where she was taking them now as his trust in her was back down to zero.

"Can't or more like *won't?*" he snapped. *"Can't...*but don't worry, because *they can,"* Rue said nodding ahead through the window and Theo looked up in time to see the huge mansion coming into view.

"Holy..."

"...Grail Bananas! Yeah I know, pretty cool, huh?" Rue said interrupting him from saying something a lot stronger than 'fruit' that was for sure.

"Uh...are we at the right place?" Theo couldn't help but ask as he suddenly realised how Harry Potter must have felt when riding in that boat and seeing Hogwarts for the first time. Okay so it wasn't a castle but it came pretty damn close!

For starters there was no saying how big the place actually was as most of it was hidden by thick forest on either side, but Theo guessed that it went much further back than it looked. Only the grand entrance and front of the house was visible, with its thick weathered stones that were half covered in a blanket of lush green ivy that looked thick enough to climb. It certainly had enough features to be filed away in the 'Horror film' creepy section of Theo's imagination because the very last thing this house screamed was *school.* Now a place people went to if they fancied making the news with the headline...Missing Boy/Girl then yeah, it would fit right in, but a place to learn? Theo didn't think so.

"Trust me Kid, this is the right place," Rue said on a chuckle and then pulled the bus in front of the building,

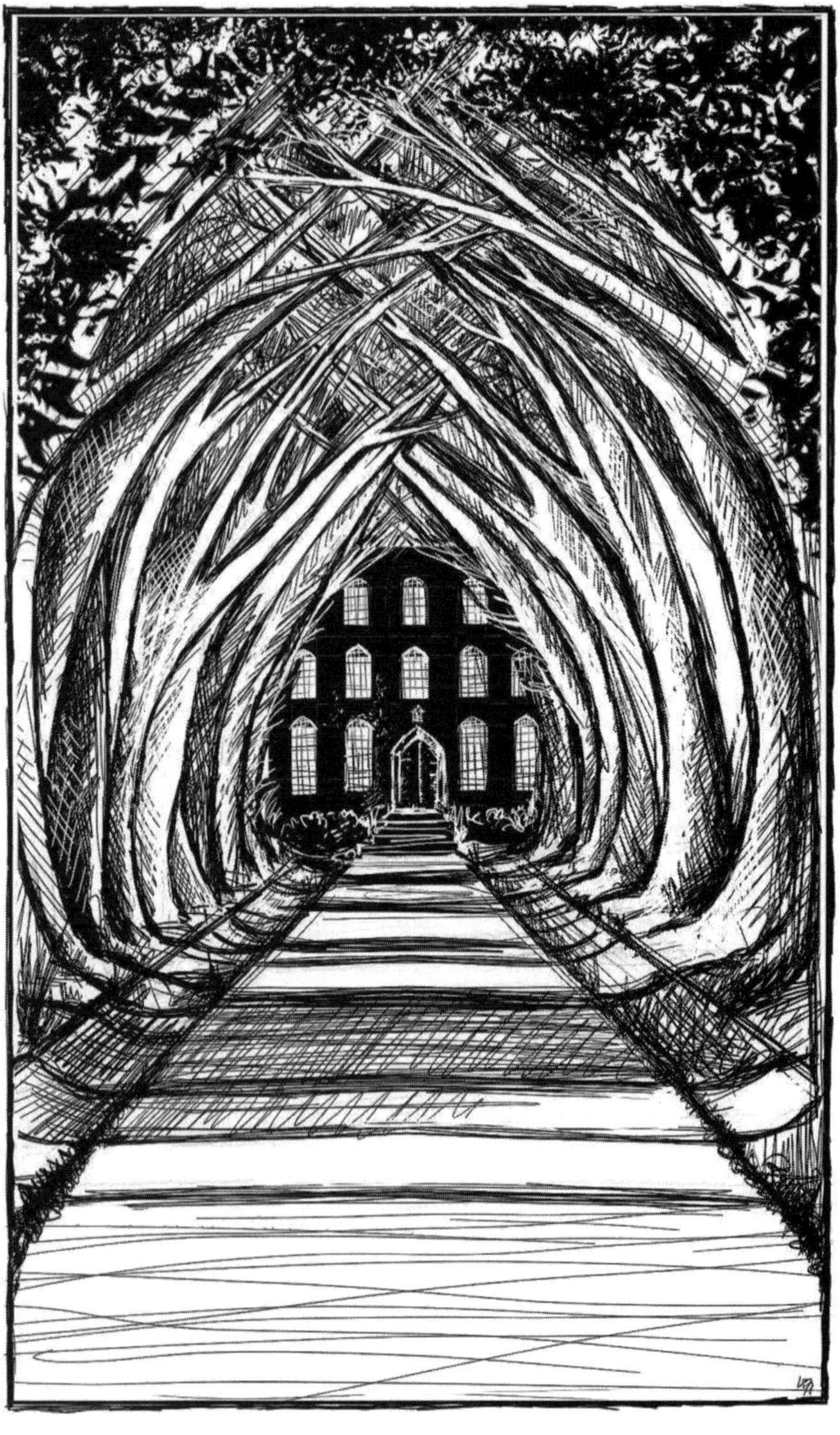

squealing the tires as she managed to pull off some spinning handbrake turn, barely keeping all the wheels on the ground. After giving her an even dirtier look, Theo looked around the large parking lot that was empty, save for one blue truck that looked to be one journey short of a junk yard. Theo looked back to see everyone was staring out of the window in utter shock, probably thinking the exact same thing he was...

This was no school!

"What on earth is this place?" Theo muttered under his breath.

"Your new home Kid, now get off the bus," Rue said shocking him.

"Excuse me?" he replied with a raised eyebrow. She cut the engine after stopping the bus right outside the main doors which definitely looked more imposing than of the welcoming kind. The entrance was just as grand as the building, if not more so with its impressive stone archway standing tall and jutting out making a clear statement, one that Theo interpreted more as *'Enter at your own risk'* than the 'Welcome home' mat he had been hoping for.

Rue pulled the lever to open the creaky bus doors making Theo jump.

"You heard me Kid, this is your last stop."

"You sure about that?" Theo said sarcastically, knowing he was actually referring to the fact that she had possibly tried to kill them all only a short time ago. Well if that's what happened on just the journey getting there, then God only knew what was in store for them when they stepped inside the place.

"Sure I'm sure or surely as I am ever going to be sure," she said winking at him with a wicked grin.

"Right," he muttered, frustrated that she was obviously finding this more amusing than serious. He looked back to the others and from the looks of things they were all waiting to see what he would do first before making their move. Well he doubted that they would be allowed to just stay on the bus, shout mutiny and kick out the blind chick before taking the bus to Mexico. So with that in mind he took a deep breath and took the first steps off the bus into Horrorville.

"Shake like a tree, people!" He heard Rue say behind him before the rest of them moved quickly to follow him into the unknown. Once they had all piled off the bus the door slammed shut behind them and Rue pulled away fast enough to kick up gravel around the tires before driving out of sight.

"Wait! What about our stuff!?" Ena shouted as the bus disappeared around a hidden road by the left side of the building into what looked like straight into the thick forest.

"Well I for one am going to be looking out for my vintage Doc Martins on ebay," Zane said dryly, getting an evil glare from Ena.

"She wouldn't dare get rid of our stuff!" Ena shouted back and Zane chuckled at her before putting their dire circumstances into perspective,

"Oh no, I'm sure the one who just tried to drown us all in a lake with some serial killer whose favourite colours are most likely beige and blood, before then dumping us outside a house worthy of a Stephen King novel, is going to take great care of our stuff!"

"Alright genius, then what are we going to do now?" she snapped back, folding her arms across her chest and tilting her head as if expecting answers. Zane held up his hands in defeat and said,

"Hey don't look at me, I'm not running this Shindig Sweetheart, I'm just dancing alone in the corner." Ena rolled her eyes before looking expectantly to Theo, along with everyone else.

"Yes! Now that is a much better choice. Theo here, he's your main man," Zane said enthusiastically jumping to Theo's side and patting him on the back, no doubt just glad that he was now off the hook.

"What?" Theo asked confused, looking from one to the other as they all stared expectantly at him.

"You're now in charge, that's what," Ena said and Theo half expected her to click her fingers after the announcement.

"Oh no, not happening," Theo said backing up and noticing the worried look that Janie gave him as if she especially needed him to take the lead on this one.

"Oh come on dude, what did you expect? We have been following your lead since you first stepped on that bus to Hell…so now it's time to man up and lead this band of merry men into the house of horrors…which just so I am clear…means him going first, right?" Zane said looking at the others this time making Theo roll his eyes right along with Ena.

"This isn't exactly what I had in mind," Theo admitted and Ena raised her hand out pointing to the house and snapped,

"And you think we did?!"

"Please Theo, can't you see that we need you?" Janie said in a quiet voice that was barely more than a whisper.

"Yes, you be leader is logical choice." Ivan said before doing as Zane did and patting him on the back, only when Zane had done it, it hadn't made Theo fall forward on a step just to keep himself upright.

"Alright, but let's at least think about our options here," Theo said taking a step back so he could look at them all, putting his back to the creepy house.

"Which are?" Ena asked putting a hand to her hip already showing attitude before carrying on,

"Because last I checked, we have no stuff, no ride, no money and oh yeah, a big fat nowhere else to go."

"Oh right, because these are the reasons to stay at the Bates' motel…put me down for a park bench," Zane said making Ena huff and Ivan look confused.

"It's an old horror movie from the 60's called Psycho." Janie told him softly making him smile down at her.

"Nice to see another cultured horror movie groupie is in the group," Zane told her, giving her a wink and making her blush again.

"Great, and I like long walks in the park, playing netball and hopefully living well past the legal drinking age …can we move on now to the more important stuff…say, are we going into horror school or not?" Ena said, first addressing Zane and then moving on to question Theo, who they had already named leader. Theo looked back at the house trying to weigh up their options. He knew he could get this wrong either way but he at least needed to try and find the lesser of two evils. On one hand, walking away might not get them very far considering no matter how annoying Ena could be, what she had said was right…they had nothing. But then walking through those doors was going to mean only one of two things, either death or answers.

"Has anyone got a phone on them?" Theo asked having an idea. Everyone shook their heads apart from Ena.

"Lucky then I didn't put it in my bag like Rue asked," she told him fishing it out of her blazer pocket and handing it over. Theo gave her a grin, admiring that she had a rebellious streak, one in this case that might end up saving their lives.

"What's your plan?" Janie asked obviously feeling more and more at ease around them.

"You'll see," he told her and like the others, winked at her. Ena walked past him to walk next to Janie but mainly to give her some advice, advice that made Theo chuckle out loud.

"Wanna know the best advice I ever got?" Janie nodded holding her one hand still hidden within her jacket the closer Ena got.

"Beware the handsome face, for they can lie just like the rest." Janie's eyes got wide as she thought about it before surprising Ena when she looked not to Theo or to Zane but first to Ivan as he walked past them both to stand next to Theo. Ena followed on, looking to the house so that she could not only hide her shock but also her knowing smile from Janie.

"So what do we do now…knock three times and say there's no place like home?" Zane asked as they approached the thick black gates.

"Seriously though, are you ever going to stop dropping movie quotes?" Ena asked sarcastically.

"I don't know, are you ever going to remove that pole from your…"

"Enough bickering," Theo said interrupting him.

"What, I was going to say nose," he argued knowing this wasn't true.

"Yeah, right you were," Ena muttered when poor Ivan was once again just left looking confused, so Janie smiled up at him and said,

"The Wizard of Oz."

"Ah, me like little dogs," Ivan said grinning, this time making Zane confused.

"Uh, he likes what now?"

"I think he means Toto," Janie said making it obvious that she was going to be the go to girl when things got confusing around them. Theo was at least glad it was giving her something to focus on other than the potentially dangerous situation they were about to enter into.

"Well, here goes nothing," Theo said holding the phone in one hand and pulling on the gate with the other. He didn't know why but he was surprised to see it was open, getting the strange sense that this only happened when it was dark. He let Ivan open the other side until both were back against the stone archway allowing them access to the heavy oak doors that *did* look as though they belonged on a castle. They were massive and for once tall enough so that Ivan didn't have to worry about ducking to get through.

They were riveted with black iron studs and large hammered iron hinges that looked more for a purpose than as a feature. Theo placed a hand at the centre, getting ready to push and noticed that the same family crest that was on the wax seal on his letter was also carved under his hand. He hadn't known what to expect but finding the door warm to the touch hadn't been it. He frowned as an overwhelming feeling came over him as though he was meant to be here and nothing had ever felt more right.

"You okay?" Theo was surprised by the way the door had affected him but he was even more surprised to hear that this concern had come from Ena.

"Yeah, just a weird feeling that's all. Come on, let's get this over with," he answered her and before taking a secret shaky breath, he pushed open the door. As they all walked in they were shocked by what they found.

"What is this place?" Janie braved to ask, speaking first and letting her voice echo around the massive open space.

"I don't know but what's our first lesson going to be, how to bury a dead body after making a round of bloody Marys?" Zane replied staring at the Gothic space which looked as if someone had turned an abandoned church into a nightclub for Vampires.

"Or maybe home economics will be how to pickle your favourite body parts?" he added, making Janie chuckle and Ena groan.

"This can't be right." Theo said also noticing the glass bar behind them which was decorated in fancy scrolled iron work. Then he looked back, taking in the high arched stone ceilings, wrought iron chandeliers and plush purple and red velvets that covered the different seating areas.

"Not unless I hit twenty-one already and I am early to the party," Ena said giving her take on the nightclub that surrounded them.

"I no understand," Ivan piped up, adding to their confusion and doing so with considerably less sarcasm than the others.

"No and that includes the rest of us, big guy," Zane said patting him on the back as he walked further into the room. But then he quickly froze on the spot when they all heard a high pitched squeal from the mezzanine level above them that was situated at the far end of the club.

"What was that?" Janie whispered fearfully, getting behind Ivan, which right then seemed like the smartest thing to do. Theo couldn't help thinking that it sounded as if someone was being hurt, so without giving it another thought, Theo pressed the ring button on the phone and called the numbers he had keyed in before entering the club.

"911, what's your emergency?" the operator on the other end asked.

"Hi, I think someone is hurt, we are at…" Theo was about to explain about the nightclub when suddenly the line went dead. He pulled the phone from his ear to look at the screen just in time to see it start to disintegrate into metallic dust and Theo dropped it before it could touch him. It landed on the floor and burst into a little cloud of dust.

"I don't think you will be needing that," came an eerie calm voice that echoed around the room. All five teenagers fearfully looked up at the same time to see a shadowed figure emerge on the balcony…

Their new Headmaster.

5
My Bad

"*How the Hell did he do that?*" Ena asked through gritted teeth as if Theo should know. At that moment he wanted to turn around and remind her that he wasn't exactly the expert on freaky crap or warped realities. Ones that especially started with them being driven here by a blind chick, drowned by a someone who would give the grim reaper a run for his money and then brought to Hell's twisted take on a nightclub. So instead he decided it best to go with a warning.

"Get back," Theo whispered to the others over his shoulder and without even thinking about the danger, he stepped forward taking his place as leader. He looked up at the shadowed figure standing tall above them knowing this guy was the one in charge. However, Theo couldn't help but notice something odd when he did this and even though the guy was stood in the shadows, he could still see the brief flash of purple that lit his eyes.

"Who are you?!" Theo ordered in a commanding voice even he barely recognised. This time he could see the whites of this guy's teeth as he grinned momentarily.

"You must be Theo," said an equally commanding voice, only his had the added bonus of age and clearly years of authority behind it.

"That's right." Theo wanted to add more to this and throw attitude his way but, looking back at his friends, he knew it would be too risky. But he thought if he could at least keep this guy's attention on him then it might give the others time to get out, as the main doors were still open. He wasn't sure what he could see from up there but it was pretty dark down where they were stood, so Theo thought it was worth a chance.

"Make your way slowly to the door, I will keep him distracted," he told the others, knowing that it would be impossible for the guy to have heard him whispering from all the way up there.

"But what about you?" Ena asked just as quietly along with Zane when he added,

"Yeah dude, we are not leaving you."

"I will make a run for it, just go!" he told them, knowing full well that his chances were next to nil. Theo looked back up to the balcony and started walking closer to try and draw the guy's attention away from his friends.

"So you know who I am, don't you think it's time I know who *you* are?" he asked, purposely projecting his voice to try and mask the sound of footsteps echoing in the room as the others tried to sneak out.

"Leaving so soon?" the man asked calmly before Theo heard the doors slamming shut behind him, making his shoulders tense knowing they didn't make it. He looked behind him to see that Janie was still cowering behind Ivan and Zane shrugged his shoulders as he came to stand next to him.

"Got any more ideas?"

"Nope, you?" Theo asked Zane back.

"Other than picking up the big Russian and throwing him at the guy, then no, I'm fresh out." Theo raised his eyebrow at the idea and looked back at the same time as Zane at the giant who was clearly protecting the girls.

"Yeah no, don't think our muscles are going to cut it." Zane said sarcastically.

"I'm thinking not." Theo agreed taking a deep breath and taking charge once more.

"What do you want with us?!" he shouted up at the man who just seemed to be watching their interaction with great curiosity.

"Fear not young man, I am merely here to welcome you all to your new home. My name is…" He was about to tell them who he was when he was suddenly interrupted by the same high-pitched squeal they had first heard when entering the club. The sound of doors bursting open came from above before a rainbow of colour started racing into view.

"AHHH they are here! OM Genius! They are finally here…oh just look at the little crumpets!" This came from a riot of colour that started racing down the grand staircase which curved down to the main floor of the nightclub. There was another one that mirrored it on the other side, both framing a large stage area.

Theo watched in utter shock as a small girl raced towards them, skidding on the bottom step and righting herself on the banister before she fell on her backside. She had bright green hair in twisted pigtails that showed the slightest hints of blue streaks high on her head. She was older than her size suggested but had a cute baby face which would still make it hard to gauge how old she actually was.

But it was her style which had everyone, including Theo, staring in awe. The whole of one arm was covered in one big tattoo that looked like a sky painted on her forearm, with swirls of blue

77

and purple storm clouds with a small V shape of birds flying past. Above that was a strange thick black ring of ancient text and different symbols that fascinated Theo, causing him to wonder what they could mean. He couldn't see more as she wore a T shirt that he couldn't help but chuckle at. It was white with black writing that said, 'Zombies hate fast food' and underneath there was a picture of a couple of Zombies trying to catch some innocent people running from them.

Rainbow tie dye shorts covered in silver glitter were also part of the outfit, along with purple tights with white stars and knee high converse shoes that were covered in white skulls. She smiled, flashing her lip ring and her nose stud which was a winking smiley face. Even the pair of mirrored goggles strapped around her head and nestled in between her two green buns had skull hands attached to the sides. She resembled a Goth who had been dipped into a vat of rainbow paint and then someone had thrown a tub of glitter over her before she had time to dry.

"Oh my Mona Lisa! You guys are soooo freakin' cute! My name is Pipper Winifred Ambrogetti, well Miss Pip to you guys but I will not accept or answer to Miss Pipper Pants or Miss Am.I.Like.Spaghetti because that's not how you say my last name and it's just mean... Well, well, well come on then, let me shake your hands!" she said reeling off this little speech and speaking a million miles an hour. After this she stepped forward and started at the back with Ena.

"And you must be Ena. Oh aren't you rockin' some style girl! Love that blazer, very eighties or is it in now...? You know all the styles come back around at some point and personally I am still waiting for the bustle dress to make it back on the block," Miss Pip said stuffing her hands in her short's pockets and rocking back on the heels of her feet like a child would.

"Uh...bustle dress?" Ena said obviously confused and taken aback like the rest of them were.

"Just think lots of layers and ruffles that equal big bums and you will have an idea...any who, moving right along the bus to our next contestant...who do we have here..." she said sidestepping to Ivan who was standing guard in front of Janie and looking down at Miss Pip like she was a rare coloured butterfly he was fascinated with.

"Wowee, you're a big guy ain't ya?" she said after raising her head up and whistling because of his size.

"I be Ivan," he said down to her making her giggle.

"You be Yoda bear, that's who...see what I did there, you know, instead of *Yogi* bear?" she asked us all with her emerald green eyes open wide and expectantly.

"Oh come on people, it's a cartoon...oh never mind, I can see I have a lot of work on my hands! At least tell me you know who Yoda is, 'cause if not then Star Wars will be first on my lesson plan!"

"I think I might like this school after all," Zane muttered to Theo nudging his shoulder.

"We know who Yoda is." Ena told her, frowning at Zane's comment and making him moan at obviously not getting his Star Wars lesson after all. Miss Pip clapped her hands together making her numerous crazy rings clash together, one of which looked like a tiny cleaver chopping through two fingers, complete with plastic blood dripping down one knuckle.

"Excellent! We will all get on just fine then."

"I know not this Yoda," Ivan said frowning and Miss Pip closed her eyes and raised her head to the ceiling muttering something to herself about strength. Then as if someone clicked their fingers, her head snapped back down to look at Zane.

"You!"

"Me?" Zane said pointing at his own chest.

"Yeah, emo boy, you're Zane right, the artist/music/movie freak which is all totally meant in the best way possible?" Zane looked to Theo as if to confirm whether or not this was an actual question Miss Pip had thrown his way.

"Uh…yeah," he said after Theo just shrugged his shoulders as if to say, 'Don't ask me'.

"Cool beans, right your job is to teach the big guy movie culture from at the very least the eighties and upwards or this…right here…" she paused a minute so she could circle her hand around, motioning towards herself and Ivan before carrying on with,

"…is gonna get Space Odyssey pretty soon!"

"What does she mean by that?" Theo asked Zane who chuckled.

"At a guess, I would say she means the word 'confusing', seeing as 2001, A Space Odyssey is one of those movies that leaves your head hurting and wondering how on earth you will ever get those wasted three hours back."

"Gotya," Theo replied, thankful to have at least one of the group who understood their new teacher, otherwise she was right, it would get 'Space Odyssey' pretty soon.

"Okay, so I feel like we are missing a girl." Miss Pip said looking around the place as if expecting her to be hiding somewhere which, of course, she was. It was only when Ivan cleared his throat that Miss Pip twigged where to look and as soon as she did, she decided the best way to approach a nervous girl in hiding was to pop out from around Ivan and shout,

"BOO!"

"Ah!" Janie screamed and moved away from Miss Pip, but in doing so she must have forgotten herself because both her arms went up in defence and now everyone could see what she had been hiding all this time.

"Janie I..." Theo started to say something but with one look at her face he let it trail off...*she looked ashamed*. Janie was born without a left hand and this was one of the reasons she wasn't just a nervous person but also the reason she usually kept herself to herself. She had experienced years of being bullied for being different and as a result, trusted no one. She also believed this was one of the reasons she had never been adopted as she would often ask herself...'Well who would want a broken child when there were plenty of whole ones to choose from?'

But what Janie didn't know, along with the other four orphans who had got onto the bus that day, was that there were reasons for everything in their lives...lives they were only now about to discover the true meaning of.

"Oh there's no need to be shy, I'm not gonna bite off your other hand...just maybe chew on your leg a bit," Miss Pip added joking and winking at her. The others meanwhile looked on in horror at not only her comment but mainly at what she did next. Because before Janie had a choice, Miss Pip grabbed her left arm and shook it, clearly not choosing Janie's one good hand for a reason.

Janie's eyes grew wide in surprise and glistened with unshed tears as it was obvious that she was deeply touched by the gesture. For a start, other than seeing a doctor when she was little, no one ever touched Janie's left arm, in fear that they would get burnt by it or something. And secondly, in just those few seconds, Miss Pip had made Janie feel normal for the very first time.

"It's nice to meet you," Janie said after finding her voice along with her courage.

"And it's a red Jolly Rancher meeting you too! By gosh but you two girls are just the prettiest dolls! You boys better behave is all I can say!" She added wagging her finger at the boys before spinning on one foot. Theo smirked, watching both girls blush right along with Ivan, who didn't seem to know where to put himself as he shifted from one foot to the other.

"Right, well without further ado and some green Mountain Dew, I can crack on with showing you guys...oh but wait, DUH! I knew I was missing someone!" Miss Pip said interrupting herself suddenly and slapping a hand to her forehead dramatically. Theo couldn't help but cringe slightly knowing that he was next and hoping he didn't have the same treatment as Janie as he knew he would have no choice but to appear rude. But what other option was there...tell her 'Sorry I can't shake your hand because you're tiny and I am pretty sure one touch might kill you'...he didn't think so.

"Well just look at you, why am I not surprised to find you as leader of the pack! And so handsome! It's almost like Thor and Achilles had a baby. Well that was if one of them was a girl and I don't just mean dressed up as one, 'cause as we should all know, that wouldn't work either. But Crackers and Cheese, I am really hoping I don't have to teach you that lesson…"

"I uh…I think we are good, Miss.," Zane jumped in to say before Janie's cheeks turned nuclear from blushing so hard.

"Phew! That's a relief!" Miss Pip said, pretending to wipe the sweat from her forehead. Meanwhile Zane leant into Theo and muttered two words, making him choke on a laugh,

"Awkward much."

"Now let's get back to it then shall we…if you would all like to follow me I can show you to your new crib," she said walking ahead and back towards the staircase, but before the others could follow Theo stepped up to the leadership role.

"Not so fast."

"Theo." Ena hissed his name, warning him not to do anything she would consider rash but Theo had gone beyond all the strange behaviour and cryptic answers. So he decided to just come right out and say what was on his mind.

"First we want to know what exactly happened to us on that bus and why we are here?" Miss Pip paused her skipping strides and they all watched as her shoulders slumped. Then, before turning back round to face them, she looked up at the man in the shadows who, until then, they had all forgotten was still there watching them.

A few silent moments passed as if they were somehow communicating with each other without speaking and it was only when Theo noticed the man nod his head that Miss Pip turned to face them.

"Okay, so you wanna know what happened?" Theo looked back to the others after Miss Pip had asked this and noticed them step a little closer so they didn't miss out on the answer...one everyone was obviously desperate to hear.

"Yes, we do." When Theo said this Miss Pip simply shrugged her shoulders and said,

"Suit yourself, I was going to wait until we had cookies and milk but no time like the one that ticks."

"I could wait 'til there's cookies." Zane said and Theo lightly punched him on the arm, letting him know now was not the time for jokes.

"Just explain what happened to us," Theo demanded again, not expecting for one minute that the next three words out of her mouth would be the ones she said...

"You all died."

6
It's Always the Quiet Ones

> RIP
> Theo
> Ena . Zane
> Janie . Ivan

"Uh...come again?" This came from Zane, who seemed to be the only one who could speak at that moment, well that was until Theo shook his head and muttered,

"That's impossible."

"Oh I think you will find it's very possible, especially with a death dealer hitching a ride," Miss Pip said snorting a humourless laugh and saying it in the same matter of fact way as she had used when telling them all something as dire as 'you're dead.'

"Carrick." Theo snarled the name.

"I think I am hearing things again." Janie said holding a hand to her forehead as if feeling faint and it seemed like an automatic reaction for Ivan to take a step next to her just in case she fell.

"Well I for one am not listening to this nonsense anymore, I am so outta here!" Ena said turning on her heel and pushing past Zane who looked concerned.

"Oh no Pickles, there is no need for that…buggar but I knew I should have done this over cookies and milk…they were chocolate chip as well," Miss Pip said shaking her head at herself.

"Ena wait!" Theo shouted after her and jogged to catch up before she got to the main doors.

"What?!" she snapped spinning around to face him.

"Look I know this is all crazy and I agree with you that we need to leave but not before we at least get an explanation," Theo argued as Ena crossed her arms over her chest in protest but when he had finished she just rolled her eyes and threw her arms back up in the air when she had heard what he had to say.

"They're lying! Can't you see that this is just some big sick joke to them?"

"But why? Come on, think about it. Why would they bring us all the way here just to make us believe we had died...*for a joke?!*" Theo asked knowing he was slowly cracking her resolve.

"Yes!" she shouted back but Theo knew it was a lie.

"Oh come on, you were on that bus too Ena, so you can't possibly believe that!" Theo said now being the one crossing his arms and raising a disbelieving eyebrow at her. It was when he saw her shoulders slump that he knew she was losing her argument.

"I don't know what to think anymore other than how crazy this all is...I mean think about what she is telling us Theo...she is trying to convince us that we all died for god's sake! So what exactly does that make us now...*ghosts?!*" Theo had to agree with her on this because as much as he wanted to take her hand and walk out of there with the rest of them, telling himself that it was all a lie, he knew he couldn't do that.

"I don't have the answers Ena, but I just know that *they do* and if I walk out of here right now then I will be doing so always asking myself what happened this day but more importantly...*why.*" He knew he was getting through to her when he saw those big light blue eyes of hers look to the side as if thinking things through herself.

"I'm scared, okay." she whispered suddenly as if admitting some big shameful secret, one that Theo already knew. It was one of the things he was best at picking up on in people...*fear.* It was one of the reasons he was so sympathetic to other people, as though if he allowed it he could feel it for himself, as if it was

something he could touch or taste without actually experiencing the fear himself. And looking back at them all now, he could feel it coming from everyone.

But Theo wasn't afraid. No...*he was angry.*

"You're not alone but if you walk out that door right now, then you will be. There's strength in numbers Ena, I truly believe that," he told her and at that moment he really wished he could have taken her hand in comfort, for both their sakes.

He found himself surprised by what a single day had done to him. He had started this day with little knowledge of his future it was true, but if someone had told him that he would end it by trying to convince others to band together, then he would have called them crazy. Theo was a loner by choice, so what was it about these four teens that made him finally feel as though he belonged for the first time in his life. He had known them for what only felt like minutes but he was ready to risk his life for them and call each of them family.

"I hope you're right about this, that's all I can say," Ena said after sniffing loudly and trying to shake off the remains of her emotions.

"Me too. Now let's go get our answers," Theo said nodding over his shoulder back to the others, who were nervously watching this play out between the two of them.

"Plus, who else is going to look after Janie and warn her about the dangers of being flirted with by handsome and charming boys?" Theo joked nudging her arm with his elbow and forgetting himself...something he seemed to do often around this lot. Ena gave him a wry look and a one-sided grin, without looking at all affected by his brief touch.

"Don't push it English, you're not that charming," Ena said walking ahead of him, making him laugh and he couldn't help but shout back,

"But still handsome!"

"Umm… debatable," she answered smirking and walking backwards for a few second to face him when she said this.

"Yay! The gang's all back together!" Miss Pip said clapping her hands to the balcony above. Theo frowned, because from back where he stood he could now see there were a lot more people up there than he'd first thought.

"Alrighty then, who wants to see their new room?!" Pip shouted bouncing back round to face them as if the death bomb she had recently dropped hadn't just rocked the foundations of their world. Theo quickly stepped back into his leadership role and strode straight past the others until he faced Miss Pip head on. "What we want is an explanation…*right…now."*

He said the last two words leaning closer down to her, making his point.

"Fine! But if I don't get to eat cookies then at the very least I insist we all sit down to conduct this little chin wig…some people were up all night painting some bedrooms you know…and when I say *some people* I actually mean *me* and when I say *some bedrooms*, what I actually mean is *yours!*" she replied before storming off in a huff to one of the booths which was tucked away next to one of the staircases at the far end of the room.

Theo looked back at the others to see that none of them quite knew what to do so he did the only thing he could think of and that was to shrug his shoulders and follow her to the booth. As he took his place he had to wonder just how many confused people before him had sat in that very same spot wondering what on earth they were doing there.

"Righty O, let's get this…oh dear, that's not good…and quite inconvenient if I might add," Miss Pip said with a slight twinge of an English accent and stopping herself as if she could sense something suddenly wasn't right. It was only when he noticed the panicked look in Miss Pip's eyes as she looked to the others, that his senses went on high alert. His whole body tensed as if he could feel the energy around him pulsating and beating as though they were all locked inside a giant drum.

"Theo! You'd better get over here…as in *now!*" He heard Zane shout and Theo was up and out of his seat in a heartbeat.

"Oh pants, it's happening sooner than we thought," he heard Miss Pip say behind him as he launched out of his chair. He ran full speed back over to the group who were all huddled over someone on the floor. Zane had his back to him but stood back up when Theo got there, revealing who it was that needed help…

"Janie?" Theo whispered her name as he bent down behind her, once again stopping himself from taking her hand. She was shaking her head back and to, muttering something he couldn't understand. It was almost as if she was speaking a different language or was someone possessed.

"What happened?" Theo asked not taking his eyes from her.

"We don't know, one minute we were about to follow you and the next she just collapsed," Ena said as she rubbed Janie's shoulder and tried to keep her head steady enough so she wouldn't hurt herself.

"Yeah, she started muttering something about 'this isn't my body' and then she was gone…it was just lucky that Ivan caught her," Zane said and Theo looked up to Ivan who was frowning down at Janie, looking upset.

"AHHHH, IT HURTS!" They all jumped when Janie started screaming in pain and she twisted her body back on itself as if something was trying to get out of her.

"Get over here!" Theo shouted back to Pip who was approaching them slowly. She didn't answer him or rush over as he'd hoped but instead she looked up at their audience in the shadows. Theo could feel his anger mounting as the helpless seconds ticked on and he stood and marched over to the centre of the room.

"Is this what you wanted?!" he demanded, stretching out his arms before carrying on,

"Is this some kind of sick spectator sport you freaks like to play or do you just get a kick out of being cruel!?" Theo shouted up at them making Miss Pip put a hand to her mouth and gasp. The shadow above them didn't respond but just folded his arms and continued to watch in silence.

"That's what I thought!" he snarled out and turned his back on them when Janie started screaming again.

"DO SOMETHING!" Ena bellowed up at them when she too let her anger overtake her fear.

"They won't help, come on, let's get her out of here," Theo said walking over to Ivan who had now backed away in a corner with his back to the rest of the room. It was obvious he was upset at seeing Janie this way and didn't want the rest of them to see.

"Ivan, I need you to carry Janie out of...*Ivan?*" As Theo approached he could now see Ivan's large frame shaking in the dark with his head tucked low as if trying to keep something in.

"Ivan, are you alright?" Theo asked quietly so as not to startle him, when he knew that he looked anything but.

"No closer!" Ivan shouted in a grating voice that didn't sound like it belonged to him.

"Ivan?" Theo whispered as he took that last step and the second he did, he quickly realised his mistake was not listening to Ivan's warning... but it was too late.

"RRRAAH!" Ivan suddenly threw his head back and roared up at the ceiling causing cracks to ripple their way along the stone arches and rain down debris. Theo covered his head protecting himself against any bigger chunks falling down before looking back at Ivan to see something completely different looking back at him...*something terrifying.*

"Oh God," Theo muttered in utter shock when looking back at the monster that Ivan was quickly changing into. Twisted horns were tearing through the back of his skull and growing up over his face, as if trying to create a mask of bone. Theo started walking backwards slowly as though expecting that any sudden movements would cause Ivan to suddenly charge at him like some demonic bull.

"What the Hell is that thing!?" Zane shouted finally realising what he was seeing. "Stay back, all of you! Just move slowly and...*Ena?*"

Theo started to warn the rest but this was when he noticed that what was happening wasn't just affecting Janie and Ivan but also now Ena. Zane also snapped his gaze to Ena who was standing on her tip toes completely ridged as if something was pulling out her limbs. She looked like some frozen ballerina, locked in the most unnatural position. Her arms were straight above her head, stretched out and her fingers were shaking erratically. It almost looked as if she was being electrocuted or at the very least an invisible electric current was touching her fingertips from above, because either way her body was pulsating from it.

"What's happening to them?!" Zane shouted looking from one to the other. Theo did the same and Zane was right, they were all changing right in front of their eyes. Janie was now surrounded by a black mist that seemed to be seeping out of the pores of her skin and floating around her still body as if it was protecting her. It also looked as though it was trying desperately to form into something but just before it did, it would burst as if not yet having enough power to do so.

"I don't know, but we need to get them out of here!" Theo shouted back to Zane as he stepped closer to Janie. But as he did this the dark smoke around her started to form into large scorpion tails and lashed out at him, trying to pierce his feet.

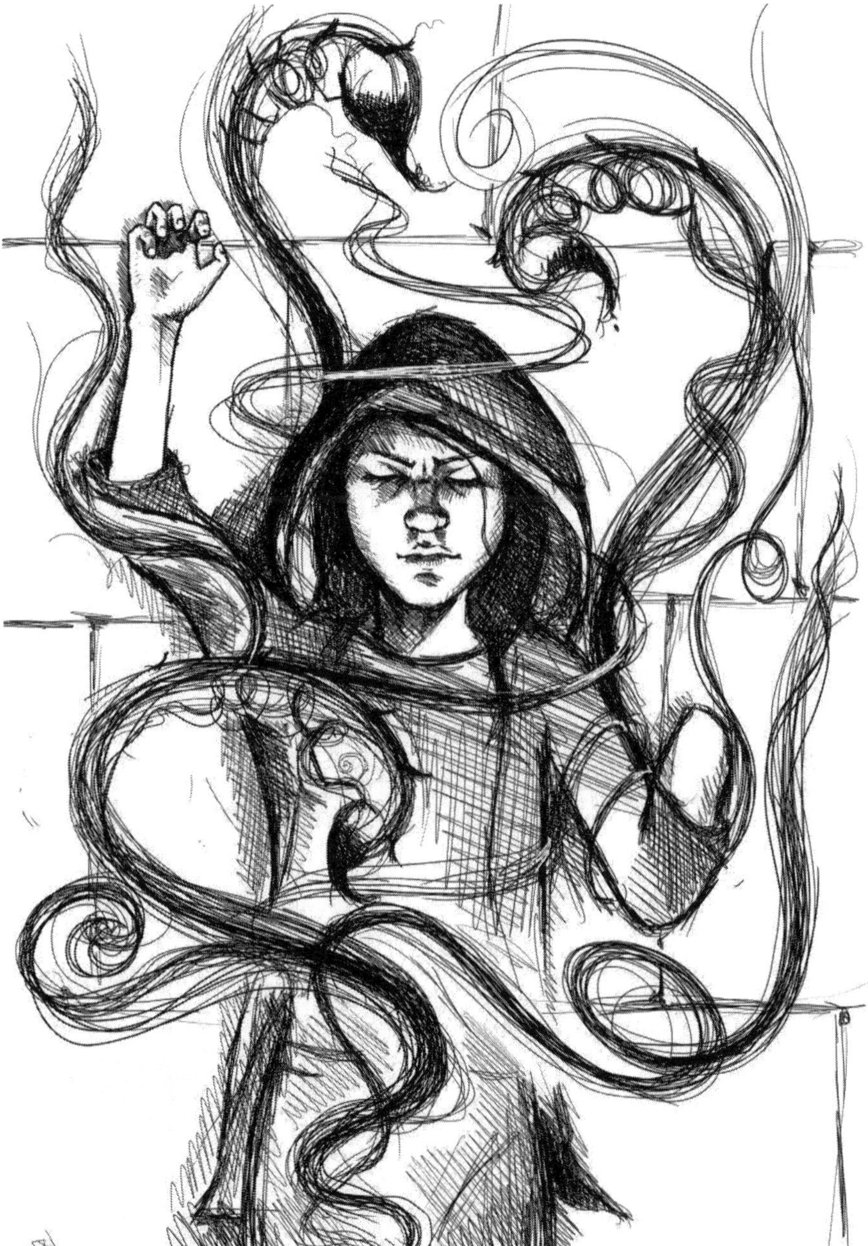

Theo jumped back just in time and in doing so must have startled the beast in Ivan, who had been quietly trying to contain himself in the corner.

"RUN THEO!" This roared warning came from the last person he expected and that was Ivan, the human part of the beast that started to charge at him now. Theo could tell that Ivan was trying to fight himself but as he lowered his head and got ready to charge, he knew that his friend had lost the battle within.

None of Ivan's features were left and it was as if the monster inside of him had completely consumed every last shred of his humanity. His face was now completely covered with twisted thick horns that interlocked by his chin and his size had almost doubled from what it once was.

What little was left of his clothes hung off his frame in shreds as he had obviously burst out of them. Even his skin had turned to smoky ash coloured rock. In some places it was even hardened the way molten lava cools rapidly when it hits the sea and his once smooth skin was now bulks of charred twisted stone.

And he looked *unstoppable.*

Theo watched as he charged straight for him with his horned head down ready to cause maximum damage and he waited until the very last second to make his move. Just before the monster could hit him Theo made a grab for Zane and rolled them both sideways out of his way. Ivan the monster couldn't stop himself in time and was about to go crashing into the stage area when Theo could hardly believe the next thing he saw. The shadowed man quickly jumped down from the balcony and whilst in mid-air a huge set of dark wings erupted from him, making him look like some dark angel falling from Heaven.

The man landed just before Ivan reached him and the impact sent a shockwave of power crashing through the room.

This not only forced Ivan's monster to go flying backwards saving himself from impact, but it also hit everyone else like a thunder wave, knocking them all out...all but Theo.

He lay motionless on the floor unable to move but unlike the others, he was still conscious. Theo looked at each of them and saw that not only had Janie's shadows disappeared but Ena was lay back on the floor as if fast asleep. Even Ivan was slowly turning back to the boy he used to be and Theo's eyes widened in shock as he witnessed the horns retracting back into the base of Ivan's skull.

"Well that didn't exactly go as party planned as we'd hoped... not like the others," he heard Miss Pip say and watched as she walked over to join the dark stranger with wings.

"Are you surprised?" The man said in a dry tone and Theo closed his eyes when he saw the man start to walk his way.

"I guess not given whose stubborn blood he carries," Miss Pip responded on a laugh. Theo could hear his footsteps getting closer until they stopped about a foot away from his head.

"Careful little Imp or I will tell them you said that," the man warned without any hint of an actual threat in his tone.

"So what now?" she asked ignoring his previous comment.

"The joining will have taken it out on their hosts, take them back to their rooms to rest, they will need it." "Aww the poor little mites, they will be plum tuckered," Miss Pip said

sympathetically just as Theo felt the man lower down on one knee next to him.

"So what about Theo…he's not asleep you know?" she asked, making Theo suck in a breath, knowing that his time pretending to be unconscious was at an end.

"No, but he soon will be." Hearing the man say this was what made Theo open his eyes and what he found staring back down at him wasn't the shadowed Angel he'd been expecting.

No, it was a shadowed…

Demon.

7
FREEDOM

When Theo opened his eyes again the very last place he expected to find himself was on the roof of his old school. This was Theo's secret place, one he would find himself going to when he needed to think and be alone from a world where he never felt he belonged. He knew that most people had a special place, but it took until the day he found the janitor's lost keys to find his. For some reason Theo could always think better when he was up somewhere higher than the rest of the world around him and for him, it was always the higher the better.

He used to have a huge tree he would climb, never stopping until he hit that highest branch before the point of it breaking. It was the only time he would feel at peace, as though he had finally found somewhere he belonged. People would often be amazed at his lack of fear and he once had a whole street outside watching as he saved a cat from the top of a roof.

The fire brigade had tried and failed, as the cat had simply moved further away from them, being more scared of the men than falling from a three storey town house. But whilst they were busy discussing new options of how to save the poor animal, Theo had already scaled up the house using the old iron drainpipe.

He remembered the gasps of fright and hysterical squeals of the neighbours at seeing him taking matters into his own hands. But before the firemen could get to him, he simply grabbed the cat by the scruff of its neck as if it was a kitten again and stuffed the scared animal into his jacket. Then he balanced himself along the narrow ridge of tiles, building up speed until he made the jump needed to reach the tree next to the house. He landed perfectly, grabbing onto one of the branches, amazingly without losing the cat. It was only when he reached the street level that he realised how unbelievable it all looked when one of the fireman dropped his helmet and said,

"How did you do that?" He was dumbstruck along with everyone else who had witnessed it, so Theo told them the only thing at the time he could think was a good enough excuse.

"I grew up in the circus," and then he unzipped his jacket, let the cat drop and he ran off, thankful that no one on the street knew who he was or that he was from the boy's home just around the corner. See that was the thing about the 'unfortunates' as Theo liked to call them. Those unfortunate souls that had been brought into the world with little to no thought on the lives they had been forced to live through the misery of never feeling wanted.

Well not until the day they finally became adopted. And even then there were those few that were fool enough to let the bitterness of their situation stick to them like a glue they never wanted rid of. It made Theo angry to know that good homes and good people had gone to waste on kids that were simply unable to ever let go of the hand that life had dealt them, instead of simply accepting the fact that they should consider themselves lucky someone had finally offered them what most his kind often dreamed of…A new hand of winning cards.

But getting back to the 'Unfortunates' such as him, that was what he had always counted on in situations like that day with the cat…it was simply a case of 'out of sight, out of mind' and that included a bunch of neighbours who had lived around the corner from him his whole life but yet had no idea who he was.

At first he didn't know why he had thought back to this particular memory but then, looking down at all those noisy school children running around like ants, he remembered why. Why he felt different as he did that day…

The man in the shadows had wings.

Since Theo could remember he was fascinated by anything that could fly and other than dreaming of becoming a hero when he was younger, he also dreamed that he would one day have wings. As a child it wasn't that strange to dream you could fly as he knew now it was a common thought for most children to have, but as he got older the dream didn't fade. No, if anything it only became worse.

Which is why Theo's secret place was as close to the clouds as he could get. But none of that explained just *how* he found himself back there because the last thing he remembered was all Hell breaking loose and a winged Angel easily stopping the chaos.

No, not an Angel...

A demon.

He thought back to the image he saw when he opened his eyes and remembered the shadowed man had what looked like purple fire flowing through his veins, making his skin glow with power. His large wings had been folded in behind him and didn't seem so threatening, but it was his eyes that burned into him with the same purple heat which seemed to singe the edges of his very soul. After that Theo couldn't remember anything but waking up on the familiar rooftop. Had it all been a dream? Had he sneaked up here to get out of doing gym and fell asleep? Well if he had then he certainly had a more vivid imagination than he first thought.

"You're not dreaming I'm afraid." A startling voice said from behind him and Theo turned quickly to see a figure was hiding in the shadows. *He was back.*

"Is this a trick?" Theo asked angrily.

"In a way I guess it is," the shadow answered him and he was surprised that his voice seemed softer, more gentle than it had been before. Was it because now they were alone?

"Who are you?"

"My name is Dominic Draven and I am your…" The man paused for a moment and Theo couldn't help but wonder why, so he finished for him.

"My Headmaster."

"Yes, of sorts," he agreed cryptically making Theo frown.

"Look Mister, I am really trying not to be rude here but if you don't tell me what's going on…"

"Then you will what exactly…sprout wings and fly away?" the man said without anger or malice.

"I wish," Theo muttered under his breath but the man must have heard him.

"Then lucky for you, in my world, wishes like that often come true." Theo looked back at him when he said this and the lack of trust was written all over Theo's face.

"You made us come all this way only to have us murdered on a bus and then all start turning into freaks for your amusement, so you will have to forgive me if I don't believe anything you have to say," Theo replied drily, hoping he had made his point.

"Then you wish to go back to this life without ever knowing what you truly are…what you, along with your friends, have now become? Because trust me when I say, you are far from what you class as freaks." Theo didn't want to believe what he was saying, he really didn't but it was getting harder not to want to listen.

"Why am I even bothering? You wouldn't understand," Theo said to himself knowing the man had no clue about how he felt or what he had been through.

"Why don't you try me?" the man said in a way that made Theo want to give him what he wanted but he didn't know why. It wasn't like Theo had a long waiting list of people he was ready to pour his heart out to...so why this man... *why this Demon?*

Theo took a deep breath and looked out to the clouds that he could only wish were at his fingertips.

"When I was seven I fell for this girl in my class. Her name was Sarah and I remember being fascinated by the plaited pigtails she always wore that were tied off in blue ribbons. They used to twirl around when she ran around with her friends and I would sit on my own and watch her with a smile." Theo was actually smiling to himself now and it only faded when he remembered who he was telling this to. He coughed as if to try and erase what he just said and carried on as if he hadn't just trusted someone else for the first time with one of his secrets.

"One day I was late getting my break time after one of my teachers wanted to speak to me. I always wondered what would have happened if I hadn't been late that day." This question was something Theo had tortured himself over, even years later.

"What happened, Theo?"

"I ran to the yard where I knew she would be and found her on the floor. She had been pushed by one of the bigger kids who was a known bully. He was walking away laughing and I remember wanting to hit him so badly that my hands shook but instead I ran to Sarah." He paused a second as if he could see her lying there on this very rooftop.

"I wanted to make sure she was alright. So I reached out my hand to help her up but that's when things went bad." He remembered back to when his hand was shaking for a very different reason as he reached out to her, wondering what she would do or if she would even take it. Of course now he wished that she hadn't.

"Your touch…it…" the man started to guess and Theo had no clue how but he couldn't bear to hear another person say it so he quickly finished that sentence for him.

"It hurt her. She collapsed back on the ground and at first I thought it had been because of the fall. I screamed for help over and over before someone came, all the while trying to shake her awake."

"Theo, you didn't know," the man said, trying to console him but as far as Theo was concerned, he didn't deserve it.

"What, that I put her in hospital? No you're right, I didn't know. And I didn't know even when I snuck into the hospital to see her." Theo snapped back, taking out his own frustrations from carrying years of guilt on the shadow behind him.

"I remember looking down after one of the teachers had picked her up and rushed her inside only to find one of her blue ribbons was caught on my shoe. It didn't feel right, her being without that other ribbon," he said as if looking down now and seeing it still there snaking around as if trying to break free in the wind.

"So like I said, I only snuck in to give it back to her." Theo paused a minute to drag a hand through his floppy hairstyle,

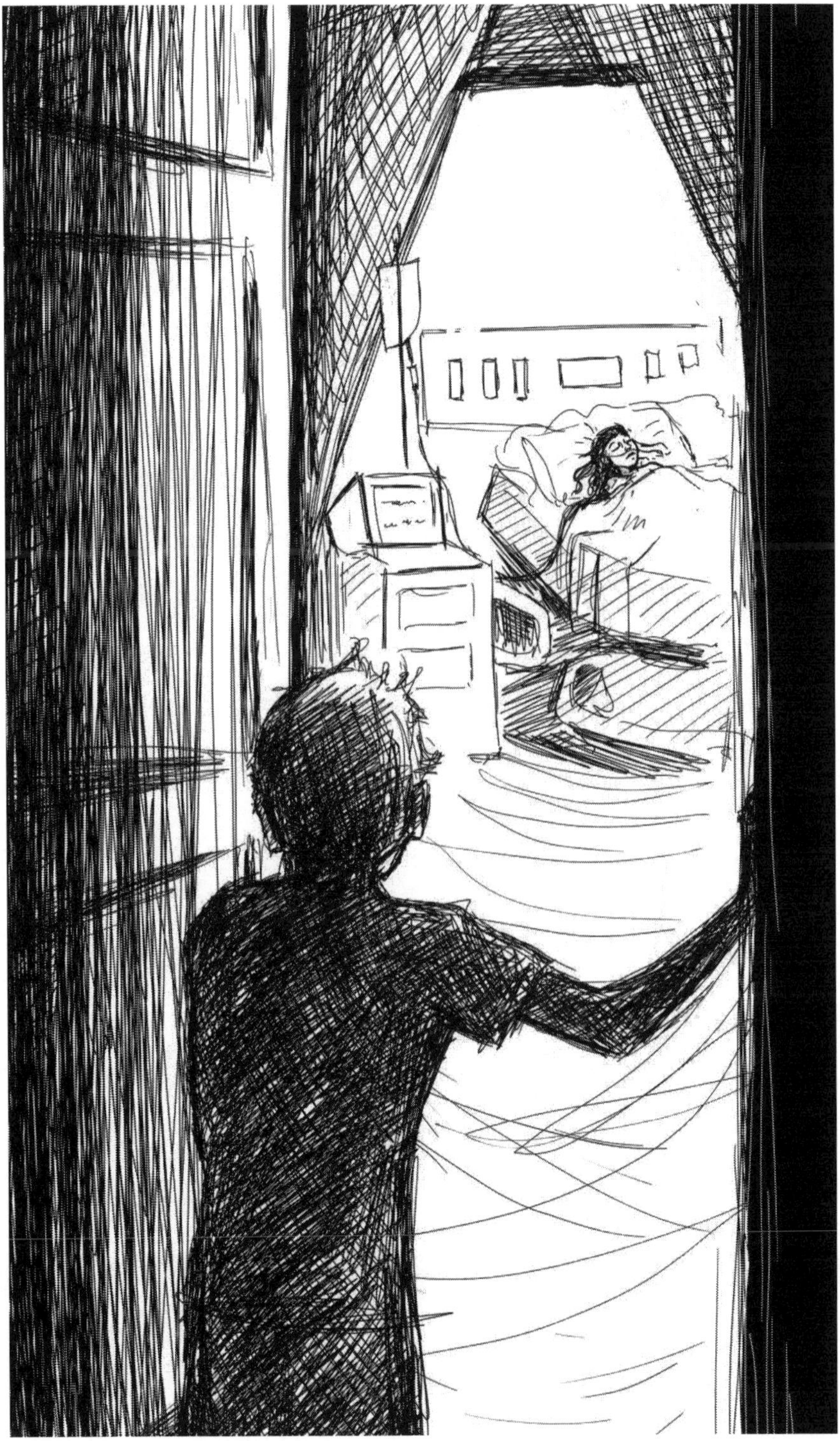

pushing it all back like he usually did when he was feeling this way.

"After that there was little doubt as to what my touch could do to someone." Theo thought back to when he uncurled her dainty small fingers and tried to place the ribbon in her hand. But then he also remembered the awful sounds of the machines beeping wildly around him and the way her fingers fell limp, letting the ribbon ripple to the floor.

After that it all became a bit of a blur, flashing in his memory bank like a flicker book of nightmares as nurses and doctors flooded the room in a panic, shouting at him to leave. But most of all he remembered not being able to take his eyes of that lone piece of blue ribbon resting there against the pale lino floor and wincing every time one of the hospital staff stood on it.

"What happened to the girl?" the man asked, surprising him with his concern for a life he didn't even know.

"She was in a coma for six weeks before finally waking up. After that, her parents moved to Scotland…or so I heard. Either way I never saw her again." As Theo finished his story he was amazed to find that this time instead of thinking back to the event that shaped his life and started him down the solitary path he had been on ever since, he felt something other than guilt…he felt *relief*. It was as though a huge weight had been lifted just knowing that someone else in the world knew the type of pain he'd experienced that day and the difficult choice he felt he had to make, to ensure that something like that never happened again.

"So you see, I was already classed as a freak before you ever showed up, so what's the difference?" Theo said looking back out to the school he never really attended and the friends he never allowed himself to make because of it.

"Isn't it obvious to you yet...there are no such things as freaks in my world, Theo."

"Then what was that? What was happening to them?" he asked referring of course to Janie, Ivan and Ena.

"It was their rebirth."

"Their what now?" Theo asked frowning at where he thought the Headmaster's face was.

"Before I explain, I want to ask you something, a question I once asked a long time ago of someone who is very special to me." Theo wasn't quite sure why he added on this personal part at the end, but for some reason he was glad. He guessed it made the guy seem more human than he obviously was.

"Go ahead, ask away."

"Do you believe in God, Theo?" The man surprised him by asking this and for a minute Theo couldn't speak. It was a question everyone asked themselves at some point in their lives and one Theo admittedly had done more than once.

"I'm an Orphan who just told you about how I nearly killed a girl because I wanted to help her off the floor...so what do you think?" Theo finally snapped, hating himself for how much that question affected him.

"That is not an answer."

"No, then how's this. I was abandoned by my parents as a baby and dumped on a doorstep like you would a stray cat you no longer wanted. Don't you think if there was a God then he would have chosen something better for me?" Theo said, trying to mask his emotions as he said this, but that deep embedded hurt was too ingrained in his heart to give up on. It was like a scar of a question mark that someone had carved onto his chest, causing it to sink its way in until becoming engraved on his damaged soul. It wasn't that he didn't want to let go, but more as though something wasn't letting him go.

"But what if he has chosen something better for you now?" It was at this point that Theo whipped around and snapped,

"Well it's too late for that!"

"Is it? Because I don't think so. You can't change who you are and nor should you ever try if what you are is something great. My own father told me that on the day that I was reborn and has reminded me of the fact a few times since," the man said with an honesty that surprised him yet again. For some reason the guy in the shadows didn't strike him as the family man type and that included having a father figure giving him advice on how to become a better person.

"Someone did this to you?" Theo couldn't help himself when asking this.

"No one did this to me Theo, just like no one has done this to *you.*"

"No? Forgive me then if I find that hard to believe," he said on a humourless laugh, thinking back to Carrick.

"Many things in this life are hard to believe when you live blinded to what your mind refuses to see."

"Anyone ever tell you that this cryptic act gets annoying really quickly?" Theo asked sarcastically but when the man laughed once it hadn't been the response he had expected.

"Yes, a certain person has told me that once or twice."

"Yeah, well did it ever sink in?" he asked defiantly.

"Would you believe me if I told you I used to be much worse?" Theo couldn't hide his grin and for a forgiving moment he felt strangely at ease talking to this man. But then as if remembering himself, he straightened up his shoulders and decided enough was enough.

"Well, as enlightening as this little chit chat has been, for one of us at least... I am still in the dark as to what on earth is going on!"

"You are right. The time has come to tell you what you are but first tell me what you see," he asked pointing his arm out ahead of him, so Theo turned around to look back at all the carefree students getting on with their lives.

"Not them, they are no longer part of your world... look up to the sky." Theo did as he was told and saw what looked like a huge eagle soaring high above the world.

"Freedom." Theo let go of the word on a breath without realising it.

"That is precisely what it is and that is precisely what the Gods have granted you. They chose you Theo and gifted you with another lost part of yourself they were merely keeping safe until now." Theo didn't want to believe what the man was saying, but with every word out of his mouth it only managed to draw Theo further down the tunnel into this man's world, a world he was sure he would never escape from.

"What are you talking about?" he forced himself to ask. Theo heard a released sigh from the shadows before the man spoke again.

"You, along with the others, were chosen long ago to be part of something my world has never known could be possible until now."

"You keep saying your world but I still don't know what that means?" Theo said frustrated.

"The world of the Supernatural and where Heaven and Hell join on earth to live their lives peacefully." Hearing this Theo's mouth dropped.

"Peacefully?" He couldn't believe it. The word Demon and peaceful just didn't mix well for him.

"Well, usually. But you have to understand, Angels and Demons are very far from the stereotypical views many humans have of them." Theo wished at that moment he could have called the guy crazy and walked away feeling as though he had wasted his time but after all he had seen today, well, how could he do that now?

"How so?" he asked instead, not wanting to blow his chance at finding out more.

"It's simple really, not all Angels are good and not all Demons are bad. There is a balance needed in all our worlds... *even in Hell.*"

"And you're telling me that they live here?" Theo asked throwing his arm out at the world below. He saw the guy's head nod, even in the shadows and Theo, trying to absorb all of this, raked a frustrated hand through his hair out of habit.

"This is crazy."

"No crazier than millions of people believing that a man named Jesus Christ walked on water." Well, he had a point there, Theo had to give him that.

"Yes, but you're telling me that the world is filled with Angels and Demons just walking around yet no one is seeing them!" The man nodded back to the bustling school yard and said,

"And how many of them really saw you?" Theo knew once again he was right.

"It is easy to hide when you don't wish to be seen. Our world is something we hide for a reason, as you cannot protect a world in chaos, only prevent it from happening and that is where lies its greatest protection." Theo knew what he was saying and could understand it. Hell, it was the reason he never got close to anyone. It was controlling the damage before the need for damage control, if that made sense.

"For example. Say you had a village full of people you had to tell bad news to but you were but one man. Say you needed to get them to leave their homes in an orderly fashion before danger could strike but you knew that most would not wish to comply.

You had a situation to control yet the fear of order from certain members of the group could jeopardise the lives of others…And it is here which lies your first test…what do you do?" he asked him and Theo thought for a moment.

"Do you tell the whole village as a collective to save time or tell them one by one in order to save lives?" he prompted him and Theo knew what he was getting at.

"You said it yourself, there is strength in numbers but by addressing each person individually, then you remain in control of those numbers and instead are not overpowered by it." Theo's eyes widened now knowing that he had heard what he had said to Ena back in the club but instead of calling him out on it, he decided to ignore it.

"I get it. People would see you guys and freak and if that happened on a big scale then it's harder to control." Which made him wonder if that wasn't what he was doing now? Had he brought them each to their own dream world to explain one by one what had happened? People often reacted badly when faced with things they didn't understand or felt were out of their control. It was after all, human nature…which brought him back to his own nature and the last question…

"So what does that make me then?"

"That you will find out in time, for I don't yet know." This wasn't exactly what he was expecting to hear after all that had been said.

"What do you mean… are you telling me that you don't know?!"

"I am not in control of this Theo, I am here, along with my people, to simply guide you through it and teach you the ways of our world. Three of your friends have merged with their chosen souls already and will soon learn what they have now become and in doing so, will take their place among our people…just like you will." Theo snorted a laugh and said,

"You seem sure of yourself."

"I have to be, for that is expected of a leader, but that is something I can see you are already figuring out for yourself." The shadow nodded at him and for some reason Theo felt his face get hot.

"I didn't ask for them to name me that." he said, feeling as though he needed to defend himself in some way.

"True leaders often don't ask to lead but simply step up when it is asked of them. They chose you Theo for a reason, just as the Gods did…that reason only you can answer when the time is right."

"Well some leader I am going to be when I can't even touch people." Theo muttered knowing that he would hear and secretly hoping that he had a solution.

"I think you will find there are greater benefits to being around other 'Freaks' as you put it." The headmaster said with the slightest bit of humour in his tone. Meanwhile Theo's heart was racing with the possibility. Could it be true, could what he was implying really happen?

"You're telling me that they wouldn't be affected?" he said, his voice clearly full of hope.

"That's what I am telling you, Theo. As I said, my world is a horizon full of possibilities brought to you with every sunrise...all you have to do is want to live each day within it, leaving this world behind." The shadow confirmed, nodding behind him back at what Theo was already considering as the 'fake world'. Theo thought about what he was saying and knew that it wasn't really a hard choice to make. Live a ghost of a life in this fake world or be a ghost *living* in the life he offered in his *real* world...in this *Afterlife* of his. No, it wasn't a hard choice to make at all.

"Alright, so where do we start?" Theo said walking closer to the man, this Dominic Draven, who was not only headmaster to his new school but also now it seemed like a mentor for his new life.

"In your case, a simple leap of faith is all that is needed." Hearing this from the shadows was when Theo had to question his mentality. He looked to the concrete below him and the drop he knew would kill any man...any man without wings that was.

"You want me to jump?!"

"No...I want you to find your *freedom.*" Theo looked back at the man and for once wished he would step away from the shadows. He wanted to look into his eyes to find the trust in them he need to see but maybe that was all part of the test? Theo didn't know and nor was he likely to ever know, but the one important thing he did know was how he felt in his heart. It was how he felt in the lightening of his lonely soul and finally seeing a future he could see himself being a part of.

It was everything he ever wanted.

So he walked closer to the man and said,

"Then I guess I will see you on the other side, old man." Then he turned with a smirk when he heard the disapproving groan at being called old. But before he could comment he ran straight for the only world he had ever known...

And jumped straight out of it.

8
Death Talk

Thankfully Theo felt himself landing not on solid concrete as he expected but instead what felt weirdly like water. At some point during his flight off the rooftop he had flipped around to see the shadowy figure above standing at the edge watching him as he descended into the unknown. If he hadn't known any better, it would seem as though this new headmaster of his wanted to be sure that his student got to where he was going and was concerned about him. And stranger still for Theo, it was a comforting sight to see that, for what felt like the first time in his life, he had the constant he had been craving. Someone who had seen even a small part of his life through something as important as this...as important as life, death and now what felt like his rebirth.

Consequently, when his body crashed through the water he let the waves his impact had created crash over him and wash away the last shreds of his old life, knowing he was going somewhere better...*or at least he hoped.* Then he did something that went against the grain of his soul and let himself sink down once more into the black abyss without a fight, one that had already seemed to have claimed a part of his life. And the sad part wasn't actually dying. No, it was letting go and killing a part of himself that he had never fully understood to begin with. To an

121

outsider this might have seemed as though he was giving up, but if you knew the true character of this young soul, then you would have known that wasn't even possible, for Theo didn't know how to give up on *anything*. But learning to let go and trust in another's words was another thing entirely and it seemed like dying for a second time was to be the first lesson he learned.

And learn he did as he let the Afterlife take him.

"Hey guys, he's awake." He heard a girl's voice say, one that he was instantly familiar with. Ena sounded relieved and again it felt strange to have so quickly accumulated people who cared about what happened to him. It brought him a warmth he couldn't explain or one he wouldn't have admitted to have even if he tried.

"Why did that strangely feel like I was being baptised into becoming a member of some supernatural cult or some crap like that?" he said as he raised himself up and in doing so feeling a sinking weight in his belly that was causing sickly bile to rise in the back of his throat.

"Ten dollars says he pukes." He heard Zane predict and he looked up to see Ena smack his chest and say,

"Just because you decorated the floor with plane food doesn't mean he will."

"Yeah well, no wonder, I mean who serves chickpeas for breakfast!" Zane argued making Theo want to laugh, especially when Ena argued back sarcastically,

"Oh yeah, and a cheeseburger would have made all the difference?"

"It's a known fact that pickles stabilise the excess acid in a stomach", Zane said with such conviction that Theo couldn't help but mouth the question, 'Is that true?' as he took Zane's offered hand to help him up further, to which he replied on a whisper,

"Hell if I know, but it shut her up didn't it?" This made Theo grin before coughing back a laugh.

"I be sorry for trying and killing you but you be fine now?" Ivan asked him in that soft unique way of his which, combined with his colossal size, was a complete contradiction to the frightening power he had displayed back in the club. Speaking of which, this made Theo take a closer look around the room to see which fantasy world he had woken up in this time. He shifted off the couch he had been lying on and after double checking his legs wouldn't collapse like he feared, he walked over to Ivan and slapped him on the back before saying,

"No worries big guy, the horned demon bull thing was sick." Of course, the second the words were out of his mouth he knew he should have thought better of it because the poor guy just looked even more confused than ever.

"He means you're cool, man." Zane translated for him with both of his thumbs up as an extra measure of reassurance. Theo then had to wonder how long it would take the gang before they finally understood each other and for some reason this thought brought a small grin to his lips.

"For me it was like taking the Red Pill," Zane said and this time it was only Theo who knew what he meant by that.

"Think Keanu Reeves wearing sunglasses, a long black jacket and kicking too many asses to count," Theo said to the group and it was no surprise when only two faces showed recognition.

"Seriously dude, we have some major media updating to do on your medial temporal lobe and lesson number one will be cult classics for sure!" Zane said causing Ena to look at him as if he had just grown another head, one that wore glasses and spoke the language of super geek.

"What?" Zane asked when noticing her gawking at him in shock.

"Oh nothing, just didn't figure you even knew how to use a brain, let alone be able to name bits of it," she said sarcastically and instead of taking offense to the remark Zane just nudged her shoulder and said,

"Don't let this handsome, cool cat exterior fool you sweetheart, there's a genius waiting to break free under the surface of it all." Ena chuckled, looking him up and down and replied,

"What, under all that paint splatter and floppy hair? Don't make me laugh." Zane caught up with her as she started to walk away and said,

"I think you will find this is called natural style..." he said referring to his hair before he continued with,

"And I do believe you will find that those are two traits that the good Leonardo da Vinci and I have in common." Ena laughed once more without humour and said,

"Oh yeah, 'cause I hear that he was such a style guru back in his heyday." This was when Theo thought it best to intervene before these two cranked it up a notch and started cracking their knuckles.

"So, I take it you all had the same awe inspiring 'go on and kill yourself' prep talk from our new headmaster then?" Theo asked looking around the room and trying to figure out whether or not they had just been magically transported into some posh English stately manor house from the 17th century. I don't think he would have been surprised to find this being the case, considering how his day was going or if a butler named Jeeves walked in right now and asked if they all wanted some freshly drained blood tea.

"Uh, not exactly." Janie said looking to her worn dirty trainers and kicking her toe against the highly-polished floor for something to do. He looked to Ivan who just shrugged his shoulders in a way that told him he either didn't understand or like Janie, obviously hadn't had the same experience Theo had before he woke.

"And you guys?" he asked looking to Ena and Zane, who out of the rest of group most likely had more to offer. Although it was only Zane who had any useful information for him as Ena just shook her head in response.

"Nope, afraid to tell you this but looks like you were singled out dude, as the rest of us just got that crazy green haired chick in our dreams and trust me on this, you definitely got the better end of the deal as that girl is straight up, grade A, bat shit cuckoo and neither of us are sure if it's in a good way or not," Zane said scratching the back of his head as if that helped him in figuring out the answer to his own question about the girl. Theo could very much believe it as from the little time he had spent in her company, he himself wasn't sure whether to shake her or just pat her on the top of the head for being so damned cute.

"So, let me get this straight...you guys still don't know what's going on or why we are here?" Theo asked but one look at each of their faces and he didn't need to hear their answers spoken aloud. It was clear that little Miss Pip was great at putting you at ease with her colourful presence but not so hot on actually explaining the important stuff. Suddenly Theo had to wonder why it was that he had been singled out? Was it because his new headmaster had seen that he had been appointed leader of the group and thought it best to allow him to explain to the others? Or was there some other reason he didn't yet know about?

"And I gather that by that look of dread that you know a great deal more than we do and as our newly voted president of this insane asylum, its left up to you to explain it to us," Zane said folding his arms and leaning back against an elaborately carved sideboard that looked as though it once belonged to some royal dynasty and not the rickety old school desk Zane was treating it as by casually using it to prop up his body.

Theo didn't know how long the others had been awake before him but he guessed it was obviously long enough to be more accustomed to their lavish surroundings than he was.

"So, you're telling me that this...this...?" Theo struggled at this point not really knowing what to call her.

"Fruit Loop?" Zane said but Theo ignored that name in favour of another one, supplied helpfully by Janie,

"Miss Pip?"

"Yeah, Miss Pip...you're telling me that she didn't tell you guys anything?!" he said, his voice thick and dripping with disbelief.

"Oh, she said stuff alright," Zane commented sarcastically rolling his eyes before Ena jumped in.

"Let's just say that her version of events was mainly focused on reciting the lyrics of 'Bohemian Rhapsody' to describe what's happened to us and then asking us questions like what our favourite superhero was and explaining that with great power comes great responsibility."

"Yeah, total rip-off of Spiderman by the way and as if anyone would pick his powers anyway, half of which were 'Invented' by a super nerd and don't get me started on wearing spandex..." Ena smacked her forehead and whispered,

'Give me strength'.

"Dude, seriously?" Theo said looking at him thinking this was so not the time to geek out on them. Zane threw his hands up and said,

"What, you're telling me the crazy chick is the only one who gets to talk nonsense at a time like this?" To this question, Theo and Ena both shouted 'Yes!' as Janie kind of nodded shyly, whilst poor Ivan just looked as if he had been dumped on a different planet altogether.

"Okay so now 'Super Geek' over there has got it all out of his system, are you going to explain what the Hell is going on or not?" Ena said getting impatient and Theo couldn't say that he blamed her having experienced that same frustration not long ago on a rooftop.

"Okay, so do you want the long-winded sugar coated version or the quick and painful…"

"Just rip off the band aid, Man," Zane said interrupting him and for once Ena seemed to agree with him. Theo decided that he couldn't put it off for any longer and he suddenly knew how hard it must have been for anyone in a profession that frequently had to give bad news. So he blurted out the only two words that came to mind.

"We died."

"Wow, brutal much?" Zane said shaking his head in what Theo knew was conflicted disbelief.

"Uh…come again?" Ena said raising an eyebrow and putting a hand to her ear as if she hadn't heard him correctly. Theo closed his eyes momentarily and held the bridge of his nose with his fingers as though he could feel a headache was about to explode there any minute.

"This isn't happening…I mean how can it when we are all here…are we supposed to be ghosts or something?" This time the disbelief came from Janie.

"I am no ghost," Ivan said joining in and adding to the weight on Theo's shoulders.

"No, you're right, you're not a ghost..."

"Well duh dude, I could have told you..." Zane said interrupting him, so Theo returned the favour by saying,

"We are Demons or Angels." Surprisingly this actually managed to shut Zane up as his only response was a spluttering sound before his mouth dropped open in shock. Ena shook her head a few times making her black bob swish around her face before she said,

"That's not possible."

"I'm dreaming...please God, tell me I am dreaming like last time," Janie said cryptically, looking up at the ceiling as though she was expecting to see the big man himself.

"I think you will find you're asking the wrong guy there, Janie." Zane said with a bitter tone and when she shot him a confused look he looked down to indicate Hell.

"That's not funny, Zane!" Ena shouted when it looked as though Janie was close to tears.

"And it wasn't meant to be, *Ena!*"

"I no understand," Ivan said and Zane rolled his eyes and said sarcastically,

"Big shocker there." Theo could see everyone was close to losing it and he knew it was left up to him to try and calm the situation before it really started to get out of hand.

"Look, I think we all just need to calm down and take a minute to..."

"To what exactly?" Zane asked now turning his attention to Theo.

"Yeah, what are we supposed to do Theo? You want us to take time out and think about this logically…is that it?!" Ena said and Janie bit her lip before saying quietly,

"Come on guys, don't fight."

"I don't know Ena, how about we turn against each other so that we each have to deal with this alone…sound like a good plan?! Anyone?" Theo shouted looking at each of them in turn, daring them to argue with him. He could feel his cool on the edge of dipping into the realms of being pissed off enough to walk out of there and say enough was enough. But at the core of his heart he knew that he couldn't do that, no he had already allowed himself to start caring about this bunch of misfits, so he knew he couldn't abandon them now.

"No, I didn't think so," he added after everyone gave him a moment of silence. Then he took a much-needed deep breath and pushed all his hair back in a frustrated gesture before saying more calmly,

"I know this is a lot to take in, but right now look around guys, because we are all we have got left in this world, one we have no clue about and if we are going to survive it, then we will only do that together." On hearing this everyone had a different reaction, Ena and Zane looked sheepishly to the side trying to avoid being singled out and Janie gave Theo an encouraging head nod and a small smile as though this was what she had been trying to say herself. Ivan on the other hand had been obviously lost in his own thoughts and asked,

"I be Angel?" Theo coughed to hide his choked surprise and Zane laughed once before walking over to him and slapping him on the back.

"I'm thinking not big man, not after what we saw but hey, even the Hulk could be a good guy...okay, one that might cost the city millions of dollars in damage after one green tantrum, but hey, no one's perfect right?" It was at this point that Theo was glad that Ivan couldn't understand half of what Zane said but that still didn't mean he didn't want to slap his forehead and pray for strength...although who exactly he would be praying to right now he had no clue.

"Seriously, do you even have a filter?" Ena said after doing what Theo had refrained from doing and smacking her own forehead.

"Of course I do." Zane said looking back over his shoulder at her.

"Then why don't you execute the right to use it, smartass!" Ena said putting a hand on her hip and giving him that 'I am not impressed look.

"Okay, so this wasn't exactly what I had in mind guys," Theo said feeling exasperated.

"Why don't you go ahead Theo and explain it to us a bit more, that way I am sure we will understand it better." Janie said obviously feeling sorry for what he was having to deal with right now. Theo gave a her a small smile in thanks but before he could say anything Zane spoke first,

"Yeah man, tell us more… especially the part about us no longer being human, 'cause that should be a riot." Theo ignored the sarcasm and continued with what he was going to say.

"Well, from what I could gather, we have all been chosen."

"For what exactly, to turn us unfortunate orphans into even greater freaks!" Ena snapped and this time her reply didn't come from Theo but Death himself…

"Well yeah, but first I had to kill you."

9
SAY HELLO TO MY LITTLE DARK FRIEND

"You!" Theo hissed at the man he held responsible for all this madness and by far the worst experience of his life so far. It wasn't just his own death he thought of, but more like the living nightmare of having to watch helplessly as others around him died without being able to do anything to stop it. For someone like Theo this was pure torture and it was as though something deep within his genetic makeup was snapping the threads holding the crucial pieces of himself together. Watching others suffer actually caused him pain, but with this group it was so much worse...it was like watching a family he had longed for being cruelly snatched away from him just as he was reaching out for them.

Watching them slip through his fingers...literally.

Well 'no more' his mind screamed at him as his fists clenched and his jaw locked in an anger he could feel burning deep within his veins. Something was coming but he didn't know what, only that he could feel the change was near, a change that felt fuelled by raw anger.

"I do not have time for your insolence boy, I have come to speak to your master," Carrick said walking past him, only Theo was having none of it. He snatched out quicker than he knew he could move and grabbed onto Carrick's arm. The silver haired man first looked down at the foreign hand restraining him and then looked down his nose at its owner. Carrick raised a single eyebrow before saying,

"What's the matter boy, do you have a second death wish?"

"Come Theo, let him go," Ena said cautiously and was quickly followed by Zane agreeing,

"Yeah man, he's not worth it." But Theo wasn't listening…or should he say, the beast inside him *refused* to listen. All he could see was the man who had caused his friends fear and death when they simply believed themselves lucky enough to be chosen for a new life. Well, at least that was the way that Theo saw it and he just assumed the others did too.

This was the reason that instead of letting go, his grip locked tighter as did his jaw the second he finally let his rage boil over and give in to his darker side that he could feel screaming at him to do damage.

"Oh I disagree…*it's worth it,*" Theo said in a voice he no longer recognised and one that seemed to have been dragged from Hell itself. Carrick's eyes widened in surprise and just as he opened his mouth to give another warning, he quickly learnt it was far too late, as it was time for something no one was expecting…

It was time for Theo's Demon.

But time only seemed to slow down for Theo and even when Carrick's lips started to mouth words of denial it was too late for that. Theo's blind rage was overriding any other logical thought.

135

It was as if years of pain and mental suffering had finally hit its limit and it all seemed to burst out of him as though he'd had a live grenade of great power in his chest all this time.

Well Carrick had just pulled the pin and he knew it. A blinding white force exploded from within Theo but as quickly as it hit, it quickly started to implode before the fingers of destruction could reach out and hurt anyone other than the person he was in direct contact with. As though some invisible black hole was absorbing all the power back inside of him and with it something else as well.

It wasn't just his own power being sucked back into his chest but also a foreign energy from Death himself. One that seemed to travel up through his veins as though Theo's heart was a battery that suddenly needed recharging and holding onto Carrick was just the power source he needed.

Theo could feel his eyes changing at the sight of Carrick falling to his knees as though he no longer had enough strength to hold himself on his feet. Theo bent lower to keep hold of him as he continued to somehow drain Carrick of his power and he couldn't say it wasn't a satisfying sight, not considering he had witnessed first-hand what that power could do to five innocent lives on a bus.

"Theo, your eyes...what's...what's happening to you?" Ena asked him, unable to keep the fear from her voice. He cut his burning eyes to hers and knew it was bad when he saw her wince, stepping back into Zane for protection. He could barely stand seeing the way they all looked at him now. Ivan with his eyes wide and at the ready, holding onto Janie's shoulders as if prepared to pick her up and carry her to safety. Zane mouthing the word 'Dude?' in a questioning manner and Ena shaking her head as if judging him for bringing a man to his knees, no matter what his crimes.

But instead of feeling enough guilt to let him go, it only seemed to morph into something darker...*crueller.* It was as though Theo couldn't find his way back from the anger, so instead of reaching out to try and release it, he was in fact running further towards it. And in doing so, his grip tightened on Carrick, his fingers digging in and trying to find root.

"Im...possible," Carrick stammered out just before his hand slapped to the floor to stop himself from falling forward and his face from slamming into the slate tiles.

"Now it's time you pay." Theo's demon threatened and just before he could allow what he knew in his heart was wrong to be unleashed fully, a cool calm voice of authority cut through the murderous tension like a burning blade cutting through a frozen lake of solid ice.

"Let him go, Theo."

"Oh, thank God." Ena and Janie both muttered in sync with their prayers for peace at the sight of their headmaster stood in the doorway with his arms folded.

Theo, without being able to do anything but give in to the command, let go of the Death dealer and the second he did Carrick inhaled deep as though finally being able to take his first breath from that icy lake. These thoughts made Theo growl as if a wild beast was beating against the inside of his chest trying to claw his way back out. It was as if another side to him was taunting him to take back hold of Carrick and inflict even more damage. Which was why Theo without being able to stop himself reached out to try and grab a hold of Carrick once more, again giving in to his other side.

"ENOUGH!" This time the demand came out as a thundering wave, blasting a power of will and control throughout the room, enough for Theo to find himself falling to his own knees beside Carrick. The rest of the group released a collective gasp at the sight of such a powerful figure commanding the room and the incredible show of dominance and power.

This time there was no hiding in the shadows or cryptic words spoken from afar. No, now he was here right in front of them, as real as the sun that shone through the tall arched windows and no longer a myth or just a name at the end of a letter. It was the masterful sight of a man who ruled a supernatural world looking like some gothic mob boss with his strange bodyguards framing his presence.

"Okay, seriously man, just when we thought shit couldn't get any weirder, enter an Albino assassin, a Samurai master and the dude that ate Goliath," Zane said leaning into Ena, a statement this time she had no choice but to agree with.

Not that the man in charge looked as if he needed back up against anyone, being as tall and muscular as they come in any decent action movie. But let's just say that if he had a battle to fight, one where he was out numbered ten to one, then yeah, his back up would certainly have come in handy.

And like Zane said, you had the mysterious hooded Albino who looked like he could have killed you with little more than a look, let alone with the killer curved blade he had strapped to his thigh. He had long bleached white hair and skin to match, well that was other than the wicked looking tribal tattoos that inked jet black all down one side of his face. One that snaked through a fatal looking scar that no doubt would have killed him if he had been mortal which, clearly, he was far from. In fact, it looked like someone had spilt ink on ice and then had dragged a blade though the frosted surface.

And as a contrast to the harsh features of the Albino was the soft knowledgeable face of the Samurai, who had earned the name, not just thanks to his hakama trousers and black montsuki kimono that seemed to have some sort of family crest embroidered just below each shoulder in two large crimson circles. No, it was the kind expression and respectful eyes he cast upon the room. Oh, and the huge samurai sword that was barely an inch from scraping the ground tucked into the material at his waist.

Now for the last and most terrifying of the three, the real-life giant who looked down at the room with tree trunk arms folded and a scowl on his scarred face.

"Holy crapola, but this guy looks as though he eats teenagers for breakfast and uses their fingerbones to pick the toenails out of his teeth!" Zane muttered to Ena who was still stood with her back to him.

"I really wouldn't speak right now if I were you...not unless you want those toothpick bones he uses to be yours." Ena warned under her breath back at Zane.

"Good plan, anyone who looks as if they spend their nights sleeping in an iron maiden coffin is obviously not a man you wanna play scrabble with." Ena looked back at him over her shoulder as though he had lost the plot, one she wasn't sure he'd had to begin with.

"Are you high?" She asked him only half serious.

"I wish, then maybe I could account for this freak out," he answered nodding back to poor Theo who was now shaking with his head in his hands.

"What's wrong with me...what's wrong with me...what have I done?!" Theo muttered over and over again to no one but his own nightmares. Carrick arose to his feet and looked disdainfully down at Theo as he brushed off his jacket and straightened it before speaking.

"I want this boy punish..."

"SILENCE!" The headmaster bellowed cutting him off and proving his words to be very effective. Then he walked over to Theo and looked down at the quivering boy at his feet before bending on one knee and placing a gentle hand upon his shoulder.

"Don't touch me!" Theo shouted pulling away from him and looking him in the eyes with nothing but sorrow in his soul. Mr Draven just raised a single eyebrow in question and he didn't have to wait long before guilt got the better of Theo, making him quietly admit his fears.

"I don't want to hurt you too." Mr Draven took a thoughtful moment to digest that before nodding once, telling Theo without words that he understood before confirming them verbally.

"You can't hurt me my boy, it isn't possible."

"Then wh...what was that?" Theo managed to get out needing to take a breath in between words.

"My mistake," Mr Draven said in response to this and Theo quickly realised that this was what he had feared all along...

Rejection.

10
Reaper's Brief Bargain

"My mistake," Mr Draven replied cryptically but Theo took his words the wrong way and the headmaster knew it the second he saw Theo's eyes close as though he was in pain.

"Have no fear Theo, you will learn to control it…*just give me time.*" He said softly placing his hand once more on his shoulder, one this time Theo didn't resist. Then he rose to his feet and held a hand out for Theo to do the same. Theo followed suit but couldn't take his eyes from the floor, too ashamed to face the others, who up until then he knew had looked up to him.

"Never feel ashamed of who you truly are, for none of my kind ever should and nor should they ever judge what is true of heart…remember that, young one." Mr Draven said so only Theo could hear but also looking back over his shoulder to his men, making Theo follow his gaze to see the three men who couldn't be more different if they tried. This made him look back at his own adopted family to see the same concern he would have for each of them if the roles had been reversed.

Ena even mouthed the question, 'Are you okay?' to which he nodded in reply, making her lip quirk to the side in a secret smile she tried to hide but Theo knew better.

"Dominic." Carrick spoke and Theo could swear he heard a small growl rise up from his new headmaster's chest.

"Go to them Theo, I will deal with this," Mr Draven said looking down to him given their height difference. Theo didn't argue but just nodded once in respect, something this man just earned from him quicker than any other man had ever done before. He had learnt that hard lesson of trust long ago and looking at the powerful figure before him now, he could barely believe he had broken down some of those barriers of his this quickly.

"Why are you here, Carrick?" Mr Draven said, cutting right to business, obviously leaving out the niceties.

"Very well I will get straight to it then, should I?" Carrick said pulling down on one of his shirt cuffs and fixing the chrome skull cufflink that had come loose.

"That would be preferable, yes." Mr Draven said in reply, folding his arms across his chest and somehow making his presence even more indisputable as the man in charge.

"The boy owes me a blood oath." Carrick said nodding to Theo who was now stood back in the protective fold of his friends. Without even looking at Theo, Mr Draven laughed once without humour and said reassuringly,

"I sincerely doubt that but please, go ahead and enlighten me."

"You obviously underestimate your…"

"Careful Death dealer of what you speak. I underestimate nothing and the proof of that is currently forgetting himself and to whom he is speaking right now in such a manner. So, if I were you I would choose my next words very carefully and explain it in a way you hope I will approve to hear." Mr Draven said in such a way that every being in the room knew he was so much more than what he claimed to be...a simple headmaster.

"Holy shit, I think I just wee'd a little." Zane whispered making Ena whisper back sarcastically,

"Ooo, my hero."

"My apologies My Lord, let me show you, for fear my words will not please, of course." Carrick replied nodding respectfully before quickly producing a suitcase Theo remembered well, only now there was a very distinct difference.

"Impossible." Mr Draven said after seeming lost in thought for a moment at the damaged he now witnessed.

"My words exactly." Carrick agreed tapping his finger against the now scorched leather where Theo's hand print seemed forever immortalised there. It looked as though he had somehow branded it with barely a touch and under the flood of lake water that had taken their lives.

"But I..." Theo started to say but one look from the headmaster and he decided against trying to understand it.

"And you believe this to be from the boy?" Mr Draven asked, obviously trying to cast doubt upon what seemed an unlikely action, that was if their reactions were anything to go by.

"I think considering the boy just had me on my knees, then it is not as farfetched as it seems. For even you can surely see the power that has been passed down to him. After all, considering where the roots of his power lie, it is not exactly surprising now is it *My Lord?*" The way Carrick said this was as though it held a hidden message and one that made Mr Draven clench his jaw for he knew exactly what it was.

"Even so, you really think a blood debt is owed to you when it was your own actions he was retaliating against?" Even Theo knew by the sound of his argument that he was trying everything to get Theo out of this new mess and from the looks of the smug smile on Carrick's face, he also knew it was useless.

"As you rightly know better than most My Lord, I don't assign the souls, I just take them and tick them off." Hearing this Draven closed his eyes briefly and surprised Theo by holding the bridge of his nose just as he himself did when he was frustrated.

"If I recall, you remember what it was like being on the other end of one of those blood oaths yourself and that didn't end too well for you, now did it?" Mr Draven said raising an eyebrow at him and Carrick laughed once and said,

"No, as I distinctly remember you making me pay for that mistake yourself, but it certainly ended well for the one who cashed it in. Speaking of which, how is your lovely soul's keeper these days, still calling my past employer a dear friend?" At this Mr Draven couldn't help but let his growl be heard by the rest of the room. However, it wasn't his reaction that Carrick stepped back from as the giant in the room took a menacing step towards

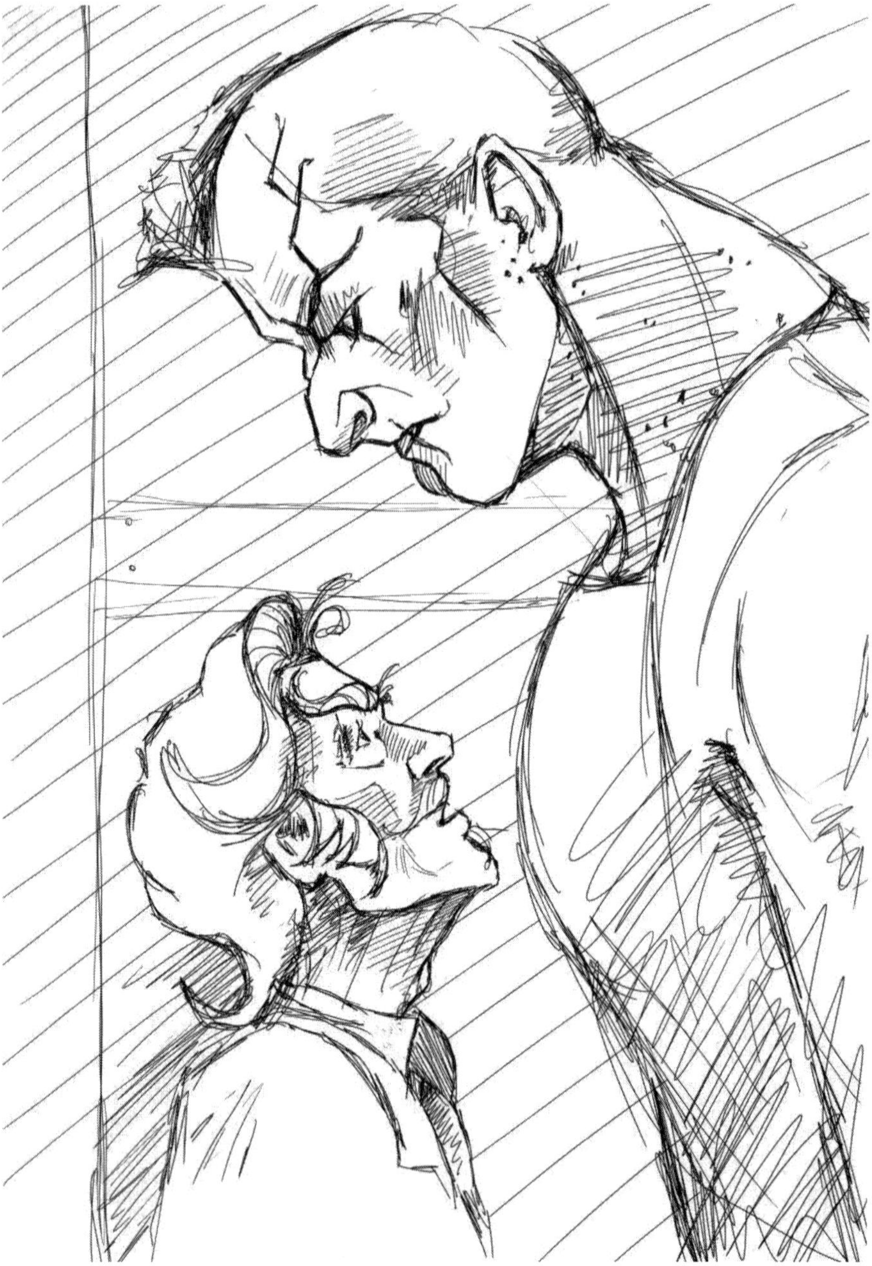

him and snarled a threat that sounded as though it came from the Devil himself,

"Speak of her again and I will finish what we started that day, Reaper."

"Ragnar," Mr Draven warned holding up a hand and making him stop before this blood oath could turn into a blood bath.

"Ah, still not forgotten about that, I see." Carrick said after making a clicking sound with the side of his mouth.

"No...I...Have...Not." Ragnar replied, no doubt spitting venom if he could.

"I suggest you put a leash on your Viking, Dominic, before he finds history repeating itself." Carrick said looking casually at his nails as though getting off topic was boring him.

"Over our dead bodies, Death Dealer." The Albino said cracking his pale knuckles and nudging the Japanese guy next to him who nodded his agreement silently.

"Well why not, it is after all the business I am in."

"Enough!" Mr Draven shouted slicing his hand through the air and looking back at his men, giving them a slight nod of his head, telling them without words to stand down.

"Does anyone else get the feeling we are missing the major plot of the story here?" Zane asked Theo, who could only nod in reply.

"Hell, it's like starting Game of Thrones at series two and wondering whose head that is on the spike."

"Eww." Janie muttered in response to Zane's unique running commentary, whereas Ena's was to say,

"Seriously, were you dropped on your head as a baby or have you always been this socially unbalanced?"

"Nah, I will have you know that these mad skills of perception and envied wit have taken years of fine tuning and hard graft, none of which is down to any injury my head has undergone."

"Just wait and give it time, I'm sure I could help you out with that last part." Ena muttered back making Theo frown and bite out,

"Hardly the time here guys, can we at least wait until after I am dead in this blood oath bullshit?"

"Sure," Zane said at the same time Ena replied with,

"No problem."

"Gee thanks guys, your concern is overwhelming." Theo said dryly and then turned kind eyes to Janie when she said,

"For what it's worth, I hope you don't die and a blood oath just means that if he ever needs surgery that you have to donate some of your blood for it…not all of it tho'!" She added quickly looking from side to side as if her innocent thoughts just slipped into the dark side for a moment.

"Theo, come here." Mr Draven's voice brought each of them back into the room, except maybe Ivan as he looked like he really needed subtitles to understand what on earth was going on. He also strangely couldn't seem to take his eyes off the other giant in the room, who was probably the first person he had ever seen to rival his own colossal size.

Theo took a deep breath and knew there was no other way out of this. All he could hope for as he took the few steps needed to where they were stood was that his trust in Mr Draven wasn't a misguided and foolish one.

"You did this...yes?" Theo looked to where Mr Draven directed his question by nodding to the now scarred briefcase and after swallowing hard, he held his head high and folded his arms across his chest before admitting,

"Yes, I did this." He then looked to Mr Draven to gauge his reaction to this news and was surprised when he noticed the obvious hint of respect flicker in his eyes along with the strange flash of purple that quickly flooded his irises for a brief moment. Carrick gave him a sneering smile that spoke volumes of his annoyance, which strangely made the giant named Ragnar growl, shocking not only Theo but the rest of his young group of misfits.

"Very well." Mr Draven said after a deep sigh, as if finally admitting defeat. He then turned to Carrick and snapped,

"Carrick, set your terms." Carrick bowed his head in acknowledgement and continued getting to the root of the matter and the reason for his intrusion.

"Theo Quinn, you have exactly one single lunar phase to make right the wrongs you have inflicted and in doing so restoring the balance between life and death. If these terms are not met or honoured by this time passed then your soul will be forfeited and used as payment for such order to be restored."

"What is that supposed to mean?" Theo gritted out hating the idea that he owed anyone anything, let alone the man who took his mortal life.

"It means you have one month to get me my power back or..."

"Or what?" Theo snapped feeling his anger once more claw away at his insides desperate to get out and free them both of this new burden. Carrick simply gave him a taunting grin, pausing for a moment, as if he could see for himself the effect he was having on Theo's inner Demon. Then he tried to snap the thread of control altogether, when he leant closer to him and finished off his deadly sentence...

"Or... *I take your soul.*"

11

A Bloody Handshake with Death

"What!? Is he for real?!" These were Theo's words exactly only this time someone else beat him to it and not surprisingly it was from his friend Zane, who this time didn't sound like he was joking around. Mr Draven held up his hand demanding silence and gave Carrick a reprimanding look of annoyance before issuing another order,

"Explain further Carrick and be done with it."

"Your soul is mine to sell to the highest bidder to use to bargain for my power back." Carrick snarled back in response to both Theo's attitude and Mr Draven's forceful demand.

"And how am I supposed to do that exactly, take a trip to the supernatural tailors and buy you a shiny new briefcase?" Theo argued back and Zane was about to take a step forward and fist bump his friend when Ena put her arm out, shook her head and said,

"Don't even think it, frat boy."

"I know not how you will do it and don't care for that matter, as it is for you to figure out yourself. Now are my terms met or should I just save you the bother and take your soul now as payment?" Carrick said, this time being the one to fold his arms.

"Oh gee, let me think on that one…death now or death later…oh how will I decide?" Theo replied sarcastically.

"Careful boy, respect for those with greater knowledge of this world is a lesson you would do well in learning…now accept my terms and be done with it."

"Fine, I acc…"

"Wait." Mr Draven said swiftly stopping Theo from making any further mistakes.

"My Lord?" Carrick questioned looking puzzled.

"You have not yet heard the boy's terms in return." Mr Draven stated frankly and Carrick, instead of giving in to exasperation or argument against someone who was obviously his superior, he simply motioned with hand and said,

"Very well, which of my terms are you opposed to, boy?" Theo thought a moment but instead of saying that what he was actually opposed to was being called 'boy' by everyone, he thought it best not to waste what was most likely his only opportunity to turn the tables round enough to not cause his death…*again.*

But the problem with this was that he didn't have a clue as to what terms he could set, as he doubted very much that he could get away with 'if I fail then you give up your soul instead'. Nope, somehow, he didn't think he would get away with that one. So, he did the only thing he could think of and that was to turn to the only man in the room who would have any hope in helping him.

Mr Draven knew the second Theo's eyes sought out his that the boy needed guidance and he had been wracking his brain trying to think of the best way of getting him out of this situation.

He would have taken his place if it were allowed and he even knew from experience with the Death Dealer he'd had in the past that if there were another way, then he too would have taken it.

Carrick wasn't a malicious character but one simply dedicated to the job which he had been cursed with. But facts were facts and Theo had unknowingly unleashed something upon that case that meant doing his job was no longer an option. Not considering the source of the Reaper's power lay mainly within the simple leather briefcase, one that was now tainted by the touch of a powerful but adolescent supernatural boy who had no control over the gift he had just had bestowed on him by the Gods themselves.

So, fearful for the boy's future in his world, he pushed the limits of terms set as much as he could in the hope that the extra time would help his cause.

"Terms will be set and carried out within three months not one."

"Absolutely not." Carrick said frowning but instead of Mr Draven getting angry and reminding him of who he was talking to, he simply laughed once and said,

"What's the matter Carrick, never heard of taking a vacation."

"Forgive me for saying my Lord, but you have clearly spent too much time around humans. Death doesn't take time off."

"Oh no, three months without Death walking around collecting souls…sounds like a nightmare to me." Zane said sarcastically to the others, after cocking his head to the side and holding up an invisible noose.

"Sounds like a great thing to…oh, you were joking weren't you, that explains the hanging thing doesn't it?" Janie said looking to Ena and correcting herself, blushing red whilst doing it.

"Uh… yeah." Zane replied leaving out the obvious 'Duh' sound so as not to embarrass her further.

"Well lucky for you you're not the only Reaper out there and I am sure the others wouldn't mind picking up the slack for a time." Mr Draven added

"Yeah, three months sounds better to me." Theo agreed crossing his arms and feeling suddenly smug.

"Fine…there goes my bonus this year. Is that all?" Carrick said grumbling to himself.

"Wow, just imagine the Christmas party, what do these guys get from their secret Santa…a scythe sharpener?" Unsurprisingly this came from Zane and this time Ena couldn't pretend not to find it funny but instead hid a secret smile behind her hand.

"What be a sc…scc…thing you speak of?" Ivan said getting stuck on the word and looking down to Janie for help.

"Seriously, after everything that's happening right now, this is the question he decides to ask?"

"A scythe. It's a weapon traditionally used by the Grim Reaper in fiction." Janie said sweetly ignoring Zane's comment after giving him a disapproving look, obviously feeling quite protective over the big guy.

"See that guy's curved blade at his leg." Ena added trying to help, nodding towards the Albino but this was where Zane butted in, popping his head around her shoulder and added,

"Yeah, think that but way bigger and on the end of a big stick." Ivan just frowned as if he was trying hard to piece together the mental image and this was when Theo took a step back and mumbled under his breath so only his friends could hear,

"Seriously guys, not really helping my case here."

"Theo, is there anything else you would like to add?" Mr Draven asked looking back at him and Theo thought on that a moment. The problem with this question was that Theo really had no clue what 'setting right his wrongs' really entailed, so what exactly could he add to his terms he didn't know. So, instead of thinking about what he would *have to do*, he decided to focus on what he knew he *wouldn't* do...

His limits.

"Yeah, there is."

"*Shocking.*" Carrick muttered under his breath before adding,

"Very well, proceed," in a bored tone that suggested he had wanted this over and done with the second he had first walked into the room.

"If I am to do this, then I refuse to hurt anyone innocent to get it done." Carrick raised an eyebrow at him, obviously intrigued by his terms.

"I care not for how you achieve your task young Theo, just that you do in the time in which you have been granted."

"He will." Mr Draven said answering for him at the same time taking a step forward, placing himself next to Theo.

"Of course, for how could he not with such a mentor as you to guide him, my Lord?" Carrick said and Theo had to supress a laugh when he heard Zane hide the words 'kiss ass' swiftly followed by an unconvincing cough. Unfortunately, Carrick didn't miss it and shot him a chilling glare before ignoring him enough to carry on.

"Now that there will be no more interruptions, let's continue, should we?" Mr Draven nodded and motioned with his hand for him to do so, no doubt wanting to get this finished along with the rest of them.

"Theo Quinn, you have exactly three lunar phases to make right the wrongs you have inflicted and in doing so restoring the balance between life and death…"

Theo quickly took a page out of Zane's book and coughed once reminding him to amend his terms as was agreed. Carrick closed his eyes and sighed before adding to his earlier statement.

"…Unless of course these actions cause you to harm an innocent soul in doing what is needed in this blood oath. If these terms are not met or honoured by this time passed, then your soul will be forfeited and used as payment for such order to be restored…are you satisfied with such?" Draven nodded and then turned to face Theo telling him the words that needed to be said in order to accept the blood oath and thus sealing his fate to Carrick's need for power.

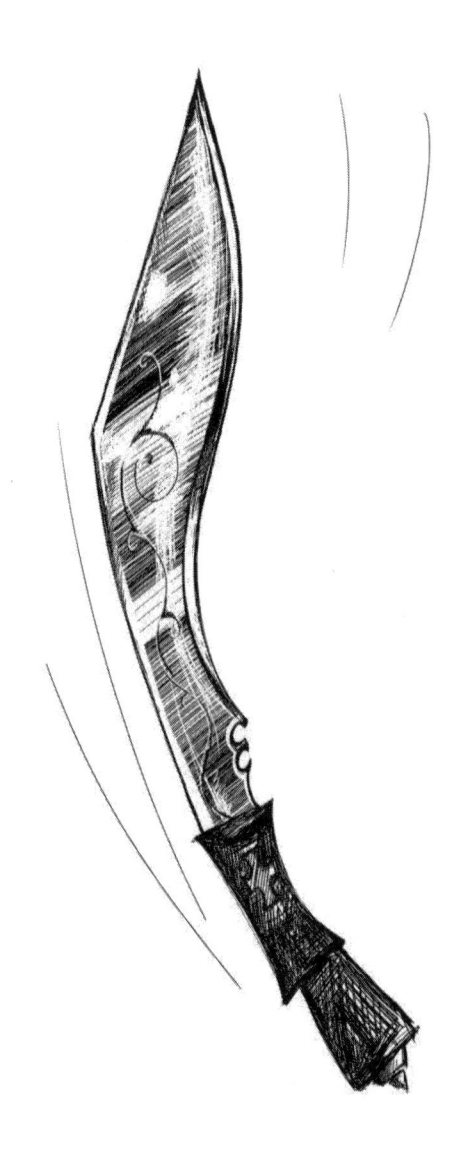

"I accept your terms and leave my blood onto you as it lays witness to our treaty made." Theo spoke the words and knew what was coming next when Mr Draven nodded to the Albino bodyguard to come forward. He took one step and at the same time drew his wicked looking blade in one swift move making the rest of the teens gasp in horror. However, before a word of protest could pass through their lips, Theo held out his hand and felt the cool steel slice cleanly through his flesh.

Carrick seeing this, took it as his cue to do the same and ran a single finger down the side of his battered briefcase releasing some kind of hidden mechanism. He then held onto the leather handle and waited for the sound of rotating cogs to click into place before an arch of deadly spikes shot through the palm of his hand, embedded so deeply that the bloody points protruded from the top of his flesh.

"I think I am going to vomit," Janie muttered quickly covering her mouth with both hands.

"Okay so now I am going to be having Hellraiser nightmares for quite possibly the rest of my life…oh and FYI big guy, it's a movie." Zane said adding this last bit for Ivan's benefit.

"FBI?" Ivan repeated making Zane smack his own forehead and roll his eyes.

"Ssshh, it's about to happen." Ena warned as Theo pumped his hand a few times to get the blood flowing. He then hissed back the burning sensation and instead of complaining about the pain he slapped his hand into Carrick's awaiting hand and all at once was hit by an immense force of binding power.

It was enough to almost bring Theo to his knees for the third time that day and each time had been in the presence of Death. Well now Death could take a break because the binding was complete and with it Theo's new life was held in a suspended state of the unknown. It felt as if his fate was twisting on the end of a single webbed thread like a spider hoping to go unnoticed by the human world, yet knowing that death might come at any moment by a crushing hand.

"It is done." Carrick stated, trying to ignore the twitch in his jaw from the immense power that just passed briefly between them. Theo squinted his eyes as he tried to make sense of Carrick's tense reaction and one look at his new headmaster told him that he was doing the same.

Theo looked down at his hand as if half expecting to see some kind of mark or residue left there by the death pact they just made but what he found surprised him even more.

"Well, with that bit of business now concluded I will be on my way." Carrick said straightening the lapels of his jacket but the Headmaster wasn't listening and nor did he look like he cared because he too was staring down at Theo's hand.

"I don't understand, I saw the blade cut through but the blood… even the blood has gone," Theo muttered to himself so lost in a million questions that when he felt a heavy hand of comfort rest on his shoulder he jolted.

"Go to them, they need reassurance and *balance.*" Theo looked him in the eyes and knew by the way he said 'balance' that he was referring to what they had spoken about on the roof top. The others looked up to him, that much was clear and Theo looked over his shoulder now to see that Mr Draven was right, the concern painted on their faces was easy to see. So, Theo nodded his understanding and turned his back on the man, who he was now blood bound to, who was walking out of the door.

"Enjoy your vacation Reaper…I hear Disneyworld is good this time of year." The Albino said after grabbing Carrick's arm and stopping him by the door.

"Very amusing," Carrick sneered back and jerked himself free before once more straightening his jacket, which seemed to be a habit with him. Surprisingly the next comment came from the silent Japanese man just as Carrick was walking through the door.

"Yes, and try not to scare the children on the Teacups." Carrick stopped, turned his head to the side and snarled like a wild cat without words, a sound that made both men smile, knowing they had hit a nerve.

"Just keep walking, Death." The Big one known now as Ragnar warned folding his arms and after a brief pause Carrick took his advice and left, looking less than happy about it.

"Really man, the Teacups?" The Albino said making Ragnar chuckle, a sound similar to that of a freight train powering its way through a station.

"October 1st, 1971 was opening day…" The Albino raised an eyebrow in question, so the Japanese guy shrugged his shoulders and finished with,

"What can I say, the Imp made me go." Hearing this the Albino mimicked his movements with a shrug of his own and said,

"Makes sense."

"Oh, I think I am gonna like those guys." Zane said looking to the odd three by the door.

"So, is that it, is it over?" Janie asked ignoring Zane's comment, taking a step closer to Theo. He watched the door swing shut behind the man in the beige suit as he walked away, leaving Theo with nothing left to do but speak his mind and in doing so, answering his friend's fears…

"No, Janie…not by a long shot."

12
Meet the Family

After all that had happened you would have thought that giving a bunch of teenagers time to process the last twelve hours would have been the best plan of action but no, not in this school. No, their new headmaster simply clapped his hands once and said,

"Right, now that's all settled, time for introductions I think." Zane looked as though he was about to say something sarcastic so both Ena and Theo gave him a look from either side of him and shook their heads, telling him 'no'. Thankfully he took the hint.

"Ragnar, call in the others." Mr Draven ordered in a way that told you he was not only the man in charge but, as Carrick had called him, Lord of the Manor. Which begged the question for each of the teens stood there waiting for the unknown…

'Who was this guy?'

Ragnar nodded as if he was used to doing anything that was asked of him, obviously having great respect for the man giving the command. Once the door closed behind him Mr Draven motioned for the other two men to step forward to stand beside him.

"I understand that each of you must have lots of questions and have no fear, for these will all be answered in time, but first I would like to introduce you to your new tutors, who will each help

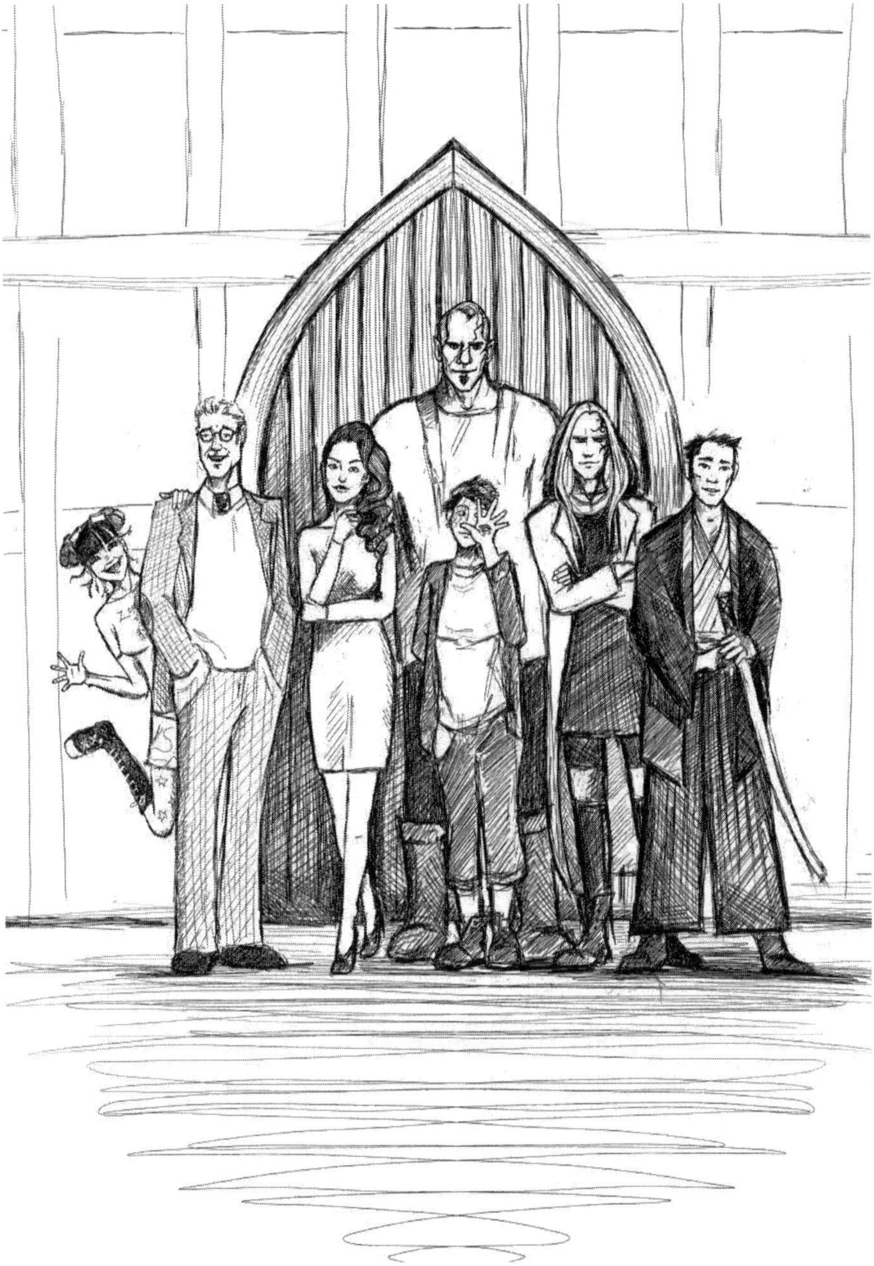

you as you walk the steps of your unknown journey ahead," Mr Draven said and as if by magic the door opened and others entered and took their places next to one another. Some they recognised, like Miss Pip and the crazy bus driver, Rue. But then there was another man and a woman they hadn't seen before. The man looked to be the only one who could pass as anything close to a teacher out of the whole lot of them as he was already dressed like some professor. This was thanks to the tweed blazer worn over a knitted sweater, the highly-polished shoes and the black rimmed glasses he wore, a pair which he kept pushing up his nose.

The woman on the other hand looked as if she had just stepped out of a glossy fashion magazine, one doing a feature on the most beautiful women in the world. It could almost be believed that she wasn't real, like a living doll of Snow White. With her porcelain skin and dark luscious curls that bounced around her shoulders when she walked into the room, it could have been believed that she was royalty.

"First I would like to introduce you to…"

"Ooo, pick me, pick me! Oh, please pick me first!" shouted out the smallest member of the group and definitely the most colourful. Mr Draven briefly closed his eyes and groaned at the interruption, almost as if he had half been expecting it. The man in glasses, who was stood next to her, placed a gentle hand on her arm and whispered,

"Patience Winnie, your turn will come soon enough."

"Oh, but that's not…" she started to say, ready to complain about how unfair it was, when one raised eyebrow from the man next to her stopped her in her tracks.

When he was satisfied she wasn't going to interrupt again he gave her a little smile, mouthed the words, 'good girl' and then looked back up to Mr Draven and said,

"My apologies, my Lord." This of course left the group of teens even more confused as to why he would be apologising for her but then he added the reason, shocking them all by saying,

"My wife will behave from now on." Hearing this was what made Janie and Ena both face each other and mouth the word 'Wife?' together, obviously surprised. I don't think anyone would have guessed that these two were an item, let alone married. Forget chalk and cheese, these two were like ice cream and hot sauce!

"It's quite alright Adam, introducing your wife first is fine," Mr Draven said causing Miss Pip to squeal and jump up and down, turning as she did this and firing pretend guns at her husband with her hands.

"Yay! Boom, boom, bang, bang! Told ya the Big Boss man wouldn't mind…in your face hubba bubba!" She said walking backwards before spinning round on one foot and coming to stand next to whom she referred to as 'Big Boss man'. Adam, her husband, just shook his head as if he had to deal with this on a daily basis and was used to her flamboyant and manic ways.

The teens all looked at each other and Zane whispered,

"Is she for real?"

"As real as a pink fairy armadillo." Pip said answering him with a wink and a sparkling grin thanks to her blue glitter coated lips. Zane gave her a look of disbelief prompting her to say,

"Shizzle be real dog…google it."

"Ooookay." Zane said dragging out the word before leaning into Theo and whispering,

"She does know I'm like a skinny white guy right, not a gangster rapper." Theo looked him up and down over the side of his shoulder and said,

"Oh, yeah man, she knows." This was when Mr Draven thought it best to clear his throat and get back on track, something that could be a challenge with Pip in the room.

"Before we begin with the introductions I want you all to know that this place isn't just a school for you to learn how to be one of us. It's a new beginning. It's a new Afterlife for each of you but above all, I want you to feel that this is your safe haven…*your home*." Their headmaster's words brought not only comfort to each of them but something far greater because for the first time they all felt as though they finally belonged and as Mr Draven had said…

They had finally made it home.

"So, with this being said, it is the reason I now introduce you to not only your tutors but to your new family, starting with your mentor Pip, who you no doubt remember meeting when you first arrived." Well that sounded like the understatement of the year as it was very doubtful that anyone would forget meeting such a character as Pip.

167

"Hello again, my pretty little young guns," Pip said giving them each a little wave. In turn, each of the bewildered teens gave their own versions of awkward waves back, all except Ivan, who decided a wave wasn't enough. He stepped towards Pip and held out his massive hand waiting for her to accept the gesture.

"I be happier in our meeting you," he said, as usual getting his words mixed up. The tiny girl barely looked older than the teens themselves, thanks to her small frame, baby face and unique sense of style. She looked up and up and up some more until reaching his face and when she found his kind eyes looking back down at her, she gave him a beaming grin. It took her no time at all to place her small hand in his, filling only a quarter of what looked like a bear's paw in comparison.

"Aww shucks handsome, I am happy to meet you too!" she said in return shaking his hand with vigour making it hard to believe someone so little had more than enough strength to do so. Ivan's eyes grew wide showing his own surprise at how strong she was and it was only when Mr Draven cleared his voice did she finally let go. Theo had to hold back a smile when he saw Ivan stretch out his hand in and out of a fist as he himself had done when they first shook hands back on the bus. It also warned him not to fall victim to one of Pip's handshakes and being fooled into believing that in this world, power was also linked to one's size.

She strutted back to the rest of the waiting adults and the other woman in the group laughed before commenting,

"Making friends again, squeak?" Pip's response to this was to pinch her white zombie t shirt with both hands, like she was snapping imaginary trouser braces and reply,

"What can I say, the big demons just love me." Then she winked at her husband, surprisingly making him blush.

"Yeah and don't we all hear about it," the Albino muttered under his breath, making the others chuckle. Mr Draven rolled his eyes before motioning him forward.

"This is Zagan. He is my lieutenant and thus being so makes him more than qualified to be your new weapons instructor. Takeshi will also work alongside him in these lessons as your personal trainer in hand to hand combat." The Japanese man also took this as his cue to step forward and bow at the waist in respect towards the teens he was soon to teach.

"Uh…our what now?" This time the comment came from Ena not Zane, however he wasn't without a response.

"I am not dreaming am I, he did just say 'weapons instructor'…right?"

"Oh dear, I don't think I will pass that class. I can't even peel a potato," Janie admitted looking forlorn and nervously scratching her shoulder with her only hand. Mr Draven gave her a kind warm smile and said,

"Have no fear young one, as you will be surprised at just what you can do when given the right teacher. Takeshi will work with each of you, not only drawing out your individual strengths but will also be teaching you how to protect your weaknesses."

"Sounds good to me, where do I sign up?" Zane said probably just seeing himself stood like a gladiator in front of the mirror with a battle axe in one hand and a shield in the other. Ena rolled her eyes at the thought.

"And this is my Captain of the Guard, Ragnar." The giant stepped forward, towering above everyone else in the room.

"I'm thinking battle studies." Theo said leaning back a bit so that Zane could hear.

"Nah, I reckon Viking demon slayer," he said back making Ena scoff,

"We are the demon's genius and so are they," she said nodding to the rest of them.

"Oh yeah, well there goes my dreams of ever making it to second base with Buffy from good old Sunnydale," Zane added making Ena shake her head and mutter 'idiot' under her breath.

"Technically though, she did date Angel and Spike and both of them were Vampires," Janie said making Zane raise an eyebrow and smile big time.

"And here was me thinking the day couldn't get any better! You a fan, shy girl?" Janie blushed and gave him a small head nod, making her hair fall in front of her face. She then jumped when Mr Draven once again cleared his throat and said,

"Let's proceed should we?" This left Ivan as the only teen not looking sheepish but mainly because he had no clue as to who Buffy the Vampire Slayer was and was left looking as puzzled as always. However, Zane couldn't help but notice the small, kind smile Janie sent Ivan's way.

"To have a bright future in our world, you must first learn the shadows of our past and to help you shed light on our vast history is your new teacher on the subject, Ragnar." For once there were no whispered comments from the group, only stunned silence as they all collectively looked up at their new intimidatingly large history teacher as he stepped forward closer to the group.

"It will be my honour to teach you the history of our people and to learn of some of our greatest ancestors," he said in his gruff, deep voice, one that matched the rough exterior of what looked like a scarred Viking warrior. None of the other teens seemed to know what to say in response to that, so it was left up to Theo to nod his head and say,

"We uh… all look forward to it." Mr Draven gave him a brief nod telling him without words that he had done well by stepping up, as it took a brave man indeed to do so in the face of Ragnar.

"Next I introduce you to your Demonology teacher." Mr Draven continued and Theo, along with the others all expected the man in glasses to step forward but each of them were yet again surprised when the beauty in the room stepped forward. It was obvious that in Afterlife nothing was as you expected, including what Mr Draven said next.

"This is Sophia, my sister." She gave them all a beaming smile, collectively making both Ivan and Zane blush, but Theo had a different reaction. He couldn't help but feel as though he had met her before. Like a feeling from a past life or something, one that grew stronger when she winked at him.

"I am pleased to meet you all," she said before stepping back and letting another teacher step forward.

"Rue, you already know from your journey here and I ask you not to hold a grudge towards her as she was only following my orders in bringing you here. As I said before, I know you must have many questions still, but please know that your encounter with Carrick was unplanned and out of our control." Hearing this wasn't easy for any of them but they also knew how Rue hadn't willingly driven them into that lake but that she had no choice and was made to do so by Death himself.

"Rue's role in your development is the most vital out of all you will learn here. She, along with Pip, is not only to be your guide to your new home, but also to your new gifts as well. She has a unique skill set that enables her to help you find and draw out the powers bestowed upon you and in doing so will help you learn how to control them. She may be blind but trust me when I say that she sees more than most." This certainly intrigued the group. However, Theo's first thought was that he knew now that he was going to have to get used to be called 'Kid', a thought he didn't relish.

"Ooo, it's your turn next, Hubba Bubba." Pip said nudging her husband in obvious excitement. He straightened the tie he had tucked into his sweater and pushed his glasses further up his nose before stepping forward when Mr Draven introduced him.

"This is Adam and as you now know, Pip's husband. He will be your teacher in Human studies."

"Oh, look Zane, someone that can finally help you out in acting more normal," Ena commented drily making Janie giggle.

"Ha, ha, at least I have a chance at passing that class, Blue Streaks," Zane retorted back giving her a new nickname.

"Can I ask, what exactly do we need Human Studies for?" Theo said, being the only one bold enough to ask what all the others were thinking.

"You may no longer be human but that doesn't mean you don't still live in the human world. And like Sir Francis Bacon once said 'Knowledge is Power', a phrase that couldn't be truer now than when it was first published back in 1597, in his book 'Meditationes Sacrae and Human Philosophy'." Mr Draven said and Zane couldn't help himself when he muttered,

"Sounds like a real page turner."

"It is but one human view of God and Man, something that is read in a very different light when you're one of us. Personally, I find it all a bit preachy but what can I say, I am half Demon," Mr Draven said with a smirk and it was the first hint the teens got that their new Headmaster had a humorous side.

"I guess it's just like the phrase, 'With great power comes great responsibility'," Zane said and the rest of the group groaned, with Ena actually slapping her forehead, a habit that was quickly forming around Zane. Of course, there was one member of the group, Ivan who like the other adults in the room, had no clue where Zane had just got that phrase from.

"I am afraid I am not familiar with the origins of who said that," Mr Draven said shaking his head slightly as if trying to remember it for himself. Zane suddenly looked sheepish before telling the rest of them,

"It was Uncle…"

"Ben! Of course, I knew I'd heard that before…it's from Spiderman, Big Boss man." Pip added, shouting out the answer in her excitement. Mr Draven hid the hint of a smirk behind the fisted hand he held to his lips as he took in the boy's obvious embarrassment.

"Well it may have originated from a comic book, but it is insightful and worthy of a mention as its principles are primarily the same…good thinking Zane," he praised, easing Zane's shame at speaking out, something Mr Draven wanted to encourage. Zane's eyes widened in surprise and upon hearing this he nudged Ena's shoulder from behind and said,

"See, totally nailed it with the superhero quote." Ena may have rolled her eyes in response to this but deep down she was secretly happy that Zane wasn't made to look foolish by the adults in the room. Coming from her it was something different, mainly done so in jest or friendly banter but by someone older, it would have just been another blow for an already vulnerable teen.

"And you, do we call you 'My Lord' or Mr Draven?" Theo asked folding his arms and making it clear that the group hadn't all missed the part in the conversation when Carrick had called him this. Mr Draven raised an eyebrow at him before saying,

"Calling me Draven will be just fine," he said which prompted his sister, Sophia to speak up.

"Yeah, he's used to being called by his last name, aren't you brother?" she said nudging his arm playfully and receiving a wry look in return, one that told Theo and the rest of them that they were missing the inside joke here.

"Aww poor Toots, she so wanted to be here," Pip said cryptically, making them wonder who 'Toots' was, especially when she received a pointed look from her husband. Adam gave her a silent shake of his head, obviously telling her without words not to go there. Of course, this just made Theo and his friends even more curious and he made a mental note to try and get it out of Pip when given the chance. Which looked as if it was going to be sooner than he thought.

"I think now that all the introductions are out of the way, it's time we let the group get settled in. Mrs Ambrogetti would you be so kind as to show them around their new home?" Draven said looking to Pip, who suddenly started rocking back and forth from her toes to her heels and clapping her hands she was so excited.

"Does a Gorgon Leech like bloody flesh fresh off the bone?!" Janie and Ena looked at each other and made 'eww' faces, whilst Zane looked to Theo and whispered,

"I'm lost, does this means she wants to show us around or feed us to a pet demon?"

"My guess is the first one, as I don't think she would have gone to all that trouble decorating our rooms, like she said she had, if they were only going to lead us to our deaths...*again.*" Theo replied applying logic in what seemed like the weirdest conversation possible.

"Righty lefty kidderly winkles, let's get our wiggle on and bust a groove on this bad boy Mansion!" Pip said turning the simple 'let's go' into the longest and most cryptically challenging sentence she had said yet.

"Does little teacher want dancing for us?" Ivan asked giving each of them a quizzical look.

"No, she is going to show us around," Janie told him and looked back to Pip, who was skipping out the room and mumbled to herself,

"I think."

As the group followed their colourful guide out the door, each of the teachers nodded in a friendly manner, putting the group at ease for the next time they would see them when classes began. They then travelled down the grand hallway that looked as if it was more suited to an English castle, not anywhere they ever expected to call home. Theo looked behind him as the door closed before he broke out into a short jog to catch up with their green haired guide. She was quick for such a little thing he thought with a smirk.

"Ask away my young Padawan," she said as Theo approached.

"A what now?" Theo had to ask.

"She means a Jedi apprentice," Zane answered for her, making Pip's hand go up as she shouted without looking back at him,

"Bingo birdie!" Theo looked bewildered for a second before looking to Zane on his right, who had now caught up with him,

"You're a geek, you know that." Zane smiled, pounded his fist to his chest twice and said,

"And proud brother, and proud." Theo rolled his eyes, like Ena often did but smiled all the same.

"So, this question your booty is just burning to ask me?" Pip said reminding him. By this time the rest of the group had caught up and not only with their faster pace but with the conversation as well.

Theo thought for a moment about asking her who this 'Toots' was but surprised himself when he opened his mouth and a different question came out,

"Why did Carrick call Mr Draven 'my Lord'?" The rest of the teens all looked to Pip, as though they too had been asking themselves the same question and were just thankful that Theo had been the one to bring it up. Pip, on the other hand, just giggled and shook her head before shocking them all with the answer,

"Because you silly bunch of jellybeans…

"He's our King."

13
Afterlife Tour

"Rightybee my little supernatural newborns, now we get to the good stuff!" Pip said clapping her hands and spinning on her heel to face them. She had suddenly stopped under an ancient looking sign hanging from the ceiling. It looked like a demonic hand pointing to a pair of double doors on their left. Underneath the words read,

'Hellish Fun
This Way'

It was easy to see that this was what Pip had wanted to show them all along but had first been obligated to get all the, in her words, 'Stuffy boring stuff' out of the way. And their first stop had been the library, which had been grand enough to rival the best

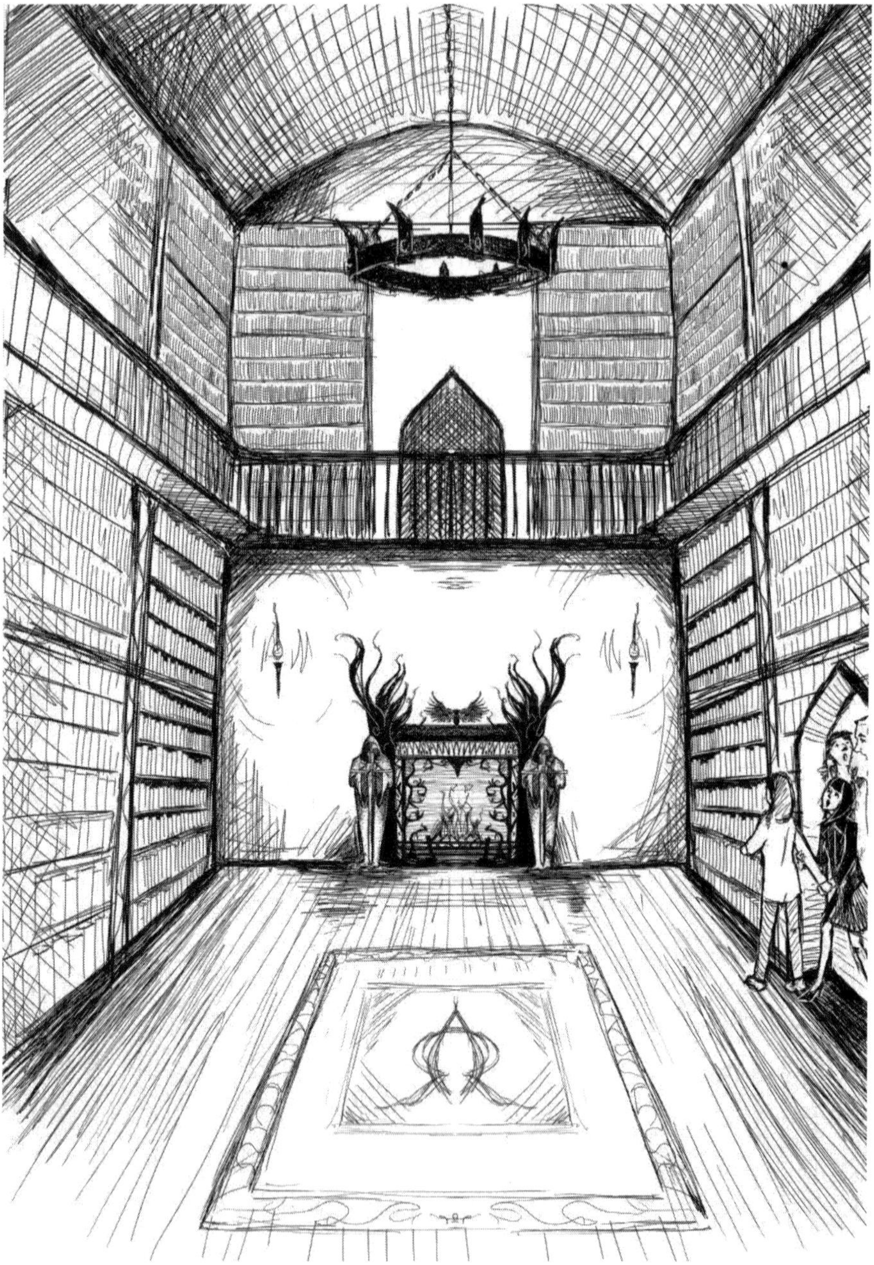

libraries in the world. The place had been incredible and even without being a book worm, you had to admire it for its grandeur and beautiful craftsmanship, something the group collectively did...one more than the others.

"This place is insanely cool," Janie had whispered as if fearing at any moment to receive the wrath of some tight lipped, old crone of a librarian. Of course, she quickly learned that she had nothing to fear when Pip broke out into song, just to hear her echo.

"I like big books and I cannot lie,

You other books can't deny,

That when a book sits there all displaced,

And a square thing in your face,

They get sprung,

From the shelf, first by the spiney scruff,

'Cause you notice that book was stuffed,

Deep in the words she's seeing,

I'm hooked and I can't stop reading,

Oh baby!"

Pip had done this after grabbing the first big book to hand and dancing with it, smacking it in time with the beat against someone's imaginary butt. As soon as she had finished the others had burst out laughing. However, Ivan had taken a little longer than the others to get it. When he did the singing echo from Pip was soon replaced by the booming sound of Ivan's laughter, making his whole body jiggle up and down as he held on to his belly.

"I be understanding at this time. Butts become books, she be clever this little one," Ivan said patting Pip on the head like some kind of big brother figure. And just like that Pip had turned what would have been an intimidating and opulent room into something the teens could use with ease and comfort.

Suddenly now the grand room, with its highly polished wooden floors and its elaborately carved spiral staircases, didn't seem to be screaming at them all to leave. However, the menacing looking black fireplace dominating the centre of the room wasn't something they were all eager to sit around telling Kumbaya stories. No, it looked more likely to swallow you whole the second you got close enough to it, as it looked like the gates of Hell themselves and for all the teens knew, it could have been!

It even had two huge cast iron statues either side that were like sentinels guarding the realm, waiting to pass out judgement and strike them down with the swords they held with both hands interlinked around the handle, cradled to their chests.

"And FYI, you will find the books about Demonology up there somewhere in between Dante's Inferno, the 14th-century poem not the computer game and Dysentery." Pip said flinging her arm out and waving it up and down pointing at the wall of books, manuscripts, journals, newspapers, and practically anything else that could be read. Ena and Theo were the only ones that screwed up their noses, so this time it was Janie's turn to ask,

"Uh…what's dysentery?"

"Oh, just some nasty little infection of the intestines that results in severe diarrhoea and blood and mucus in the faeces…in other words not the nicest of poos, certainly not one to be proud of like those phantom wipes!" Pip added making the boys laugh, all but Ivan who was still looking at the fireplace as if it was drawing him in. Pip noticed this and nudged him once saying,

"Leave those voices alone big man, you will only get burned and by more than just the flames." This seemed to snap Ivan out of whatever it had been that had captured his attention so intently and he shook his head as if banishing the rest of the dark cobwebs that had clung to his mind for a short time.

The next stop on the list had been what Pip had called the games' room. Of course, the five teenagers had all been expecting something close to an arcade or at the very least something with a TV and a pool table in it, but what they got couldn't have been further from that dream.

"Now this piece of prime real estate right here is where you will be doing your bad ass ninja training," Pip said bouncing into the room, spinning once and then doing a round house kick into the chest of one of the training dummies, making it bounce back on its stand. She landed and just before the others could shout look out, she shouted,

"Hi ya!" Then she slashed an arm out sideways, stopping the dummy before it sprung back and smacked into her and turned her head to the others and winked, saying,

"Slippery little Budgerigar."

"Budgerigar?" Zane had to enquire.

"Yeah, I mean I wanted to say the dude without a daddy but I have been told to keep my mouth PG 13, so I went with the cute little birdy instead."

"As you do," Zane muttered under his breath making Theo chuckle.

"Hey what are these for?" Ena asked walking over to a row of six wooden poles that each had three arms and a bent leg at the bottom.

"Ah, now that little beauty right there is what we in the Kung Fu business like to call a Mak Yan Jong," she said over exaggerating the accent like she was in an old martial arts movie.

"Although my man Takeshi, an all round bad ass, will be teaching you all sorts of cool beans, even my fav the art of Wing Chun," she told them as they all walked through what was clearly a training room, one that looked as though it could have also doubled as a movie set for one of those martial arts films or from the Matrix, Zane thought with a smirk, thinking back to when Neo was first in training.

"What's Wing Chun?" This time it was Janie's turn to ask.

"Oh, I just love how eager all you pickles are at being tasty. Wing Chun is best described by the master himself."

"You mean Takeshi?" Theo asked but Pip shook her head.

"Nope, by the one and only legend, IP man."

"She be hiccupping now?" Ivan asked making her laugh.

"Nah big dude, IP man isn't a hiccup, it's a way of life! I could explain it to you but way better to show you," she said walking further into the room. The others stopped, expecting her to break out into some Kung Fu style moves but she kept walking. When she realised the others weren't following she turned around and said,

"Oh, you thought I meant now. No, no, I meant you will have to watch the movie, its wicked sick cool...I will add it to your movie collection, it should be here tomorrow...*I got Prime,*" she added whispering behind her hand as though it was some big secret Amazon were trying to keep to themselves.

"Okay, let's get a wiggle on people, this tour won't show itself." Pip said clapping and once again spinning on her heel before shooting imaginary guns at the door. They followed behind but as they walked past one wall Ivan looked up in awe and said,

"I like walls here." The boys both laughed and Ena did her usual eye rolling bit but it was Janie who looked up to the wall and shivered. Thanks to her past she hated blades, only remembering that brief flash of metal before feeling the pain, and then there was nothing. The memory was as though it had been snatched away and all that was left was the edges of puzzle pieces with the image missing.

The wall had been covered in every type of edged weapon imaginable. Some even looked so far out there that they could have once been used as props off a Sci Fi movie as the only thing that looked to be missing was a Lightsaber. The number of swords alone would have been enough to fill the hands of every soldier fighting at the black gates of Mordor, or at least that was the way Zane saw it when he walked past.

"Well you can't say life here is going to be boring that's for damn sure. Most exciting thing that happened at my old school was when my old biology teacher stole a turkey from our local supermarket and claimed aliens made her do it…to be fair, after today I feel a little guilty that I didn't believe her," Zane said talking mainly to himself as they followed Pip down a new hallway.

"Seriously?" Theo asked,

"Yeah dude, and you know the weird part?"

"You mean it gets weirder?"

"Yeah, like the whole time I was thinking, did she at least steal the potatoes to go with it or did she already have them at home…I mean it wasn't even Christmas." Theo shook his head and chuckled at his friend's unique sense of humour. Ena on the other hand nudged Janie and said,

"How could it be boring around here when Zane's always able to entertain us with pointless stories like that one." Janie smiled knowing she was joking and Zane turned to face them both and bent at the waist after saying in a posh voice,

"At your service, Miladies."

After the weapons/training room there was only one place Pip needed to show them before they could finally relax in their own space, one Pip was most excited to show them. But first came the classroom.

"I'm betting my Iron Maiden limited edition picture disc collection that it smells old and has a lot of wood in it," Zane said and Theo had to agree,

"I'm thinking, based on what we have seen so far, that it's a safe bet." They had all been expecting the same thing, but they soon discovered that in Afterlife it could be a dangerous thing, as Pip soon reminded them,

"I would have taken that bet but it would have been like stealing candy from a sloth and those things are too cute for words! Have you ever seen the man taking a selfie with one, the sucker is actually smiling!" The teens all looked at her until she finally realised she hadn't made her point yet.

"Oh yeah, where was I? That's it, Big Boss man…A very good friend of mine once said that 'assumption is the mother from where all mistakes are born'. Of course, she got that from someone else but you catch my drift, so welcome to your first lesson in assumption." Then she opened the door and proved that she was right, they had all assumed wrong.

"Welcome to your new classroom," she said letting them all walk in before her. The room was a massive open space that was flooded with light thanks to the wall of windows bouncing light off the pale grey walls. It was the first room they had seen that didn't look like they couldn't swing a cat without it hitting an antique.

"Ho…ly…"

"Cheese on a cracker Batman. Yeah I know, it's the bomb ain't it?" Pip said coming up behind Zane, patting him on the back and finishing his sentence for him. Then she skipped right past him into the room and spun around with her arms out showing them the modern looking space.

"Okay, so this nice and smooth here is where the teacher of the day sits," she said after moonwalking backwards and running her fingers over a clear glass desk that was in the shape of a giant S on its side. It flowed back in on itself to create the flat part that was big enough for everyone in the room to sit on, all except Ivan of course. Currently, all it held was a fancy high tech screen that at a guess, the teens would have said was a computer. But with no mouse or keyboard for all they knew it could have been a security system to keep an eye on them working at their desks. And speaking of their desks, that's what came next.

The room didn't have much in it, other than the awesome teacher's desk, one piece of art work that hung over it and these strange looking pods. They were all joined together, making it look like a giant rounded piece of a honeycomb in the centre of the room, raised up on a slight platform.

"Umm…Miss Pip," Janie asked raising her one hand like class had already started.

"Yes deary, oh and you don't have to call me Miss Pip, unless you want to of course, but Pip is what most of my peeps and homies call me," she answered.

"Okay Pip…I was just wondering…umm, well…"

"We want to know, if this is our classroom where we will all be sitting?" Ena said taking over from Janie and relieving her of her obvious shyness.

"Ah ha, now this you are gonna like!" Pip shouted dancing back over to the desk.

"Thanks for that," Janie said taking a step closer to Ena.

"I got your back, Jay," Ena replied nudging Janie's half arm and giving her a nickname for the first time in her life. So, the beaming smile she gave her wasn't just for speaking up when she was struggling, it was also for touching her half arm, something that no-one had ever done and becoming the type of friend who would care enough to grant a nickname to someone they'd just met. For a loner like Janie, this was huge...in fact,

It was way bigger than dying.

"Tada!" Pip shouted after tapping on the screen a few times and suddenly the pods all started to move, making the group jump back as each of them rotated around on the platform until they all faced the front. Now they could see that they were like individual workstations, with big comfy seats integrated into the desks in front of them. They even had their own smaller touch screen computers and little multi-coloured pockets filled with stationary tucked away against the sides of the pod.

"The different colours were my idea but you guys will only get to know which is yours on your first day of class," Pip said looking proud and referring to the inside of each of the pods.

"And when will that be?" Theo couldn't help but ask, which made him wonder…was it something he was actually looking forward to?

"That glorious day will be only one sleep away from greatness…tomorrow," Pip added when everyone was just left looking confused, especially Ivan.

"Okkie dokkie, now time for the piece de resistance."

"I no understand." Ivan said,

"The best chocolate in the heart shaped box," Pip simplified for him after grabbing his little finger and giving it an affectionate shake.

"I see, best is last is better…yes?" Ivan said smiling now that he understood.

"Something like that…so what's next?" Theo said first answering Ivan and then turning back to Pip before she bounced out of yet another doorway.

"Next…well my lovelies, it's time you won the lottery… *Supernatural style!*"

14
Winning the Supernatural Lottery

Theatre Open

Finally, it came time for them to see their own personal spaces and by the end of the tour they were more than ready for it. It was a bit of an unnatural overload on the senses, as there was literally too much information to take in. For starters, they felt like they would need GPS just to get from A to B. And just thinking about how much time they would need getting between the two, well Zane had been right when asking how good they all were on roller-skates as they would most certainly be needing them if they didn't want to be late for class.

"Or better yet, Segway's!" Ena had shouted popping her head in between the two boys, getting in on the conversation.

"Erm, you know what, that's not a bad idea, Blue streaks." Zane agreed calling her by her unwanted nickname.

"Whatever, skater boy," she answered back before re-joining Janie. As usual, Ivan was at the back as it was obvious this was what he preferred. Janie couldn't help but wonder if he hadn't appointed himself protector of the group as he always seemed to be on rear guard. Which prompted the question, who was she to the group?

It was obvious who Theo was as the rest of them all knew the first time they laid eyes on him that he was a natural born leader. And then there was their comic relief, one she had to admit during all this crazy she was more than grateful for. And then there was her friend Ena, who was obviously as strong minded as she was smart, which only left her...*the shy one.* She didn't really know yet what she brought to the group and she was getting paranoid that the others would soon be asking the same question.

"Rightybee my little supernatural new-born's, now we get to the good stuff!" Pip said bringing them full circle and in front of the door they knew they really wanted to see behind. Even from the moment they first stepped foot inside Afterlife they had heard Pip talk about their bedrooms and now knowing Pip a little better, they had a feeling they wouldn't be disappointed.

She had seemed to go out of her way to make the teens feel as at home as they possibly could given their circumstances and once she finally opened that door and saw each of their faces light up, she knew she had hit the ball out of the ballpark once again.

"Oh my," Janie whispered putting her hand to her mouth as it had dropped open.

"It's...it's..." Ena tried to find the words but soon realised there weren't any.

"Now that is a holy cheese on a cracker moment," Zane said, easily finding the right words and Theo just whistled and said,

"Toto, I don't think we're in Kansas anymore."

"Balls!" Ivan shouted making all the teens look back at him in surprise.

"Not what I was expecting but okay, I will take it," Pip said shrugging her shoulders.

"Basketballs!" Ivan shouted again pointing at the tallest wall that had nine basketball hoops all spread out, with one closest to the floor which was ideal for little Janie and the tallest one at least two storeys high.

After seeing this Ivan was lost and practically ran over to the wall, taking nothing else of the room in thanks to his tunnel vision for his obvious passion. He quickly started picking up balls from the big basket situated under the hoops and started shooting them through each like a pro.

"Okay, so we lost the big guy," Zane said making Janie giggle.

"Wow, he's really good," Theo said and he couldn't help but notice how happy Pip looked just watching Ivan getting lost in his own slice of heaven.

"Oh no! Oh no! Now that right there is a holy cheese on a cracker moment...no scrap that, and let's just go with Holy Crap my pants Batman, but look at that beauty!" Zane said noticing what he would call his own heaven. Then he ran towards a flashing neon light that read 'Theatre Open', skilfully dodging anything else in his way.

"Now that is cool," Ena said walking over towards the wall of shelves that housed the biggest collection of DVDs that she had ever seen, one that Zane was already scanning his way through.

"I didn't even know they'd made that many movies," Ena said turning back to Pip who was now looking at them with the same happiness Theo had seen when she had been watching Ivan. It quickly became apparent to Theo that even though he didn't know if she was an Angel or Demon, there was no denying that there stood a soul who found great pleasure in giving to others.

Theo walked around the different seating areas that were a mixture of funky looking chairs, to where the others were stood. The 'Theatre' part of the room consisted of a row of six reclining seats that all looked like Lazyboys, with everything from speakers in the head rests, to cup holders and even USB ports. They all faced the large white projector screen that was yet to be filled with the colourful world of Hollywood. Each seat even had its own quirky table for snacks next to it which were classic movie themed. There was a giant metal Alien from the movie, that held up a glass top and even a life sized R2D2 that did the same thing. There was also a giant hulk hand that smashed through the metal top, giving you places to put your drinks around the top of his green fist.

A zombie dressed like a dead butler holding a bloody cloth over one arm whilst the other held a piece of red glass that looked to be overflowing with fake blood.

Then there was the tamer looking bucket with hearts that spilled over and climbed up over the glass, creating its own heart shape in doing so. They even had an Alice in Wonderland style one with a stack of tea pots and china tea sets all coming from the upturned Mad Hatter's top hat. Theo had to wonder where someone would even buy furniture like this!

Even the walls were covered in framed classic movie posters and the far wall held every teen's dream room accessory...a snack bar! This came complete with popcorn machine, glass jars filled with pick 'n mix sweets, a fridge loaded with every type of soda you could think of and...

"A bowl of fruit?" Ena asked picking up a banana and showing it to Pip.

"I was told to add something healthy," she said shrugging her shoulders and smirking at the small bowl that held no more than three pieces of fruit.

"Oh, this is so awesome!" Zane said finding yet another movie he wanted to watch and adding it to his growing pile, one he was struggling to hold steady.

"You know you live here now and those movies you can watch anytime." Ena said trying to get it through to him but he just shook his head and leant in closer to her before saying,

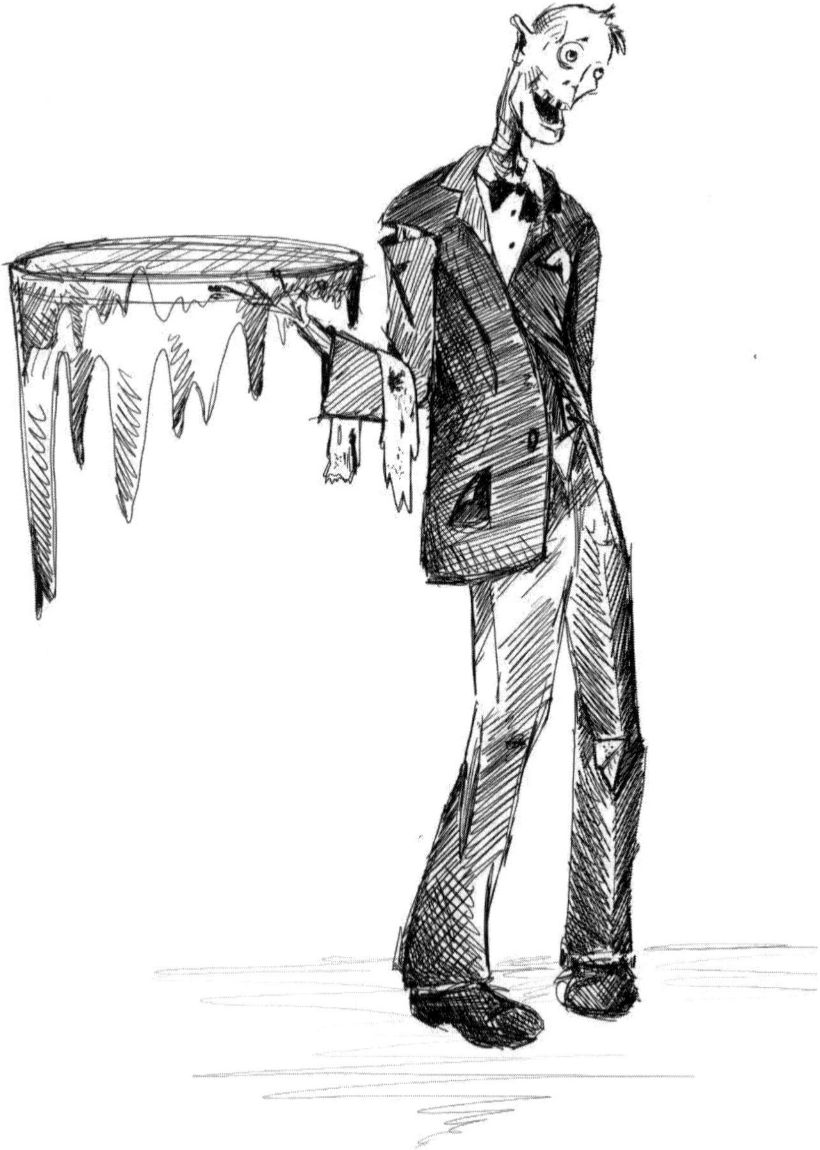

"But what if this is all a trick and they take away this carrot for bad behaviour? No, I can't risk it, I will just hide these away in my room just in case." Hearing this Pip burst out laughing.

"Most of your teachers are demons, Dude...what type of bad behaviour do you think a demon would ever punish you for? Besides, they still have their hands full with me, so don't sweat it, sweetie. No one will ever come into your space unless you ask them to, well other than the cleaner of course."

"Uh...our what now? I'm sorry I think my ears might be playing tricks on me, did she say cleaner?" Zane said to Theo as both him and Ena took a step closer to Pip.

"Are you for real?" Ena said finding herself on the same page as Theo and Zane in the cleaning department and like them it probably had something to do with growing up in a children's home.

"I told you, Supernatural lottery treacle tots, besides, you guys have more important things to do, like learn Mary Poppins style how to clean your rooms without even lifting a finger...Now that's what I call Supercalifragilisticexpialidocious!"

"You're joking...right, she's joking...she's not joking." Theo asked only adding this last part when a smirking Pip shook her head.

"I like be clean." Ivan said, only now coming to join the rest of them after he had finished shooting hoops.

"That's the spirit big kiddo, now why don't you each go and check out your rooms, whilst I order some pizza, 'cause I don't know about you but I wanna make like a turtle." Pip said and then parted with a little wave like the queen before disappearing out the door.

"I no understand."

"Yeah, you and me both, big dude." Zane said in reply to Ivan's confusion, one that matched the rest of the group.

"Seriously guys, I mean can you believe this place?" Ena said turning back to the room and looking up at the second floor, which was a large mezzanine level. A very cool spiral staircase connected the two floors and thanks to its modern design, it looked as though each of the clear plastic steps was floating mid-air.

"It's very cool." Janie agreed quietly, whilst the others were clearly more vocal about it.

"Me like place like this, it be like playground," Ivan said looking back to his obvious favourite part… *the hoops*.

"Then if you like that, you guys are gonna freak out when you see what I just found!" Theo said after taking a better look round. He had walked behind the staircase and found a whole other room and this one he had a feeling they were all going to enjoy equally.

"Holy Mother and her cleaning lady! This is freaking AWESOME!" Zane said as he joined Theo after skidding around the corner and holding onto the banister to steady himself. The room opened out like some sort of ultimate mancave and the huge sign on the wall said 'Choose your Weapon'. Of course, this was in reference to what filled the room and it was far from weaponry.

"Would you check out that set up, they must have every Xbox One and Ps4 game ever made. And look at those gaming chairs, you know what this means dude?" Zane said slapping Theo on the back.

"Plenty of time to rot your brains killing Zombies and then becoming one," Ena said winking at Janie when she giggled.

"Well I was thinking more hours of gaming without a dead ass, but yeah, killing Zombies sounds like fun too."

"Trust you to focus on that part," Ena scoffed.

Other than the main gaming station, which dominated the room with its 98inch HD smart TV, the wall also held every popular gaming console since the early 90's. Each of these were hooked up to their own smaller TV's, complete with themed shelving surround housing the games for each. Expensive looking leather gaming chairs were positioned in front of them, along with a cool seating area behind. This was complete with a huge Pac Man seat that looked as though it was trying to swallow anyone who sat in it and a huge coffee table in the shape of a giant PlayStation controller with glass on top.

There were other popular games situated further in the room all on a high polished, oak wooden floor that had multi coloured arrows painted in different directions around the room. You had pool and foosball tables, dart boards, air hockey and table tennis and all were framed around the room with a mixture of old school and new video arcade games. These included some of the classics like Donkey Kong, Centipede and Ms. Pac-Man, mixed with the new stuff, which drew in the teens like moths to the flame.

Movie themed pinball machines like the Hobbit and Ironman were just begging to be played, that was until the teens saw the Star Wars battle pod, Aliens Armageddon shooting game and a Dance Revolution X, complete with neon flashing lights. Even the walls had retro entertainment stuck to them, with classic board games hung there by Velcro with the pieces hidden behind.

"Okay, so I know we all died and I can't speak for you guys but I definitely did something right in life because I know I just woke up in heaven!" Zane said and Theo walked further in the room and said,

"No, no dude, we are all there right along with you." And this was where the fun really began.

"I think I speak for all of us when I say...LET'S CHECK OUT OUR ROOMS!" Ena said shouting this last part and running for the staircase ahead of the others.

"Where we go all?" Ivan asked looking around as if there was something he couldn't see. Janie looked back and smiled at her new friend, feeling protective and liking his naïve kind nature.

"We are all going to check our new rooms, should we go together?" she said nodding to where the others had run off to.

"I be liking that much very," he told her, grateful that he had a friend who seemed to understand him better than anyone he had ever met before. She seemed to know just what he was thinking, even though he knew that his words came out all jumbled.

"Janie, I..." he was just about to tell her how he felt when he was cut short by an almighty scream that came from above.

"Ena!" Janie said but Ivan was already gone. Janie ran towards the staircase, zig zagging around the table top games until she was just in time to see something incredible. Ivan was looking up at the balcony one second and then disappearing the next. Janie ran the rest of the way to see that Ivan had suddenly leapt to the second level and was now hanging from the railings like an overweight Tarzan.

"What the...?" Janie heard from above before seeing the others all appear.

"Uh, dude, crazy question I know, but what are you doing?" Zane asked looking over the metal rail to find Ivan gripping on for dear life.

"What happened?" Theo shouted down to Janie who was looking up at them from below just as bewildered as they were.

"I don't know, we heard Ena scream and then he was gone. I think he just leapt up there," she told them and Ena popped her head over and said sheepishly,

"I was just excited at seeing my room...Oops, sorry Ivan," she added when she saw Ivan still hanging there.

"Okay, so it's all good, just a misunderstanding," Theo said expecting Ivan to have moved by now.

"Uh...if it's all good then what is the big guy still doing there?" Zane whispered to him and Theo shrugged his shoulders.

"Alright big guy, come on up," Theo said trying to prompt him to move.

"I... cannot," he forced out and Theo, Zane and Ena all exchanged confused looks before looking back down to Ivan when

he said the last words they ever expected to hear from such a big guy…

"I scared of… height."

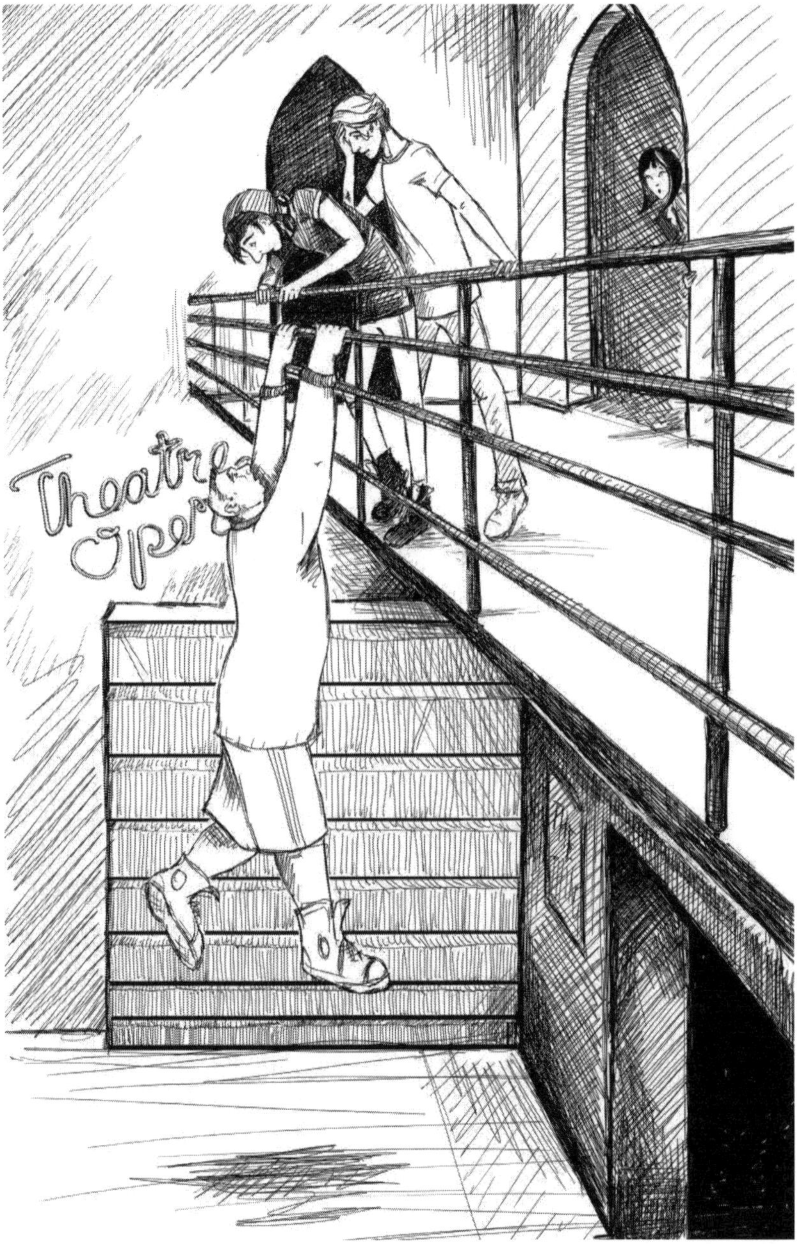

15
Russian King Kong

"Come again?" Zane said after hearing that the big guy was scared of heights. He looked down at a terrified looking Ivan and then back again to Theo, who he was hoping had an idea to get their friend back over the railings.

"I no like…" Ivan tried to finish that sentence but one look down and he stumbled on his words, this time out of fear and not his lack of knowledge for the English language.

"Okay, okay, Ivan look at me," Theo said taking charge and trying to get him focused on coming back up, not the possibility of falling down.

"Right, I need you to reach up and grab this top rail and then pull yourself up…Ivan?" Theo quickly noticed that one look at where Theo wanted him to put his hand and Ivan was too lost in the labyrinth of his fear to find his way out of it again.

"I…I…sorry," he stammered shaking his head in little frantic movements telling the others that for the moment, he was going nowhere.

"What's happening, why is he still hanging there?!" Janie shouted up obviously becoming increasingly more concerned as the seconds ticked by.

"He's a bit…" Zane stopped for a second as he saw Ivan wince, obviously feeling ashamed for being so afraid, so he whispered behind his hand,

"Scared."

After hearing this Janie was off on a mission, grabbing anything and everything she could find that was soft and would make a significantly better landing than the hard floor. She struggled one handed to grab cushions off chairs, but she managed to strip sofas so that only the bare frames were left. She even managed to pull all the bean bags from the sunken seating area and started piling them on top of one another. Zane didn't say anything but he couldn't help wonder what it was going to look like if Ivan was to fall and if there would be an explosion of tiny white polystyrene balls like he suspected there would be.

Well it certainly looked a sight down there, with everything from a Burger shaped bean bag to a whole Millennium Falcon one. There was even one that looked like a giant shark with its mouth open where you would sit. However, given what it was now being used for, it wasn't the best image to instil confidence in someone dropping from above into its waiting mouth. It had to be said that Pip certainly had a unique sense of interior decorating, Zane thought with a hidden smirk.

Theo looked back down at Ivan and then back at the three of them, knowing without a doubt that there was no way they could pull him back up, even with their combined strength. Now, maybe if they had been here a while longer and had learned some of what they all hoped were some cool, kick ass powers they might have had a chance. However, in reality, it had been a day and the only thing they had learned so far was how not to get lost, thanks to Pip's tour and for Theo, the added bonus on how to piss off a Death Dealer.

Now they were faced with one of their own in a sticky situation and for once, Theo didn't have a clue how to help someone. So, when it was Zane who spoke up, he was both surprised and thankful…oh, and a little confused at that.

"King Kong!" Zane shouted making Ena frown and Theo raise an eyebrow.

"Just work with me here…Okay, listen up big man, you're no longer Ivan."

"I no *Ivan?*"he said in such a way that if he hadn't been using his hands to grip on for dear life then he would have scratched his head in confusion.

"No, you're not. You're freaking King Kong man!" Zane said in such a way that if you were blind it would have been believable.

"What?!" Ena hissed.

"I said work with me here… *I know what I'm doing."* Zane insisted, muttering this last part to himself. She was about to say more when Theo intervened and shook his head, telling her silently not to go there. Then they all watched as Zane worked his magic, something that shocked them all.

"Now close your eyes and listen to the sound of my voice."

"But I…" Ivan started to say but was quickly cut off when Zane grabbed his hand that was quickly turning white from gripping onto the railing for ages. In fact, none of them quite knew how he had been holding on for so long as it was, not considering how heavy he must be.

"Look at me. You. Are. Not. Ivan." Zane said forcefully, squeezing his hand and finally getting him to stop looking at the ground.

"I no Ivan?"

"No. You are not Ivan. And do you know how I know. Because Ivan didn't just leap up here to save the girl without thinking," Zane told him.

"I did not?" he asked obviously as confused as the rest of them.

"No, you didn't. Ivan is afraid of heights but King Kong, now that is a hairy ass dude that isn't scared of anything! And he was the one that just wanted to save the girl without thinking. Now that girl is still in trouble and needs your help," Zane said sounding his most serious yet. It was astounding really, considering all the things he had faced since first stepping foot on that bus and it took seeing one of his new friends too terrified to move to get him to finally act like life wasn't just some big joke.

"Girl needs your help!" he said through gritted teeth, rolling his hand in the air and trying to prompt a suitable response from Ena, who didn't know it but was supposed to be playing the damsel in distress right now.

"Eh?" she said not getting it until Theo leaned in closer and said,

"I think this is the point where you scream." So, she rolled her eyes and kind of yelped, this time making Zane roll his eyes before shooting her a scathing look.

"Really?" Zane said making her shrug her shoulders.

"What, I suck at 'I'm the whole helpless girl' crap okay!" she snapped. Zane looked to Theo and he held up his arms and said,

"Don't look at me dude, I suck at it as well."

"Amateurs," Zane muttered before swearing at the sight of Ivan's fingers nearly slipping.

"Come on Dude, work with me here, you gotta just believe it! You're King Kong! Now just reach up and jump over...come on I know you can do it!"

"I...I...not do it," Ivan said with his voice shaking under the strain of fear. Zane closed his eyes feeling the bitter sting of defeat, knowing that there was only one place left for him to go and that was down. Of course, falling was only ever going to increase his fear and he knew what that felt like and didn't want it for his friend...*not like last time.*

A painfully memory flashed in his mind of the face of someone he cared deeply for and the last time he saw those eyes asking him why. He tried to save them but had failed and right now that sinking feeling that lingered deep within his soul was clawing its way back to the surface. He was so close to admitting defeat when something magical happened...

An almighty, ear shattering scream erupted behind them all and time stood still for everyone but Ivan. The second he heard that sound coming from someone he had already started to feel close to, he felt something inside of him snap into place. The scream was quickly followed by a blood curdling roar that sounded like it had come from the very depths of Hell, as a demonic beast was being let loose on Earth in the form of one large Russian boy. He was quickly up and over the railings before his mind even registered the action and he quickly stood as protector over the one the scream had originated from.

They all turned to see the big guy stood in front of the person responsible for such dramatic actions and one look to see Ena looking just as confused as Theo and Zane, quickly told them that it didn't come from her as they had first thought.

"Are alright you be?" Ivan asked so softly it was surprising that it came from someone so large and only seconds ago, someone who had sounded so scary.

"Yes, thank you… *my King Kong*," Janie said adding the cute pet name and looking up at him as though he was her true-life hero. He nodded once and stepped aside for the rest of them to see her stood there looking suddenly bashful.

"Now that was what I call a scream!" Zane said beaming at her and now making her blush.

"Yeah, I will say! That was brilliant, Jay!" Ena also praised giving her a high five and this time adding a smile to those rosy cheeks. Zane walked over to Ivan, slapped him on the back and said,

"See…totally King Kong my man!" Suddenly Janie wasn't the only one blushing as Ivan's face started feeling warm. Zane and Ena walked back along the corridor to continue what they were doing before Ivan turned all ape on them, leaving Theo and Janie stood there alone as Ivan had followed the others. Theo looked down below at the 'landing pad' Janie had created just in case and watching her struggle with all those large cushions one handed hadn't been easy for Theo but she had done it.

"Silly I know but…" she started to say, doubting if it would have worked or not but Theo quickly interrupted her and said,

"It was brilliant." Then he gave her shoulder a squeeze as he walked past, leaving her stood there biting her lip and feeling for the first time in her life, as though maybe she wasn't…

Useless.

16

Dreams Come True for Stolen Souls

"Well it's gotta be said, but in my book, that crazy little green haired chick is right up there with Gandhi," Zane said after being gobsmacked opening the door to his new room.

"Enjoy Zee, I am gonna check out mine," Theo said christening Zane with his new nickname before going in search of his own idea of heaven.

"Uh, uh," Zane said for once being lost for words the further inside the room he walked. It was like Theo had said only this was Zane's own version of heaven. It was easy to guess that Zane was an artist but how Pip had known was a mystery to him. However, one look at the room and it was clear that she knew him better than anyone else in the world did.

The room was huge, with tall ceilings and a north facing wall made of glass, flooding the room with light, but as any artist would prefer, not direct sunlight. The room was split into sections and one looked more like an artist's studio than a teenager's bedroom.

There was a whole wall dedicated to art supplies and every tool of the trade. Old crates turned on their sides built up a quirky shelving unit that was filled with everything from glass jars filled with different colour powder paints to metal tins of Turpentine, vases filled with every size paint brushes like an artist's bouquets of flowers and of course, tubs and tubs of paint.

Then there was a whole other section of stuff hanging from hundreds of hooks on the wall that held larger brushes and tubes of paint held there by bull clips, which any artist would tell you is the easiest way to get all the paint from your tube as well as a nifty way to hang them up.

Zane's eyes nearly popped out of his head when he started reading names like Michael Harding, Schmincke and Daler Rowney Georgian, along with some of the oldest suppliers like Old Holland and Winsor and Newton.

There were shelves up to the ceiling filled with stuff, like Montana's spray can selection in every colour he could dream of and canvases in every size just begging to be painted. The shelves were so high that the only way to reach most of the stuff was via the industrial looking metal ladder hung on runners above.

In the corner of the room was a circular desk that filled the space like a wave of colour thanks to even more supplies, in the way of pencils, pastels, pens and charcoal sets, all spread out in their own wooden display cases. Paper in every size and grade lay piled high like white skyscrapers and above were wooden squares hanging down which were covered in empty pegs awaiting artwork. They almost looked like crude chandeliers without the lights and Zane smiled, knowing that he had once made something simpler in woodwork to dry his pieces without fear of damage.

He couldn't believe the level of thought that Pip must have had when picking all this stuff as it was the best of the best in art supplies. He couldn't even do the maths in his head when he tried to imagine how much this stuff must have cost them. He had only ever seen a room like this in his dreams of maybe winning the lottery or better yet, making it big with his art one day.

But it wasn't just the endless amount of art supplies or even the high-tech gear that sat on his new desk just begging to be played with. It wasn't the easels, the canvases, the hundreds of artist's pens, the watercolours, the oils, the acrylics and every type of brush known to man. No, none of this meant more to him than the bare wall that held one single piece of art.

The wall was like a giant blank canvas to display his work and at its centre it held two simple words spray painted on a jagged piece of driftwood and now it was one sign that summed up his new life...

'Art immortalised'

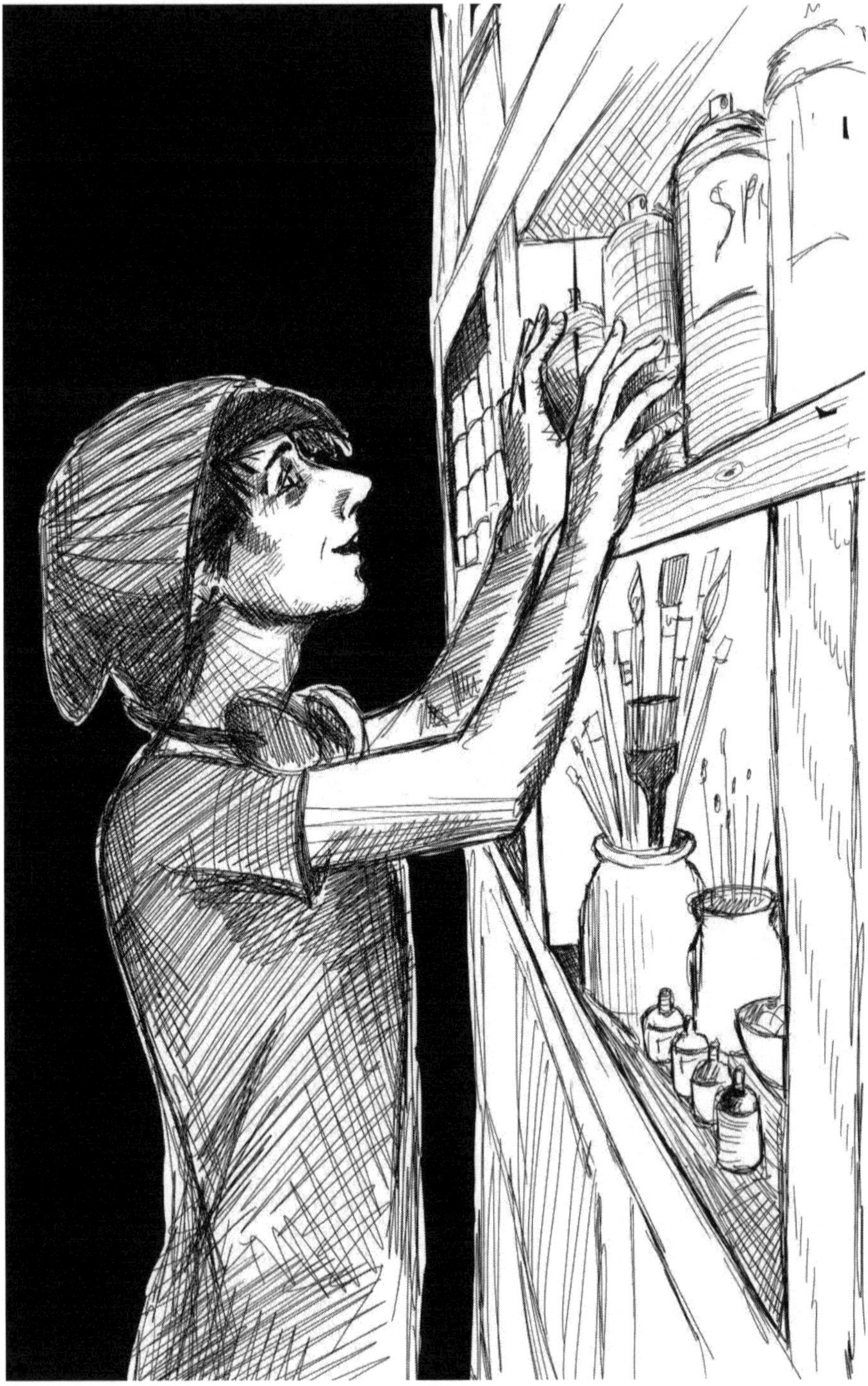

"Wow, I can see why you screamed," Janie said after Ena dragged her into her new room.

"Isn't it fabulous!" she said referring to what she thought was the most perfect space she could have ever imagined. It was girly but in a subtle way, without being childish. Full of soft pastel colours and delicate swirl designs on the scattering of rugs and matching cushions on cute quirky little chairs. One looked like a giant egg that hung from the ceiling and was lined with white fake fur. Another one was a Chesterfield wingback chair that was covered in a patchwork design, one made up of the cutest pieces of fabric so that it looked far too expensive to even sit on.

Then there was nearly every girl's dream as one whole corner of the room held nothing but make-up and every type of beauty product known to a woman. It was all arranged in a way where even the makeup filled jars, pots and display cases looked pretty, matching the décor of the rest of the room. A huge mirror framed in lights hung above the vanity that was any make-up artist's dream, with its sleek slide away compartments that each held every shade of lipstick, to a rainbow colour of eyeshadows. Next to this space was a beautiful canvas with more of her favourite flowers, waterlilies and the words written in white...

'Be your own kind of Beautiful.'

What Ena was yet to discover was the hidden switch under the vanity that revealed a doorway into her own walk-in wardrobe, complete and fully loaded with her favourite designer clothes, handbags, shoes and too many accessories to mention.

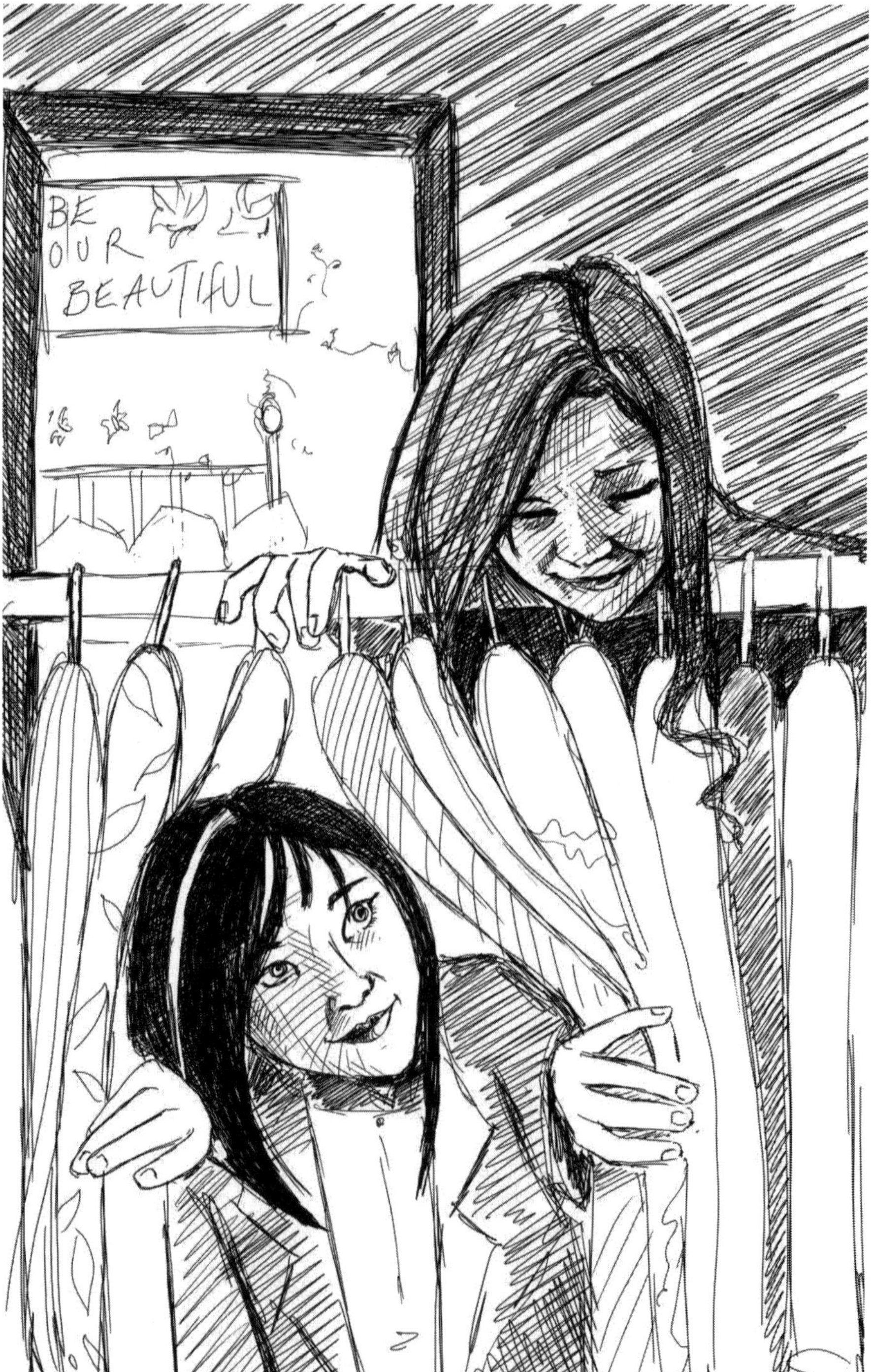
BE OUR BEAUTIFUL

It was true that Ena loved fashion but it wasn't just about following a trend for Ena as more about the opportunity it granted the individual to fully express themselves to the world. It was like waking up in the morning and not feeling whole until you put on your armour to face the world.

This was Ena's escape from what she knew could be a hard, cruel world, especially for an orphan who grew up knowing that she had been given away to face a life alone. So Ena had created another version of herself as a way of protecting her fragile soul. She would wear her new skin like stepping out onto the stage every day, playing the part of a hard ass. She didn't make friends. She didn't cry. She didn't grant smiles like throwaway gifts. She didn't hug or speak of her inner thoughts. She didn't do gushy feelings or swapping 'woe is me' life stories. And she *never* let anyone into her personal space allowing just a glimpse of the real her…until now…

Until Janie and the guys.

So, what it was about the others that made her feel different, she didn't yet know but for the first time she felt like she was shedding her fake skin. Like it was slowly being peeled away by them, leaving something beautiful underneath and to go with this new her, was her new perfect space…a space she finally wanted to share.

"It's so you," Janie said, for some reason knowing this like it was a fact, not the guess that it could only ever have been. Ena looked back at her with shock on her face and for a moment Janie thought she had upset her by what sounded like an assumption, one she knew deep down that it wasn't.

"It is and it's my dream," Ena admitted freely, smiling so big it almost felt like her face would crack from happiness. Janie smiled back at her and then did something so out of character she could barely believe what came over her, so lost in a moment that she had been dreaming about herself…having a friend.

Janie nodded to the huge bed behind her, which had an ornate carved headboard that was painted pearly white and decorated with cute fairy lights. Even the bedding matched the colour of the lights with its large pink waterlily at the bottom that evaporated, transforming into hundreds of tiny butterflies.

Ena looked back and smirked, knowing what she was silently thinking, so instead of saying a word, she just nodded, giving Janie the go ahead. Then they both did something they had never done but always wanted to do with a friend. They ran for the bed and both fell back on it like angels with their wings out feeling for the first time on top of the world and remembering this day forever as not the day they died, but the day they were both *reborn.*

"Come on, let's go check out your room," Ena suggested nudging Janie after they'd had their fun.

"You know that's the best thing I've heard all day," Janie said laughing. Ena laughed as well and replied,

"And here was me thinking it was the roar of King Kong just before he leapt to save you." Then she winked making Janie blush an unhealthy shade of crimson.

"Anyway, I wonder what his room is like?" she asked Janie as she scooted off the bed. Janie follow and muttered,

"Yeah, I wonder too."

Ivan shook his head, rubbing the back of his neck with what he knew was a massive hand. He couldn't help the way he looked and often wondered what it would feel like for just one day to look like one of the other guys. He hated what his size had offered him in his short lifetime and the violence he had been forced to inflict upon others. He shuddered just thinking about it and looked back over his shoulder at the others as they disappeared into their rooms. They must never know…no one must ever know the things he'd done.

He still didn't fully understand what he had become but he knew one thing for sure and that was this was his one chance at a new life and he wasn't doing anything to jeopardise that. He would be taking his inner demons with him into Hell if that was where he needed to go but never again would he let them loose upon the world.

No, he would need to learn how to control it and hide that part of himself away forever. He didn't care what the headmaster expected of him, he knew he would never be able to give him what they wanted. Because his demons had been inside him for a lot longer than when he first stepped on that Godforsaken bus, that was for damn sure.

Hell, he felt as though he had been fighting them since the day he was born and today was no different. No, if anything it just gave a demonic face to the beast inside of him, one he had been trying to keep caged for seventeen years. Growing up in the orphanage had almost been as bad as his time on the back streets of Moscow and he would have said he had the scars to show for it but Ivan never scarred. No matter how many times he got hit whether by something blunt, sharp or pointed, it didn't matter as he felt the pain but the scars only ever remained immortalised on his damaged soul not his outer shell.

But no, the others can never know. He said this again to himself over and over because for the first time in his life he felt as if he had a chance. A real chance at a family and people who cared about him. The way they had included him because they wanted to and not because of his size and what they could gain from having him at their backs. The way they explained things to him that he didn't understand thanks to the language barrier. In fact, if it hadn't been for his unfortunate connections with the Bratva, the Russian mob, and his keeper's love of American sports, then he probably wouldn't know a word of English. Thankfully it was where his passion for basketball was born and his only pleasure in life.

Speaking of which, he opened his door wondering what was waiting for him behind it, hoping it was better than the damp broken bunk he had been used to…

He wasn't disappointed.

In fact, he was so overwhelmed by it all that he only managed to take a few steps before he fell to his knees, thanking any God he thought had forsaken his dammed soul. It was his dream room and everywhere he looked there was some reference to the game he loved so much. There were basketball shaped chairs, there was a row of metal locker room wardrobes, there was even a mini version of a basketball court on the floor.

Everywhere he looked there was something he would have sold his soul for and now the ironic thing was that his soul had been taken against his will and granted him all his dreams without him even asking for them.

Something in one corner caught Ivan's eye and he scrambled to his feet, cursing his size for taking longer to move than he wanted. He ran over to the farthest wall and nearly wept for joy when he saw all the signed pictures of his all-time favourite players. There were the greats like Bill Russell who played for the Boston Celtics, Magic Johnson who played for the Lakers, along with Kareem Abdul-Jabbar, Shaquille O'Neal and Wilt Chamberlain who were other Lakers' legends, which also just so happened to be Ivan's favourite team.

But then in the centre was by far the world's best player even to this date, basketball God, Michael Jordan. He might have played for the Chicago Bulls but Ivan didn't care. He thought the man flawless in the game and looked up to him as an idol.

His assigned Bratva mentor had talked about basketball none stop and watched reruns of all the best games, so naturally Ivan had picked it up and fell in love with his only shred of normality. So, seeing all those autographs hanging on his wall was beyond a dream come true, it was unbelievable.

The rest of his room was spread out into different sections. There was a lounge area that had huge basketball beanbags that even he would look small in. In front of this was the biggest flat screen TV he had ever seen hung on the wall and under this was

the latest games' console, complete with games and DVDs all tucked away neatly in a custom-built entertainment system.

Next to this was a NBA arcade basketball game, where you won tickets for every shot you made through the hoop. He couldn't wait to start playing this but first he wanted to check out the rest of his room. He turned around and saw what looked like the coolest bed he had ever seen on the opposite side of the room. It was round and it too looked like a giant basketball, one that was big enough for him to sleep in with room to spare. He had never slept on a bed big enough for him before, so he was looking forward to trying it out later and seeing what a good night's sleep would finally feel like.

He sat on the edge of the bed before falling back, proving that the bed could take his weight and when he didn't hear it creak or groan under the strain, he smiled and thought one single happy thought...

Oh yes, he was home.

17
'Underwood'

Theo had left Zane to drool over his new room, whilst he went in search of his own. It didn't take him long to find it as each of the doors had their own names on them in a style that suited their individual personalities. Zane's had been written in graffiti, representing the artist in him, whilst Theo's name had been written in a heavy metal band style, representing his love for music.

Growing up he only had an old Walkman cassette player he found in a box of random junk when he was snooping in the attic once. He would never forget the bitterness he felt when he saw that the box had been labelled with a case number, not a name like the person had deserved. It had obviously been left there by an orphan and usually when a box ended up in the attic it meant that its original owner had come to the end of life's journey. It was sad to know that whoever it had belonged to had no one in the world to pass these meagre possessions on to. All Theo could hope for was that they had at least reached a better place in death than Earth had given them in life.

At first, he had left the box and kicked it back under the old rafters in anger, but then later that night his thoughts still plagued him. He couldn't stand the thought that the last piece of someone's life in this world was wasting away in some dark dusty place, soon to find its final resting place dumped on a landfill some day. At least if Theo had it he would treasure it and the poor life it once represented, even if it was filled with old 80's rock band cassettes and a few faded heavy metal t-shirts.

However what Theo didn't know that day was that it would then spark a passion for rock legends such as Jimmy Page, Eddie Van Halen, Jimi Hendrix, Slash and many more. He had always wanted to learn how to play guitar but who was going to buy him something like that when he had to rummage through old boxes in the attic just for something to do. Instead he would listen to the likes of ACDC, Iron Maiden, Queen, Led Zeppelin, Guns n Roses and Metallica. So of course, stepping through his door right now and he couldn't help his reaction,

"Holy... shit...no freakin way!" Then his mouth dropped open in awe. It was as if someone had plucked all the things he had ever wanted in life straight from his mind and arranged them all around this one huge room. Okay, so he may not be able to play guitar yet but he was certainly set for when he did because there, hung up on the far wall, was what was on every guitarist's wish list. There was a 58 Gibson flying V, a 60 Gibson Les Paul standard with a sunburst paint finish. There was also a 68 Fender Stratocaster in Olympic white and he knew it was just like the one Jimi Hendrix played. Also, hanging there was the amazing creation by Eddie Van Halen, the Frankenstrat, his personal favourite for what it represented, a monster of a guitar!

"Oooh, now you're a thing of beauty," Theo said referring to the stunning aqua paint job on a PRS custom 24 that reminded him of waves on a beach. He loved them all, even though he couldn't play them he knew it wouldn't be long until he was rocking out on these bad boys, as he would make it his mission. And with the wall of Amps next to them, then he would certainly be heard, thanks to the makes of Fender, Mesa boogie and the classic Marshall. This room looked like the place all guitarists would go when they died and made it to Heaven.

There was even a corner dedicated to acoustic guitars by the likes of Martin, Taylor, Washburn and Gibson, which were the crème of the acoustic crop. A shelving unit next to them also held all the other bits you would want when playing the instruments, like tuners, capos, packets of strings and plectrums galore with every design you could imagine.

Jack leads were looped on large hooks on the wall and hard back cases were used as part of the furniture but it was what

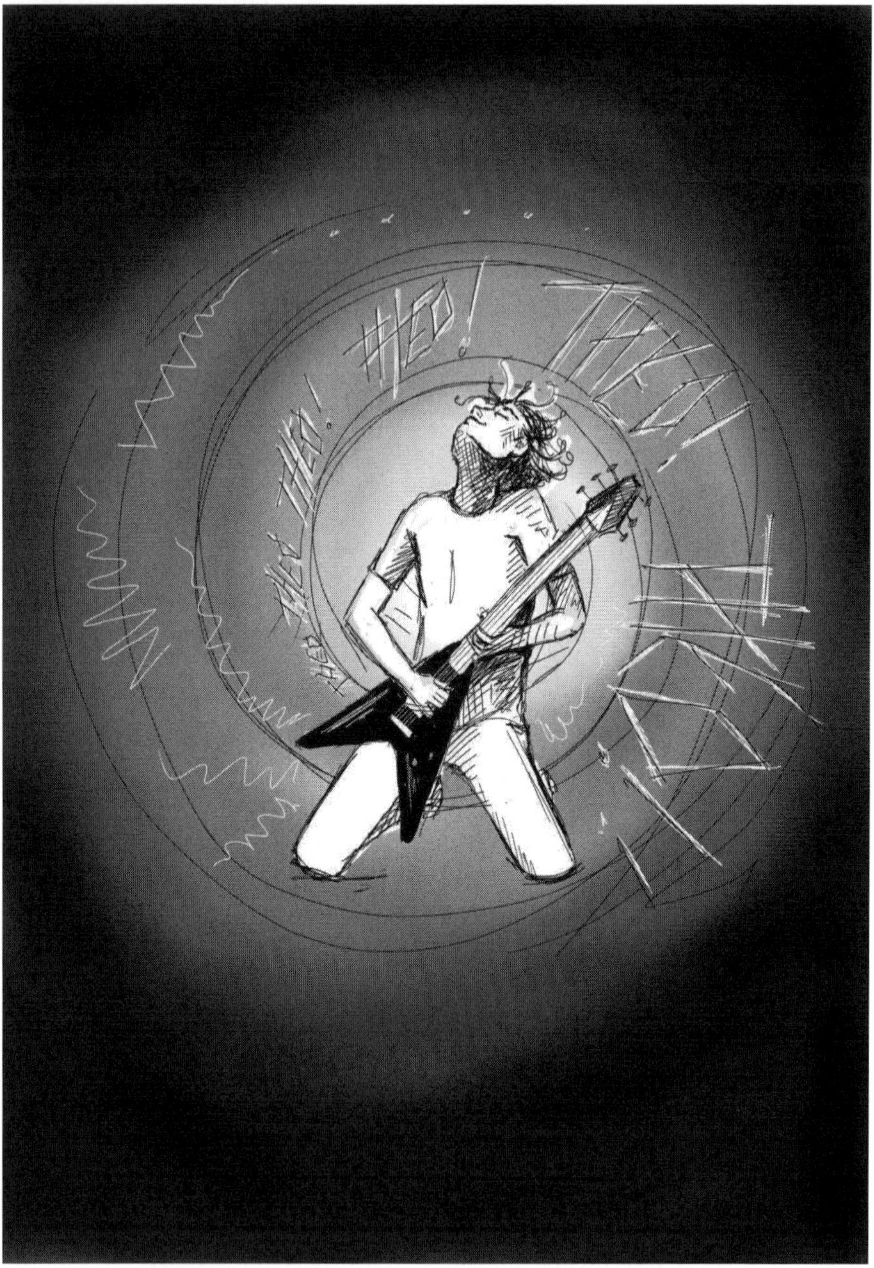
THEO!
THEO! THEO!
THEO

looked like every book ever written on how to play guitar filling most of the shelves that he was most interested in. Because he had to face facts, the guitars were cool but unless he knew how to play them then they were nothing but extremely expensive art work hanging on his wall.

Then he turned to face the opposite wall and was once again blown away by where he would be both sleeping and relaxing. His bed was raised up high as if someone knew that he preferred to be up on the highest point of the room. It was a massive wooden structure that was also a great means for a work out, something else that Theo enjoyed. There were thick metal bars for doing pull ups attached, along with knotted ropes for climbing and hanging rings from the ceiling so that you could jump up and pull yourself up to the bed's platform.

The was even a punching bag hanging down and a weights' bench all under the bed, like some mini gym. Theo couldn't help giving it a try by jumping up and reaching the hoop easily before hoisting his body up with one hand. Once up there he liked the look of the navy coloured bedding as it looked comfy and inviting.

There was also a quilted comforter folded at the bottom which was a vintage union jack flag design that was frayed where the different colours met. He put his hands behind his head and let himself fall back looking up at the high ceiling that was decorated with an ocean of license plates from all around the world.

Then he looked over the side and down at his room, releasing a sigh of utter bliss and trying to picture his life here from now on.

He could see himself in the small seating area for relaxing and was loving the giant denim hand chair that would be perfect for all those long hours gaming. He saw his new friends all in here, hanging out together and who knows, maybe some of them would be interested in learning how to play guitar as well. It would certainly be an awesome place to start up a band, he thought with a smirk thinking back to the gothic looking nightclub they had first walked into. But it was from this vantage point that he first noticed something weird.

He saw that his suitcase had been placed on a metal chest that looked like one of those you would fill with vinyl records. It would make sense that was what it contained considering it was next to a huge shelving unit filled with too many CDs to count and what looked like a kick ass stereo system, which included a mixing table.

His suitcase just reminded him of his old life and he just hoped that he didn't look as out of place in this room as that old case did. But it wasn't this that he found weird, it was that the case was open and some of the contents were spilling out onto the floor. It almost looked as if someone had rummaged through it, but for the life of him he couldn't think why they would have

bothered. It wasn't as if he had anything of value, just the few items of clothing he owned and some personal items like his Walkman and an old Gameboy, one with a green line across the screen thanks to hours of being beaten by Donkey Kong.

He shrugged his shoulders before rolling to one side and jumping down, landing on his feet like he always did. It was more than likely that the prehistoric luggage had finally given up and burst open thanks to its rusty latches. He didn't think much of it, that was until he started picking all the items up and saw something he never expected to see again.

"What the…" He didn't finish off that sentence as it no longer seemed to hold the same weight as it used to, not after the day he and his new friends had just had. But I guess there was always room for something a little 'stranger' he thought as he ran his fingers over the front cover and traced the words,

'THE GLASS DAGGER'

Meanwhile it was in Janie's room, after Ena had just left to go unpack, that those stranger things started happening to her not just Theo, connecting them in a way she wouldn't fully understand until it was too late.

Janie's reaction when seeing her room for the first time was just like the rest of them…she was overwhelmed. She didn't know about winning the supernatural lottery because if she was being honest with herself then she didn't really understand what had happened to them all. But she knew by that one glance at this room and she had definitely won life's lottery, whether she had died or not.

Her room was a lot different from Ena's but then again, so was she and her new room screamed out those differences. It was true that Janie liked to hide herself away wearing dark clothes, but this wasn't the only reason for her goth style. She didn't do it to be different or out of some teenage angst that was expected of her for being an orphan or for living each day with a broken body. No, she simply just liked the style, the music and instead of being scared of the darker side of life, she simply embraced it...

And until now she had always done so alone. Well not anymore, she thought with a smile and now looking around the room she knew that she would be doing so in her own style. Her room was beautiful in a gothic meets girly girl kind of way. A huge wrought iron bed dominated the room and at each corner large metal trees twisted up and entwined their vines at the top, joining together to make up the canopy.

Floaty soft grey material hung twisted from the top and brushed the bottom of the dark slate floor, with wide panels of lace skulls. This matched the bedding that had different shades of grey flowers which also made up a skull the size of the bed. In fact, skulls were definitely the main theme of the room but each seemed to have a feminine element to them that Janie loved. Like the huge black and white striped rug that had a funky hot pink skull raised in a shaggy style. Or the white chair that looked like paint was dripping at the back, making the outline of a skull's eyes and nose.

There was even an old tall glass case that had been hand painted with sugar skulls up the sides and the inside was packed with CDs from her favourite bands.

And then there was the wall of old typewriters that she started to freak out about. If there was one thing that Janie loved more than anything else in the world, it was writing. She would often lose herself to the beauty that could be found in the written word and fully immerse her mind for a short time in the worlds she would create. It was the ultimate step taken in escapism and for an orphan with no money, it was also the cheapest option.

So, for Janie seeing all those timeless classics in all shapes and sizes, sat there just waiting to have their own stories written on each, then she had certainly found her personal slice of heaven. She didn't know much about famous manufacturers or how old they were but she just knew that she had always wanted to write on one, like stepping back in time and hoping for a masterpiece to be born.

She walked over to them and couldn't help but push down on a few of the keys, trying to get a feel for them, smiling whilst doing so. She wanted to sit down with one, which prompted her to take a better look around the room, hoping to find what she was looking for. And there, right in front of the window, was where she found it. An old green leather topped desk that looked as old as the typewriter that sat upon it, facing the outside world for inspiration.

Oh yes, she couldn't wait to start something and walked over to the desk wondering how they had known about her secret passion for writing. It also made her wonder how long exactly these people had known about her as she knew that it had been at least more than a year since she'd last written anything, also begging the question, did they also know the reasons for that as well?

She shuddered just thinking about it and couldn't help the frown that quickly replaced the smile. The seeds of doubt were starting to take root and unfortunately, as she took her place at the desk and touched the keys, those seedlings began to sprout and reach the surface.

The old matt black typewriter sat before her and she read aloud the golden letters above the platen roll, where paper sat awaiting her visions to be born into ink.

"Underwood." This was clearly the name of the typewriter and when she reached out her one hand to touch the keys something changed.

"What the…?" She didn't know it, but these same words were at that same point in time being uttered by another. Theo had said the same thing when he saw the book in his hand, one that should never have been there. And now Janie was also saying these words referring to the impossible and like the book, something that shouldn't be happening. But no matter how much she wanted to give reason to it, she just couldn't. Because keys on a typewriter didn't move without being pressed and words didn't appear unless they were written by hand. But that's what Janie's eyes were seeing right now.

At first, she thought that she had triggered something and her logical brain tried putting it down to some kind of sensor, which in today's modern technology could be accountable, but back in the 1920's, then no, there was no logical reason for what was happening now. But seriously, after today, then what could she offer logical reasoning to ever again. Because nothing had made sense ever since she first stepped off that train and got onto that bus. And the way the keys had started to move on their own certainly didn't make sense.

The second it started happening Janie was out of her seat and standing back. It had been the clunk of one letter first hitting the paper that had made Janie second guess her sanity...had it been real? So, she leant in closer to check the paper when it suddenly started up again.

Janie jumped back in fright and soon it was letter after letter, word after word and sentence after sentence as the keys hit the paper at incredible speeds. The ding and chink sound fired off one after the other when each new line was done and the next had found its turn.

"Stop...stop it..." Janie muttered over and over, getting scared and shaking her head as if it would help rid her ears of the terrible sound. It was almost like rapid gunfire going off in the distance, like the haunting echo of a World War One battlefield reaching out and finding her room. But it didn't stop and in place of her fear she started to feel something uncoiling in the centre of her belly, as if it was something deep within her that was waking up...

And it was angry.

"SHUT UP!" she shouted as she felt it burst from within her, something black and cold. It lashed out and hit the walls around her, transforming the room into a moving mass of shadows. This darkness started to split into smoky serpents that each slithered down and started circling her. It was almost as though she was their mistress and they were simply waiting for the order to destroy.

Janie seemed lost to her darkness but she wasn't too far gone that she couldn't read the words written on the page like some mad mantra, which had been chosen for the new name of the typewriter. Gold letters that no longer held the name 'Underwood' but had now morphed into the chilling dagger pointed letters making up the word...

'UNDERWORLD'

But being lost to this darkness didn't make her weak, oh no, it made her feel powerful and most of all... *brave*. Brave enough to rip the page from the typewriter's clutches and hold it up to the window so she could read it. And without needing to speak the words, the serpents slithered away from the glass, providing enough light for her to do so.

Then she read out the single line that had been written enough times to almost fill the page.

"Lies are all you know, find the truth that's hiding below." And just like that, those seeds of doubt fully blossomed into black poisonous flowers named...

Afterlife.

Lies is all you know, find the truth thats hiding below.
UNDERWORLD

18
BLACK LIES

Back in Theo's bedroom...

Theo just couldn't understand it. He remembered holding that book in the airport, right before that creepy...

"It must have been her, she must have slipped it into my bag," Theo said talking to himself, then dropping the book back on top of the suitcase. He turned his back on it, shaking his head, quickly deciding that the guitars looked a lot more interesting than trying to figure out why that book was now in his possession.

But he couldn't get his mind off it. It was as though something was secretly calling out to him. Which brought him back to thinking about the old gypsy woman. It was true that she had seemed a little unhinged to say the least, but just because the old girl had been persistent about the book it didn't mean there was anything at the time to concern Theo with...well that was up until now, he thought wryly staring back at it over his shoulder.

"Did that just...*move?*" he asked himself when he thought he saw the book's cover vibrating. Unbeknown to him, but just like his friend in the other room, he looked to the window first searching for the most logical reason. But it wasn't open.

He looked back to the book to gauge if what he had seen had been real or not. In his mind it had moved as though something had been alive beneath the pages and was trying to get out. He frowned and stormed back to the suitcase unafraid of what he may find and after today, then really what did he ever need to fear again.

He thought on that a moment as his hand paused over the front cover. It didn't take long to know he was wrong about fear and he looked over to the door to where those fears now resided in their own rooms. Because now the major difference in his life was that for the first time he cared about people and he had a family to protect. So, with that in mind he opened the front cover and read that first paragraph again...

'Our story begins in the not so distant future, when legends are written in the sands of time, like footsteps left there to follow. When the heroes of this world are children who rise above the strength of men and bend the will of their blind elders. For this story is only the beginning, so before you continue, you must ask yourself...

He suddenly slammed the book shut, unable to read anymore, angry with himself for doing so in the first place. He must have imagined the book moving and after the day he'd had, who could blame him. But he still had to ask himself about that book. It just seemed like too much of a coincidence that in the first paragraph alone it spoke of children that would rise above the strength of men and that they would become the heroes of the story.

Theo looked down at his hands and saw that they were shaking and he couldn't explain why. Was it because they reminded him of all the pain they had unwillingly caused or was it because he wanted so badly for them to belong to a hero worthy of having his own story told?

"This is such BS!" he said once more just as he had back in the airport, only this time the book decided to speak back. It suddenly flipped open and all at once the pages started flickering back and to, over and over and over. It was as if the spine had been nailed down but the pages were still free to get blown around in the invisible storm overhead.

The room went dark as if some shadowed force was feeding from the words deep within. Theo looked to the wall of windows to see the sky was now filled with the evidence of an impending storm headed this way and the thunder was raging in the distance with brief flashes of lightening.

It was almost as if someone had flipped a switch on what had been a bright and sunny day but the second that book had opened, it felt as though nature was responding to its inner darkness…*And Theo was right*, because the next thing he knew,

That darkness spoke.

The book suddenly stopped flipping erratically through its pages, coming to rest open at the very centre of the book. Theo stepped closer to see what it obviously wanted him to see and the second he did the words started to disappear from the page. He couldn't believe what he was seeing and in a moment of logical thinking he picked up the book just to check it wasn't his eyesight that was starting to blur.

He raised it up and the moment he did the book started to bleed. It was as though the disappearing words had seeped into the pages beneath and because of this it caused black ink to overflow, dripping to the floor and all over Theo's hands.

"What is this!" he shouted down at the book, shaking it and expecting it to tell him... *and tell him it did.*

As soon as he made this demand, words started to reappear on the pages and on the one he held with his left hand scratchy looking letters soaked through forming the words...

'Lies are all you know,'

And the rest started to appear soon after in the centre of the page he held with his right hand...

'...find the truth that's hiding below.'

Theo slammed the book shut and threw it, tossing it across the room where it hit the window with a thud. The black ink splattered against the glass and smeared a black line down its length as the book slid down the window defying gravity. But the way it did this made Theo wonder if it was ink after all?

This made Theo look down at his hands and he rubbed his forefinger and thumb together, testing the black substance covering his hands. It was a thick, sticky substance but also strangely smelled a lot like blood, with its metallic tang that made Theo want nothing more than to run to the nearest bathroom and scrub his hands. Well whatever it was, it certainly wasn't black ink as he'd first thought.

He snarled back at the book, knowing that whatever it was, it was clearly something demonic. Although that in itself could mean anything these days and Theo could no longer automatically assume that it was something evil. Man, but it had certainly been a lot simpler being able to put a label on things in a time before he stepped foot on that bus.

"Demons equal bad, Angels equal good but oh no, not anymore, that would be *waaay* too simple…what's next, the tooth fairy that kicks your teeth out, then sells them on the black market?" Theo muttered, talking to himself again and trying to defuse some of the tense craziness of what had just happened.

"So, come on, what's the next cryptic message?" Theo said sounding unimpressed, cracking his neck to the side and getting ready to tear that book up into tiny sticky little pieces for even thinking it would work in casting doubt on this place. He was just about to reach his stained hands to retrieve it from the floor where it had finally slid down to rest, when he noticed something above him.

"What now?" he asked frowning hard and wondering if this had anything to do with that douche bag, death dealer Carrick.

"What is it…what do you want me to find!?" he shouted losing his patience.

The black substance still stuck to the window started to bubble and crackle as if the glass beneath it were scorching hot. It hissed and started to spread thinner, shrinking down from the intense heat and creating new words as it moved…

'me'

"You? But where? Where do I find you?" Theo couldn't help but ask, giving into his weakness, the one that compelled him to help others.

'imprisoned below'

"Below? Below what...below this place? And why, why do I need to find you?" Theo asked all at once, pounding his hand against the window in some desperate need to know. The second his fist made contact with the glass it started to shatter and the answer to his questions came from the furious action. The last two words were spelled out by the travelling cracks, branching out like lightning bolts and forming a person's final sentence...

'Death awaits'

The tiny fine fractures continued to travel, cracking further outwards around the words, like little forked tongues licking at the glass. Theo stumbled back a step to the sound of it shattering further and he looked back over his shoulder to see that what once held a picture of the stormy sky was now a giant milky white jigsaw puzzle. The sound was a haunting one, as usually there was little good that could ever come from that particular song of destruction.

Just then a knock sounded at his door and Theo shot a panicked look in that direction. He didn't want any of the others seeing this so he called out in a voice he had to force to sound calm,

"Just a minute, I will be right out!"

"Theo? Are you okay in there?" It was Ena and it didn't sound like she bought his calm and collected act. Theo was torn as to where to look next as he heard both the sound of the door handle turning and the sound of the glass that had finally hit its limit. The explosion happened so fast that Theo barely had time to react, although it felt like everything around him was happening in slow motion.

He just had time to shout towards the door,

"ENA NO!" Then he spun around, lowering to his knees as he went down in the crouched position and covered his head with his arms to protect himself.

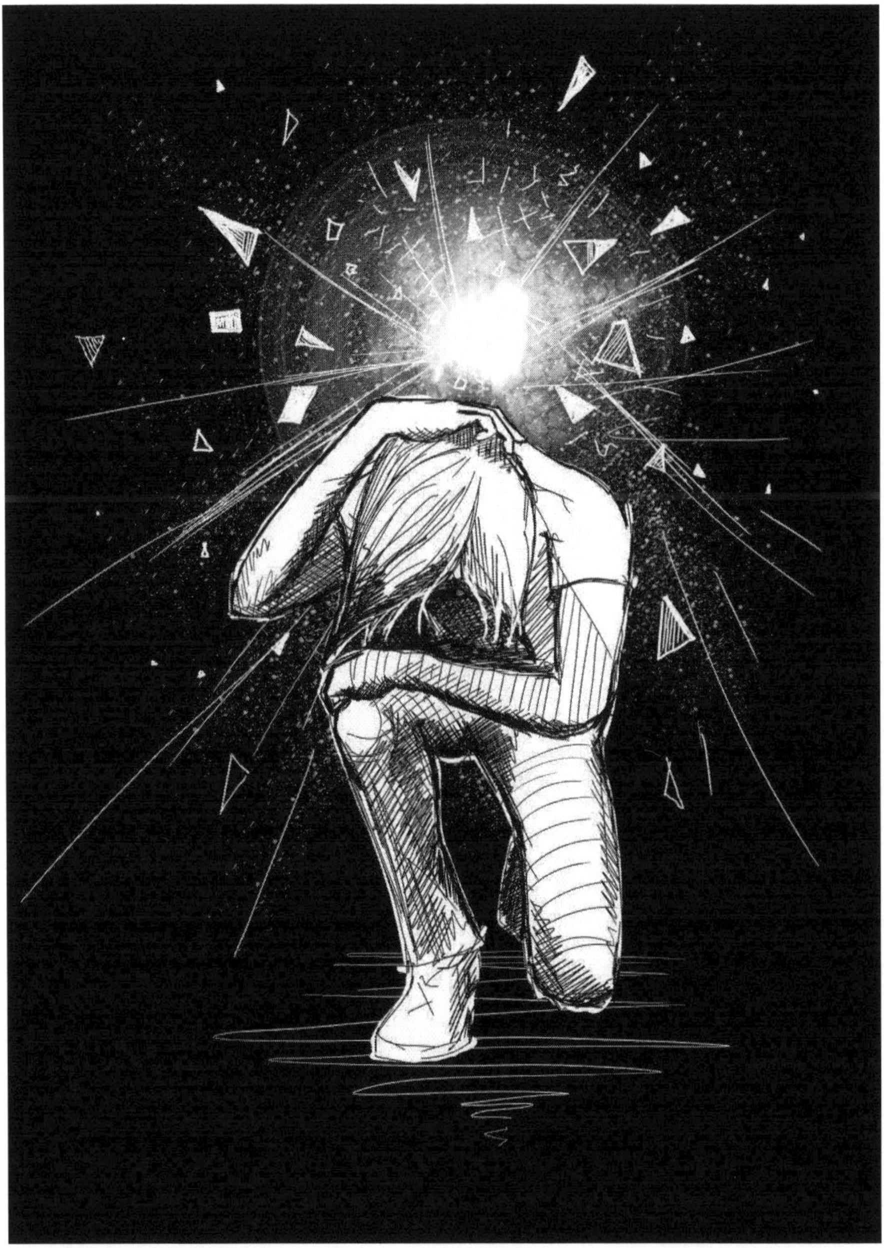

The window erupted in an explosive arc around him, falling with the grace of snow only with icy fragments with deadly intentions. Just as he should have started to feel the first wave slicing into his back or hear the first musical death notes of shards chiming against the floor, Ena opened the door.

"Uh...Theo? What are you doing?" The sound of Ena's obvious concern wasn't the panicked strain he had been expecting and thinking about it, shouldn't he have felt pain by now? He looked up slowly, finding himself still in the protective cocoon he had chosen as being the best course of action at the time, but it had been for nothing. He first looked to Ena who was stood before him with a hand on her hip and looking down at him with one eyebrow raised. He then snapped his head around to look back at the window to see the impossible...

Not one single crack.

'How is that possible'? he asked himself silently in his confused mind. The window wasn't only flawless but so was the clear sky that no longer had a cloud in sight. He looked to the floor to see that even the book had disappeared and Theo had to ask himself the embarrassing question...*had he imagined it all?*

What else could it be? There was not one single shred of evidence to suggest otherwise. There was no demonic ink, no cryptic words written by the very destruction of the glass, no storm or even any signs that there had even been one. So, what the Hell was going on around here or going on with him? Either question was one that needed an answer.

"Theo?" Ena said his name again, alerting him to the fact that he was still knelt on the floor looking around the room like a crazy person. He didn't quite know what to say other than thinking quick on his feet but first he had to get up on them. So, he stood and said the only thing that came to mind.

"I...uh...must have nodded off." Her face said it all.

"Are you trying to tell me you fell asleep like that?" she asked sceptically nodding to where he had been huddled on the floor like a scared kid. Theo inwardly winced and then looked to the bed.

"No, I was up there... I must have been sleep walking," he added quickly when Ena folded her arms.

"Do that often, do you?" Ena asked sounding not the slightest bit convinced.

"What are you doing here?" Theo ignored her question, asking his own instead, throwing the ball back in her court and slamming the door shut on his own.

"I just wanted to tell you that the pizzas are here and if you didn't get down there soon then there will be nothing left."

"Ivan?" he asked thinking this would be the reason but Ena corrected him.

"No, that would be Zane who is currently trying to eat his own body weight in pepperoni." Theo laughed and ran a shaky hand through his hair as he was secretly still trying to make sense of what just happened.

"Then I guess I'd better get down there and try and beat him."

"Oh great, that's all I need to see, two alphas competing over sliced sausage…must be my lucky day." Ena muttered as she walked out the room leaving Theo chuckling, but the second that door closed Theo's smile dropped. He looked around the room once again needing to see that damn book or anything else that proved he wasn't going as crazy as he thought he was. But it didn't take him long to see that the room looked exactly as it had when he first stepped foot in there and there was nothing other than his shaky hands to indicate otherwise.

He decided he needed to splash some cold water on his face or in this case maybe just dunk his entire head in a bath full of ice water…either way he needed to get a grip back on reality because he felt like his sanity was running on quick sand.

So, he went in search of a bathroom and guessed he found the right place when he saw an old painted sign above a door that said, 'Boys Locker Room'.

Inside he was yet again shocked at the level of thought that went into something as simple as a bathroom. One wall was all brick, painted with navy and white stripes and this matched the theme throughout. There was hand painted writing on another wall near a walk-in shower unit, that looked like a line from the dictionary, making Theo laugh when he read it…

'**Boy**, meaning: A noise with dirt on it'

Oh, he would be thanking Pip for that one he thought wryly as he walked over to the vanity unit. It was a long wooden sideboard that had been dry brushed with grey chalk paint and had a large navy glass bowl sat upon it as the sink. A basic copper pipe was bent over the centre with two valve taps either side of it for hot and cold.

Theo loved the modern fixtures mixed with the basic raw materials that were used throughout the room. Like the copper pipes being used to hold the plush looking navy and white towels. Or the sleek glass shower wall, with its crude hammered copper shower head that would be like taking a shower under a metal rain cloud. Even his tooth brush holder and soap dish were made from glass and copper.

In fact, Theo would have appreciated the room more if the whole reason for him being in there now wasn't to try and wash some of the madness he felt still lingered on his skin. He turned the valve wheel and filled up the sink after finding the small hidden button that worked the stopper for the plug hole. Then he placed his hands in the cool liquid and scooped up as much water as he could and just before he could splash it all over his face, he looked down. It was only for a split second but it was long enough to see what he had been hoping to see when back in the room...

Evidence.

It was back when Ena had just walked in the room and asked him what he was doing crouched on the floor. And back before he felt himself going mad looking for any evidence to prove that it had all happened. He didn't know whether to laugh or scream but either reaction wouldn't make a difference. Because right there, down in his hands was the diluting string of what looked like black smoke snaking away from one of his fingers and mixing with the water.

He looked up at himself in the mirror above the sink, saw all the colour drain from his face as he uttered the only two words that mattered right then,

The truth.

The… "Black Ink."

19
AND ALL BEFORE FIRST CLASS

That night Theo didn't think he would sleep and for a long while he just stared at the ceiling above his bed flicking the reading light that was fixed to his bed frame on and off. He had it aimed at all the licence plates, reading all the names of places he wondered if he'd ever get to see. He had always wanted to travel but now, well he wasn't sure what options for a future he had left. He had dreamed of the day he was old enough to get out of the system, shedding his 'Lost Boy' skin and making it out in the world, far from the streets of London.

It wasn't that he didn't like London, he just didn't like that it was all he had ever known. But now he was here, across the pond in a place he didn't know, with a future ahead of him he couldn't foresee and more importantly, *couldn't control.* And for someone who had mapped out his life once he had done his time and survived, making it to eighteen, he was finding not knowing wasn't as easy as he had hoped.

He had tried talking to Zane about it when they were playing the latest Gears of War game on the Xbox One together, but one sceptical look told him Zane was not only not on the same page as him but they were obviously reading a completely different book! Zane's would have been called, 'How to make the most of your lottery win'. However, Theo's would have been called, 'Ten signs to tell you if your lottery win was real or not'.

"Dude, look around you, does it look like the type of place I would wanna leave anytime soon? For all I care they could tell me I was never allowed to leave again and I would still wanna do cartwheels, sing hallelujah and sign any cult joining contract they shoved under my nose." And just like that Zane confirmed it.

"But what if it's not what we think it is?" Theo asked hating that small amount of doubt inside him that the damn book had forced in there. Zane raised an eyebrow and instead of answering his question, he asked another.

"Is there something you're not telling me, did something happen?" Theo didn't know that Zane could be so perceptive.

"What, you mean other than becoming blood bound to some uptight, arrogant asshole named Carrick, who grants out death wishes for fun?" Theo said shooting a particularly ugly locust, making its whole body explode thanks to picking up a Boomshot.

"Nice." Zane said complimenting him on his kill and walking around half of the reptilian torso.

"Yeah, but to be fair what did you all expect a grim reaper to be like, Mary Poppins?" Ena asked as she threw herself down onto a giant burger bean bag and then covered herself up with the cheese blanket that was attached.

"Streaks has gotta point," Zane said making Ena scowl.

"Do you have to call me that?!" Zane's only answer to her was to tip a fake hat her way and give her a wink. Theo looked side on at her knowing she was trying not to smile and instead faking a groan and eyeroll.

"I think if I had his job I would be just as uptight," Janie said quietly coming to join them along with her towering shadow Ivan. It had been the first thing Janie had said since coming down to eat pizza and Theo couldn't help wonder if something had happened to her too. He also couldn't help but notice the way she kept looking down at her missing hand as if she was half expecting something to start growing from beneath her empty sleeve at any moment. Theo wanted to ask her about it but really, what right did he have prying like that. And besides, it wasn't like he was preaching on about his own creepy literature experience.

"Frag out!" Zane shouted, warning Theo of the grenade he'd just thrown that had ricocheted back after hitting one of the buildings.

"Too late," Zane added after Theo was too slow and was now crawling on the ground needing medical assistance. He took one look at the guy and almost felt his pain, but hell at least that guy knew who his enemies were, Theo thought dryly.

So, with all these doubts playing on Theo's mind he was surprised to find the sound of an alarm waking him up from a deep, dreamless sleep. He rolled over groaning and looked down over the bed frame, trying to locate where in the room that annoying noise was coming from. He grabbed hold of one of the bars and let his body roll off the bed, swinging as he went before dropping to his bare feet.

He followed the sound and had to laugh when he found six sticks of dynamite and a timer flashing, telling him it was seven in the morning. He pressed the red button but this just started a countdown of ten seconds. He raised an eyebrow wondering what happened next but considering he didn't have to wait long, he just folded his arms and leant back on his cool desk. He was just looking down at the legs that were made from extended guitar necks when his ten seconds were up and there was no way for him to miss it.

The alarm that had been blaring before was nothing compared to the ear-piercing sound that was screaming out now. It sounded like a banshee was giving birth to a Tasmanian devil! Theo grabbed the fake explosives and started pressing buttons but nothing worked. He dropped it back on the desk and covered his ears as he couldn't take it any longer.

The next thing he knew his door was flung open and in skipped a happy looking Pip wearing a World War 2 military helmet, one that had an angry cartoon face with buck teeth painted on the front and pink glitter stars all around the sides. There was also a sticker on the back that said,

'I fought in Hell and Won,
Boo Yeah, She Dogs!'

In other circumstances Theo would have asked about it but considering his ears felt like they were close to melting off, he decided it could wait…Oh and not forgetting the steampunk goggles she had resting on the rim, although Theo wasn't sure that metallic pink was very steampunk, with or without the cogs and rusty nails she had glued to the sides.

Pip was also wearing a black T shirt with bold pink writing that said,

'Do I feel lucky,
Well, do you,
PUNK?'

She turned to face the alarm clock and picked it up but Theo wasn't looking at what she was doing because he was too busy reading the back of her T shirt. It had a picture of a fat Unicorn on it with writing underneath that read,

'Hell, yeah I feel lucky,
Cause I'm a four-leaf clover
Pooping Unicorn!"

Theo grinned and shook his head thinking she was certainly quirky. And with her ripped tie-dye rainbow leggings and big heavy biker boots that were covered in flames, spikes and skull toe caps, then maybe quirky wasn't a strong enough word for it.

"Dude, it's always the red wire," she said showing him by waving it in front of his face and saying with a chuckle,

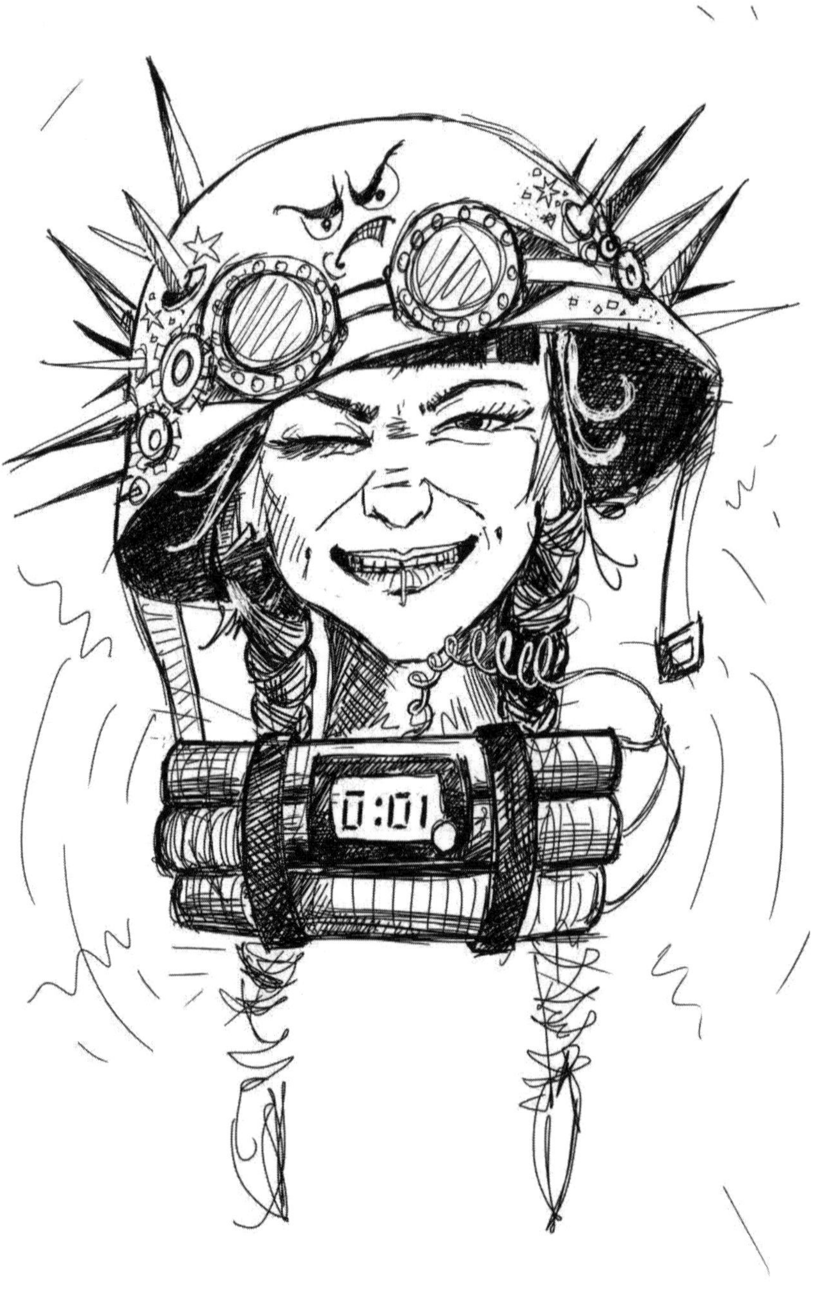
0:01

"You little pickle you." Then she straightened her helmet as it was slightly too big for her and breezed out of the room just as she had entered it. Theo exhaled a whoosh of air he didn't know he had been holding onto, in the way one would do when faced with someone who was as far from the 'normal' spectrum as you could get like Pip was. It wasn't just the way she dressed either, but more like someone who was clouded by a demonic aura only also happily trapped inside a glittery rainbow for all eternity.

She reminded Theo of someone who had a split personality and one was a goth and the other someone who Theo would have expected to see dressed up as My Little Pony at some cartoon convention.

"Hey doll face, you coming?" she said after popping her head back around the corner and fanning her fake pink eyelashes that also had silver stars glued to the ends, after granting him a girly wink.

"Yeah, just let me put on some pants though," Theo said looking down as he was still just wearing his boxer briefs and feeling more uncomfortable by the minute.

"Groove'itude on the plan! Now you go and hide those budgie smugglers and I will see you in two shakes of a monkey butt," she said winking again and then grabbing herself from behind the door to make it look as if someone else was pulling her out of sight. Meanwhile Theo was still stuck on the whole 'budgie smugglers' bit and couldn't help but do the guy thing and readjust himself out of habit.

"Righty O, my winkle tiddlers, are we all ready for our first lesson, now we are all fed and watered?" Pip asked clapping her hands just as they were all finishing breakfast. When Theo had walked out, this time wearing jeans and to his delight, a vintage looking Black Sabbath T shirt that he had discovered in his new walk-in wardrobe, he had found a breakfast feast waiting for him. Of course, the first thing Zane had said was,

"Cool Tee Theo…and for three points can anyone name the movie this rich genius was wearing this very same T shirt in…I will give you a clue, he totally digs wearing metal pants?" Theo laughed and pushed his shoulder as he sat down, saying,

"Come on Zee, I know its early but don't just give up trying…that's easy."

"Easy? I am still trying to work it out," Ena said pulling a piece off her Danish pastry and dipping it in the jam.

"It's Iron Man, in Avengers Assemble," Janie said shyly, after buttering a piece of toast by pressing the slice up against her cereal bowl and spreading it upwards so the bread couldn't go anywhere. You could tell this was second nature to her and it amazed Theo just how much skill she had using one hand in every day to day things.

"Ding, ding, ding! Three points for JayJay!" Zane shouted tapping his glass of orange juice for sound effects. Janie bit her lip and let her dark hair fall forward so it would hide her blush.

"I know not this game we play," Ivan said. Ena patted him on the hand after at least licking jam off one finger first and then said,

"Don't worry about it, I'm not that good at movie trivia either." This was the point that Pip had bounced back in the room and Theo had to wonder if she ever entered a space like a normal person.

"Oh, it's so exciting! Isn't this just so exciting!? Afterlife's first day of school…it's just too brain licking good!" Pip said and then lifted up the plastic heart hanging from the thick gold chain around her neck. One that was actually a green, pastel coloured brain that she then licked to emphasize her point.

Ena shot the rest of them a look and saw the same confusion being reflected back from the others and one that made Pip bend double, letting out a full belly laugh.

"Oh, you should see your faces! I don't mean we are gonna lick your brain, jeez we're only demons, not zombies! Now let's go and learn about some flesh-eating Gorgon Leeches!" she said snapping her teeth twice making her black skeleton hand, lip piercing more prominent. One that Ena noticed matched the black bones that covered the tops of her fingers from the skeleton bracelet she wore. It flexed when she moved her hand thanks to the five rings attached that kept it in place, doing so when she gave them all the peace sign.

"Ebay, sweet chickydees," she said after catching Ena and Janie staring at it, then flashing her pink eyelashes again as she winked.

"Right those tail feathers aren't going to shake themselves…well unless there's an earthquake, but no worries 'cause we don't get many around here, unless my husband broke loose that is," Pip said, talking mainly to herself as everyone stood up.

"Uh…just to elaborate here but your husband was the dude wearing glasses and rockin' tweed right?" Zane said looking slightly worried.

"That's my Hubba Bubba," she said boastfully and then thrust her fist out that had ADAM, her husband's name tattooed proudly across her knuckles, surrounded by hearts and flowers. Then she placed a big smacker on his name, kissing it twice for all to see. Janie and Ena both looked at each other and mouthed the sound 'Aww' at the same time.

"Isn't Hubba Bubba a bubblegum?" Theo asked Zane ignoring the mushy stuff unlike the girls.

"I don't know but why am I the only one concerned with the part when she said a word like 'earthquake' and combined it with even more words like 'husband' and 'broke loose'?" Zane asked the others, making Pip giggle before she said,

"Oh, my little Padawans, you have so much to learn and speaking of that itch, let's go and have a scratch, shall we." At least this time Theo knew what she meant but with the usual confused look from their favourite Russian, she looked seriously to Zane, pointed to Ivan and said sternly,

"You need to get this one Star Wars and stat." Then she turned abruptly and stopped before she walked out the door and added an afterthought,

"Oh, right…let's change that 'stat' into a 'statute pending', we gotta get you crumpets to your first class and guess what…"

She paused for dramatic affect and motioned for the rest of them to come in close before she whispered...

"It's Demonic History."

20
SUPERNATURAL 101

Pip led them all to the modern looking classroom that they guessed they would be seeing a of lot of in the future. Each of the techno pods (as Pip had called them) had been assigned to them, but when they all just stood around waiting to be told which was theirs, Pip just said,

"Well go on then pickles, pick your buns."

They seemed to automatically pick their favourite colours, all except Theo, who stood back and waited. Ivan went for the orange one that was the same colour as his beloved basketballs. Ena went for the blue that was the exact colour of her streaks and Janie the hot pink one that matched the raised skull on the rug back in her room. Zane's was a deep blood red colour as it was always a paint he chose for his art work, being something that morbidly always drew the eye in.

That only left Theo and as he had never really thought about his favourite colour, he naturally just chose the remaining one, the rich purple one positioned at the front. Their individual work stations had everything they needed for the academic side of whatever it was they were here to learn, but first Theo needed some clarity. So, after they had all settled in their pods, Pip asked,

"Is there anything else I can…?"

"Yes, you could finally tell us what we have changed into and what we are doing here," Theo asked abruptly, cutting Pip off.

"Dude, blunt much," Zane said popping his head around the adjoining pod.

"It's about time we got answers Zee and I don't know about you but I have hit my limit on waiting for them," Theo replied knowing that deep down this had all been fuelled by that damn book.

"I uh...well...I..." Pip started to try and find the answer to the question, when a musical voice finished it for her.

"I think I will take it from here, thank you Squeak." An elegant woman said after entering the room as one could only image an Angel doing. There was simply no other way to describe her graceful beauty. She had a timeless look with her soft, pale porcelain skin, big dark eyes and long ebony curls swept back off her face, cascading down her back.

Ena couldn't help but admire her classic style, with her navy and white thick striped pencil skirt, white wrap around shirt and tailored navy blazer, complete with matching heels and a string of pearls. She looked just like a film star walking on set ready for her close-up with Cary Grant and Grace Kelly.

"Ice cool beans, sister boss man," Pip said giving her a high five and surprisingly it didn't look out of place when she returned it, as it looked as if it was something that had been done a few hundred times before. Although this was Pip they were talking about, as she probably high fived the janitor and made it look cool.

"Laters, you Supernatural legends you," she said firing imaginary guns at each of them in turn before she twirled out of the room like a five year old girl dressed as a princess would do.

"For those of you who may not remember, I am Sophia Draven, your Demonology teacher," she said in a sweet voice and Zane coughed once to clear his voice and muttered,

"As if we could forget, eh Theo?" Theo laughed once but didn't agree as it felt strange thinking of her that way, no matter how hot she was. No, Theo was more into the quiet, shy type of girl and as soon as he thought this he couldn't help but snatch a glance towards Janie, who was hiding herself away under a large hooded sweater.

Sophia hid a smirk behind two fingers as she walked to the front of the classroom tapping her red lips in thought.

"We remember you, you're the King's sister," Theo said speaking up and making it known that he knew who the headmaster really was, thanks to Pip. She raised an eyebrow at him and said,

"Among other things, yes I am." Theo frowned wondering what that was supposed to mean. Thankfully he didn't have long to wait, as the answer came from a high-pitched voice at the other end of the room.

"Oh yeah, I'll say. This awesome chickadee is also married to the pale albino, kickass assassin Zagan, whose hotness also controls a shed load of legions in Hell…what? Okay, okay, my bad, I'm going, I'm going!" Pip said after she received folded arms, a raised eyebrow and a tapping foot from Sophia. She had obviously been listening by the door and couldn't help but add something to Sophia's introduction, letting the others know that there was more than meets the eye with this one.

Theo couldn't help but wonder what else they were going to discover about their new teacher by the time their first lesson was over. Well, as long as she started by giving them answers then he didn't care who she was married to. Although he had to admit, he would now be even more careful not to piss her off as it couldn't be denied, her husband was one scary looking dude.

"That crazy little Imp," Sophia muttered smiling after Pip had thrown her hands in the air in defeat and had walked out the door pouting like a child refused ice cream.

"Excuse me Miss, but what's an Imp?" Janie asked raising her hand.

"Ah, excellent question, Janie, as I am sure you are all curious to know what *you are* but also what *we are* as well…oh and you can just go ahead and call me Sophia sweetheart, the 'Miss' gig makes me feel old," she said winking and putting them all at ease with her friendly nature. It had to be said, she was certainly less intimidating than her brother.

"Okay, so if you would all like to look at your screens we shall see what history has to say about explaining Imps," she instructed before turning her back on them and walking behind the desk to start tapping away on her own touch screen computer. Seconds later each of their screens illuminated into life and showed a series of old pictures of artist impressions of what they must have believed an Imp looked like.

"So here we have everything from an old lady depicted as someone feeding little creatures from a chest to one hiding in a tree that looks like a little winged furless rodent from Germanic folklore. And even this one from Japanese folklore, which I wouldn't let Pip see as it looks more like a dog sized toad with dodgy eighties hair." They all burst out laughing, not expecting her to have a sense of humour. She tapped a few times more on her screen and a paragraph popped up with a mythological explanation of exactly what history had dictated an Imp's origins were.

'Originating from Germanic folklore, the Imp was a small lesser goblin. Imps were often mischievous rather than evil or harmful, and in some regions, they were portrayed as attendants of the gods. Imps are often shown as small and not very attractive creatures.'

"That right is not, small my friend be but pretty she is," Ivan said standing up, surprising them all. Ena couldn't help but pop her head around to see Ivan's screen filled with Russian words telling him what the others had also read and he, like them, was not happy.

"That's not very kind," Janie said and Sophia agreed,

"That's right, it isn't very kind to our lovely Pipper, but it acts as a good first lesson for you to learn," she said coming to stand in front of her desk before leaning back against it, casually crossing her legs in front by the ankle and folding her arms.

"In this new life you face, you will soon learn that a human's history about our kind is far from the truth. You must first unlearn everything you think you know about Heaven and Hell, and in doing so embrace your new life by accepting our own history in its place." She took a minute and nodded her head before adding,

"Now this doesn't mean we are asking you to turn your back on humanity, quite the opposite actually, as you will need to wear it often to veil your true selves…that of course will be where Pip's husband, Adam will come in handy," she said pausing, knowing that there would be questions.

"And why exactly do we need Human Studies, 'cause last I checked, we have all been there, done that and you guys were the ones to take the T shirts off us, so no offense but what qualifies you guys to teach us about the human world when you have never been human?" Theo asked the question that he knew everyone else was too afraid to ask. However, there was nothing but a look of respect in Sophia's eyes as she gazed upon the brazen teen, a hidden smirk emerging before she answered.

"It's true, I have never lived a single day as any of you have in the human world, but I have lived among humans long enough to know the importance of fitting in, something great power gained and increased age can erode from memory through time. Losing touch with humanity is a dangerous thing when you still have to walk hidden among them." Theo understood what she was saying but still needed to know more.

"So, we will be allowed to go outside and interact with the rest of the world?"

"But of course. In fact, you will be encouraged to do so. My dear Theo, Afterlife is your new home, not a prison. How do we expect to teach you about the world if we are to keep it from you? And besides, Pip would never forgive me if she didn't get to show you Evergreen Falls' shopping mall and movie theatre," Sophia said looking to each of them and feeling bad on seeing surprise flickering in their eyes. What had they been led to think coming here. By putting herself in their shoes she realised that they had certainly failed with their first attempt at meeting them down in the club. But no one could have foreseen that outcome…well other than maybe the Oracle, but having her around right now would have been way too simple, Sophia thought bitterly.

"You never know, one day you may even wish to attend the college here and experience a human right of passage, as most teenagers do. I am sure Pip will be more than happy to help you learn the rules of beer pongs," she said, hoping to further alleviate their worries.

"Sign me up!" Zane said laughing with the rest, but it was Theo who almost sighed in relief. He didn't know much about the others and how they felt about their uncertain futures, other than Zane's wisecracks about signing cult contracts this morning. But for Theo, well he had felt lost not knowing if he was still in control of his own destiny and able to make his own choices freely.

"But before we get too ahead of ourselves, let me explain more about what you are now in our world, instead of what you may want to become in theirs," Sophia said, knowing this wasn't going to be easy for either her or them.

"I like we know," Ivan said and for once, as Theo often did, he was speaking for the rest of them.

"Of course, you do. And I understand how very strange all this may be for you, but please remember we only have your best interests at heart and we are so pleased to be able to welcome you into our family." They all listened to Sophia's kind words but none of them could help feeling as though she was also trying to prepare them for what would be hard to hear facts of what they had now become.

"So, what are we exactly?" Of course, this question came from Theo, who quite frankly had had enough of beating around the bush.

"The truth...?" Sophia said making Theo frown at her as his only answer to that stupid question.

"We don't really know yet." And with that bombshell dropped the others decided they too had hit their limit.

"What do you mean you don't know?" Ena asked with her voice slightly raised, showing her panic was barely being controlled.

"I was trapped, unable to move, suspended in the air!" Ena continued and Janie also jumped in and said,

"And what about those things that came out of me? That black smoke...how could you not know?"

"I be bull like charging creature...I no like this thing I did," Ivan said standing again and this time raising his hand. Sophia held up her hand and closed her eyes for a moment, trying to get peace back into the room.

"I understand your concerns, I really do, but what I mean is we are yet to find out which…well…which…" Sophia paused, finding it difficult to word the sentence right when Theo decided to wound it up for her in a dark, scary nutshell,

"Which side we are from, Heaven or Hell…right?" he said making Sophia inwardly wince before voicing the only answer she could give…

"Yeah… pretty much."

21
Which Side Are You On?

"Yeah... pretty much," she said after shrugging her shoulders and agreeing with Theo's statement about which side they were on. Of course, this quickly caused another outburst from the group.

"What?!" Ena said at the same time Zane said,

"You gotta be kidding me."

"So, is that what happened down there in the club, was it like Hell trying to drag us down there or something?" Janie asked looking around frantically, focusing on the windows and the walls as though she was expecting something to happen at any second.

"Okay, okay, guys, let me explain. First, nothing is going to drag you up, down, sideways or anywhere else you don't wish to go. And secondly, what happened down in the club was just your other selves reacting to this place...as if it was finding home for the first time and feeding from its power," Sophia said trying to calm down the group.

"Like turning on a light bulb?" Zane asked but Theo shot him an 'Are you for real' look.

"Yeah, just like that actually," Sophia agreed smiling.

"Explain the bit about our 'other selves'. You mean if we are a demon or an angel...right?" Theo asked, pressing for more.

"Alright, so let me try and explain this the best way I can. A lot of humans believe that when you die, your soul goes to Heaven or Hell and your body remains as it's something you no longer need...like shedding an outer shell that kept your soul safe until it was time to pass on." Theo thought about this and couldn't help but think about that box in the attic and that depressing case number written on the side. Is that what had happened to him? His body was no longer needed and his soul finally found peace?

"Well, our bodies are just that. They are the outer shell that houses what we truly are. The face we display to the world that we hide our true natures from."

"But why hide? Would it be so bad if humans knew the truth?" Janie asked once Sophia had finished, but it was Theo who answered that one, remembering what Draven had told him on the rooftop and repeating the same words,

"Your world is something you hide for a reason, as you cannot protect a world in chaos, only prevent it from happening and that is where lies its greatest protection." Sophia laughed once and said,

"You sound like my brother." Theo looked down to hide his awkward reaction and ignored the obvious stares from the others.

"The world today has changed from the days when Gods were powerful from worship and named the makers of this world without question. And science was decades away from giving people alternative answers. Those days of strong belief are simply not strong enough now to overcome the fear of something that people find hard, if not impossible, to understand. So, we keep the peace by restoring and maintaining the balance between our kind, so humans remain unaffected as well as protected, to live as the Gods intended...with free will granted."

"So, you're like the Supernatural police?" Ena asked tucking her blue streaks behind her ear, only to have the short strands fall forward again.

"Sort of, yes," Sophia replied with a smirk.

"And your bodies, you mentioned them being like 'outer shells'?" Janie asked this time and Theo looked to Zane, wondering for once why he was so quiet.

"Yes, we call them vessels or hosts."

"That sounds a bit cold," Ena said hugging herself as if, unbeknown to her, she was trying to hold onto hers.

"Not at all, I can assure you I am quite fond of mine, as we have spent many lifetimes together," Sophia corrected.

"Uh...you don't look that old, not at all," Zane said after clearing his throat, something he seemed to have to do a lot when around the beautiful Sophia. She gave him a warm smile and said,

"Thank you sweetheart, but I am a lot older than I look." Theo remembered Rue saying the same thing to him before he got on that bus...of course now he felt like an idiot.

"You no age your body time?" Ivan asked in his own unique way.

"My host does age, but at an incredibly slow rate. Our essence regenerates our body's cells constantly although we still have to take care of it," she said answering the questions freely.

"How so?" Ena asked.

"Well as one would a plant, we still must feed it, give it water, although not as much or as often as a human would have to, but we still need to rest it and give it time if it needs to heal from very large and deadly wounds."

"So, uh can you…like…die?" Zane asked suddenly having the strange urge to cut himself and to see if it healed like Wolverine.

"Our bodies can be damaged beyond repair if we are not prepared to protect it, or do not have the power to do so…for example if we are fighting someone with far greater power. Well, then they could do enough damage to our host but death…" She thought a moment, trying to find once again the best way of describing it.

"…Well our demon, angel sides would only be banished back to where we came from in the hope of someday being granted a new vessel…but depending on our rank, the punishment, our power, things like that, then that would depend upon many factors as to what could happen to us. Death can come at the hands of Gods above or below, if it is deemed so, once back in their domain," Sophia said, knowing she was going to need a large glass of Absinthe after this first class, as she had hoped to ease them into it, but all hopes of that were quickly sinking down the supernatural wormhole.

"And on Earth, do the Gods punish?" And there it was, another doozy of a question for her to answer, surprisingly by the shy but inquisitive Janie.

"This may come as a surprise but the Gods have no power on this plane."

"What!?" This outburst all came at her as a collective from the teens.

"Earth is human territory, first and foremost, which means it is untouchable by any greater power from above or below. The Gods gave humans free will to choose their own path and whether it be right or wrong, it is not for us to decide or more importantly *to intervene.*" Sophia could see that they all found this shocking, which wasn't surprising given that it was the complete opposite to what had been taught about most religions.

"So, you can't punish a human?" Theo asked frowning when thinking about all the wrong doings by human hands that were getting away with great evil.

"Punishment for humans is left to humans, always has and always will be. Whether it be in the form of revenge or a justice system."

"But think of the good you could do?" Theo argued again and Sophia granted him a soft look before saying,

"Think about it Theo, it would be like a heavyweight champion punishing a child for hitting another child and where do you draw the line. After all, innocents go to jail everyday just as the guilty go free. It is an unfair world you live in but for most, it is a *free world*. We keep our own kind in line and are left only to hope that the humans do the same with theirs."

"So, what's the point of even believing in Gods, if they have no power to help people?" Theo asked again, getting frustrated.

"Oh, but there is great power in faith and hope. Believing in something bigger and better than yourselves can help to make humanity better. That is the power that Gods have on earth. Believing can join a nation in times of devastation. I have seen men do great things in my time on this Earth," she said looking to each of them and seeing a flicker book of too many histories to count flash by in her mind.

"I have seen them rebuild cities after the destruction by both men and nature and that was all driven by their belief that the Gods would help them through the devastation. That they had enough faith that when the time came, a better place awaited them if they did right by the Gods they believed in. So, as you see, religions can better a person enough to guide them to do right in this world and not to walk down the path of evil," Sophia said, hoping this was all she would need to say on the matter but of course, there was one boy that wouldn't let it go.

"But it can also be the cause of war and death," Theo said, throwing another argument back at her.

"Very true. As we all know religion can be used as the excuse needed to manipulate men into following blindly a cause which was never their own. All a King had to say was how God had spoken to him and told him to destroy the heathens in the south. And before you know it, thousands are dead and all for land, wealth and power gained for a single man wearing a crown who wanted more. Something the common man would have died for without ever seeing a single thread of good come of it." Sophia knew the second she finished what Theo would say.

"And this is something your kind could have stopped," Theo argued, thinking of the injustice of it all and what was worse, knowing that they had the power to stop it but didn't.

"War will never stop when greed drives those in control of nations. History will repeat itself, whether it be classed as more civilised or not. But if we were to involve ourselves in human disputes, then there would be more carnage. I can guarantee you of that." She knew by one look at the frustrated teen that she needed to prove her point further.

"Tell me Theo, how do you chose a side?"

"What do you mean?" he asked frowning and all the rest were left to do nothing but watch this dispute in silence.

"Alright, take the Second World War for example. If we had intervened, then whose side should we have taken?"

"Well ours of course, the Germans were trying to invade," Theo said sounding sure of himself but Zane smirked, knowing what was coming next.

"And those Germans, you think they all deserved to die by our hands, because they were following orders from a tyrant dictator who would have killed off his own people if they'd rebelled? You think we should have wiped a whole nation off the map because of a single man's rise to power?" she asked folding her arms across her chest and making her point enough that Theo had to admit defeat himself.

"As I said, it is not that easy a question to answer when faced with all the facts. Each person who died in that war, whether on one side of the battlefield or the other, was a father, a husband, a brother or a son. They were loved by someone in the world and they died for another man's cause. We accept this as the way of the human world, but just because we accept it, it doesn't mean we want a part in it. Another lesson learned I think," Sophia added looking to the others and then resting her eyes on Theo, who was now thinking about what she had said and most of all, admitting defeat himself.

"Okay, so I get it. Biggy rule number one, no interfering with human life," Theo said making Sophia laugh.

"I would ask if there are any more questions, but I am starting to fear the many more disputes I will have on my hands…and you are far too good at debates," she said nodding to Theo, making him blush.

"I am sorry, Miss. Injustice is a bit of a sore spot with me," he admitted honestly.

"And that is not a bad thing Theo, for it will serve you well. We certainly have our fair share of injustice to act upon in our world. Have no fear of that, as once trained, we will keep you busy." Now this definitely piqued all their interest, as it was a hint of what their future there held.

"Are we going to become like…supernatural soldiers?" Ena asked and Zane piped up and said,

"I would prefer the Superhero status …if we are choosing a name that is."

"I think that will be better explained by Rue, as she will be the one helping you discover what you are and what powers you have buried deep within your hosts," Sophia said thinking she had at least dodged another difficult question for the day, when another one soon took its place making her want to sigh.

"So, this host of ours, what exactly are you expecting to find lies beneath it?" Ena asked tentatively.

Okay, so this was where things got tricky for Sophia as every one of her kind was different. Even the combined races didn't always look alike, let alone throwing Angels and Demons into the mix. Hell, but she had seen enough scary looking angels in her many lifetimes to know a spoon wasn't always a spoon and can in fact be a killing blade just hiding behind the innocent looking spoon...if that made any sense?

Being of royal blood granted from both Heaven and Hell meant their family often had to face difficult decisions. It also meant trying to control the world's supernatural races not only to get along without killing each other but also to do so hidden from inquisitive and suspicious human minds.

But that all seemed like a piece of cake compared to being faced with five innocent teenagers all looking up to her to tell them the impossible was real and life was about to get a whole lot scarier...in the form of one day looking in the mirror and seeing your other self where once your human face used to be. Because in her world, monsters didn't live under your bed or in the dark looming corners of your mind dreaming up such things. No, they were your neighbour, your colleague or even your friend. And even though Sophia knew she was beautiful on the outside, on the inside she was what any one of these teens would have called...

Terrifying.

So, she did the unthinkable, not knowing any other way of explaining it to them other than showing them...

Her true demon form.

22

Demon Disco Dancing

"Alright, let me try and explain this the best way I know how," Sophia said knowing this was a risky move but at the same time she needed to test them.

"And that is?" Theo asked and Sophia cocked her head slightly to the side and replied,

"I'm going to show you." And just like that, with only a single sentence as their warning she changed...

Into a monster.

The girls both let out high pitched screams and the boys scrambled out of their seats with open horror etched on their faces.

"Janie, no look!" Ivan said turning her around to face the wall and Theo shouted out,

"Whoa! Holy..."

"Shit!" Zane said finishing off Theo's sentence, whilst Theo pushed the others behind him in case *it* decided to attack. Because no matter how much warning they might have had, nothing could have prepared them for the sight that faced them now. The Sophia who had spent their first lesson talking to them with ease and kindness now looked as though she could rip their faces off and smile doing it. And with that disgusting grin facing them, they

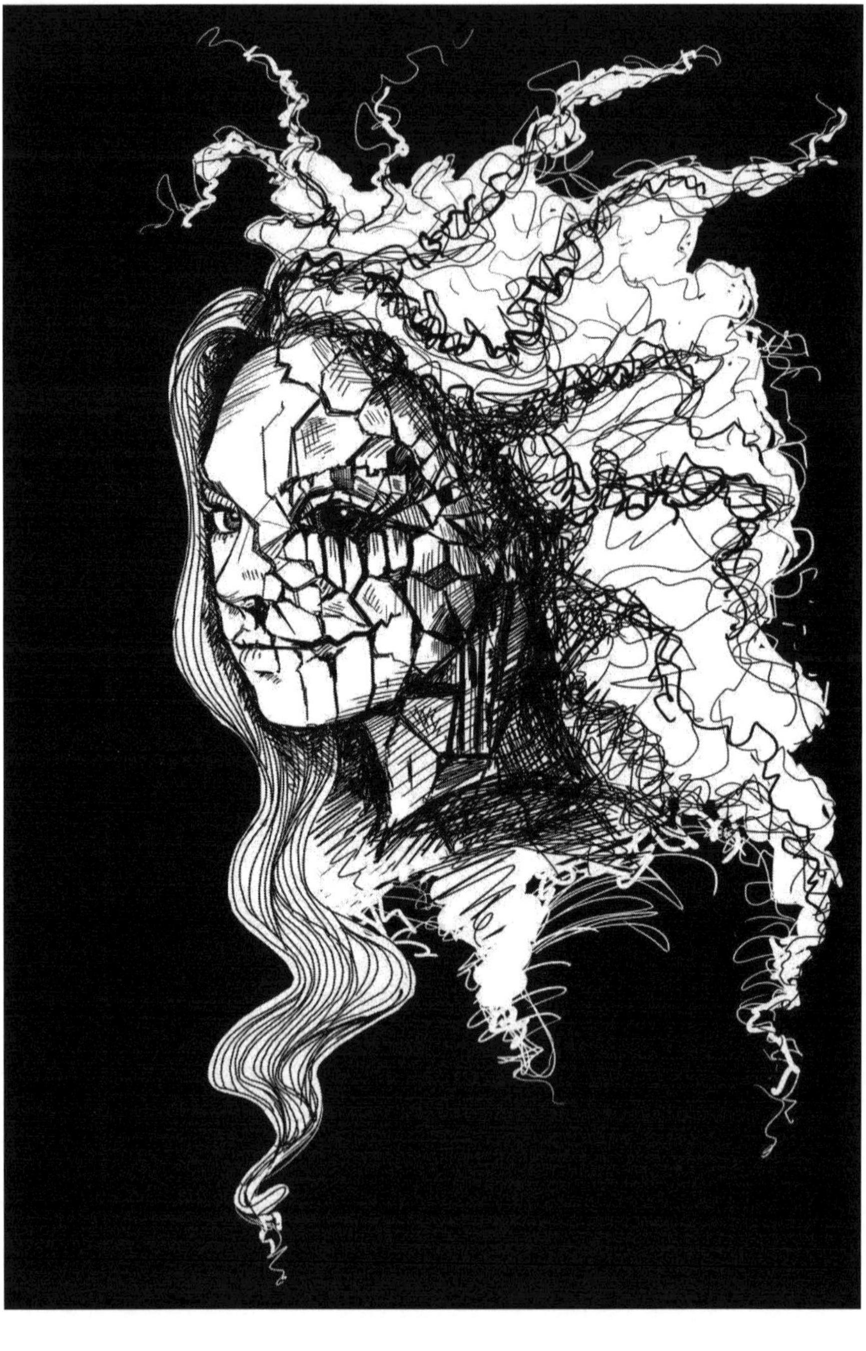

would have no chance to escape either as they were more likely to slip on their own vomit.

In fact, Ena had a sickly green tinge to her skin and Zane looked half way to choosing whether to swallow bile or spit it out. Sophia's face had morphed into a grotesque and hideous version of herself, with skin cracked as though made from the hard desert sands left to bake under the hot blazing sun.

She looked grey and lifeless as though she was a living corpse, with eyes of milky white as if she had been blinded by extreme light. Her smile, if it could be called that, looked as though a blade had slit along the corners of her mouth and up her cheeks, held together by a strange black substance oozing from beneath the many cracks in her flaky skin. It almost looked as though her black soul was trying to escape by any means possible, even if it meant seeping through her eye sockets and from the cracks in her eyelids, running down her face like mascara tears.

Theo swallowed hard as he looked at her soulless eyes, when they transformed from white to onyx black, giving her demon form a more sinister depth. It reminded Theo of a horror movie he once saw, when some scientists were infected with a deadly virus, one that turned their blood black as if it had rotted in some way. But it wasn't just her appearance that had changed, it was the addition of what followed her from behind, like a living shadow that was shaped like a pair of giant smoky wings.

She held up her hands and started to walk towards them, her wings following her every step like magnetic vapour holding its shape but also looking like ink under water with the way they moved.

"AHHH!" Ena screamed again, proving that when scared enough, it was certainly a convincing sound when she meant it to be, unlike when they were trying to get Ivan off the railings.

"Okay guys, please, I know this looks bad but..." she never got chance to finish as this time Janie just happened to glance her way again and was soon left screaming once more like Ena did. The next thing they knew the door burst open and in ran Pip.

"Holy Rip Van Winkle Batman, what the freak is going on?!" she shouted after coming to a skidding halt. She then looked to Sophia in her demon form with her raw, flaky hand tapping on her cocked hip and said,

"What, what's the biggy?" Sophia didn't look impressed and nodded to the huddled group of scared teens for Pip to follow her gaze.

"Oh...I see."

"Yeah, and so do they," Sophia commented dryly.

"I thought we talked about this. You know, in the meeting we had and my idea about..."

"I am not juggling flashing balls, Pip," Sophia said cutting her off and slicing a hand in the air, giving her obscene appearance a very human trait.

"Yeah, but look at them, I told you that if we pull a scary then we have to back it up with a funny. Juggling balls is a classic, it's that or..."

"No Pip... I am not line dancing to Billy Ray Cyrus' Achy Breaky Heart either," she added before Pip could say more. It was at this point that an amazing thing happened and that was the faintest sound of a giggle coming from Ena. Pip heard it and nudged Sophia.

"See, told you dudette, it could totally work," she whispered and even though in this form the others wouldn't be able to see it, she still rolled her eyes out of habit, knowing that Pip was right. She needed to make the point that she was still the same person they'd first encountered but in order to do that she had to show them that no matter what her appearance, she still had her humanity. And this lesson in trust would be one of their most important ones. So, she did something she didn't really want to do, not without a few bottles of absinthe down her anyway. She nodded for Pip, giving her the go ahead.

"Oh, Jiminy Cricket, this is gonna be awesome sauce on a hotdog!" Pip said before running out the room, leaving everyone looking as if they didn't know what to do. An awkward silence fell upon the room and after three minutes waiting they all looked to Sophia and she could think of nothing to say, so instead she just shrugged her shoulders.

The next thing they knew Pip was back, running into the room and this time carrying a huge 80's style, silver boom box over one shoulder and a massive hot pink tutu fluttering behind her over the other.

"It's time to go to funky town!" she said placing the boom box down and looking to each of them before saying,

"Now would a scary ass demon, gonna kill you dead and tear your faces off do this first…" Then she pressed play and the room quickly filled with the 80's machine drum beat. Then she quickly kicked into her massive skirt, wiggling it up her body and threw her helmet to one side, letting it slide along the floor, releasing a mass of tight green curls. After this she snatched out a pink sweatband she had stashed in her leggings waistband and snapped it around her forehead, now looking like she was ready for some radical 80's rave.

"Lucifer help me now," Sophia muttered, looking to the ground as if praying in her despair when hearing the twangy base sound, that was the unmistakable opening surf guitar riff with added cheesy synthesiser.

"Seriously Squeak…Kenny Loggins' *Footloose*?"

"What, it's a classic! And you freakin' loved this song at last year's Christmas party…come on, you remember that thing we did, with our feet…oh can't you just feel that awesome beat infecting your brain!" Pip squealed as her hand went to the side of her head and her little bum started to shake to the side.

"Not really" Sophia commented dryly but Pip just ignored her and started singing,

'I been working so hard, I'm punching my card, eight hours, for what, oh tell me what I got, I got this feeling, like times still holding me down'…" Then she stopped and cocked her head to the side to tell Sophia to start dancing.

Once again, the others couldn't see thanks to her black eyes, but she certainly rolled them before her foot started to move. It was ever so slight at first but Pip lowered her hands, shaking them closer to the ground just before the chorus broke.

And then she let loose! She raised her hands back up and started to shake them round in time with her behind, swinging her body out and back in again.

"Oh, who am I kiddin', I love this song!" Sophia shouted and just like Pip, she started to really let herself go on the chorus. The others seemed stunned and glanced first at each other looking before back to a sight they never thought they would ever see. A bad ass, scary demon, wearing a posh outfit dancing in time with the colourful, tutu wearing Pip.

Their moves were in sync as if they had done this a hundred times before and the foot thing ended up with them linking their arms and stepping over each other's legs, as though they were walking as one. Then Pip grabbed Sophia's flaky hand and spun her round a few times before breaking free to do her own thing. Sophia's wings followed her every move, clouding them both for a moment in black smoke before they formed wings once again. Even they looked like they were having a good time, swaying back and forth with Sophia's sidesteps.

Meanwhile Pip looked as though she could have been the star on some Broadway musical. She took off doing her own thing, kicking up her legs and clapping under them, all the while singing her little heart out. Sophia also started doing her own thing, letting herself go and swinging her arms from side to side, clapping her hands in time with the beat.

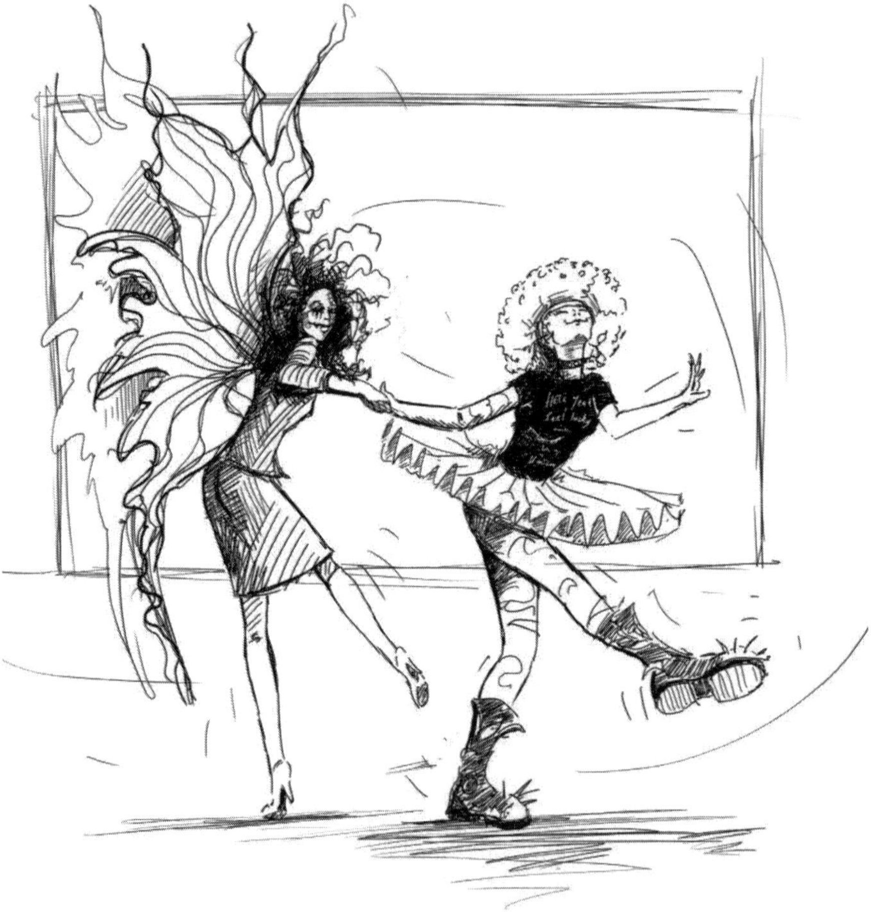

The others watched fascinated, no longer able to find her scary and getting used to the way she looked in this form. Ena and Janie even started dancing along with them, laughing and giggling as they did. The boys just looked on in awe at what was the last thing they ever expected to witness in their first class.

Then the song kicked it up a notch and Pip stepped it up a notch (if that was possible) and started going crazy, shaking her head round from side to side, making her massive green afro blur as it went around and around. Then the next thing they all knew she was on the floor break dancing.

She spun her little body round in a tight ball and then landed up on her head, to kick her legs out, creating V shapes with her body. Then she spun back and flipped up just as the song was finishing, so that she could run into a power slide along the floor, pretending she was holding a guitar up in the air when coming to a stop near the door.

It was at this point as the song was just about to finish that her husband walked in, followed by Sophia's. Everyone froze, along with Pip, who looked to the door and said,

"Too much?"

"Are we interrupting something?" Zagan said with a smirk looking at Sophia and Adam couldn't help but ask his own wife,

"I didn't know dancing was on the curriculum darling?" Pip backflipped up skilfully, walked over to her husband, patted his cheek, and said,

"You don't teach dancing sugar pop...*you live it.*" It was at this point that Ivan shocked them all and started clapping and with hands as big as his, it created quite an applause. The rest burst out laughing and joined in, clapping with him.

She gave them all a graceful bow, raised herself up and then pushed her wild hair back with both hands before saying,

"And my work here is done." Then she left the room giving them all a salute. Adam shook his head, obviously used to his wife's strange outrageous behaviour, and said,

"I'd better go and make sure she doesn't start dancing on the roof, like she usually does after that song."

Zagan watched them leave and then walked up to his own wife and said,

"Nice moves beautiful, wish I had turned up sooner." Then he placed a gentle hand on her cracked face and kissed her cheek being completely unaffected by her appearance. If her skin hadn't been a deathly grey colour you might have seen her blush.

"And what are you doing here so soon?" she enquired, unable to keep her smile to herself. And the teens soon realised something, what should have been a creepy, spine tingling sight was no longer something scary to them at all. Pip had been right, *it had worked.* They could no longer look at her and feel revolted but instead they just accepted it, as though this was a different part of her, one that didn't change who she was inside.

"Time's up sweetheart, it's time for their next lesson."

"Already? Wow, that did go quick," she replied and the group had to agree, their first lesson went by in the blink of an eye.

"Just give me a minute to finish up." Zagan looked down at his wife, tapped her chin once and nodded with a smirk. Then he left the room, leaving them wondering what their next class was.

"So, what do we think, did Pip make her point?" Sophia asked folding her arms and the second she did, she was back to her human form, looking as radiant as ever. Suddenly the teens all started to look a bit ashamed at their reactions to her demon form.

"I think I speak for everyone when I say we are sor..." Sophia held up her hand and stopped Theo in his tracks.

"There is no need to apologise Theo, for I know what I am and I know how it must look seeing me like that for the first time. My actions weren't done to scare you all but to *prepare* you. I will not lie to you but my world can be a scary place to an unknown like each of you. However, given time and education, then I promise, there will come a day when seeing demons in their natural form will be like second nature to you and you won't even flinch..." she said, pausing a moment at the end as if deciding whether or not to say what she wanted to say next.

In the end she sighed and then went for it, knowing that to be forewarned was always better than to be blindsided.

"...After all, soon there might come a day when you yourselves look in the mirror and gaze upon your own true forms...and they might not be pretty but one thing I am damn sure about and that is they will be kick ass!" she finished, smirking at the boys grinning but also hoping that when the time came, the girls especially wouldn't find this too difficult to grasp.

They certainly didn't look as convinced as the boys did but that was only to be expected. If a girl got a scar, it often meant she felt as though she was ugly, but if a boy did then in her experience it often meant they were cool. For her though, as someone unable to scar, she only had a dear friend to go by and they once told her,

'Scars are just the diary you carry with you, showing you of your past mistakes to learn from, heroic actions to be proud of and past adventures to remember.'

Oh yes, her sister-in-law and now queen was a wise woman indeed…although she had also seen her fall over trying to put two legs in one trouser leg by mistake, but she just assumed that everyone had their 'off' days…well humans that was anyway.

"So, what is our next lesson, Miss?" Zane couldn't help but ask and Sophia smiled, giving up asking them to call her Sophia and said something she knew the boys really wanted to hear…

"Weapons training."

23
DEMONSTRATION

The group soon found themselves walking into the huge training room that they had been shown on their tour with Pip, only this time they were dressed for the occasion. They had each been given light grey trousers to wear that were wide legged and tied at the waist, falling to their ankles.

They were called Hakama and traditionally they were worn over a Kimono. These were jackets in the same colour and material that crossed over and were tucked into the high waistbands of the trousers. Theo and Zane looked at themselves in the mirror before walking out and both as if like they were about to star as extras in a martial arts movie. Whilst the girls looked at themselves and pulled awkwardly at their sleeves and collars, feeling out of place.

Janie was particularly nervous, having no idea what awaited her and wasn't looking forward to being made a fool of. But really, what other outcome was there for her in hand to hand combat seeing as the 'hand to hand' part was going to be a problem. Everyone would know she would be at a disadvantage in a class like this and she hated it, but what was worse was having to respond to those pitying stares.

"You'll do great," Ena said nudging her shoulder knowing what dark place her friend's mind was quickly wandering off to. It wasn't hard to guess after watching the colour drain from her face when Sophia had first told them what their next class was going to be.

Janie gave her a small smile that wasn't reflected in her eyes, telling Ena very quickly that it was faked. Ena couldn't say that she understood how she was feeling, as not many would unless they faced the same handicap, but she knew what it felt like to be looked at differently. She knew what it felt like to be pitied and at the same time ridiculed. But the difference here was that no-one in this room pitied Janie, they only wanted to support her and that meant not treating her any differently than any of the others.

"I can't even throw a ball without smashing a window, so God knows what will happen when they give me a weapon, but if I were you, I would stand well back," Ena added looking to the far wall of weapons that decorated the large space with lots of shiny, sharp metal.

This time when Janie smiled, she knew it was for real.

"And besides, I don't think we are the only ones who feel awkward," Ena said nodding to the last one out of the changing rooms and Janie looked over her shoulder to see poor Ivan who looked as though he wanted to go run and hide. Janie bit her lip and felt bad that she had only been thinking of herself, when she clearly wasn't the only one the thought of doing this class was affecting.

Ivan walked in last and hated every step that took him closer to violence. He didn't know how he was going to explain to his new teachers that he didn't want to do this... *that he couldn't do this.* In fact, he was so lost in the midst of his inner turmoil that he didn't realise at first that someone was talking to him. He looked down, as he had to with most people, and saw little Janie looking up at him with a beaming grin on her face. He liked it when she looked up at him because all the loose hair she usually wore down to hide herself, fell back and he could see all of her beautiful face.

It was a sight that made his fears slowly slip away until all he focused on was the way she touched his arm, pulling at it so that he would go with her. He let himself be led to the others and this was when he finally decided to ask what it was she had said to him.

"I sorry, I no listen there." She laughed once and repeated herself.

"I said that Ena and I think you look great, very heroic," she added winking at him, something she never did with anyone else. Well, hearing this was enough for Ivan to completely forget his fears and instead focused solely on trying to make himself look even more heroic.

"So, what now?" Zane asked looking around the room like everyone else and wondering where their instructor was. Rue had been the one to show them down there and to their individual lockers, which not only had their names on but also had brand new training gear inside, which included everything from running gear and gym gear, to what they were wearing now. They had even got everyone's sizing right, which wasn't the most difficult task for most but then when you threw Ivan into the mix, then yeah, that couldn't have been easy.

They had asked where Pip was and Rue laughed once and said,

"Busy with her husband." Now none of them wanted to know what that meant but I think their faces said it all, which was when Rue laughed even harder and corrected them all by leaving the room saying,

"Disco dancing on the roof."

It had been the first time any of them had been alone with Rue since the bus drive, but each of them had taken Draven's advice and not held it against her. Knowing now of course, that she'd had little choice and was just following orders. And speaking of orders, theirs quickly came from above.

"Welcome to your first lesson in weapons training and combat. If you would all please move to the sides, I think we should start with a demonstration...Takeshi, if you would be so kind," Zagan said from a small balcony above the door they had just entered through. They looked towards the other side of the room to see the Japanese man entering, walking down the centre with purpose.

He wore robes very similar to the ones he'd had on the day before when they had been introduced, only this time instead of wearing black, he wore red with white symbols embroidered with silk thread down the long panels at the front.

"Uh...guys, I think moving would be a good idea," Zane said as he looked back up to Zagan who looked like he was getting ready to do something. The others didn't need telling twice and all moved to the side to watch this from a safe distance. Just as they did Zagan, who had backed up, ran towards the edge and jumped down to the fighting arena below, landing hard on one knee.

The impact caused the floor to ripple around his knee before sending a shockwave of cracks outwards like vines growing beneath the bamboo floor. Shocked gasps came from the girls and they all looked for any damage to their new teacher, as there was to the floor beneath him. Although they were soon to find out that it would take a lot more than that to hurt a high-ranking demon like Zagan.

He looked up at his approaching opponent and pushed his black hood back, reminding Zane of some of his favourite computer generated assassins, in that bad ass awesome, superhuman way. His long white hair was half tied back by a thick band of leather cord and his pale white skin made for a startling contrast with the long black Kimono style jacket he wore. He stood up and as he did the deeply gouged floor started to repair itself, as if he was using his power to suck back the damage, and soon the cracks were no more.

"What do you say my friend, shall we dust off those old Rōnin bones of yours?" Zagan said in jest and Zane, having seen a movie about the famous 'Rōnin', knew what this meant and the importance of the name. The name Rōnin was given to those who unfortunately became a samurai without a lord or master due to their death or fall in combat.

According to the 'Bushido Shoshinshu', also known as the Code of the Samurai, one suffering this loss was supposed to commit seppuku, a ritual suicide after his master's death. Of course, not everyone was so quick to want to fall on one's sword until disembowelment. So, those who chose not to honour the code were deemed 'on their own' and were meant to suffer great shame to their name and family.

It meant that a lot of very skilled Samurai warriors ended up becoming mercenaries. However, Takeshi took a different path, one that led him down the supernatural road and pledging his loyalty to a very different master...*Dominic Draven.*

In response to Zagan's provoking banter, Takeshi held his hand out to some nearby staffs that were positioned in racks at the far wall with the rest of the weapons. The long pole shot out to his hand as though there were some physical connection the group couldn't see. As soon as it was in Takeshi's possession he spun it round like a propeller at an impossible speed then swept it low to the ground before coming back up into a ready stance. Then he blew some lint off his shoulder and motioned for his cocky opponent to come closer using two of his fingers that also had hold of the weapon.

Zagan cocked his head to the side and smirked when Takeshi's only response to his goading had been him showing off his skills with the weapon. Zagan not being one to keep a challenger waiting bowed at the waist, keeping his eyes on his opponent at all times as he'd been taught. Takeshi did the same and the second he rose back up ready for him, Zagan ran towards him full speed.

He held his hand out as he went so that one of the staffs could swiftly gravitate to his hand just as it had done with Takeshi's. Then he jumped the second he had it in his grasp, so that he could bring it down with the sole intent of cracking it over Takeshi's head.

Everyone gasped expecting it to make contact, but that's not what happened. Takeshi, knowing Zagan's old tricks, was more than ready for him. He simply raised his staff up in time to counteract the move, filling the large space with the echoing sounds of wood clashing against wood.

"Wow! Did you see that?" Janie said, amazed that they could move objects with their minds.

"Well, Zane's mouth is still hanging open, so I am going with a yes on that one," Ena replied making her laugh.

Then the fighting really began.

Zagan spun back round so that they faced each other once more.

"Let's see what you've got, Samurai." Zagan said with an amused glint in his pale eyes and a grin playing at the corners of his mouth. Takeshi nodded his head, silently telling him that he was ready after taking another stance. Zagan did the same, first spinning his own staff and in doing so, showing off his own unique set skills.

Only Zagan didn't move like Takeshi, in what seemed like a more traditional way. Because as Takeshi came at him with hit after hit, each was blocked in the most unusual way. Zagan's style was definitely his own, as he and the staff seemed to move as one with each other. In fact, he moved so fast that he looked as though he was actually bending the wood as it flipped around his torso, passing it back around his body and to the front again.

Each time he did this it would end up blocking Takeshi's hits, no matter where he tried to land them on his body. Zagan's strange technique seemed to place the long staff wherever the next hit came from and protected him in a way that wouldn't have been possible had he been human. To begin with, the speed in which he did this would have made it impossible to be effective as it was all so quick it sounded as though the wood was clapping whenever it hit Takeshi's.

Then Zagan suddenly lashed out, throwing kick after kick his way but Takeshi was just as quick and stepped back one, two, three and on the fourth kick he changed tactics and caught Zagan's bare foot. Then he flipped it over with his hands and Zagan's body followed, spinning six times in the air. The teens all thought this was it, he was going nowhere but landing hard on the floor but they were wrong. Instead Zagan used his staff, hammering it into the ground at a right angle and in doing so propelled his body back upright to a standing position just before he fell.

"Nice," Zagan complimented and Takeshi smirked and bowed his head in thanks before going at him once more. The two hit out at each other in such a way that it was almost dizzying to watch. It was almost like watching a well-choreographed dance on fast forward. They broke away from each other one last time and Zagan looked to the group of teens all watching in awe.

He thought of what his enchanting wife had showed them earlier that morning and now knowing that their limits had been pushed, he decided to push them just a little bit more...*alright, so maybe a lot more.* Zagan looked back to Takeshi to see him nod, as he must have also been thinking the same thing, that it was time to step it up a notch. And what was the best way for two Supernaturals battling it out to step things up a notch...

Supernatural powers.

Zagan smirked, thinking this was going to be good and from the look of his cool, calm, collected friend, that tiny glint in his eyes told him that he thought the same. So, he spun his staff around and felt the release of a dark power trying to rise up from deep within him as it too wanted its turn and he would let it, giving it the go ahead when he suggested to Takeshi...

"Let's make this more interesting, shall we?"

24
Fire and Thorn

"Let's make this more interesting, shall we?"

The group all looked at each other, wide eyed and wondering what Zagan meant by making things more interesting? As far as they were concerned, you couldn't exactly have made things any more interesting than they already were...*or so they thought.*

"Very well, General," Takeshi said with respect and then ran his hand up his weapon, igniting it in a distinctive white flame that looked deadly against the dark red wood of his weapon.

The collective gasp from the group confirmed that they had been wrong, round two was like taking the impossible into the realms of incredibly possible.

"General?" Zane mouthed the word to Theo, receiving a shrug of his shoulders in return, as he too had no clue what it meant.

"My turn," Zagan said and then looked up at the ceiling, twisting his neck to the side in what looked a painful way. Then his eyes started to fill up with a white liquid, almost as though paint was filling his irises. He then held out his staff straight ahead of him with one hand and started to twitch his head, as though he was allowing something to happen and was trying to help it along.

"Oh...*my*...G..."

"I think the last word you're looking for doesn't apply to this," Zane said interrupting Ena and then started shaking his thumb down towards Hell. In this, she couldn't disagree with him as there was only one word for what was happening to their teacher right now and it was far from Heavenly...It was truly,

Demonic.

"I think something is trying to come out of him," Theo whispered to the others, unable to keep the awe out of his voice, whilst watching Zagan twist his neck side to side, as if readying himself for something, until doing it one last time before it started to happen.

Bumps suddenly appeared under his skin and started rippling along in waves, as though whatever was emerging was using his veins as a passageway. It continued to do this, travelling up his neck until it reached the black, barbed, tribal tattoo that ran down one side of his face. As soon as it got there, the ripples stopped and instead the black ink started to break away from the long, mean looking scar that marred his face, one it had been entwined with.

Then it came alive!

Unbelievably, it slithered down his face and out of sight for a moment as it travelled down his neck, shoulder, and arm. The group had only a second to wait before they watched it remerging from under his sleeve. It started to branch out, attaching itself onto the staff and re-forming it, effectively covering it in some kind of deadly looking black vine. It quickly grew up the length of the pole he held until it consumed it all, leaving only a part untouched where his fingers were still grasping it.

Then it finished. It was done. And his weapon was ready.

And to prove this he spun it once and when it came to rest he made a slight twisting motion, releasing a string of deadly and wicked looking thorns all over the vine like demonic barbed wire. In fact, it almost mirrored what his tattoo had been, only now it was three dimensional and had been given life.

"Mm." Takeshi made the slightly impressed sound, whilst cocking his head to one side as if this was something new. Then, after a brief exchange of respect in the way of just a look, they went at it again, this time though…

Supernatural style.

However, now their weapons barely even made contact and the teens quickly assumed that this was the whole point. Unlike before it had all been about hitting and blocking an attack, but this was obviously all about how to avoid contact, which made the group wonder what would happen exactly if they did manage to make a connection. They didn't have to wait long to find out.

Both their bodies bent, swayed, swooped, and crouched low to the ground every time their unearthly weapons came close to hitting one another. It looked to Theo as though they were both biding their time for the right moment in which to strike. But what was most unexpected was that the right time came for them both simultaneously as they finally made contact. Their Hellish staffs clashed with a boom, echoing in the room like the sound of Thor's hammer hitting an anvil. It caused a wave of static to vibrate throughout the room as their supernatural sides took over.

The deadly vines tried to invade Takeshi's staff by gripping onto it and climbing up and over the flames. Takeshi saw this and slammed his second hand over his weapon, causing the white flames to transform into a more lethal and traditional looking red hot fire. This in turn started to burn and scorch the vines enough to cause damage and they quickly backed off for fear of complete destruction. Zagan retaliated by backing off also, spinning on one foot and coming to rest on the ball of his other foot behind him.

They gave each other a moment and once more there was a silent and respectful nod between them before they began their attack once more. This time their hits became that little bit faster, that little bit more powerful. Something the teens witnessed when Zagan hit downwards with such force it not only cracked the floor again, but it also made the vines branch out along it. It was as if to test for the possible threat, leaving scored marks on the floor in their wake. Of course, Takeshi was too quick and side stepped away from the hit. But with Zagan's staff momentarily positioned the way it was, it gave Takeshi the upper hand…or so he thought.

Takeshi swung his pole around his head with both hands and raised higher, gaining more momentum with each spin until it was travelling around at a blurring speed. It looked as though a helicopter's propeller was on fire but still rotating.

Then when it had reached the right energy level, he hammered it down, hitting the ground with devastating effect. The flames erupted from the end of the staff and were quickly heading towards Zagan in a direct line of destruction. But this happened just as Zagan was raising his own weapon from where it had momentarily been trapped, due to the cracks he had made in the floor.

He managed to dislodge it just in time before he was engulfed in Takeshi's firing inferno but instead of moving his body, the vines on his weapon did it for him. Black tentacles shot out from the staff as if also sensing the danger and attached themselves to one of the beams above, propelling Zagan's body upwards. He too used this to his advantage as the vine spun him round, so that he could then kick himself off the wall and swing towards Takeshi's body.

Zagan was just coming down on him ready to deliver a kick to the head, when Takeshi folded his body backwards, so that Zagan had no other option that to continue his descent over him. Takeshi flipped his body back up and faced Zagan where he had landed gracefully behind.

Then came the last round.

They both held out their weapons straight and suddenly charged at each other, reminding Ena of two knights about to joust on horseback. Janie winced, looking away as she couldn't watch, but the rest seemed fixated and held their breaths waiting to see who would be classed as the victor.

The two poles hit each other head on, which was nearly an impossible task. But what was more amazing to watch was the way they both crumbled on impact. Zagan's deadly vine quickly retreated into his body as the wood splintered back towards Zagan's hand. On the opposite side, Takeshi's flames extinguished themselves as that too was crushed, bowing in on itself from the

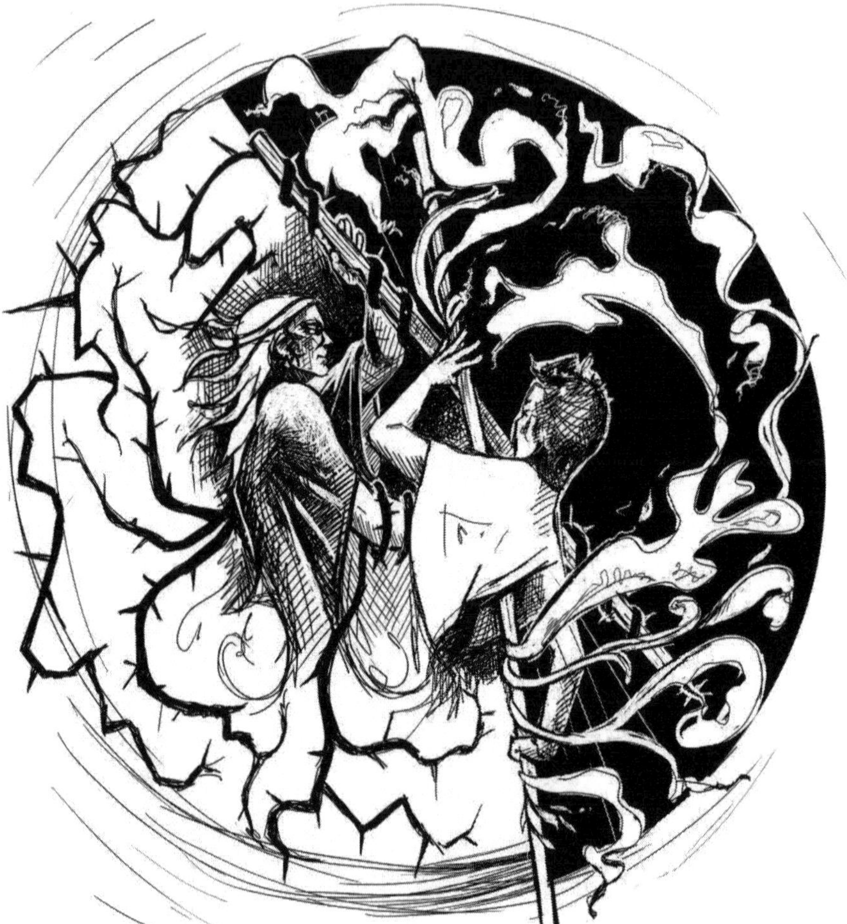

pressure just as Zagan's staff was doing the same. In the end, the fight finished with each of them holding the small piece that was left of the staffs. Their gazes fell to all that remained and they looked up at one another then both smiled at the same time.

The group collectively breathed deep after holding their breath for so long and Janie who was still looking at the wall said,

"What...what is it? Who won? No one is bleeding, are they?"

"Fighting is dusted. Winner there is not," Ivan said getting his sayings mixed up.

The two men bowed to each other for the last time, signifying to the rest of them that Ivan was right, the fight was finally over. However, they were quickly reminded that this hadn't been a fight at all.

Zagan turned to face the group and by the time he reached them his facial tattoo had made its way back up his cheek and was resting once more where it belonged, nestled amongst his long scar.

Their new teacher was just about to speak, opening his mouth to do so when an enthusiastic Ena couldn't help herself,

"Wow...just wow! That was amazing...no, no, that was epic!" she said bursting with excitement, as though she had been suddenly transformed into a demon fighter, champion groupie. Zagan looked taken aback and for a minute didn't know what to do with himself other than say,

"Thank you, Ena. And the rest of you, did you enjoy the demonstration?" They all nodded but Janie, who was looking everywhere else but at him, just did so at the wall.

"That was totally sick!" Zane said granting him a raised eyebrow from his teacher.

"Sick? You were revolted?"

"He means that we all thought it was cool," Theo added, clarifying Zane's slang for someone who was probably older than the Oxford dictionary, let alone the urban one.

"Ah, I see. But I also see that not everyone was a fan of the show," Zagan said nodding to Janie who blushed scarlet.

"I uh…well, it's not that it wasn't…you know…okay." Zagan burst out laughing and said,

"Well my fighting skills have never been referred to as just 'Okay' before but don't worry, I will try not take it personally. Although my wife is sure to get a kick of out hearing about this later." This made Ena chuckle and Janie feel guilty.

"But, regarding the fight, I understand that not everyone who walks into this Dojo is drawn to violence and they don't have to be as that is not what I teach here or what Takeshi will teach you either."

"But that was…?" Janie started to argue that what they had been doing looked very violent but her teacher got there first.

"That was nothing more than a demonstration showing you how to try and anticipate your opponent's moves and skill level, which in this case Takeshi's was evenly matched to my own. It is about keeping good balance, blocking what comes at you and counteracting it if you can. It was also about showing you how to use your powers, incorporating them, not only your weaponry as we did, but also in your environment. It is about using your own unique skills to your advantage... when the time comes in discovering them of course."

"And when might that be?" Zane asked as, like Theo, he hadn't seen anything resembling supernatural coming out of his body, not unless you classed the mammoth offering he made to the toilet God that morning which was the size of Tyson's leg...gross, he knew but he was proud all the same. Of course, Zane blamed it on the amount of pizza he'd consumed!

"It is hard to say, as I know for some of you it has already seen the light of day but has yet to develop further. That is where Rue will come in. She will help you learn how to control it, until eventually it will become second nature," he said purposely making the tattoo on his face move and slither around for a few seconds.

"But for today we will start off light. First do you have any questions for me before we begin?"

"What's a Dojo?" Janie asked wanting to know thanks to the answer he gave her about violence.

"A Dojo is a Japanese term which means 'place of the way'. But in the Western world the term primarily refers to a training place specifically for Japanese martial arts such as aikido, judo, karate, or even Samurai."

"What about Kung Fu?" Ena asked, thinking they were all the same.

"Kung Fu is Chinese and did not refer to the martial arts as it is known today. It's simply a name given in reference to any study or practice that requires great patience, energy, and time to master such a skill."

"And will we be learning to fight with those staffs today?" Zane asked crossing his fingers behind his back.

"They are known as a Bō and are typically used in Japanese martial arts. However, they started life very differently and were originally used to balance buckets or baskets either side of the shoulder."

"So how did they become weapons?" Ena asked truly curious and surprising herself that she actually cared to learn the history of a weapon.

"It started in 1477 when Emperor Sho Shin came into power. He was determined to enforce his philosophical and ethical ideas, so introduced a ban on weapons in an attempt to prevent an uprising.   It became a crime to carry or own weapons such as swords, so the people became more inventive, giving birth to a new fighting style," Zagan said giving them a brief history into Japanese weaponry, one he was surprised to see they all looked very interested in.

"What else did they use?" Theo asked, looking to the mass of weapons at the end of the room and seeing if he could spot anything that looked like it could be classed in that same category.

"The people of Okinawa looked to simple farming tools as new methods of defence, ones which the samurai warriors would not be able to confiscate. This use of weapons developed into Kobudo, or "Ancient martial way" as is known today." He paused for a moment and looked back to the far wall, where traditionally most weapons were kept in a Dojo. It was a little off topic and not how he expected his lesson to start but they were here to learn after all. And who was he to stand in the way of their enthusiasm when an opportunity for them to learn presented itself.

He knew he had made the right choice when their eyes lit up after he asked the question they all wanted to hear…

"Would you like to learn more about these weapons?"

25
Golden Age of the Dagger

"Would you like to learn more about these weapons?"

"Does a one-legged duck swim in a circle?" Zane said receiving strange, confused looks his way.

"Dude, did you just say that?" Theo asked smirking and Zane shrugged his shoulders and replied,

"What? I was gonna go with the whole 'is the Pope catholic?' thing but I didn't want to rock the God boat and find out that the Pope is actually a demon." The teens all burst out laughing and Zagan had to try and keep a straight face, as he knew exactly what the Pope was. But that was something they definitely weren't ready for.

"Follow me," Zagan said motioning with a nod of his head for them to join him.

"These here are called a Sai." Zagan said pointing to a set of three-pronged weapons that they all recognised.

"Pip keeps telling me that a famous fighter by the name of Raphael uses them." It was at this point the teens all burst out laughing but one look at Zagan's confused expression said it all...he had no clue who Pip had been referring to.

"Am I missing something?" he asked folding his arms and raising an eyebrow. All laughter stopped and this time all the group looked to Zane instead of Theo.

"What?"

"This one's on you Zee," Theo said nudging him with his shoulder and Ena couldn't hold back a sneaky giggle after the nudge pushed him forward a step. Zane groaned looking back at them all and scrubbed a hand down his face before saying,

"Uh…okay so how should I put this?" Then Zane thought for another moment before having an idea.

"Do you have a phone?" At first Zane thought he would refuse him but he must have been too curious to know, so instead he nodded towards a mirror on the wall. The rest followed, not wanting to miss this.

Zane didn't know what to expect but it certainly wasn't the mirror turning into a computer screen the second his teacher touched it. Zagan tapped on the internet browser icon and up popped Google.

"Okay, so this is who Pip is talking about," Zane said typing the name and four other words after it,

"Teenage… Mutant… Ninja… Turtles…have I got that right?" Zagan asked and Zane nodded as he clicked on the image tab so that his teacher had a picture to put to the name. He took one look at the cartoon tactical human sized turtle and groaned.

"That little Imp should thank her lucky tattooed stars that we are all scared of her husband," Zagan said, shocking them all.

"Uh…you are talking about the same guy we think you're talking about…right? Oxford scholar be his choice of style and cute and wacky be his choice of wife?" Zagan laughed aloud this time, liking this kid and his sense of humour. He would certainly need it around here especially if this damn new prophecy was anything to go by.

"Oh no, don't look at me like that kid, that is one story you will definitely not be hearing from me but don't worry, I am sure Pip would be more than happy to tell you all about it." He turned back, ready to continue their lesson, when an afterthought made him pause.

"Of course, she would do so against her husband's will but that is often the way of it." And then he shrugged his shoulders signifying the end of it.

"So, as I was saying, these weapons you recognise, thanks to green ninja reptiles, they along with many others that you see here were mainly disguised as farm tools. Although looking at ones such as the Nunchaku, I can imagine not very convincingly," he said pointing to a set of short wooden poles attached in the middle with a chain. Janie automatically got the giggles which in turn set everyone else off again.

Zagan turned to look at her and she raised her one hand to cover her mouth. However, it didn't take Zagan long to work out what was so funny…*again.*

"Let me guess, another cartoon character's choice of weapon?"

"His brother, Michaelangelo... he, uh... wears the orange mask," Zane said nodding back to the picture of all four of them still on screen. Zagan closed his pale eyes a second and rubbed his forehead in a sign of frustration before muttering,

"But of course." Then he looked back to them and said,

"Let's try this a different way, which ones do you *not* recognise?" It was at this point that the teens felt bad for him, so they all started pointing to the ones on the wall they didn't know. Zagan held up his hand to stop the bombardment and said with a smirk,

"I get the idea."

"Will we learn how to fight with them all?" Zane asked looking at the only one that looked like it could pass as a farm implement and nodding to the one that had a handle like an axe but had curved metal at the end.

"Ah the Kuwa, it is an Okinawan weapon based on a hoe. It is also used in Okinawan Kobudō."

"A hoe as in the gardening tool?" Ena asked and Zagan laughed.

"Yes, as I said, they had to protect themselves without seeming like a threat and trust me, when used properly, it can be just as deadly as all the rest. Although I wouldn't recommend it against anything big," Zagan said, thinking back to a particular battle in Tartarus, one that involved some rather angry Cyclopes brothers the size of four storey buildings.

Oh yeah, Zagan could just imagine it, entering Tartarus, the lowest level of Hell, armed with nothing more than a glorified gardening tool. He was a good fighter to be certain, but damn, even *he* wasn't that good!

"What's a…uh…Okin…a…wany…kobo something?" Ena asked and Zane shot her a look and said,

"Shouldn't you know how to say this stuff?" She frowned giving him daggers and snapped,

"That's racist!"

"No, it's not! You're Japanese, aren't you?" he asked and looked to Theo for back up on this one, but Theo had already guessed her secret on the bus when he first met her. That being that she didn't speak her native language and was obviously embarrassed about it. So, he shook his head slightly, telling him to drop it…but this being Zane, of course he didn't get the hint.

"Yeah, so! Just 'cause you're from the Netherlands it doesn't mean you speak Dutch!" she snapped again.

"I do speak Dutch and I also speak German and French…and anyway is it really so bad of me that I assumed you are intelligent enough to speak one of the hardest languages to learn?!" Zane argued and doing so in such a way it was hard for Ena to fight back against that sort of compliment.

"Well I don't!" she said trying anyway with a huff and folding her arms as her only defence.

"Well then lucky for you, now is the perfect opportunity to learn then, isn't it?" he added and Theo rolled his eyes hoping one of them would soon drop it.

"Well maybe I will!" Ena said, not being the one like Theo had hoped.

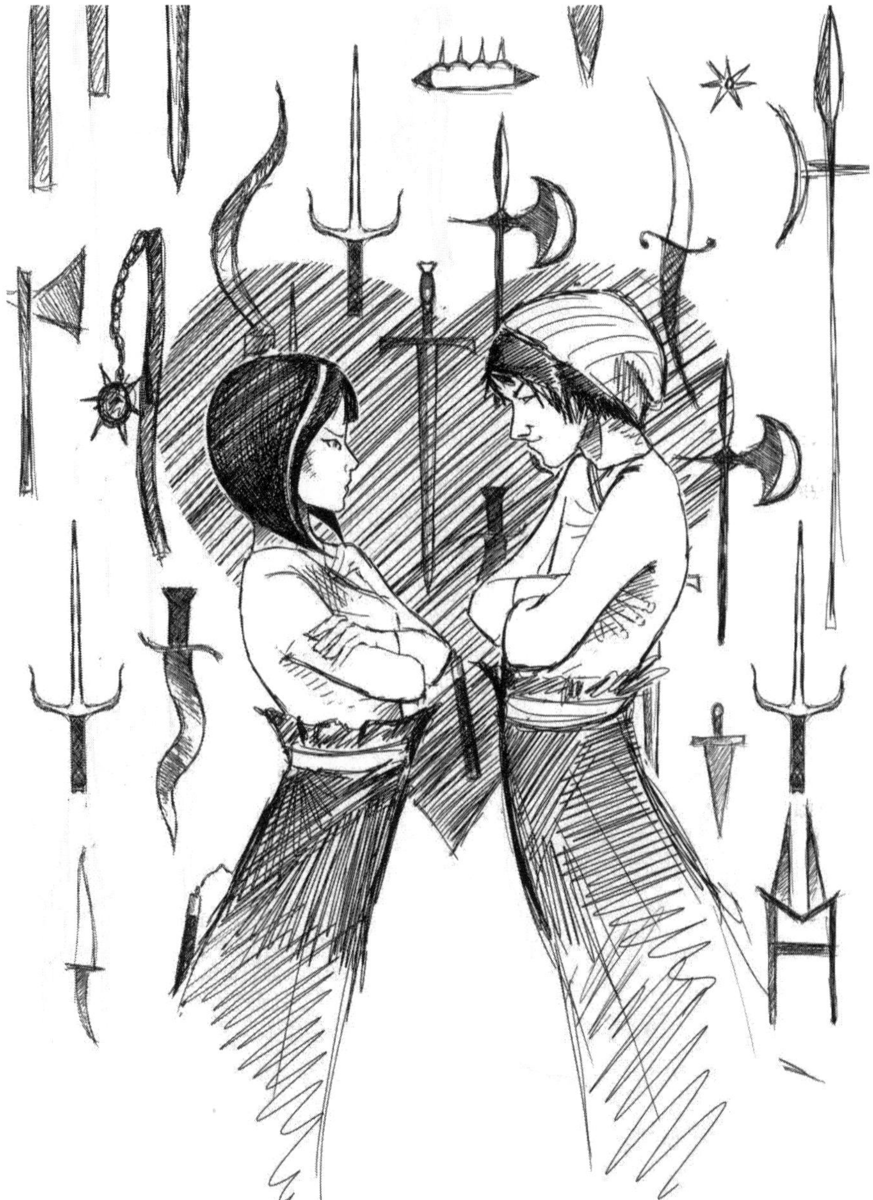

"Very good then!" Zane said, mimicking her stance and Theo decided it was time to pull out the big guns. So, he looked to Zagan, hoping he would get the hint when he nodded at the two of them. It was in that moment that Zagan's face said it all and he must have realised, 'Oh shit, yes, I forgot, I am the authoritative figure in all of this.'

"Fine I…"

"Daggers!" Zagan shouted interrupting Ena's pointless reply and not knowing any other way of dealing with arguing teens other than using a tactic he often used with his wife… diversion.

"Moving on from the Okinawan Kobudō which, in answer to your question Ena, refers to the weapon systems of Okinawan martial arts…and before you ask Janie, it is named this because it originated among the indigenous people of Okinawa Island," he added quickly, just before Janie could open her mouth and they once again found themselves off subject. He was starting to think his wife's idea of a lesson plan wasn't such a pointless endeavour now.

Only he had to say that he doubted letting her demon self be seen had been on her own. That was something he would have to remember until later if the conversation arose. After all, any argument he could actually win against his wife was something he classed as a great victory, considering how rare a thing it was for him.

"So, getting back to the lesson, first we are going to start with the oldest and most basic form of weapon. But don't be fooled, it may be basic but it is far from ineffective against a foe," Zagan said, leading them over to a table that was covered with a cloth but above it attached to the wall was every size and form of dagger you could have imagined.

"The earliest daggers were made of materials such as flint, ivory or bone in Neolithic times but when the world entered into the bronze age in the 3rd millennium BCE, copper daggers were forged."

"Uh…question," Ena said raising her hand, this time more tentatively, due to already feeling Zane's ridicule. But Zagan nodded for her to go ahead.

"I was never that good at history, so this might sound dumb but…" Zagan held up his hand and stopped her.

"Remember, there is no such thing as a stupid question, there are only stupid actions which come from those who are too foolish to ask. After all, knowledge was born from the first man who asked why." Ena smirked and then couldn't help but add playfully,

"Or woman." Their teacher smiled and said,

"Please beg my pardon. 'Knowledge was born from the first man *or woman* who asked why'," he corrected before continuing,

"Now let me hear your question, young lady." Ena blushed at this and bit her lip a moment before asking,

"What does BCE mean?"

"Good question. Alright, this is how it works, BCE means Before Common Era and BC means Before Christ, both of which are the same thing."

"So, basically any time before Christ was born?" Zane said letting the rest know that he was not only good with languages but also history as well. Theo was beginning to think that there was more to Zane than the artistic, comedian dressed like a punk rocker.

"That's right, Zane. Can you also tell the rest of the group what CE and AD mean?" Zagan asked knowing that he did thanks to his skilful photographic memory, that the others knew nothing about yet. Zagan had read all their files before they arrived. So, he also knew about Zane's ability to paint or draw an exact replica of anything he had ever seen, just from memory alone. This also meant that Zane never forgot anything he learned, which would be an ideal skill to have in this new world of his.

"CE just means Common Era, which is anything after this point, including now. AD means the same and is short for 'Anno Domini', which is Medieval Latin, simply meaning 'In the year of the Lord'." Zane said wowing the others with his knowledge, including Ena if that wide-eyed look was anything to go by.

"So now that we know the correct terminology for time, let us continue with the history of the dagger," Zagan said and continued to explain about daggers of ancient Egypt. Like the two recovered in the tomb of Tutankhamun, one being made of gold, and one of smelted iron. Then moving on to the middle ages and the most common use of the cross-hilt dagger.

Zagan pointed to the section above which held all the ones that had a cross guard on the handle. This was a bar that had been placed between the blade and the hilt for protection of the wielder's hand.

"But for now, these are what we will be learning with," Zagan said pulling back the cloth that hid six daggers. Zane and Theo both picked theirs up, more eager than the rest to start fighting but each frowned when they bent back the blades on their palms, realising that they were made of rubber.

"I thought it wise not to let you all go at each other with real ones quite just yet. After all, I am just your instructor, not a medic," he teased making them laugh.

"So, if you could each pick one up, we shall practice some basic defence moves and stances that are better served for protecting yourselves," he said picking up the last dagger and getting them to stand in a line at the centre of the room, so that they could each face him.

"First I want to see each of you hold the blade in a defensive way, one that you think will help you get ready for an oncoming attack." They each did as they were told, with Janie being the one who looked the most awkward of them all. However, it was Ivan who was the only one who had it right, which wasn't surprising to Zagan, not considering the violent past that was written on the pages of his personal file.

"Alright, now watch this," Zagan said letting that be the only warning before he took his blade and demonstrated how easy it was to reach their weak spots. He moved in a swift, fluid motion, catching them all off guard as he pretended to slice away at them one by one. He started with Theo's throat, slashed at Zane's wrists and then through Ena's eyes finishing with Janie's belly before coming to Ivan and stopping.

"I no show weak spot, I know this," he said looking down at Zagan, reminding him of Ragnar in many ways and knowing that it was quite possible that their demons could be of the same race.

"That's right, you didn't. Look at his stance," Zagan instructed and then walked back along the line, first lowering his head to Theo, telling him,

"Tuck your chin down, so that you protect your throat...that's it." Then he moved to Zane and twisted his arm around so that his wrist was turned in.

"Hold your arm this way round so that it can protect your face but also your wrist, so that the veins won't get cut. This will also protect your eyes Ena, as you can quickly raise your arm."

"But I would get cut," she said frowning.

"Yes, but defensive wounds can get stitched and heal, however losing your sight is more devastating in a fight, as it would no doubt be swiftly followed by your death." They each nodded and even though Ena didn't like the idea of getting her arm sliced open, she liked the idea of death far less.

But Janie, well she felt as though she wanted the earth to swallow her whole, just to save her from the shame that she thought was coming. However, she was wrong.

"Now Janie's stance is nearly perfect, see the way she is slightly lowered, holding her leg this way, ready to bring it up to protect her belly."

"But that's where you got me," she stated, both confused and shocked, mainly that she had done something right, even with her disability.

"Yes, because you were too concerned that I would go for your face, because you are one handed and feel vulnerable there. But if you stand this way..." He gripped her shoulders and turned her side on, so that her shoulder faced him and the hand that held the blade was positioned further back.

"...See this way you can step into your thrust and at the same time protect your vital organs in your torso," he said bringing her hand forward towards him and making her step into the action, showing her the ease of the move. She looked up at him and grinned, making his heart melt a little.

"I did it," she said utterly bewildered by such a thing. He gave her a little tap under her chin and said,

"But, of course you did and you got me good as well," he added looking down at his torso and her eyes followed to see that if it had been a real dagger it would have been impaled firmly in his gut.

"I really did that," she said again, mainly to herself as she never thought she could have accomplished such a thing.

"Just wait until I get you throwing the boys around, then you will have more faith in yourself."

After this Zagan showed them some more moves on how to defend a blow and follow it up with an attack. They went over it again and again until the move felt more natural to them.

However, Ivan only had to be shown once, unlike Ena who managed to fall down a few times, unable to get her feet in the right position. In fact, it was on her last fall that Zagan offered them some words of wisdom,

"Nana korobi, ya oki"

"How mean that?" This time it was Ivan who asked.

"It is an old Japanese proverb that simply means 'fall down seven times and get up eight'." This answer didn't come from Zagan but from the Samurai master who had walked up behind him... *Takeshi.*

They all looked to him, waiting for him to say more but it was actually he who seemed to be waiting for something. Thankfully though Zagan helped them out with this one, as he mouthed the word, 'Bow' and sure enough they got the hint.

They all moved at once but some, like Zane and Ena did so more dramatically, bending further down and really getting into the culture. Whereas Ivan and Janie did so looking more awkward and feeling out of place, just hoping they weren't insulting him at the same time.

Theo, on the other hand, bowed first for Takeshi's culture, and then for his own, he took a step forward and held out his hand for Takeshi to shake.

Takeshi bowed back at them all and then took Theo's offered hand, giving it a shake but the second he touched it, something startled him. He let it go, looking down at his palm as though whatever Theo had done, he had left an invisible mark there when doing so.

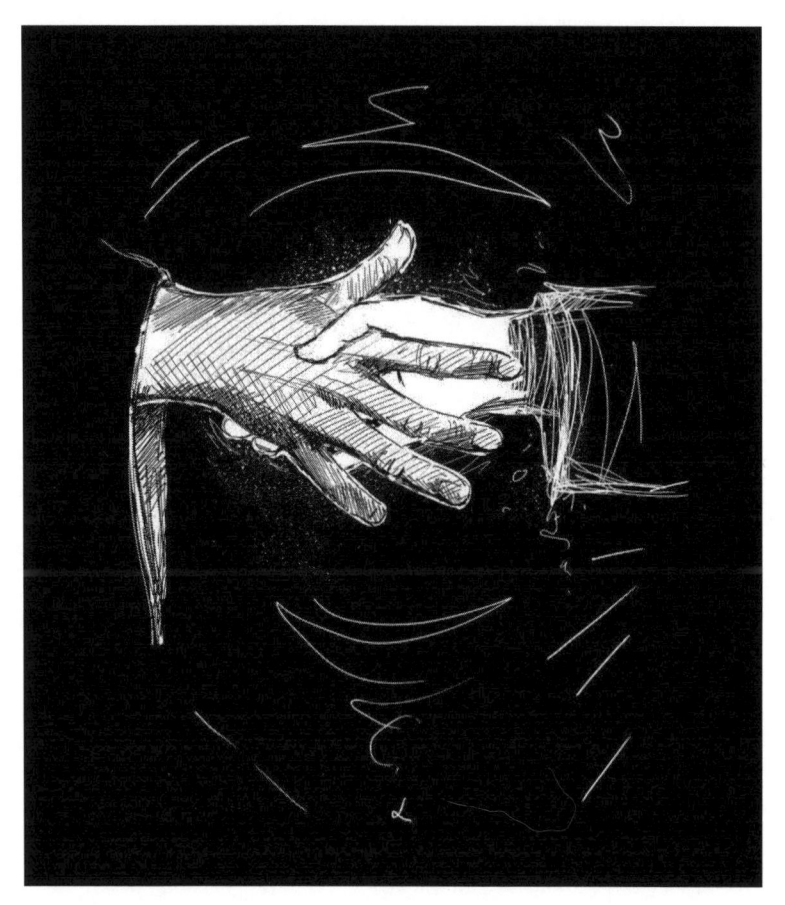

Theo frowned, thinking back to Draven telling him on that rooftop how touching people wouldn't be an issue in his world as it once had been in Theo's.

But looking at Takeshi's reaction to his handshake and well now...

He wasn't so sure.

26
The Warning

The lesson continued but Theo's mind was elsewhere the moment he saw Takeshi excuse himself just after shaking his hand. It could have just been a coincidence and Theo was being paranoid. But it hadn't just been about the look from Takeshi, it had also been the look Zagan had given them...*as though he knew something too.*

Theo wasn't stupid. He knew that look, having spent a teen's lifetime receiving it. It was the look of uncertainty and for these guys who, let's face it, were the ones who were supposed to know everything about this type of thing, then that was far scarier than Theo wanted to fully admit. Which was why that night, when lessons were all done, he couldn't shake the feeling that something big was coming...something that would happened *to him*. And because of it, for the first time in his life, he wanted to talk to someone about it.

"Come in! Unless you're a chick, then you can pay a toll with Tootsie Rolls and Jolly Ranchers," Zane replied after Theo knocked on his door.

"Dude, seriously, do you ever stop eating?" Theo said on a laugh, thinking about an hour ago, when they had eaten dinner. They had thought that as with breakfast and the meal the night before they would have their meals brought to their common room but oh no, that privilege was over for what was named 'Class days'.

So, instead of comfortable eating in front of the TV, or in Zane's case, not having to watch his manners, like trying to burb all the villains in Batman, they had to eat dinner in the main dining room. At first, walking in there had felt strange for the teens, as if they didn't belong. And it didn't help with feeling this way the second they saw all their teachers sat there waiting for them.

Of course, it wasn't surprising that Theo was the first one in the room and was literally pushed to the front of the others, as though he had been appointed their spokesman for the group. However, all awkwardness seeped away as soon as their headmaster stood up and welcomed them.

"Please come and join us. Zagan tells me you all did exceedingly well in your first defence weapons class, which means you must all be hungry." None of them knew what to say after this so instead they all nodded and sat down at the obvious space that was waiting for them.

Once they were settled Draven clapped his hands once, signalling that food should be brought out for everyone. Theo couldn't have said what was on the teachers' plates but whatever it was it looked fancy and not exactly something that Theo would have classed as 'Teen friendly'. For starters, he knew that it had way too much green stuff on it for his liking, let alone Zane's, who

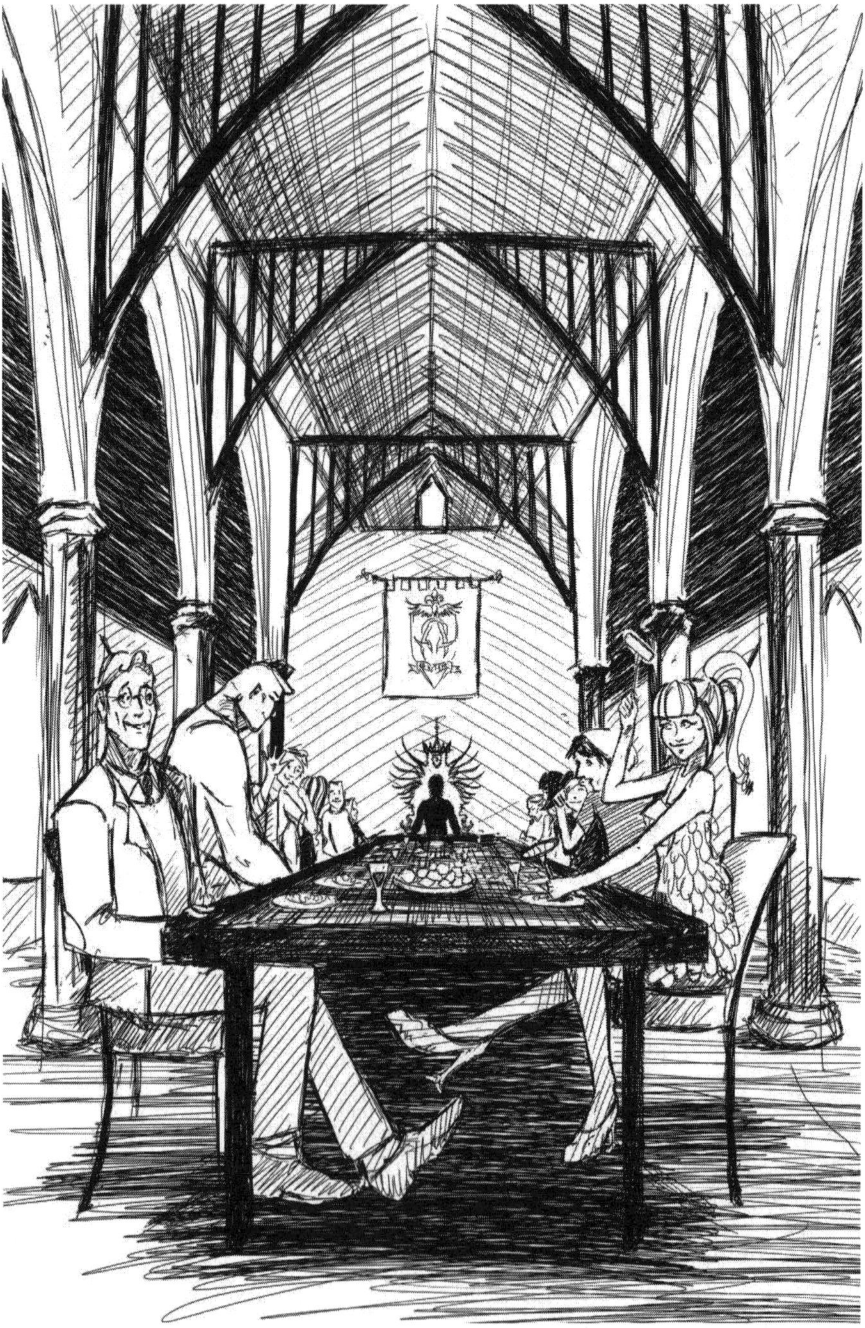

had openly declared the night before about the 'No green rule', stating clearly,

"If its green, then it ain't James Dean." Theo, along with everyone else, had needed some clarity on this but Zane only offered one word,

"Cool".

"You're so weird," Ena had said, shaking her head, whilst Janie had admitted,

"I don't get it." But in true Janie fashion, ten minutes later she finally said,

"Oh, now I get it, James Dean is cool and green veg isn't." Theo had smiled down at his plate, when Zane had ruffled her hair, saying,

"If you weren't so cute I would say something right now to take the piss but nope, one look at that wide-eyed kitten look and I just can't do it!"

"Oi, what about me, you take the piss out of me all the time!" Ena said frowning but Zane just laughed once and said quite openly,

"Yeah but you're cute after I do it, so it's just the price you have to pay...besides, you love it, Streaks." Theo looked up to gauge her reaction, wondering which it would be this time, freely expressed outrage or a hidden smile followed by a lame comeback.

"You're a dork," she said quickly biting her lip after. This was something Theo knew she did to try and stop herself from smiling openly, the blush however, was new.

After that their dinner continued and thankfully there wasn't a green piece of food in sight. And Zane's eyes lit up when platter after platter was brought out, full of burgers, hotdogs, fries, subs, burritos, and golden, crispy fried chicken…so basically Zane's version of food heaven.

"Seriously, how are you so skinny?" Ena asked after Zane devoured his fourth piece of chicken, two hotdogs, two pints of soda, half a meatball sub and she lost count of how many handfuls of fries. She was half tempted to ask if he would have eaten the 'partridge in the pear tree' if there had been one.

"It's all about the brain power Streaks, burns a lot of calories being at this level of genius." Once more her only response to this was an eye roll and a muttered 'geek' under her breath, but Theo knew that inside she was laughing. He didn't know how he knew this, as Zane most certainly didn't, but he could just tell that Ena had a soft spot for her bantering friend. Now just how much of a soft spot that was he didn't know but for Zane's sake, he hoped it was one that ran deep, as he thought they would have made a good couple. She would certainly keep him on his toes that was for damn sure. And besides, it certainly hadn't taken her long to forgive him for assuming she could speak Japanese anyway.

The rest of the meal hadn't been as bad as the teens first thought as everyone seemed pleasant and laidback with one another. At his old school, watching the teachers having lunch which each other had looked more like a funeral wake than a bunch of co-workers eating together.

But these guys seemed more like one big family and Theo had to wonder just how many years had been spent working together. It was obvious this was their first teaching gig. Not saying they weren't any good at it but having an epic duel, with

flaming weaponry and one of them turning into a terrifying demon just to make a point, wasn't exactly what you would call typical first day material. But who knows, maybe that was their idea of easing them in...well the demonic disco dancing had certainly worked.

However, there were two things about the dinner that Theo couldn't help but feel was odd and it was clearly who was missing in the room. There were two empty chairs either side their headmaster who was sat at the very top of the long table on his own. Theo couldn't help but wonder who usually filled these seats. And from the way Draven kept glancing sideways, he could only guess that they were meant for someone important to him. In fact, Theo could easily recognise when someone was trying to hide their disappointment. Then it suddenly hit him, who else was missing from the room, which just added another reason why he had knocked on Zane's door later that night...

Takeshi was missing.

The second the thought had entered Theo's mind Draven looked up at him from down the end of the table, where Theo was sat opposite. There might have been a massive space between them but Theo couldn't miss the slight shake of his head, as if telling him not to go there. Which begged another question...

Could they read their thoughts?

Theo didn't know what came over him but once the meal was all done, it was as if he needed some answers. He didn't know why but ever since seeing that damn book, all that he couldn't think about were his doubts about the place. He didn't want to think this way and even felt guilty when doing so. Especially after all the trouble people had gone to in trying to make them feel welcome.

He thought about the added personal touches Pip had gone to with their rooms. He thought about how important it had been to Sophia that they not find her terrifying. To the point of making a disco dancing fool of herself in hopes of alleviating that fear.

And then there was the way Zagan had taken Janie to one side and spent some time working one on one with her, giving her the confidence she needed when being faced with handling the weapons.

Theo looked back up to Draven and thought of how he had dealt with things when Carrick had made his demands. He'd never had anyone have his back before, not the way Draven had done. Knowing deep down that if Draven could have taken the blood oath himself, then he would have. So, why now was it that he was having doubts about being here and why was he having doubts about them?

Deep down Theo knew why and it was for that reason that when the meal had ended he lingered behind, waiting to ask the question that was almost bursting out of him. At first, he had wondered who the best person to approach would be but then it was obvious when a flash of colour caught his eye…Pip.

She was wearing what looked like a dress made up of hundreds of deflated balloons in every colour imaginable! Theo could only imagine what it sounded like every time she sat down, as he couldn't get the image of a giant whoopie cushion out of his mind. The top part of the dress however looked like a giant pair of red lips with white fangs hanging down and piercing through the under layer of rubber balloons. He couldn't have imagined why, but to this she decided to add knee high socks covered in little cartoon avocados talking to one another about the weather and dinosaur feet high heels. These matched the little open mouthed t-rexes she had attached to her ear lobes, making it look as if they were taking a chunk out of her.

"Uh Pip?" Theo said her name and tapped her on the shoulder quickly, not really feeling comfortable touching anyone again after Takeshi's reaction. She jumped around, put her hands together in what looked like a prayer and said in a Japanese accent,

"Ah, master Theo, 'of flowers, the cherry blossom, of men, the warrior.' or 'Hana wa sakuragi, hito wa bushi', depending who you're speaking to...you don't speak Japanese do you?" Pip asked as an afterthought.

"Uh, no," Theo said with a half grin, surprised that someone as scatty as Pip could.

"So, the first one then," Pip said winking a painted eye that made her look like a doll. She had drawn long cartoon lashes on with black eyeliner and on the other eye, little black cat ears and a tail peeking over her eyelid.

"What does it mean?" he asked, knowing that it would have bugged him all night if he hadn't.

"It means as the cherry blossom is considered foremost among flowers, so the warrior is foremost among men…I was basically calling you a warrior, not a flower…just in case you were confused, were you confused…? I only ask because you looked confused," Pip said, speaking at her usual pace of a hundred and one miles per hour.

"I get it," Theo said smirking and Pip nudged him and added,

"I knew you were a smart and fizzy soda pop. I told her, I said that one is…" This was the point where she stopped suddenly and slapped her hands to her mouth but the damage had already been done. And Theo hadn't missed it.

"Who? Who did you tell about me?" Theo asked as she started to turn away, shaking her head and murmuring over and over, "No, no, no…I didn't say it, can't get mad, I didn't say it." Theo could see that she was heading towards her husband but he had to find out who she had been talking about before she got there.

"Please, just tell me…just…" he caught up with her and touched her shoulder this time not being so cautious. She stopped but kept her back to him. She didn't look at him but instead kept her eyes on the floor as if what she was thinking caused her pain. Theo could only think of one reason why she would feel this way, so he went out on a limb and asked,

"Is it someone beneath…is it someone in the lower levels?" Pip's head shot up, she turned to look at him over her shoulder. Then Theo's blood ran cold when her green eyes flashed crimson and her pupils slit for a second like a wild cat thirsty for flesh. Theo quickly pulled back, letting go of her shoulder and her eyes turned back to their original forest green colour.

She shook herself as if trying to come out of a daze, frowning as if she too didn't understand what just happened. Theo backed up further and turned around ready to walk away but stopped when she called his name.

"Theo..."

"Yeah?" he answered frowning, knowing from just one look that the next thing out her mouth wouldn't be something he would want to hear...and he was right. "Never go down to the lower levels..." she warned and Theo shuddered feeling the hairs on his neck stand on end when she finally finished her sentence...

"...You won't like what you will find."

27
Voices

After this, Theo almost ran out of the room. What was supposed to alleviate his doubts had only ended up doubling them. And now that warning about the lower levels had not only got him thinking about what was down there, but about actually being stupid enough to find out himself.

He just couldn't seem to shake this crazy feeling that he was needed down there. Which in itself was unnerving. Because if this turned out to be true then it could only mean one thing...Afterlife wasn't the safe haven he and the others thought it was.

He continued to think about the possibilities of what he may find down there, when he first realised that he was lost. He looked one way and then the other trying to see if he recognised anything in the long hallway, but there was nothing. There was a massive pair of double doors at one end and a single door at the other just before the corridor curved around in a dogleg. He decided that those double doors looked way too intimidating for there not to be something important behind them. So, he decided it best to stay clear of them and go the other way.

He started walking in the opposite direction, towards the single door at the other end but then stopped dead when he heard an angry woman's voice. He didn't recognise who it belonged to, never having heard it before but whoever they were, they didn't sound happy about something. He slowly crept closer to the single door, all the while looking back, making sure the coast was clear.

"You can't just keep me here forever, locked away like some princess stuck in a tower!" The voice demanded and Theo had to wonder why this girl was obviously being held against her will.

There came a murmured reply, one Theo couldn't make out but whatever it was, the girl certainly didn't agree with it.

"Oh no! Don't start that again! I am not a child and I wish you would stop treating me like one!" she said louder this time and Theo could tell that things were certainly heating up. Yet again he couldn't hear the reply but whatever it had been, it hadn't worked in trying to calm her down, in fact, it just had the opposite effect.

"I don't care what you say! I am leaving and you can't stop me this time!" He saw the door handle start to move and he was ready to jump out of sight, around the corner. But then came a loud thud from behind the door and the handle suddenly snapped back upright. Theo was startled, as he wasn't expecting it and wondered if the girl was alright. As now all there was, was an eerie silence.

Just as Theo was struggling with his inner self whether to get involved or not, there came an almighty high-pitched scream in frustration and then an angry demand,

"LEAVE ME ALONE!" The sound of glass shattering quickly followed, along with the sound of someone sobbing.

"I think you might be lost." A cool calm voice spoke behind him and acting on instinct, he spun around and hit out, quickly finding his fist caught in someone else's strong grasp.

"Who are you?!" Theo demanded, wrenching his hand free and finding himself staring into a pair of crystal blue eyes. Eyes that belonged to someone who could have only been an Angel.

The tall man had a halo of golden curls, pushed back in an attempt to tame them. But Theo couldn't manage to stray far from that gaze. His eyes were incredible, like looking into a pair of topaz stones, and seeing a light shining through from the other side. Theo didn't know how he knew but he could tell that this person was letting his power be known and it felt intense.

"I am Vincent and you must be Theo," he said surprising him.

"Why does everyone keep saying that, was there like a news bulletin with my picture on it in the Supernatural Weekly or something?" Vincent laughed and whether it was intended or not, it instantly put Theo at ease.

"I wasn't eavesdropping," Theo said after Vincent looked to the door with a frown.

"No?" he questioned, as though he didn't believe Theo.

"I got lost and heard shouting, so I stayed because I was concerned," Theo said, folding his arms and showing this Vincent with his body language how he didn't like anyone questioning his good intentions. Vincent laughed once and patted him on the back, saying,

"Relax kid, I know how easy it is to get lost in these halls. Besides, you're not the only one with thoughts of concern," Vincent said, looking back to the closed door once more as if trying to listen out for signs of further distress but it was silent.

"Run along now Theo, the others are wondering where you are and you don't want them getting lost too when they come looking for you." Theo looked over his shoulder to see that the hallway continued past the door around a small bend and then looked back to Vincent. This time he couldn't help but ask the same question again, only doing so in a more forceful tone, letting him know the depth of what he was really asking.

"Who are you?"

"My name is..." Vincent started to say but Theo cut him off.

"I know your name." Vincent grinned knowing what he meant and also that what he had heard about the kid was proving true. Theo had a relentless nature but at least had the bravery to back it up. Enough to turn it into his advantage at least. But it was also his heroic nature that had Vincent more intrigued and knowing that without a doubt, it was something he would definitely need in his future here. So, knowing this, Vincent gave him what he wanted...answers.

"As I was saying, my name is Vincent..." Theo rolled his eyes and Vincent nearly laughed but instead he opened up the door he really didn't want to walk through and finished his sentence before closing it again,

"...Vincent Draven..." He paused, waiting for the penny to drop before adding the obvious,

"Dominic Draven's brother."

28
Eyes He Knew

"So, what you working on?" Theo asked after making that crack about Zane always eating and closing the door to his room.

"This baby right here is a Wacom Cintiq 22HD touch screen with interactive pen display," Zane informed him shaking a little digital stylus before going back to what he was drawing on screen.

"Cool," Theo said, this being the only possible response given that he had no clue what Zane was talking about.

Theo had gotten back to the room and found Vincent had been right, they were all getting ready to come to look for him. They had wanted to know why it had taken him so long, so he made up some lame excuse. Of course, Ena had wanted to know the ins and outs of it, being the nosiest one of the group and all. She finally got off his back when she found out it was nothing more interesting than asking Pip if there was ever going to be any tests. Of course, this then meant he had to lie about the answer, saying he gave up waiting in the end as they were all busy having a big discussion about something he didn't understand.

He hated lying as it wasn't one of his strong points, but thankfully he had come up with this excuse on the way back to the common room, so he'd had time to think about his answers.

"So, what's up?" Zane asked getting right to the point. Theo scanned the room and admired the city loft vibe that it had going on. There was the obvious art studio thing that commanded half of the space, which Theo gathered Zane preferred to be the case. But it was the relaxing side of the room that Theo liked. It was the rustic oak used to make his low bed frame and the half iron girders that came out of the wall to create a staircase to the small space above. Theo looked up to see a comfortable reading nook there, filled with large floor cushions and a book shelf integrated into the same framework used for the bed.

"Awesome bed covers," Theo said, never thinking he would be complimenting anyone on such a thing, but faced with a bedspread that cool, he couldn't help but mention it. Zane finished what he was doing and turned to face him, replying,

"Yeah, when I finally stopped freakin' out over my art studio, I finally looked at the rest of the room and nearly wept like a baby. Does beg the question exactly how many years Pip was stalking us for, though doesn't it?" Theo nodded looking once again to the vintage looking Godzilla poster that had been made into a cover for Zane's massive bed. Theo especially liked the title 'The Titans of Terror' that was written above the picture of Godzilla fighting other monsters.

"That was the one where Godzilla fights Mothra and Ghidorah…it's a great monster movie."

"No doubt, knowing stalker Pip, it's in our collection," Theo said in reply.

"Already clocked it and written it in for monster movie night on Thursdays." Theo smirked, remembering when Zane claimed the day and was the first one to write it down on their common room memo board that had the words 'Time is precious, so waste it wisely' written above.

"So, what's really going on? Because as nice as it is to show off my awesome room and chat about monster movies, it's not really why you're here is it?" At this Theo let out a deep sigh and slumped down on the bed, covering his face with his hands in frustration.

"What is it?" Zane asked, this time with more concern in his voice.

"I don't know…no, that's not true, I do know, but I am not sure."

"Sure about what…*this place?*"Zane said, his guess being an afterthought.

"Yes, no…maybe, I don't know but something just feels off to me." Theo admitted, hating that he might be casting that same doubt onto another.

"Okay, so I know the place is…well, let's face it, it's no Hogwarts, but come on, what exactly do you think they are hiding here?"

"Oh, I don't know, people locked up in the basement," Theo said before thinking about it and Zane didn't take it as a joke like Theo had half hoped. His eyes widened in shock momentarily but then looked side on as though he was now thinking about the possibility of such a thing. Theo wished he hadn't said anything and slapped his hands to his knees before getting up.

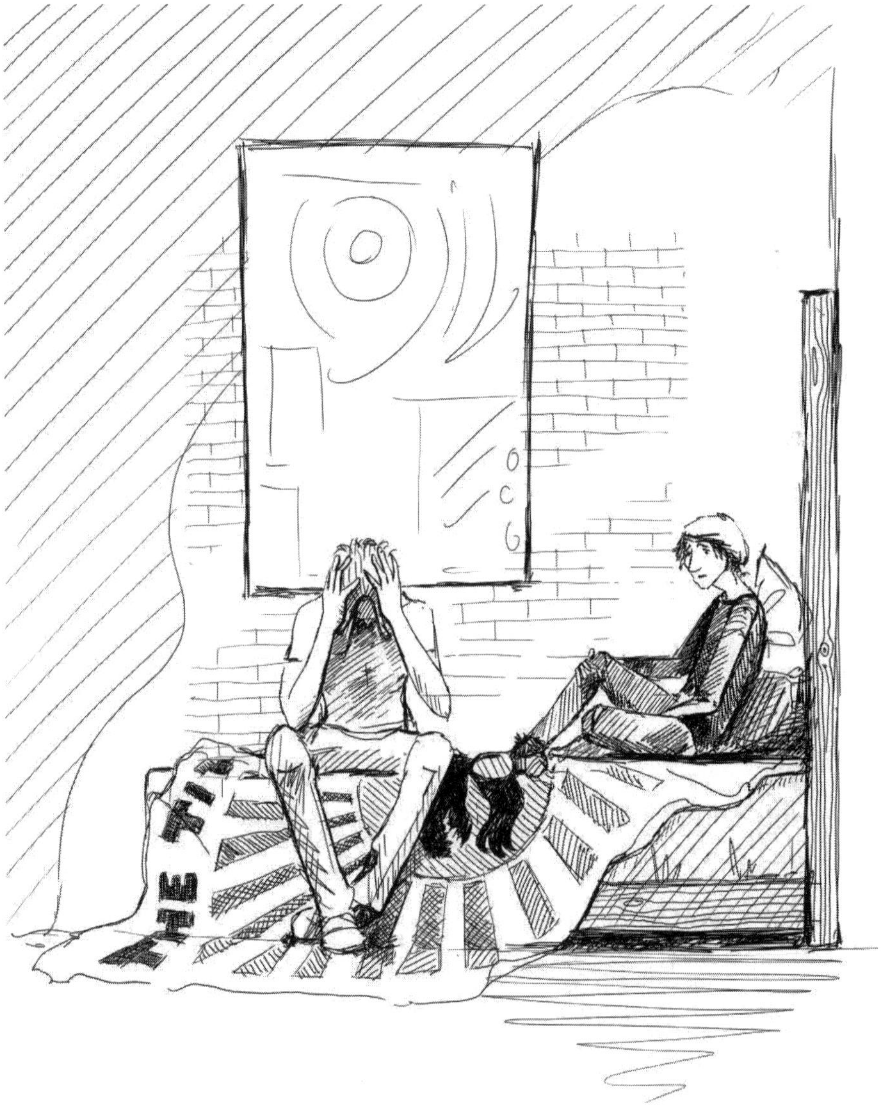
THE

"Look, forget I said anything. I'm just being paranoid and clearly having trust issues or something." Zane granted him a sceptical look, one that clearly said, 'Yeah right'.

"Look, don't let my comedic genius fool you, I'm actually quite perceptive and even if I wasn't, it's not hard to know something happened the other night that's got you all woggie."

"Woggie?" Theo raised an eyebrow.

"Freaked, spooked, weirded out, in a funk... Look whatever you wanna call it alright... all I am saying is you were as psyched as we were when first seeing this place and now, well now you kind of look like..."

"Like?" Theo asked when he paused.

"Like you're about to do something stupid and you came in here so that I would subtly talk you out of it." Okay, so it was true, he was observant, Theo thought dryly.

"Dude seriously, I am gonna start thinking you're actually like a Jedi or something," Theo joked making Zane smirk, before leaning back against the wall and saying,

"Flattery will usually get you everywhere but you're not a chick, so nice try." Theo laughed once and decided to just go for it as Zane was obviously not going to let this lie.

"Fine but it's gonna sound crazy." This time it was Zane's turn to laugh.

"Dude, are you being serious right now? A few days ago we all stepped on the bus from Hell driven by a blind chick, met Mr Death himself...who just so happened to pop by and KILL US..."

he said raising his voice at this part for dramatic effect before carrying on his valid point,

"...then snap, we are here and being told we have been reincarnated into kick ass Demons or Angels and are being trained to protect the world, like some supernatural super soldiers..." He paused a second and then counted down the facts with his fingers,

"...Whose first lesson, I might add, consisted of a disco dancing demon and some demonic, shaolin monk style fighting by an albino Legolas lookalike, who we also had to explain to who the freakin' Teenage Mutant Ninja Turtles were! Seriously, you think you got shit any weirder than that, then be my guest and amaze me."

"Okay, so you might have a point there," Theo admitted, amazed that Zane had said all that and didn't even sound out of breath.

"Ya think?" Zane replied sarcastically.

After this Theo decided to take a chance and do something he never did, which was confide in someone. So, Theo told him all that had happened. He told him about the book and the warning it bled out. He told him about Takeshi's look after shaking his hand. He also mentioned what happened earlier that night, when getting lost. Hearing the girl crying and meeting Draven's brother and also what Pip had said to him, warning him against going down to the lower levels.

After he was done he looked to Zane to judge his reaction and finally after a few minutes Zane said,

"Okay, so my rant seems tame compared to the creepy shit that's happened to you since we've been here...and I am not even gonna mention a certain 'blood bound' incident we are all trying to forget."

"Dude, you just did." Zane ignored Theo's comment, passing it off with just a shrug of his shoulders and then asked,

"So, when are we going down there?" Theo laughed in response but then saw that his expression was serious.

"What...you're joking right?"

"Oh, come on, what are they gonna do, kill us...*again.*" Theo rolled his eyes and said,

"I thought you said that I came in here for you to talk me out of doing something stupid."

"Yeah, but I didn't say you made the right choice," Zane said, slapping him on the shoulder and winking at him. So, what was supposed to be Zane talking Theo out of doing something crazy, ended up with roles reversed. Which meant he didn't walk out of Zane's door until he was sure that his friend wasn't going to follow him down the road of insanity. So, to accomplish this, he did the only thing he could think to do...

He lied...*again.*

He left letting Zane believe he had changed his mind and hoping that his friend wouldn't be stupid enough to think about going down there by himself. And until he reached his own room he believed that he would be doing the same.

Of course, *he was wrong.*

Theo was back in his room and his eyes automatically went to where the book had been but there was nothing there. So, with this in mind, he decided the best thing for him to do was to relax in front of his TV and fall asleep. He went into the bathroom and completed his nightly routine, which mainly consisted of using the toilet and brushing his teeth, but this time, he added a quick shower to the short list. He had already had one today, as they'd all done after being dismissed from their last lesson with Zagan.

He had worked them hard and they hadn't realised it until they looked at the time but they had been in with him for three hours, so no wonder he was feeling it. But this time, he wasn't showering to get clean or to feel the relaxing heat ease his strained muscles. No, this time it was to sooth his soul.

He let his head fall under the blast of cascading water and closed his eyes, letting the cool liquid wash away his mental torment. He knew what he *wanted* to do and he knew what he *should* do but neither of these two were the same. There was something down there, he just knew it and he wanted to find out what. But he also knew that he should just leave it and speak to the one man who could grant him answers...

Dominic Draven.

But through that option brought forward the fear of lies for Theo. For now, he trusted Draven and he wanted to keep it that way. But something told him deep down in the pit of his stomach that if he went to him with this, then that trust would be shattered in a second. Because he knew that Draven was the type of man that if he felt it necessary, he would lie and had many times in the past, even to those he cared for deeply.

Theo didn't know how he knew these things, he just did.

He ran a frustrated hand through his wet hair, smoothing it all back before pushing off the wall in anger. He hated not knowing what to do and wished he had a sign, anything to tell him what he wanted to hear.

He got out of the shower, grabbing a towel off the rack to wrap around himself before walking back into his room. He grabbed a clean pair of underwear and a comfortable pair of flannel pyjama bottoms to put on. Then he sank back into the giant denim hand chair and grabbed the used towel off the floor and reused it to dry some of his floppy hair, that pretty much fell where it wanted and stayed there.

He grabbed the remote off the cool side table that was an old vintage amp, which had one side replaced by glass so you could see all the workings inside. Pointing it at the TV he pressed the button and went back to drying his hair. But the lack of sound filling his room made him frown under the towel. He lifted it up over his face and continued to rub the back of his head with it, catching the droplets falling down his neck. But none of that concerned him as he just went through the motions. However, what did concern him was the snowy static on the screen that seemed to be on every channel he clicked through.

His logical brain told him that it just hadn't been programmed in yet, but then that same logical train of thought quickly led him to this being an unlikely reason. After all, you don't go to such lengths as picking out people's favourite music, movies and even colour schemes, to then kitting out rooms with the latest tech, without setting it up as well. And besides, this was only a flat screen we were talking about, it should have just been a plug and play type of deal.

Which begged the question, why was he now faced with hundreds of channels that all showed the same grainy black and white fuzz that occasionally had a white line running through it.

"Great...just great! All I wanted was five minutes of normality that can only be found in trash TV," Theo said speaking aloud and letting his head fall back with exasperation. He didn't know what happened next but he must have fallen asleep this way, because the next thing he knew a buzzing sound was waking him up.

"Oh, what now?" Theo asked rubbing his eyes in annoyance and trying to focus on where that noise was coming from. He first looked around the room after seeing briefly that the TV still showed nothing but static. His first thought was the book and he looked to the window half expecting to find another message written there waiting for him. Theo let out a sigh of relief when finding nothing there, but this turned out to be premature when a flickering on the TV caught his attention.

It looked as if it was trying to find a signal of some kind as grainy shapes started to emerge. Theo lent forward trying to make out what it was, when an image started to zigzag across the screen in white lines. The image was a haunting one, as the second it snapped into place it looked like surveillance footage of some medieval prison.

There was a long stone corridor with heavy iron cell doors running along each wall. But it was the door at the very end that held Theo's attention and his mind quickly snapped back to another door at the end of a hallway. One he had seen only hours before. The two images in his mind started to merge into one until the one on the screen in front of him won the battle.

The screen started to flicker as it had done in the beginning, but this time when it snapped back into place it showed the door even closer. It continued to do this, crackling in and out from the picture to static, only to once more re-emerge closer and closer to the door. Theo was transfixed waiting to see what it wanted to show him. His breathing became laboured and beads of sweat gathered on his forehead before dripping down the sides of his face.

"What...what is it you want me to see?" he demanded, getting angry with the creepy dramatics, when all he wanted it to do was get to the point. But it continued to play out, over and over with the same sequence until Theo knew the last time was coming. The image was so close to the door now, there was only one image left...

Theo watched with breath held firmly in his lungs, not letting it go again until he saw the horror he knew was coming. Slowly at first, small fingers started to reach up through the bars as one hand was trying to take hold. The second those fingers

355

found metal and curled around the iron, Theo gasped as a desperate face quickly followed. They slammed their face against the small opening and Theo couldn't believe his eyes as he recognised the face behind the veil of terror…

"No…it can't be…it…" he started to murmur his denial but nothing could hide the truth, nothing could hide those eyes.

Eyes he knew belonged to…

"Janie."

29

GOING TO NEED FAITH

Theo didn't think, he just ran. He ran out of his room and found himself in front of Janie's door in seconds. He had to know. He had to find out. So, he knocked on the door, never in his life praying for something so much. Not since he was seven and little Sarah ended up in hospital after his touch.

"Come on, come on," he said knocking again, but trying also not to wake the others. In the end, he couldn't wait for what was most likely her getting out of bed and stumbling around for a robe or something. At least that was what Theo was hoping to see when he opened her door and walked in.

Her room was dark, which at first Theo took as a good sign. The full moon was high in the sky and casting shadows in her room, giving him at least enough light to see. He slowly approached the bed, not wanting to frighten her if she woke to find him there. He squinted his eyes, trying to see if he could make out her form on the bed which would have been hidden by the floaty material that surrounded it.

He frowned when feeling the slight breeze, as though a window was open somewhere. Theo's hand reached out to touch it but the mysterious breeze blew back the material attached to the tall metal bed frame.

"*Janie?*" he whispered as he took that final step closer, but as the material whipped across his face, he pulled it back to reveal her bed was empty and Janie,

Was gone.

He frowned, briefly scanning the room before placing his palm on the mattress to see if it was still warm. A chill ran up his spine the second he realised it had been a while since she had been there as, like his blood, the bed was cold. He let out a growl of frustration, before hitting the switch on the wall letting light flood the room in hopes of giving him answers. And he didn't have to look far.

"No Janie, not you too," he said as that chill turned his body to ice, frozen at the sight of the same message he himself had received. He looked at the destruction on the table in front of the window that held the remains of what looked like an old typewriter. Then he looked up to see cracks in the glass, spelling out the same words of desperation he had also read in his own room.

DEATH AWAITS ME,

IMPRISONED BELOW,

TONIGHT, IT ENDS,

TONIGHT, I DIE.

Theo closed his eyes as the guilt he felt morphed into anger. He was so stupid. How could he have let this happen? He knew something had happened to Janie, even asking himself if it had been the same that he had experienced. Then why not ask her? Why not push her on the matter? He should have been honest with the others, maybe that way, she too would have opened up or confided in him. Then he could have convinced her to leave it be or at least leave it up to him to take action. But now what? Where was Janie now?

He asked himself these things with clenched fists, wanting to scream out her name in hopes that she would answer. But once more the moon answered his silent questions and cast shadows along the floor. Theo frowned, wondering if he was seeing it right, as it almost looked as though elongated words were stretching out, trying to tell him the answer. He stepped back, once, twice, three times until he was far enough away to read what the shadows were telling him, as the missing piece of the sentence started to take shape,

TONIGHT,

YOU WILL

SAVE ME OR...

SHE DIES.

Theo ran out of the door as though someone had lit him on fire. It had been confirmed. Janie had taken it upon herself to go down to the lower levels and become someone's saviour. Theo's next actions took him back into his room, where he grabbed a pair of jeans and a t shirt, dragging them over his body in a hurry. It was as if he was on autopilot, going through the motions and not even thinking about what he would do once he got down there.

To start with he didn't even know how to get to the lower levels, let alone know where to find Janie once he was there. For all he knew it could be like a bloody labyrinth in Hell down there!

Once dressed he rammed his feet into some high top, red and white converse shoes and ran out the door. He only paused for a second outside Zane's door, battling with himself on whether or not to knock. Eventually he thought of the dangers that he could possibly face and he knew he would never have forgiven himself if he was the reason any of them got hurt. So instead of shouting for them all to wake up, as he selfishly wanted to, he didn't.

He was blaming himself already for not talking to Janie when he had the chance. Maybe if he had, then she would be sleeping in her bed now, where she belonged. He shook his head, letting his anger fuel his need to get to her quicker, but looking at all the doors he passed he started to doubt he would even get there.

"Which way?" Theo said to no one...or so he thought.

"That all depends on where you are trying to get to?" A girl said behind him and he turned to see a beautiful girl about his age, stood with her arms crossed. She had long, wavy, raven black hair and a pair of startling blue eyes. Theo had to mentally shake himself out of being dumbstruck by a stunning pair of eyes, a colour he could only imagine was close to a tropical blue shade. Ones that were currently framed by a pair of thick black rimmed glasses.

She also had soft, cute features that, at that moment, Theo thought were contradictory to her frown and body language. She pushed her glasses up her nose once, twice before clearing her throat and saying,

"Well?" Theo didn't know whether or not to tell her the truth, but when she groaned and said,

"Look, I don't really care either way, as I have my own problems to deal with." Then she turned around and started walking in the other direction towards a row of arched windows that looked out onto a balcony with steps going above and below.

"Hey wait!" Theo shouted after her, which was when she snapped her head back to him and hissed a warning,

"Ssshh or they will hear you!" Then she looked all around her as if expecting to see someone watching them, only relaxing when she found the hallway empty.

"Who will?" he asked and she rolled her eyes once.

"Oh, I don't know, the same people you don't want to find out you're sneaking around here at two in the morning," she replied sarcastically, making her point.

"Alright, so you got me there," he admitted, making her smile momentarily and he had to admit, it suited her far better than the fake attitude that looked out of place.

"I'm Theo, one of the…"

"I know who you are…everyone does," she said, cutting him off and adding this last part as though she was being made to swallow a bitter pill. Theo decided to ignore the last comment as he was too interested in who she was to argue.

"And you are?" Theo asked and she looked out of the window for a moment before answering him.

"In the wrong place and with the wrong people," she said cryptically and that's when it all clicked into place for Theo.

"You're the girl I heard shouting earlier, aren't you?" Her head snapped round to look at him and her red cheeks weren't hard to miss, even in the low candlelight, thanks to lit torches on the wall.

"You heard that?!" she hissed horrified. Theo put his hands out in a symbolic gesture of peace and justified himself.

"I was walking back from the dining room and got lost, I heard someone shouting and…"

"Yeah, yeah, I get the idea," she said, obviously too embarrassed to hear more.

"I was angry," she said, this time being the one to justify herself.

"And now?" Theo asked, seeing that she had opened the window, and it didn't take a genius to guess what she was planning.

"This isn't anger, this is clarity." Theo could understand that, having found it quite a few times before himself.

"Fair enough. Look its none of my business I know, but I need to ask you this for my own peace of mind…do you need my help?" Theo asked, knowing that time was of the essence, so if this girl said yes, then he would help her but convince her to do whatever she was planning at a later time. She looked thoughtful for a moment and a small smile played with the corners of her mouth, as if she knew a secret that he didn't. However, she didn't say what but instead said,

"Thank you, Theo but I will be fine. I know this place better than most people."

"You do?" he asked, surprised by her answer, but even more by her next reply.

"I grew up here." She laughed once when she saw his shocked expression. Yes, she supposed it would be a hard thought to grasp, considering she was roughly the same age as the teens but had still not joined them. Not through lack of trying, she might add. But oh no, there was always some lame excuse in her world… 'the stars are yet to align', 'the fates have not yet decided', 'the Gods have yet to cast judgement on such things'…yada, yada, yada…Well she was sick of it.

For once she just wanted to act like a normal teenager and actually have friends that weren't old enough to remember things like, 'Oh remember when that dude, JC turned up who could walk on water and rocked the civilised world.' Okay, so mainly that would be Pip saying that but still, was it too much to ask for someone to talk to that had been born in this century? In fact, if she stayed there any longer she would be saying things like 'Thee vexes me' and 'I do declare'.

But Boy Wonder here wouldn't understand she thought bitterly, as not many would, instantly feeling guilty for thinking such things. Especially about someone who was only trying to help her.

"Then maybe you can help me instead. I am looking for a way down into the lower levels." Her eyes widened after Theo said this.

"Why on earth would you want to go down into that vile place?" she asked, shuddering and pulling her oversized, long knitted cardigan around herself in comfort, one that was made from chunky, soft grey wool.

"I have a friend who went down there and could be lost." Theo said, thinking it best to just keep it simple.

"Then you'd better hurry or…" She paused as if what she was going to say next was tactless and insensitive.

"Or what?"

"I am sorry, I shouldn't have…let's just say your friend obviously needs your help more than I do." Hearing this didn't fill Theo with masses of confidence, that was for sure. But then at least she took pity on him enough to tell him the way. She even went one step further and after fishing around in her bag, she wrote down on a piece of paper a few tips for him, telling him not to look at it until he was down there, as only then would it make sense.

"Thanks. So are you gonna tell me your name before you run away," he said and she blushed again.

"That obvious is it?" He nodded to her bag that was almost bursting and said,

"Well, you are packed and about to crawl out of a window...it's not the most conventional way to leave otherwise."

"Look, like I said, its none of my business and I..." he started to say, having pity on her, when she suddenly blurted out her name,

"My name is Faith but my friends call me Fae." Theo smiled and said,

"It's good to meet you, Fae." And before he knew what he was doing he was extending his hand for her to take. He didn't even realise his mistake until she had placed her slender hand in his. But instead of causing her pain and weakness like he was afraid of, she simply shook his hand.

"Warmth." The word whispered past his lips before he could stop it, as he had never felt anything like it before. It was as if her touch had awakened something deep inside him, as if opening up the door to a secret chamber he had unknowingly locked shut. Her smile quickly disappeared and she pulled her hand free.

"I am sorry, I shouldn't have..." She didn't finish but shook her head and looked away, as if suddenly ashamed of herself.

"Hey, it's okay, you didn't do anything wrong," he reassured her, now seeing something in her that he saw in himself...*self-doubt*. But she wasn't listening and instead she pushed open the window and climbed up, using her foot on the stone ledge. She was halfway out and looking down at the balcony when she stopped.

"Theo..." She called his name without looking at him and Theo paused himself.

"Yeah?"

"It's true what they all say, you know..." she said and Theo could hear the smile in her words even if for the moment, he couldn't see it. So, he went on to ask,

"Yeah, and what's that?" She took another moment and this time looked back at him over her shoulder and said something that in that moment he had never needed to hear as much...not where he was going.

She grinned big at him and said,

"You do have a hero's heart."

And then she was gone.

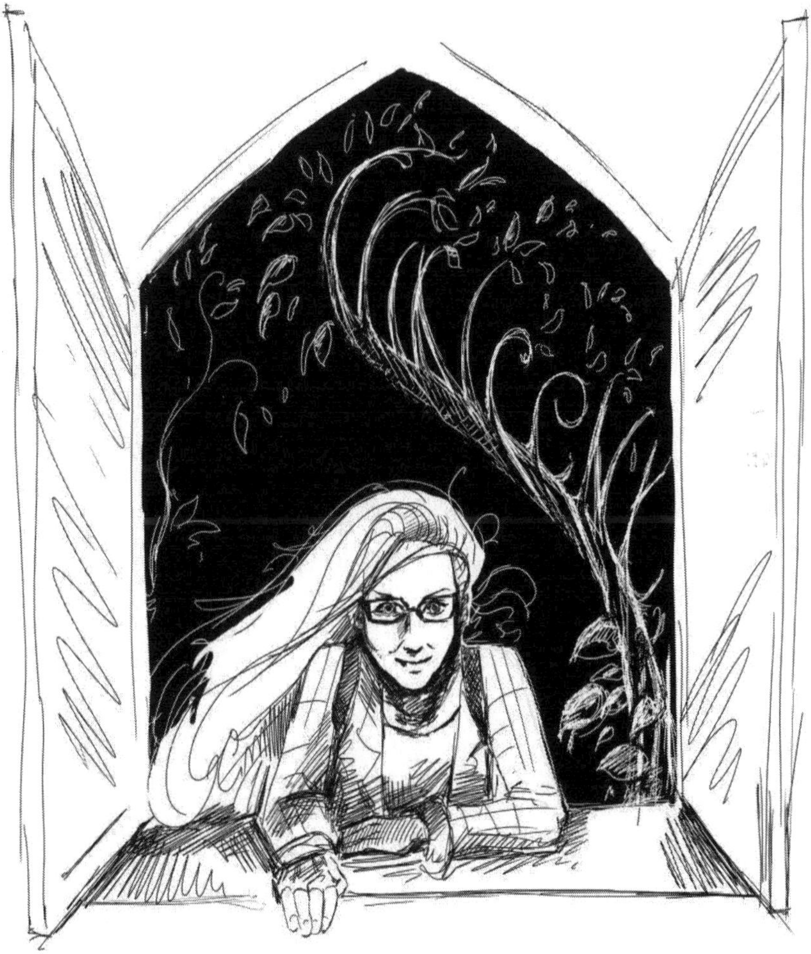

30
THE GLASS DAGGER

Theo followed the route that Fae had told him about and other than making one wrong turn, when he had to back track, he found the main staircase that led him down. And boy did it lead him down he thought, looking over the side of the spiral staircase and not seeing an end.

It reminded Theo of something better suited to a castle and he had to ask himself how long this place had been there, as it seemed centuries older than it could have possibly been. From what he could remember from history class and the basics they had touched on world history, America was only founded on the 4 July 1776, yet this place looked like something from the 13th century!

"We're not seriously going down there, are we?" Theo heard a voice from behind him and nearly jumped out of his skin. He spun around, holding a hand to his heart as though this would help in some way to slow it down.

"Zane, you scared the shit outta me!" he snapped but Zane just raised a sceptical eyebrow and said,

"Yeah well you fed me a load of BS about not coming down here yet came yourself, so I think we are even."

"Point made," Theo said swallowing his guilt.

"So, are we really gonna do this?" Zane asked nodding to the spiral staircase that looked more like a giant stone corkscrew that could have led straight into Hell.

"I guess we are," Theo said before taking the first steps down.

"What do you think is down there?" Zane asked, no doubt trying to concentrate on anything but the creepy descent.

"I'm not sure, but my guess is it's nothing good," Theo replied, trying to not let his head spin at the sight of how far it went down. The height didn't affect him, it never did as he loved to be up high, but this was more dizzying thanks to the continuous circling motion it took to get down there. They seemed to go on forever but at least they could see what they were doing thanks to the full moon shining through the slits for windows, that were positioned at every turn.

"Whoa!" Zane said slipping on a step and saving himself just in time.

"You okay back there?" Theo asked as he too had noticed that the further down they travelled the more damp and slippery the stone steps became.

"Yeah but come on, you would think with all that money they would have at least put in a lift or something." Theo didn't reply but silently had to agree with his friend, asking himself a few times, when would it ever end.

"So, the hot chick with glasses, did she say anything about what could be down here then?" Zane asked making Theo groan.

"Just how long were you following me?"

"Pretty much since I saw you coming out of Janie's door like someone had a gun to your head." Well that had been entirely possible considering his mind had been too focused on finding her than who was watching him.

"And since I knew you weren't going to face danger in tartan flannel trousers and bare feet, I just waited for you to leave your room," Zane confessed and Theo had to admit that he was impressed. He hadn't known anyone was following him, so it had to be said the boy had skills…although for now Theo thought it better to keep that to himself as knowing Zane he would take that as the go ahead to make sneaking around his new hobby.

"Finally," Theo muttered as soon after they reached the last step and came face to face with a door. The door was jammed a little but when they both put their weight behind it, the stubborn wood gave way. They walked through and both took in a deep breath, as it no longer smelt damp. Their eyes also had to adjust to the new, brightly lit room they had just entered and Zane's must have cleared sooner than Theo's as he heard him whistle before he knew what it was about.

"What is this place?" Theo asked aloud, even though he knew Zane wouldn't have the answer to this one.

"I don't know but I am sure of one thing."

"What's that?"

"That if Indiana Jones was a real dude, then he would be peeing his antique man pants right about now." And Theo had to agree with him as the place was a treasure trove of everything from historical artefacts to strange glowing orbs. It looked like a shrine to both the world of the supernatural and its history combined. It was a long, wide room that had holes carved out of the rock walls and each were used to display something of great value. It kind of reminded Theo of walking into some supernatural museum, with everything from exquisite jewels, to half broken pots covered in symbols.

"Wonder what used to be here?" Zane said, nodding to a strange black pool of water that looked as if it once had something sat on top of its now empty plinth that could just be seen under the veil of liquid.

"I don't know but my guess is it wasn't anything you're likely to see in the British Museum on Great Russell St, that's for damn sure." Theo said, thinking of home and the busy streets of London.

"Let's keep going," Zane said, nodding to the door at the other end and Theo agreed. But he was unable to help his wandering eyes from taking in each and every object housed in the carved holes, being utterly fascinated. He had no idea what they were or the significance of each piece, obviously needing the man who owned the collection for that information. One he very much doubted would happily do so when they weren't even supposed to be down there in the first place.

Theo carried on walking…or so he thought.

"Uh…dude, you coming?" Zane asked and Theo didn't know what had happened, but he strangely found himself standing opposite something he had no memory of even walking up to. It was as though his movements were suddenly a blurred reaction of what he thought he was doing.

"I don't think that's a good idea, Theo, it could trip an alarm or…oh okay, so too late," Zane said and once again Theo looked down to see he was now holding something. But when did he move his arm?

"I don't know…" Theo was suddenly cut off when a series of age old images slammed into his memory bank, as if it was being branded there for all eternity. Scenes of the sky clouded with arrows, raining down on an ancient army below. A barbaric King that led that army falling to the ground after taking a spear to his shoulder. And then a heroic beauty with hair as golden as the surrounding sands of time.

She held in her hand a glass spear, plunging it into the chest of a living monster, letting the glass fill with blood before telling it that even a God could die on Earth.

She had been incredible. Like a warrior Goddess fighting against the evils of the world. But it all ended with an eternal scar left upon the earth and Theo was stood at its very core. Black sand started to slowly rise up all around, as though some invisible force was trying to take it away and cleanse the earth of its lasting evil.

Theo began to feel something in his hand and he looked down to see he was holding the glass spear. It was the same one that he had seen embedded in the King's shoulder and the same one that was then plunged into the chest of an unearthly being.

Only now, it had been made into a glass dagger and one filled with the blood of an evil God.

Theo asked himself why. Why him? Why had he been chosen? But as if it could read his thoughts, a voice spoke to him from above the black dust that was still funnelling around him.

"The blood of yours, is now the blood of mine, and the blood of mine, will rise again… *to take it back!*"

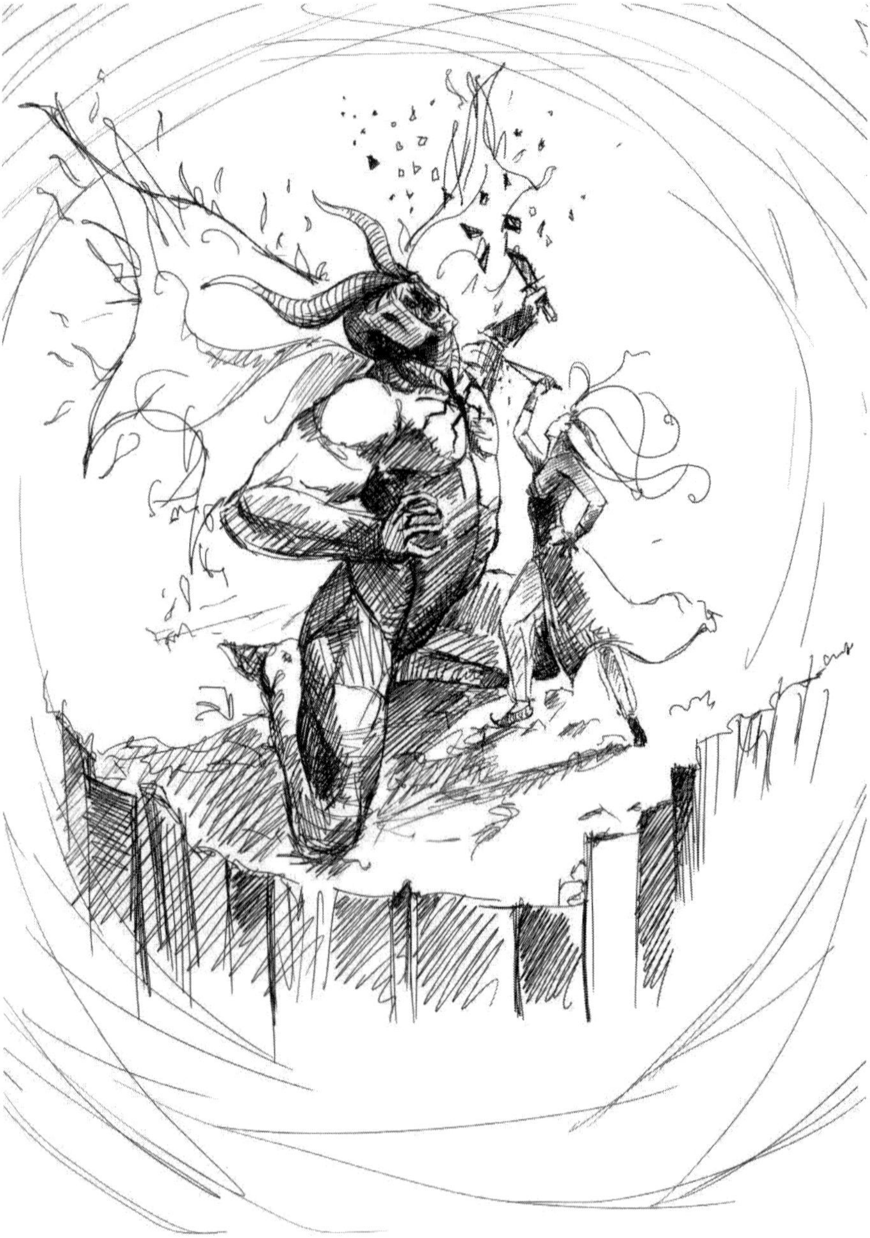

"THEO?!" He heard Zane's voice calling him from a distance but when he looked around he could see nothing but ancient sands of time, once scorched upon the earth, telling him the story of how they came to be. Then came the pain.

Theo screamed out, landing on his knees as he felt the burning in his hand. He looked down at the blade to see the handle had fused itself to his skin so that he couldn't drop it. Its metal spikes cast upon the handle had also twisted round and embedded themselves into his hand, like a locking mechanism, so that he couldn't let go. The glass started to crack, signalling for the ritual to begin. This was when the once blood filled dagger started to drain away, seeping through the cracks and running down the glass onto Theo's hand, as though his inner power was drawing in, sucking it from its once empty vessel, and now into the depths of a living breathing one... *Theo.*

He screamed again, feeling it travelling through his veins like venom burning his cells in its wake. Theo felt as though he was both dying inside and getting stronger with each fill of his lungs. Like two powers were fighting each other for dominance and in the end so as not to destroy each other, they simply merged together, as if good was no longer fighting the bad.

Like Demon no longer fighting Angel.

It felt like...

Like destiny.

31
STONE EYES WATCHING

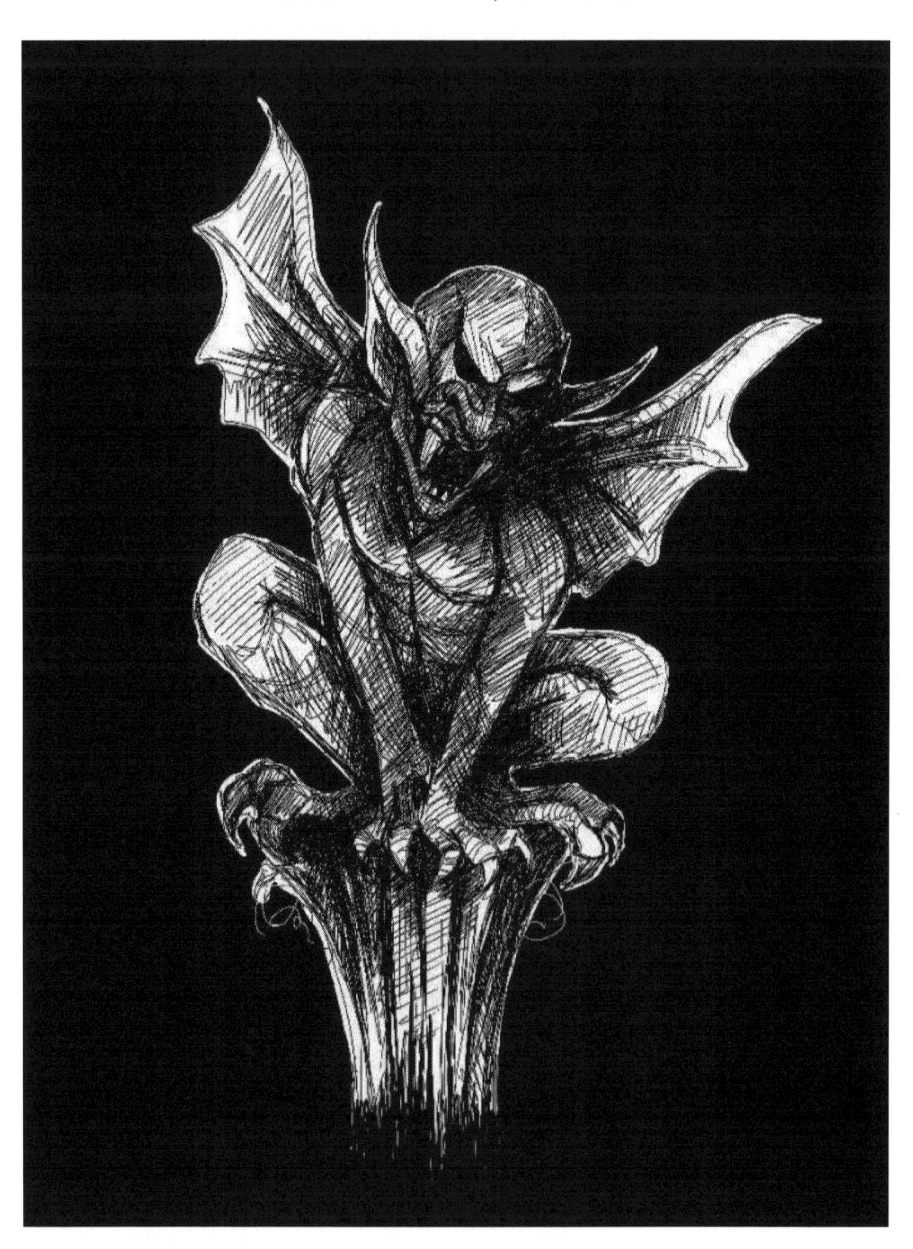

"Theo...Theo?!" Zane shouted his friend's name, as the second he picked up that dagger he knew something was wrong. In fact, the second Theo had moved towards it Zane knew his friend wasn't acting of his own accord. It was as though something was compelling him towards that glass dagger, almost like the blood trapped inside it was speaking to him. Zane knew it sounded crazy but even he himself could feel the power buzzing around it like it was conducting electricity or something.

He had called his name a few times but there had been nothing. It was suddenly as if he wasn't in the room. His body was still there but his mind was locked away in a place Zane couldn't reach.

"Uh Theo man, I think maybe you should put it...whoa, what's happening to all the red stuff?" Zane asked not knowing whether Theo could even hear him. But Zane didn't take it as a good sign when his friend started crying out in pain before dropping to his knees.

"THEO!" Zane shouted his name and ran back to him, shaking his shoulders as if this would help to bring him back. He looked down at the dagger and tried to pull it from him but Zane ended up crying out himself as it burned his skin the second he made contact. He cradled his hand to his chest and looked down, feeling helpless to do anything. No, it seemed that it would only release its hold on Theo once all the liquid had drained away, only Zane couldn't see where it was disappearing to. But as he'd guessed, the second the very last drop had gone Theo gasped in air, as though he had been close to passing out. He fell forward on his hands just as the dagger skittered across the floor.

"Theo?! Are you alright?!" Zane asked placing a hand on his back, letting him know he wasn't alone. Theo took a few minutes to compose himself enough to move. He just nodded at first, letting his concerned friend know that he was okay.

"What the hell was that?!" Zane asked once he managed to get Theo back to his feet. Theo looked down at his hand to see a new red mark had appeared, like an ancient scar from the past had made its way through the vision. It was the symbol of the Alpha and Omega combined and Theo was trying to think of where he had seen that symbol before.

"Hey, that kinda looks like the school's shield, I remember seeing it on the letterhead that was on our acceptance letters," Zane said, never forgetting what he saw.

"You're right," Theo agreed now remembering it as well.

"So, what happened, what did you see?" Zane pushed again.

"I think it was memories of how the dagger began," Theo said looking down at it and bending to pick it back up.

"Uh, do you think you should do that?" Zane warned but Theo knew that the danger had passed.

"I can't explain it, but it's almost as if it's telling me to take it, like I will need it or something," Theo said after picking it up and looking down at the now empty glass dagger. It looked like a giant shard of clear crystal that had once been blood red, as though it had been chipped off a glass boulder. In fact, the only thing that looked manmade was its handle.

It had six hooked claws made of gold, holding it secure to the metal it appeared forged to. Then its T bar held a fan of claws reaching outwards on either side, which looked like deadly spikes ready to injure anyone who didn't wield it right.

The handle itself was decorated with embossed gold lattice work and its pommel end piece looked like an Aztec sun, arching round like some Sun God's headpiece. It was stunning and deadly looking all at the same time.

"And that liquid?" Zane asked making Theo look at him when he said,

"It was blood," Theo answered feeling as though he was back there, seeing it seeping into himself all over again. But it wasn't just this that was playing on his mind. It was all the images it had shown him, like a storyboard when all put together. He didn't know who the monster had been or the girl who had defeated it but he knew one thing, that fallen King, well that King had been…

Dominic Draven.

One from a different time.

"Well that's comforting to know," Zane said sarcastically in response to Theo telling him it was blood.

"We'd better go," Theo said gripping the handle once more before hooking it through the belt on his jeans being careful of the gold spikes that were likely to do damage.

"Yeah, let's just hope the rooms beyond this point don't get any weirder," Zane said but down there, well they were asking for a lot. They pushed the next door open and found themselves faced with a huge hallway, one that cars could have driven down with room to spare on either side.

"Wow, it makes you wonder who their architect was and if they have like a demon company they go with?" Theo had to laugh, as it was true the place was incredible, but in a gothic, creepy way.

"For starters, I don't think you could walk into Macy's department store and pick out your favourite Gargoyle," Zane said looking up at them all as they walked past. Well if Theo thought that the upstairs looked like part of a castle then down there it looked as if it was straight out of a Greek temple.

There were carved stone pillars that looked like sandstone warriors running down the length of the space. Each was holding up the ceiling above with muscles bulging with an eternal strength. Theo looked up and saw massive arches covered in gilded flowers. It now seemed as though those stone hands were holding up precious artwork on the ceiling, along with the stone arches.

But like Zane had said, it was not only beauty to be found because in between these pillars were the twisted faces of grotesque looking gargoyles. However, they weren't the weathered ones Theo had been used to seeing on buildings like Westminster Abbey or London's Natural History Museum. No, these looked as though they could have been carved yesterday.

"I swear those eyes are following us," Zane said as they walked down the massive space, feeling like a couple of small intruders in comparison.

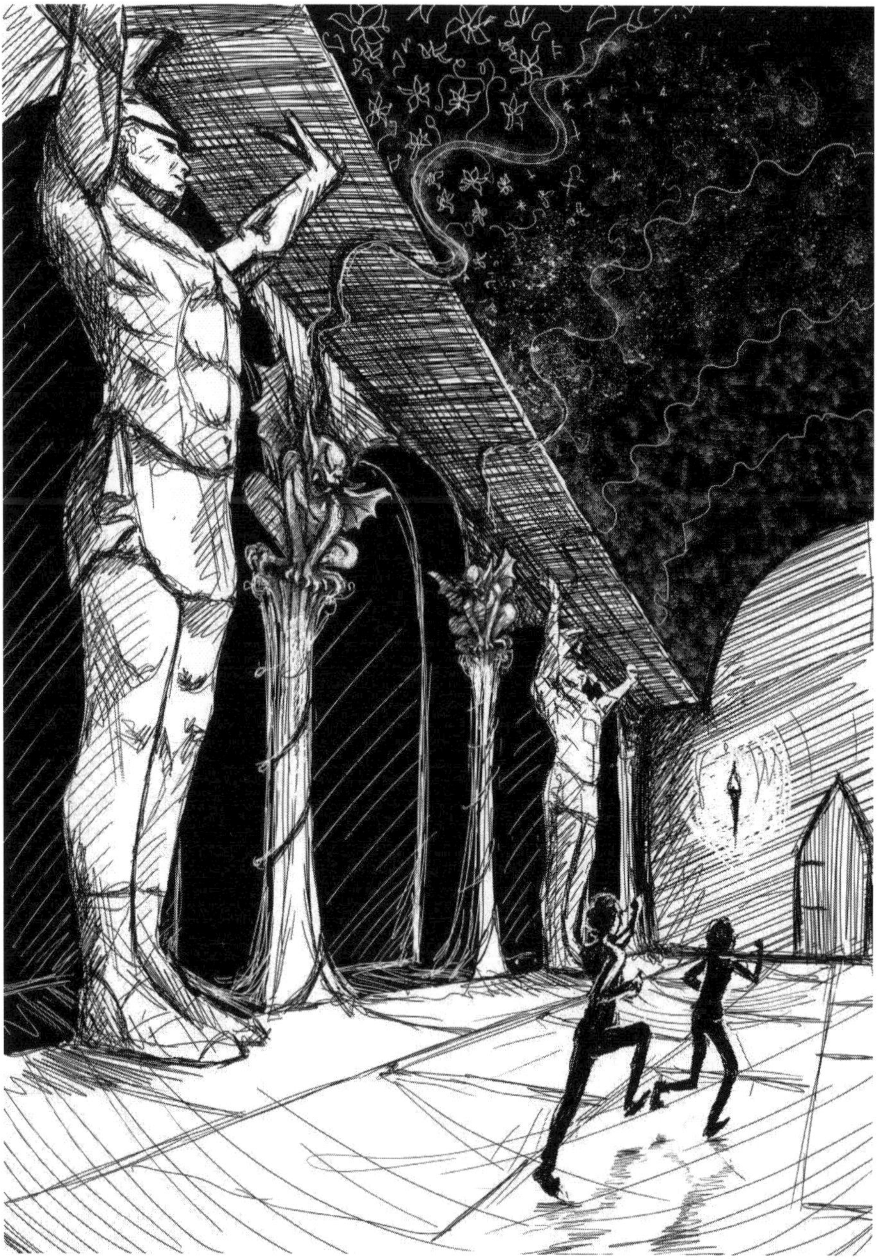

"I think that's because they are," Theo said side on to his friend as he noticed the first one turning its head as they passed.

"Great…just great, even the freakin CCTV here is demonic," Zane said looking cautiously up over his shoulder at them.

"Ignore them," Theo muttered between gritted teeth.

"Easier said than done my friend, seeing as they keep looking at us like the human take-out just arrived," Zane murmured in reply, turning on his heel to make sure no one was following them.

"Then let's make it fast food and get a move on," Theo recommended and they both started making a run for it, as being watched by those stone demons had become too much. The door at the other end started to get closer and closer just as they could hear the frantic movements of stone grinding
against stone, as the monstrous gargoyles tried to keep up with their fast pace.

They both landed hard against the door, falling through it but saving themselves before they hit the ground. They both turned and slammed the door, shutting out whatever those things were.

"Oh good, out of danger," Zane said leaning against the wood, trying to catch his breath. Theo on the other hand turned around to take in the room and gasped before informing him,

"I think you spoke too soon." Then he grabbed Zane's shoulder and pulled him, so that he was facing the right way and could see what Theo was now seeing.

"O...h, you have got to be shitting me!" Zane said after first stuttering to find the right words to express...well, the unbelievable they were seeing right now.

"Seriously it can't be, it just..."

"Calm down," Theo said, trying to keep Zane cool along with dealing with his own. But then Zane lost it and screamed what they were now both stood inside,

"Calm down, calm down...are you insane? How the hell can I calm down when we are in...!" He took a breath, looked around the vast space and screamed,

"...A GODDAMN CRYPT!"

32
BLOOD IS THE KEY

Theo had no choice other than to slap a hand over Zane's mouth in hopes of calming him down.

"Okay so yes, it looks like a crypt but at the moment it looks like a very *quiet* goddamn crypt and we really…*really* want to keep it that way. So, I suggest we get to the other side as quickly and as quietly as possible before we find out who rests in those holes," Theo said, emphasising the word 'really' again and then looked towards the man-sized holes that covered the walls of the room, just to make his point. Zane didn't try and say anything but just nodded behind his hand letting Theo know that he understood.

"Are we cool?"

"Yeah for now, but just so you know, if anything crawls out of those holes, then I'm not ashamed to say I will probably shit myself before screaming out of that door like a little girl, 'cos at this point, give me creepy ass gargoyles any day, at least those bitches can't reach me!" Zane said making his own point very clear.

"Gotya," Theo told him as he didn't want to admit it, but if something did come out of those holes, then in all likelihood he would be right there running alongside him…minus the crap filled pants and screaming like a girl of course.

The room they were now stood in, if it could be called that, was the size of an enclosed football field. The floor was a series of broken tiles that created a picture which neither Theo or Zane could make any sense of. It almost looked as though the sky itself was engaging in a battle of light and dark, creating clouds of grey in between.

The huge walls looked tall enough to keep an army out, but for all they knew a dead army was what lay inside them. For there were floor to ceiling holes cut out of the bare rock that were the perfect size for hundreds of coffins to fit inside, widthways. But even this wasn't their biggest concern right then, as it was what the room held at its core that was their main focus.

"Okay I was wrong, this place officially just got weirder."

"Amen to that. What the hell is that thing?" Theo agreed with Zane as what they were seeing now made even less sense than the dagger, gargoyles and coffins combined. At the centre of the room stood a gigantic pillar, reaching up to the roof, as though it could have held an entire city… or what they at least thought was a pillar.

The closer they got to it they soon realised it wasn't a manmade structure at all, but instead a Jurassic looking tree that seemed as if it was still trapped in the stone age. Theo had never seen giant redwoods before but looking at the size of this thing, then this was what he would have expected. Something big enough you could have fit three cars through if someone had cut a tunnel through its centre.

"I think it's a tree…or at least it was at one time," Zane said looking it up and down just as Theo did the closer they got to it.

"It looks…"

"Fossilised?" Zane finished for him and he was right for it no longer held any life inside it that it once had. The colossal trunk was grey, void of energy as though it had been locked down there that long. And without any sunlight, it had simply started to fade from the earth, becoming stone like the rest of the room. Even its vast network of branches that travelled along the ceiling above were dead, as though they too were still searching for that important lifeforce…the sun.

"I think it's wise if we just leave it alone," Theo suggested.

"Good plan, although I don't know about you, but I don't see any doors around here…do you?" Zane agreed and like Theo, was looking around the place for a way out, other than the way they had come in.

"Maybe we made a wrong turn or missed something?"

"No, this is the way she said to go but wait, I didn't check the note," Theo said, only just remembering what Fae had written down for him.

"So, the hot geek did tell you something?" Zane remarked but Theo just shot him a look as if to say not to go there as he fished the piece of paper out of his jeans' pocket.

"Well that's interesting," Theo remarked sarcastically, something Zane didn't quite pick up on the first-time round.

"Yeah?" Theo looked up and said,

"No, not really. It just sounds like it's really gonna hurt...*again!*" he answered, walking over to where she had directed in her note, a place that simply looked like a wall of stone vines.

"I don't see a door," Zane said but he didn't know what Theo knew thanks to that note and the horrors that awaited them. So, instead of telling him what was written, he just handed it over for him to read for himself. Zane's eyes widened and he looked back up at the thorn covered vines all entwined there. It looked like a curtain of razor backed snakes had been draped down to hide what lay beneath.

"Okay, so hey, look it was nice knowing you and all but..."

"Gee thanks, your concern is overwhelming but you'd better stop now before I cry," Theo said lacing his words with sarcasm.

"No, you crying will be when you stuff your hand in there and let it feed from your blood like the note said. I mean how do we even know it's not going to get a taste for you and think...um, I like this vintage, I think instead of a sip, I shall just take the whole bottle?"

"Well, there is only one way to find out now, isn't there?" And before Zane could talk him out of it, he suddenly plunged his hand in and prayed he tasted foul. He touched the cold stone and for a second he wondered why he'd bothered as the things were obviously dead but then what was it that Pip had said, about presumption being the mother from where all mistakes are born.

Well this turned out to be true when Theo started to feel movement on his fingertips.

"What's happening…*is* something happening?" Zane asked repeating himself. Theo turned to look at him with one hand still feeling for something more, but just as he was about to answer his eyes went wide, telling Zane all he needed to know. The vines slithered along his palm and up around his wrist, entwining itself as if trying to find a pulse on a sleeping corpse. The second it found what it was looking for Theo started to feel it pulsate and vibrate along his flesh just as it produced its wicked thorns.

"AHHH!" Theo cried out just as Zane predicted he would as it started to pierce Theo's palm over and over again, extracting his blood with each thrust. Theo tried to yank his hand free and when Zane saw what Theo was doing he tried to help; both of them putting a foot on the wall, trying to get leverage. But there must have been a certain amount of blood needed because as soon as it had taken its fill, it released him, making them both fall backwards.

They landed with a painful thud but Theo cared more for the throbbing in his hand, not his behind. He cradled his hand and looked down at the injured palm, seeing now that the strange symbol the dagger had left was back, only this time it was bloody.

"Look!" Zane shouted to Theo. He looked, not knowing what to expect, just as the vines started to thrive once more. It w as as if they had found just a drop of sunlight, enough to breathe lush green life back into their roots. The grey vines started to bloom into a wave of forest greens before each one looked like the tree it once belonged to. They slithered up to the ceiling and back to the fossilised tree only managing to make it to the very tips of the branches. Theo couldn't help but wonder what would happen if it had made it all the way down the mighty trunk, but this fleeting thought was quickly consumed by the sight of the massive doors emerging from behind its veil.

"Alright, now that is a freakin huge door!" Zane said, getting off the ground as Theo did but being just as transfixed as he, unable to take his eyes from it. It was huge and looked as though it would have needed thirty men to move it! But in the end, as if by his thoughts alone, the door started to open and Theo half expected to find some giant standing there behind it, being let out of its prison. Thankfully though, all that faced them was a bright light that was as blinding as if they had been walking out from the darkness.

"Do we dare?" Zane asked and Theo nodded and replied,

"Why the *Hell* not." Then he walked forward into the void with Zane following him saying,

"That isn't funny, for all we know this could be the gates of Hell." Theo didn't answer him as he obviously made it through to the other side first, ready to inform Zane of what faced them the second he made it through the blinding tunnel of light.

"Oh, we're in Hell alright, just one that's controlled by the Dravens," Theo said and Zane rubbed his eyes to see that Theo was right. They had just stepped in to none other than a Demonic prison!

"You got that right," he agreed as the place they were now stood was no doubt many people's idea of Hell considering they were now staring down the centre of a room which held demonic prisoners either side. They were literally surrounded by the world's most dangerous demons and supernatural beings on earth!

"Well, we ain't in Kansas anymore," Zane said looking from side to side, making sure no one was going to fly out at them and attack at any second.

"Mmm, I smell young flesh, fresh for the picking." A demonic voice said, making them jump further away from one of the heavy metal doors that was the only barrier between them and IT.

"Then where are we?" Theo asked after they both gasped when the door rattled frantically.

"It's freakin' 666, House of the Dead, on Elm street, in Amityville, on Friday the 13th in Hell…that's what this is!" Zane said and he had to agree with him, because even though it took a lot to scare Theo, this was right up there on the top of his list!

The crude doors looked like hammered metal with bolted rivets used to reinforce the strength in each. They all held small openings with bars fixed inside the arched windows. But it was the locks that puzzled Theo the most, as some held small flat dishes which looked ready for something to be placed there for the door to be opened.

"Come here little boys, I won't hurt you, just a little kiss for granny." One withered old voice said and Zane reached up on tip toes from a distance to see a hideous old woman, bleeding in between hundreds of wrinkles with pointed razor-sharp teeth, grinning sadistically at him. But it soon got more sickening when she gave him a little wave and he found that all the flesh on her fingers had been eaten and all that was left were the bones that had been gnawed, filing them down into sharp points.

"Nope, I don't think so," Zane said giving Theo a little shake of his head, telling him not to look.

"What was it?"

"Well, let's just say that if Wolverine had a crazed, demented grandmother, with a major skin problem, then I think we just found her," Zane replied swallowing down the bile that also threatened to bring up his food.

"Let's carry on, Janie must be down here somewhere…oh and stay away from those dish things, the note said that they are the locks and blood is what can open them," Theo said after double checking the note again and knowing now that the P stood for *Prison*. No wonder she had been shocked to find him going down there by choice.

"Well, not only do I not intend to go anywhere near those doors, but I also think that unless I am haemorrhaging and bleeding to death by some freak accident involving my batman belt buckle, that just happens to spray my blood up there, then I think we're good." Theo didn't answer as he agreed, it was pretty obvious neither of them were going anywhere near those doors, that was unless…

"Is that Janie?" Zane asked as they walked around a corner to see that the door at the end was different in several ways. To begin with, it was much bigger. But apart from being more heavily fortified, it was also covered in several symbols that looked to be branded into a series of metal bars, ones that had been added to the original door.

Almost as though when they caught this prisoner, they knew they would get out of any other door they had. So, they had no choice but to reinforce this one, not only by bolting twenty metal strips the size of 2x4s across it, but also by using magic.

However, all of this crude metalwork framed a small hooded figure who stood in front of it looking through the gaps as though they were listening to a God speaking.

They couldn't hear what was being said but the second they saw a hand moving towards the small dish, they both cried out.

"NO, DON'T DO IT!" It was at this point that their question of who it was, was quickly answered as they turned and looked over their shoulder. Zane had been right. It was Janie but not as they knew her, not as anyone knew her. Because this Janie was clearly possessed.

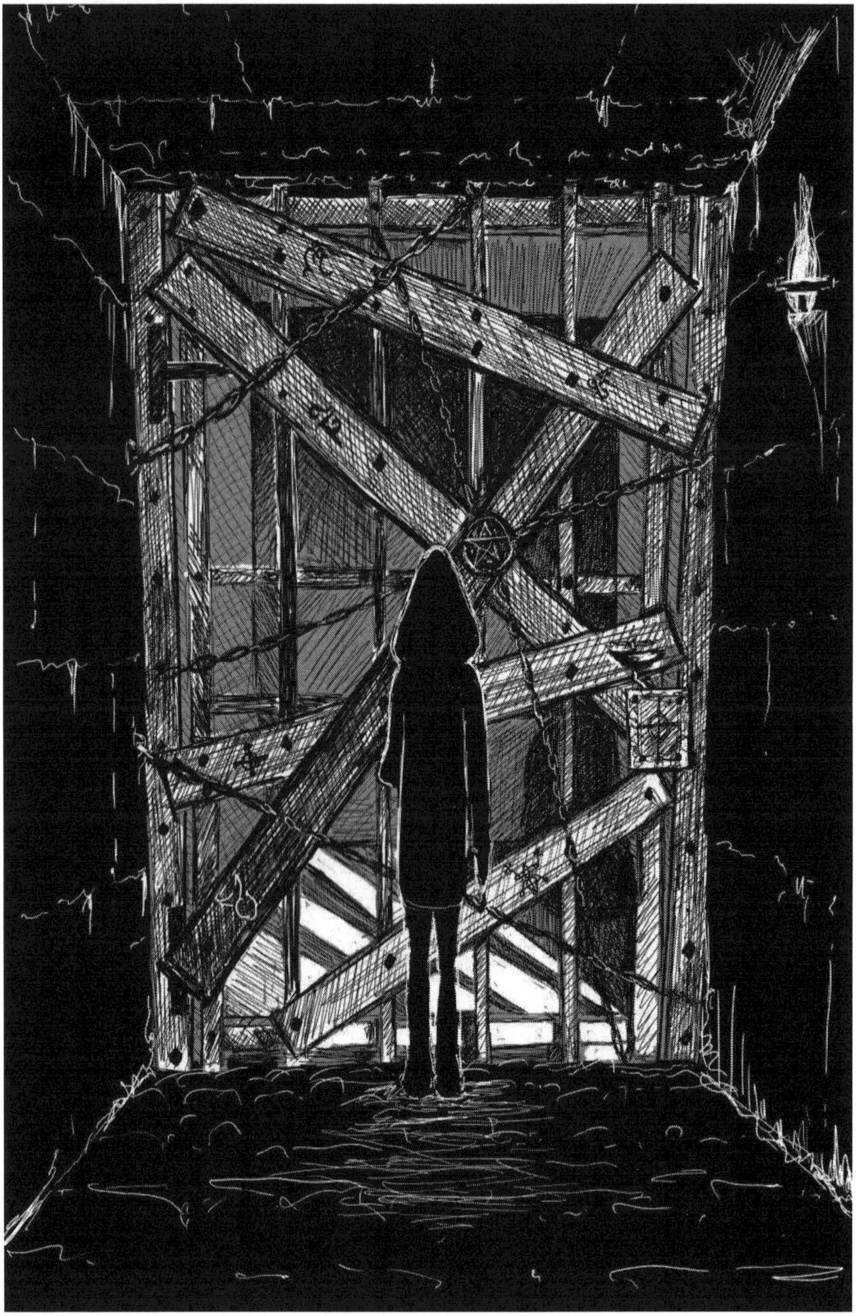

Her eyes were full of blood coloured fire and glowing as though she was drawing in a demonic energy from whatever was locked away behind that door. Then she started to speak to them, first opening her mouth a few times as though she was testing the action. Because the horrifying reality was simple, her body no longer belonged to herself but to the Demon that possessed her.

And soon came it's warning,

"My time has come, time of the Blood Master to arise and you will all…"

"Die. For. Me."

33
Blood Rage

Theo and Zane were both stunned into silence at the sight of little Janie possessed. It almost looked as though someone had draped an evil veil over her head and what they saw now was it mimicking her human side, using it as a host to do its bidding. A bidding that meant setting whatever was behind that door free. Something that Theo and Zane didn't need to be a couple of genius' to know was most likely a very bad thing indeed.

"Janie? Janie it's us, it's Theo and Zane, can you hear us?" Theo asked slowly trying to approach without alarming her. At this she turned her head to the side and let out an ear-piercing screeching noise, like some demon underling was crying out to its master. Her eyes still weren't her own but now neither was her skin, as it had started to crawl as though something was digging at her insides to be let out.

The last time they had seen that was yesterday when Zagan had called forth his powers in the fight with Takeshi. Was this what was happening now? But better yet, was it the monster trying to get in or was it their Janie trying to get out?

"I wouldn't come any closer if I were you or your little friend here will smile at you while she slits her own throat," the demon said, once again using Janie's lips. It sounded as if it was from a foreign land, but one not of this Earth. Almost as though it was trying to remember how to use a mortal language, it had been that long.

Theo would have called its bluff considering Janie didn't have a knife but then, as though reading his thoughts, she lifted her arm, the one missing the hand, and folded back her sleeve using slow creepy stilted and mechanical movements. Then she twisted her body as though something was moving and writhing inside her before producing the same black smoke they had seen back in the nightclub. It seemed to seep out of her pores and combine at the end of her flesh, joining together creating a large point where a hand should have been.

But surely it was only made of smoke, Theo thought, but then as if testing him with that knowledge her arm moved closer to her face and she grinned at them as she dragged the blade down the side of her face.

"NO!" Theo screamed and was about to run forward when Zane stopped him. Theo hadn't seen see what Zane saw as he was too clouded by his anger. But when that blade had cut her face it also carried on, slipping down to her own neck, threatening the life they both cared about.

"Now you will watch me rise," she said before plunging the black smoke dagger into the door, making it disappear up until it reached to her actual flesh.

"But the door, surely that won't be enough?" Zane asked Theo but he didn't need to answer him with any predictions because in that moment nothing was on their side...not even fortified metal and magic combined.

Janie's body started to go rigid as her back bowed and her head shot up, looking to the stone ceiling as if she were trying to concentrate on drawing in more power. She screamed again and again, but once more the sound wasn't coming from her but from the Hellish minion, whoever was behind that door.

The next thing they knew even more black smoke started to come from within her, adding to the force that was trying to open the door. They didn't know if it would work or not but if the sounds of metal splitting were anything to go by, then it didn't look good.

"What are we going to do!?" Zane asked, once more looking to Theo for answers.

"I don't know but it doesn't look like we have long so we'd better think of something quick as that door won't hold out much longer." And Theo was right, for the metal looked to be heating up, turning red hot and making rivets and bolts burst out of their holes due to pressure building. One of them tore into Janie's face but she obviously didn't register the pain, not with the demon inside of her.

"Look, now the symbols are melting away!"

"We have to do something!" Theo said, seeing that Zane was right as not only was the magic nearly gone but now there was molten metal dripping from the door, creating a hole at its core.

"What about the dagger? What if you..." Zane never finished his sentence as they were too late. Suddenly the centre of the door exploded inwards, thankfully causing most of the damage to fly inside the cell and not into Janie's body. Now the hole was big enough, Janie bent her head slightly and disappeared inside the cell making both Theo and Zane scream out,

"NO!" Then without giving it another thought, they ran towards the cell ready to discover who or what was behind this evil game. Because Theo knew now that was all it had ever been. Just some sick twisted game to get one of them down there so that Janie or himself could be manipulated enough to get close to them. Then once in range, bam! The game completed and the unwilling soul was trapped within themselves, ready to do the prisoner's bidding.

Well, they may have used Janie to set them free but Theo would do everything in his power to stop them from stepping one foot out of that cell and hurting anyone else. For Janie may have been lost to them already but he wouldn't allow them to reach the others, not if he had a single breath left in his body!

They had made it to the door, ducking inside themselves only to come face to face with what looked like death. They found a body hunched on the ground. It looked like the remains of someone who had starved long ago, as they were practically withered away to nothing. Janie was hunched over him and as soon as they entered she turned to look over her shoulder. They expected her to lash out at them in some way, but what they found was confused frightened tears.

"Theo, I don't understand," Janie said to him as if a small part of her had just broken through and it sounded utterly heartbroken.

"It's alright Janie, we will figure this out, just…" Theo started to say but Zane's panicked voice cut him off.

"What's that…on his arm?" Zane asked, sounding disgusted by the sight and Theo squinted in the low light, trying to make it out himself. It looked as though the withered body had once been some sort of human machine hybrid.

One arm looked like rusted pieces of metal, and cogs that hadn't turned in quite some time. Underneath this was dead flesh missing skin, as though that had been the part to wither first. It was like a skeletal body of flesh and bone had been experimented on and after dying it had been dumped in there as some kind of afterthought, throwing it away in some barren junk pile.

"Janie... step back, walk towards us slowly," Theo warned, not liking how this felt. Not one little bit. Janie shook herself as if something inside her still lingered there, hidden beneath the surface.

"I don't get it...why would something want this door open so badly, there is nothing in here but a mutated, rotting corpse and why now is Janie..." Zane was cut off when Janie screamed as that rotting corpse they had been so sure about, suddenly reached out and grabbed her ankle.

"Theo! Theo help me!" she shouted and Theo reached out just as her eyes started to turn white.

"Janie, no!" Theo was just about to grab her arm but Zane pulled him back quickly and just in time as those smoke serpents were back and snapped out at him, trying to take his hand off. They would have succeeded too if it hadn't been for Zane's quick actions. Theo fell back a step and watched wide-eyed and helpless as Janie's face was frozen in a mask of horror as the energy was quickly drained from her.

The colour of her skin started to fade into lifeless grey and the hand that had been drawing that lifeforce was now turning into more than a few strips of flesh against brittle bone. Theo and Zane started to take a few steps back as it started to gain enough strength to move its twisted limbs.

"We need to get out of here...Zane run!" Theo shouted just as it lunged again, catching them unaware of the immediate danger. Theo moved out of reach but Zane tripped and cried out for his friend as he was quickly dragged backwards.

"Zane!" Theo shouted, going back for his friend but soon scrabbling back as the figure rose up to his full height, taking Zane's body with him, suspending him in the air by his throat. Zane's eyes too seeped into a white void as though someone had just taken his soul.

Theo was torn between running and screaming the place down until Draven or the others could hear him. Or he could do what he was born to do...to fight.

"LET HIM GO!" Theo threatened, feeling his anger bubbling up inside him, ready to burst free when it reached its peak. The demon's head was down, hidden by the shadows and just as it drained the last of his friend's body he let him slump to the ground, discarding it like a useless dead carcass.

The creature took in Theo's threat and twisted its head as if it had amused him to hear such a thing from such a lowly being. Theo could now see, by draining the power from two people, what must have been the demon's usual form. The man cracked his neck to the side before stepping out of the shadows and allowing Theo to take a good look at the enemy he faced...and it was terrifying.

403

The creature looked like some kind of demonic version of a civil war brigadier with its double-breasted jacket, the colour of charcoal, that tapered down into a wide belt. One that looked to be made from demon skin and worn like a trophy as it was decorated with teeth and horns, held in loops of hellish leather.

The buttons on his jacket held runes from some ancient language and were connected to leather straps that continued around his back. This also served the purpose, along with the strapping across his chest, of holding his mechanical arm in place. But there was nothing robotic about it as it looked more like someone had raided a junk yard in Hell and pieced together something in a hurry. It mainly consisted of large hammered brass plates, riveted onto pieces of leather, that fit various parts of his arm. This was then joined together by chains for stability and copper pipes that led back to a steam piston that hissed every time he moved.

There was also a series of cogs that were fitted at the elbow which Theo gathered was supposed to aid in his movement there. This was also the same theme by his hand and once again, it looked like an unfortunate monster in Hell had been skinned, having its hide used to fashion a glove. Attached to this were chains that had been bolted straight through his fingers and these all gathered together at his wrist, which turned by a barrel of cogs.

And if that wasn't creepy enough, old bloodied, medical tubing ran the full length of his arm carrying some sort of oily red fluid. It was as though his veins were on the outside of his body, weeping black liquid at the joints that smelled like old blood mixed with oxidised copper.

As he stepped further into the light, Theo felt revolted to see that the few patches of his own skin that peeked through looked burnt and deformed. Pieces of twisted flesh that barely looked useful enough for movement, let alone anything else. It seemed to weep a yellowish liquid at the cracks while other parts resembled what happened to skin when it had been submerged in water for too long.

Theo wanted to gag but was too frightened when the rest of him came into view. Half of his face was covered by a metal plate that had been screwed into his skull. You could still see some of the flesh on the bolt heads that had risen when the metal had been driven deeper into his skull.

A flexible coil framed up and over his bare eye and joined to moving cogs at his cheek. His covered eye was hidden behind a black mesh but the demonic iris could be seen glowing amber. As though he were some kind, of cyborg nightmare that was alerting you to the fact he had been switched on. His other eye was ice white, with a black ring around the outside of his iris and tiny dot of black at the centre, giving him a Marilyn Manson vibe.

"I be General Gruen, second-in-command to the true Lord and Master of Hell, Ba'al Zəbûl, for he will rise again!" A voice bellowed out, reminding Theo of a clip he once saw on YouTube of Adolf Hitler delivering a speech. He sounded of Germanic descent, mixing this with a demonic growl at the end of his words. Theo wasn't ashamed to say that it made the hair of the back of his neck rise.

But no matter how terrifying he was, Theo couldn't extinguish the flames of rage building inside of him and he quickly acted on this before his fear could override his actions. He grabbed the glass dagger from his belt and ran at him. The General laughed, underestimating Theo and swung out his mechanical arm towards him, in hopes of knocking him off his feet.

But Theo remembered his training from Zagan and ducked at just the right moment, following the defensive move by bringing up his dagger and embedding it in the demon's shoulder. He managed to catch him just between the plates of metal, driving it deep enough into his mangled flesh, so that when Theo dived out of the way, the dagger remained.

The demonic General first looked at Theo with a shocked expression, obviously surprised that he had actually managed to inflict damage with a weapon. Then he turned his head slowly towards the dagger still embedded in his flesh and his eyes started to glow in a way that were responding to the sight. The General bent his head to the side, turned back to face Theo and smiled, showing him that over half his teeth were metal.

"The Pertinax, ÙRI ISKAKKU..." (Mean's 'Blood Weapon' in Sumerian) He uttered the ancient words, this time as though they were the first words ever whispered from new born lips. It certainly flowed better than his English, that was for sure.

"...My Master, Ba'al Zəbûl will thank you for this... when your soul is rotting in Hell that is," he said calmly before lifting a mechanical boot and kicking Theo square in the chest with it. Before he knew what hit him, Theo was flying backwards through the broken door, snapping the rest of it clean off its twisted hinges. His back smacked into the prison wall opposite the cell before he fell forward, his face landing on the dirty cobbled floor.

"You younglings, so naive, so easy to manipulate...I knew at least one of you would release me and grant me access into the treasury, but never did I imagine you would deliver to me the very reason for my being here," the General said sounding amused as he pulled the dagger from his shoulder. But that

sadistic smile soon left his lips when he looked at the dagger more closely.

"No...no...this can't be...where is it?" he shouted and stomped his way to where Theo was lying against the cold stone. He saw him coming closer, only now noticing his limp thanks to his larger mechanical leg.

"WHAT DID YOU DO?!" He screamed down at him in a purely demonic voice that sounded as if it had been bellowed from Hell itself.

Theo spit out blood on the floor, landing on the General's foot and started laughing before saying,

"Take a good look asshole, it's on your boot!"
The General wasn't in a laughing mood and picked him up by the back of his neck. He held him next to his face, lifting him from the ground.

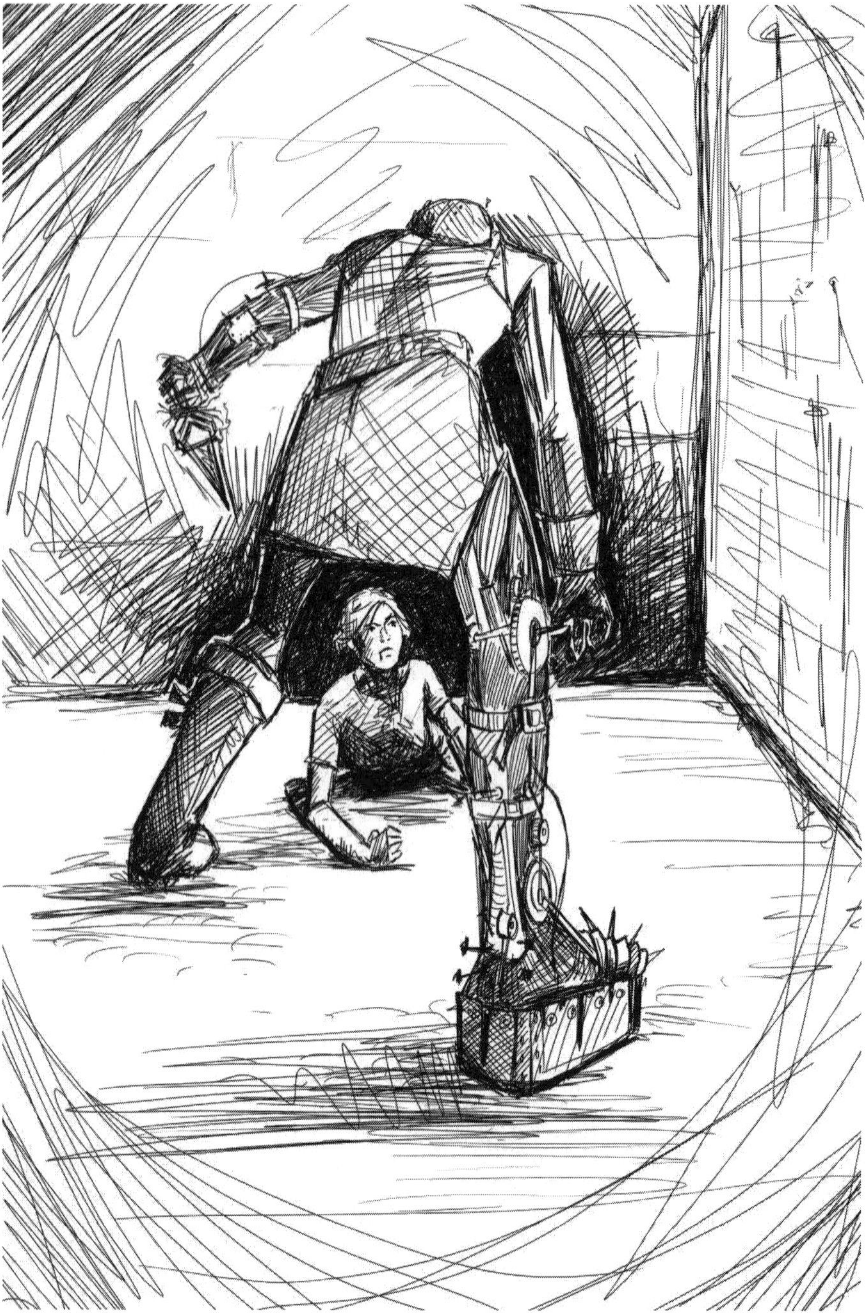

"YOU LIE!" he snarled, snapping metal teeth at him. Theo knew that he should have been scared in the face of death, but considering he had already faced that twice in the last few days, he just couldn't find it in him. However, when he looked back into the cell and saw both Janie's and Zane's bodies lying there all lifeless, then what he did find was something a lot more useful...*rage.*

Suddenly a flash of memories invaded his mind all at once, every single time his touch had hurt someone or affected them in some way. It started with Sarah and became a montage of nameless faces, until finally it came to Carrick, the last person his touch had affected. Then something clicked into place. Like slotting the last puzzle piece into position, creating the clearest of pictures in his mind. He finally knew what he was...

A Demon.

34
Stolen Power

"GIVE ME THE BLOOD OF A GOD!" The General roared in his face. Theo smiled and replied,

"Try and take it from me, bitch!" Then he raised his hand up and thrust it onto the unprotected side of the General's face. Theo didn't know what he was doing at first, as he had spent most of his life trying to control what he always considered a curse. But now, well it was the first time he was considering it a gift, one he was willing to use to its maximum potential. So, he concentrated on drawing in on the energy he would always feel when touching someone, breathing deep as if mimicking the action his powers were inflicting.

The General's face went from rage to shock and finally to panic when he felt his own stolen power being drained back from deep within his dark soul.

"You can't do this…I am a God among mere men and you are but a youngling." He felt the presence of Janie and Zane there as it flowed back into him and this only angered Theo further. He gripped his face and dragged it closer. Once there he uttered the same words the warrior woman had done from his visions…

"Yeah, well even Gods can die on Earth, asshole!" Then he used the last of his strength to draw in even more, until the General's grip released him, severing the connection. The General's knees gave out and he dropped to the floor with a crack. He fell forward and Theo pushed out of the way, watching as his flesh started to wither, turning grey once more.

"It…it isn't possible…you can't be…Electus," the General said but Theo wasn't listening. Instead he got to his feet and ran over to his friends, knowing now what he must do, even if it left him vulnerable.

"I hope I'm not too late," he said landing hard, first next to Janie as he skidded to her.

"Here goes nothing," he said placing the same hand on the side of her face, and doing what he had done with the General, only this time what he hoped was in reverse. He let go of the power and energy he felt nearly overflowing in him and pinpointed the aura he knew was Janie's. It was like a lingering shadowed essence inside of him that he was trying to give back to her. Her stolen gift returned.

"Come on! Come on Janie!" he shouted down at her when nothing happened, but then after one last push of power she gasped desperately for air and opened her eyes wide, reaching up for him.

"Theo?" Her sweet voice uttered his name and he wished he had the time to comfort her but he didn't. He had one more friend to save. He had only enough time to grant her a wink before racing over to where Zane's body lay slumped on the floor.

"Time to wake your ass up, my friend!" Then he slapped a hand to Zane's face, invoking the stored power inside of him. But this time it was different. Instead of shadowed serpents like Janie's, it was the light he found. It was bright and blinding and much easier to find. It flowed out of him the same way, but this time it left him feeling almost completely drained.

"I bet you didn't slap Janie like you did me," Zane said, before opening his eyes. Theo laughed once and then fell backwards.

"Theo!" Janie shouted and Zane sat up, reaching for his friend.

"What's happening to him?" Janie asked and Theo could hear the concerned tremble in her voice as though listening from a distance.

"I don't know but I know who will," Zane replied nodding to the hallway and at first Janie thought he meant the demon that had done this to them.

"Here they come," Zane added before they came into view. It was as though Zane had somehow detected their presence. The General looked up and saw it too, coming closer towards him. So, in his desperation and with his last shred of power, he got up and ran back into the cell.

"HE WILL RISE AGAIN! THE BLOOD GOD WILL RISE!"

"Look out!" Zane said, grabbing Janie and pulling her out of the way. She landed on top of him and they both looked sideways to see him run at the wall, disappearing into a cloud of ash the second he hit it.

The two entwined teens then both looked to the door and saw their headmaster, Draven, standing there looking down on all that had happened. Theo managed to open one eye to see the blurred vision of their Supernatural King stood in the doorway.

"And so it's begun," Draven said in a sombre voice.

"What has?" Zane asked after Janie scrabbled off him. Takeshi walked into view behind Draven and picked up the fallen dagger. He handed it to Draven over his shoulder and their headmaster's eyes widened in surprise. He took a moment to look at the dagger in his hands, noting the lack of blood when running a finger down its length.

He then looked down at Theo and just before he passed out, Theo managed to hear Draven's horrifying answer…

"Blood… of the Infinity War."

To be continued…

Acknowledgements.

We would first like to thank all the fans of The Afterlife Saga who have shown us all their support during this time and continue to do so by spreading the Afterlife Chronicle word.
We can't thank you enough.

We would also like to thank those closest to us and each have a personal message to give...

From Caroline,

The biggest thank you for me to give easily must go to my wonderful husband, Jamie Brooks. I simply couldn't be where I am today without all your love, support, tea making, technical wizardry and never-ending belief in me.
I love you x

To my daughter Amber and son Marley, thank you for not treating me like a nutter with all my booky weird requests from modelling to pulling faces. I know you love it really 😊

Thank you to my mum. It all starts somewhere and you taught me how to draw...plus babysitting xxxx

Blake Hudson for being amazing by supporting two nutty gals with a dream and your always honest opinion.
Thank you to Elizabeth and Hazel Pescatore and Ashfield Park Primary School, where the Chronicles all began. Who'da thought young kids love horror!
My legal and marketing team Jo Beattie-Edwards and Sarah Jane Lomas.
You are just awesome!

...And finally

To my 'beastie' Aka Stephanie, you are the most generous, kind, inspiring and brave person I know. Love working with you

(Apparently, I have to call it that even though I have far too much fun).

What would I do without you?

From Stephanie,

I would first like to thank my amazing husband, Blake, for not only supporting me but encouraging my crazy imagination and making it bloom into something great. Words will never be enough to describe how much I love you!

To my Mum and Dad, whose support is never-ending and their love is unconditional. And my sister, Cathy and brother in law, James who each offer their support in many ways.
Love you guys!

And a very special mention needs to go to the awesome and beautiful Elizabeth and Hazel Pescatore, who two years ago planted the creative seed in my mind and inspired me to write this first instalment to the next level of the Afterlife saga.
You guys are epic!

I would like to thank all in the Brooks' household for loaning me their wonderful mother and letting her join in my brand of crazy. Also, a special thanks goes to Mr Brooks himself, Jamie who has been our tech genius throughout this endeavor and been with us every step of the way.
You are a tea making star!
P.S...I don't have sugar in my tea ☺

And last but not least is my partner in crime, Caroline. Quite simply put this would not have been possible without you as no one could have created my vision and plucked Afterlife from my mind quite like you could. Your talent knows no bounds and I consider it a gift being able to call you friend.
To my 'beastie', who I love dearly.

We would both like to thank Claire Boyle, for her tireless effort in helping the world see our dream come true the way we always hoped it would. You are a rock star in our eyes!

Once again thank you to all Afterlife fans for spreading the word!

We love you x

Printed in Great Britain
by Amazon